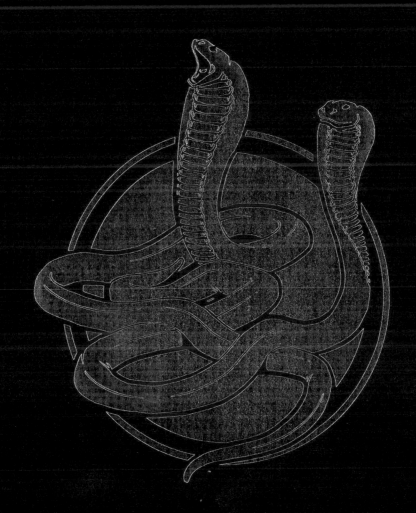

Also by Gary J. Cook

Graveyard Rules (1988)

Blood Trail

A Novel

Gary J. Cook

Gary J. Cook

Dennis McMillan Publications
2006

FIRST EDITION
Published March 2006

This first edition of *Blood Trail* consists of 1,000
copies bound in Brillianta (100% rayon) cloth and
104 copies bound in quarter-morocco pigskin
with hand-made paper-covered boards.

The dustjacket design & artwork, interior design,
and all interior artwork but the two-cobra image
was created by Michael Kellner. The line drawing
of the two cobras was done by Jeff Siedlik.

ISBN 0-939767-53-8

Dennis McMillan Publications
4460 N. Hacienda del Sol (Guest House)
Tucson, Arizona 85718
Tel. (520)-529-6636 email: dennismcmillan@aol.com
website: http://dennismcmillan.com

To

Mikio Noma, Captain, Imperial Japanese Navy

Manfred Koczur, Lt. Colonel, USAF

And to all those men and women scattered
around the world, walking the Trail.
You know who you are.

Acknowledgments

Thanks to:

John and Linda Quinn who got me off the Trail, and onto another one–one without grizzlies or the Frenchman in it.

Bob, the OSS Guy, for all the great stories about the real Terry and the Pirates.

Darryl Graham, USMC sniper extraordinaire. Among the bipeds, snipers are truly unique.

Frank and Archie for their stories of grizzly bear hunts.

Rod Carlson, USMC helicopter pilot and hockey player from Duluth, for his unflagging encouragement and sense of humor. Rod wrote the jacket copy. Feel free to blame him.

Rick DeMarinis and Kent Anderson who, inexplicably, got me started writing.

The original members of the Region One Anti-Drug Team–Barney and Gale and John and Roundhead.

The Friday afternoon crew of vets and other reprobates at Red's in Missoula–especially Jerry and Bob, Dale and John, Mark and George and Roger. A lot of the humor in this book is their fault.

Dr. Duncan Hubbard, physician, hunter, one of the unsung who goes above and beyond in his efforts to keep the holes in the dike plugged.

And first, foremost, and always, Yasuko and Kali, who not only permit but–why do they do this?–encourage my eccentricities.

Prologue
Laos, 1973

The mountain on the far side of the valley stood dark green and massive. Tendrils of mist clung to folds and finger ridges and to the jungled tops of vertical limestone outcroppings. Once upon a time, the small valley must have produced rice, but now the valley floor—maybe a thousand meters long and not more than four hundred meters wide—was a lake of waist high, yellow-green grass. Mist like slow smoke drifted across the tall grass.

To his right, in the direction the Huey would come, the mountain descended to a heavily forested saddle. Behind him rolling hills covered with a patchwork of grass and dense brush and, here and there, remnants of canopied forest, rose toward the distant, impossibly rugged ridges of the Annam Cordillera.

It had taken him a day and a half, staying off ridges and trails, snaking his way through forest and bamboo and elephant grass, to work his way down out of the hills to the small mound at the edge of the valley.

High grass and the branches and leaves of an ancient tree growing in the center of the mound allowed him to stand concealed beneath the tree.

Normally he would stay away from such an obvious spot, but because the grass was so high he needed the little bit of elevation that the mound offered to see across to the treeline on the other side. The slope of the hill behind him was where

1

he wanted to be, but the slope was too open, the nearest stands of brush and bamboo too far from the valley floor. He'd never make it to the helicopter if the meet went south.

There had been no need to insert him so far from the valley, except that he'd wanted a day or two to get reacquainted with the bush. But from the moment he'd jumped out of the helicopter, he'd felt at home. The rich, pungent smells of growing, living things overlaid with the stench of rot and decay. The sting and cut of elephant grass. All of it had been as familiar as yesterday.

He'd quickly moved away from the insertion point, through thick bamboo and grass taller than he was, into the forest. Dark, damp forest. Mold and moss and spider webs. Sunshine flickering in the leaves and branches high above, like the light from an old-time movie arcade.

In the morning, he'd waited for three deer, graceful and fragile and twitchy all at the same time, to move on. That afternoon, he'd been eyeball to eyeball with a green viper nearly invisible in the leaves.

Mr. Slide come home again.

A half klick or so from the mound, a cobra had appeared—the first King Cobra he'd ever encountered in the bush. Seriously spooky that snake. Pucker factor of at least twenty on a scale of ten.

He'd been sitting hidden inside a stand of thick bamboo on the other side of a nearly dry streambed, waiting for the afternoon rain so he could move down the open slope to the small mound with the big tree, and the snake had emerged from the grass on the lip of the far embankment. One second there'd been him and the mosquitoes and the ants and before his brain could even process what he was seeing a huge cobra, black at the head, flowed down the embankment to the streambed, gliding over and around and between moss-covered rocks and debris. Nearly fifteen feet of horror.

It had stopped and, for what seemed like a long time, lay motionless, its olive body nearly invisible in the rocks and debris. Finally it had raised its head slightly and flowed back up the embankment. At the top, a third of it still exposed on the embankment, it had sensed or smelled him and had risen, its small sleek head like a malignant periscope above the grass, and rotated toward him, exposing an underside of gray-brown. It searched forty-five degrees, back and forth, swaying from side to side, locking on to where he sat hidden and not even blinking in the thick, leafy bamboo. He could see white crossbars beneath an orange and yellow and black throat.

No jungle animal or human would have known he was there. He knew that from experience. But the cobra had known and had locked onto him, its jet-black eyes glinting. He'd clearly heard it growl. No hiss or spit or any of that. Growl. The most frightening sound he'd ever heard. He thought for sure it was going to come for him. Huang had taught him that King Cobras had no fear. They were known to attack any living creature in their territory, elephants included. And for sure he was in its territory. And not only was he in its territory but the terrain was too rough, the grass and low bamboo too thick for him to outrun it.

He'd eased the selector switch to full auto and pushed the safety off, and as he did the remainder of the cobra had retracted up the embankment, the head elevating even higher, hood spread white on the inside. It swayed from side to side, growling, its eyes pure black death. Angry and no fucking doubt about it. He'd had the eerie feeling that it could read his mind.

Sweat trickled down his back and along his rib cage, dripped from the corner of his right eye. If it came, it would go to ground—out of the grass and down the embankment and on him in seconds. He'd have to shoot it, and then the whole world would know he was there.

3

Even now, just thinking about it, he could feel the hair stand up on the back of his neck. Folklore said that King Cobras mated for life, and sometimes hunted in pairs. Kill one, and the other would hunt you as long at it had a trail to follow. Where had he heard that? Kipling, maybe. The other one was in the bamboo with him; he'd suddenly been sure of that. That was why the one he was watching hadn't gone to ground: it was waiting for its mate to sneak up on him.

He'd fought the nearly uncontrollable urge to see what was behind him. Was it cobras or black mambas that mated for life? There had been cobras in the Kipling stories his grandfather had read to him. The cobra could smell his fear; he was sure that it could. And he tried to hunch his back without moving, not taking his eyes off the snake swaying above the grass, hoping that if there was one behind him, it would strike his ruck and the radio inside.

The cobra rotated its head away from him, its hood no longer spread, and moved farther into the grass, its head smoothly sinking out of sight.

He sat there for a long time, more than an hour, waiting for the afternoon rains and the cobras to come. When the rain finally came, gray sheets of it obscuring even the embankment on the other side of the stream, he stood and forded the stream, and climbed the embankment and hurried through the grass on the other side, down the long, mostly open slope to the small mound.

He suspected that the cobras—he thought of it now in the plural—knew the tree and the mound. They probably hunted here.

And all through the long, wet night, he'd hoped that was all they did here—hoped that it was not also their home.

The rain had stopped before first light and he'd eaten some rice and *nuoc-mam,* had a drink of water, stashed the poncho in his ruck, and then, by touch, broke down the M-14, and

4

with a silicon-impregnated cloth wiped the parts. He reassembled the rifle–the same rifle he'd used before; God alone knew how Peter had managed to hang on to it. Ran a couple of patches down the bore. Unloaded the eight magazines, seventeen rounds per twenty-round magazine. Wiped each round. Reloaded the magazines. Seated a magazine in the rifle.

Quietly cycled the bolt. Made sure the safety was on. Put the other magazines back in the ammo pouches on his web gear. Put the cleaning gear back in the ruck. The usual drill.

It was like old times–except that he was light grenades and extra boxes of ammunition. And instead of the bulky 7X50 binoculars, he was making do with much smaller, plastic, nine-power Nikons.

He poured a spoonful of black, sandbag ash into his hand from the old, yellow plastic tobacco pouch that had been his grandfather's, added water, and mixed it into a thick paste. Dabbed and smeared the paste onto his face and neck and hands. In his opinion–an opinion not shared by Peter– sandbag ash beat the hell out of grease sticks. He wedged the tobacco pouch into one of the ammo pouches. If things got hinky, he'd leave the ruck and the radio, take only the rifle and web gear.

Finding a good hide had been impossible given the parameters of the mission. The grass was too high for him to lie prone, or even to sit, and he'd settled for standing in the bend of a branch that was at least a foot in diameter, solid as a fence rail. In the night, he'd cut branches and leaves so that he'd have a field of fire that included most of the other side of the tiny valley. By widening his stance and crouching slightly, he was able to wedge the branch between the back of his left arm and side. He'd adjusted the sling so that when he put the rifle stock into his shoulder, his left elbow was pulled solid and tight under the magazine and receiver. The sling plus the branch gave him a position as solid as resting the rifle on a sandbag. The flash suppressor was well back inside the hole he'd made in the outer branches and leaves. Being on the only elevated spot on the entire valley floor was not where he wanted to be, but at least the muzzle flash would be hard to spot.

Holding the rifle with his left hand, arm and hand wrapped in the sling, he lifted the Nikons and scanned the other side of the valley. Nothing moved. Only the slow creep of mist across grass. The forested mountainside had taken on definition, and the mist escaping from the forest made it look as if there was a ground fire.

According to Huang, there would be only three or four Chinese advisors. But there had to be a big unit nearby or the Chinese wouldn't be here at all. If there were more than five, the helicopter would not land and he'd have to hike back out.

Damn. He hadn't thought about that, hiking back out. AKs and RPGs and mortars were one thing, King cobras another. No way he wanted to walk back out through country inhabited by two snakes that size, with that kind of attitude.

He heard a rustle off to his left and saw grass ripple away from the base of the mound. He glanced slowly around. Nothing moved. No cobra periscoped above the grass. Something was watching him; he could feel it. He looked up into the branches. Nothing there, either. That's all he'd need, a giant cobra to fall out of the tree on him. This was getting weird. Serious weird. He'd spent *beaucoup* time in the bush and nothing like this had ever happened before. The actors in this little play hadn't even appeared and already he was as twitchy as the deer he'd seen.

There was movement across the valley and putting the Nikons to his eyes he saw four Asians in camouflage fatigues come out of the mist. Tall. Too big for Vietnamese. Some kind of Tiger-stripe camouflage. Floppy bush hats. Three with AKs slung barrel up. One–the one closest to him–with an AK slung so that it rested at his hip, barrel pointed forward. Extra magazine pouches were worn at the chest on the first three; a pistol was strapped to the waist of the one with the AK at his hip.

The guy with the pistol and one other were carrying what looked like half a body bag. The bag was square and from the way they were carrying it not heavy. The other two were carrying a full body bag, one at the head, one at the foot, the bag sagging into the grass between them. The front guy on the big bag had his hands behind his back holding onto a strap; the man at the rear was holding another strap with both hands in front of him. The large bag probably contained the heroin. The square bag the remains of a U.S. Special Forces Lieutenant.

He was there to help recover the remains. Peter had brokered the deal with the family. The heroin was part of the deal for use of the helicopter and pilots. Nothing was ever clean when spooks were involved–and the spooks were always involved. For some reason that he could not fathom, the heroin was worth more than money to the spooks.

The four men walked a hundred meters out into the grass, and dropped the bags. Maybe Huang and Peter were worried about nothing. Maybe for once this was going to go off without gunfire.

He dialed the scope for 250 meters. No windage. The helicopter would be putting out a lot of rotor wash, but at that distance it wouldn't make much difference.

From the direction of the saddle, the unmistakable thump of a Huey inbound reverberated across the valley. And a white Huey, blue at the tail and along the top of the fuselage and engine hump, thudded over the saddle, skimming the trees as it flew nap of the earth down into the tiny valley, the white fuselage stark against the rich greens of the saddle.

A white, Air America Huey. Fuck Oh Dear. How could you miss a white helicopter? Peter was thumbing his nose at the Chinese again. *Damn.* What an asshole he could be.

The Huey leveled out thirty feet above the grass on the other side of the tiny valley, rotor wash pushing grass and mist down and to the side behind it, like the wake from an airboat, rotor disc flashing against dark forest. It powered past the four Chinese, down to the far end of the valley, and banked into a sharp turn, the edge of the rotor disc only a few feet above the grass, the top of the helicopter visible beneath the disc.

He reached down to the ruck at his feet and keyed the radio twice, letting them know he was there. The Huey completed the turn and came straight for him down his side of the valley, the dark Plexiglas windows and the jungle behind it making it look like some gigantic prehistoric bug. As it flashed past, rotor wash buffeting leaves and branches, he again keyed the radio twice, marking his position so that the pilot would not put down between him and the four Chinese.

The helicopter continued to the base of the saddle and again banked into a sharp turn, tracing its way around the valley. It leveled out and headed toward the figures in the grass.

He'd glimpsed Peter alone in the belly, looking out the other side. He hadn't seen any guns. No M-60 hanging at the door. It was just like Peter to ride in on an unarmed helicopter. A snow-white, unarmed helicopter. Face, Peter was going to tell him—and then give him another of his long, involved, oh-so-boring lectures on the importance of face to the Oriental mind.

The helicopter slowed as it approached the waiting figures,

skids just above the grass, holding a hover about fifty meters from the four Chinese.

He put the rifle to his shoulder and leaned across the tree branch, cheek on his thumb on top the grip, and squirmed around until the crosshairs were dead steady on the chest of the Chinese with the pistol. The scope was dialed to the full nine power. At that distance he could make out facial features. The Chinese looked like an arrogant bastard. He'd lost his hat to the rotor wash. He pushed the safety off, but kept his finger away from the trigger. The other three Chinese were staring without emotion at the helicopter. One had lost his hat, but the other two had stuffed their hats behind their magazine pouches. Wind from the rotors rippled their fatigues, pressing the Tiger-stripe material tight against their bodies. The rotor wash was also serving to keep the mist away.

All of the Chinese still had their AKs slung. The lead Chinese had his pointed toward the Huey, but his arms were folded across his chest.

More face, no doubt.

He moved the scope to a point between the helicopter and the waiting Chinese, and watched as Peter—wearing jeans and a bright red Hawaiian shirt with yellow flowers—jumped out, a metal ammo can held in one hand. Peter's Browning HighPower was in a shoulder holster under his left armpit. Jesus. A Hawaiian shirt and a 9mm in a shoulder holster. Face, my ass. This was going way beyond face. What Peter was doing was comparable to throwing rocks at that cobra. The shirt and the shoulder holster and his black skin made him look like a Jamaican gangster—whatever a Jamaican gangster looked like.

The lead Chinese gave an arm signal and the crosshairs again settled on his chest. One man stayed put, and the other two bent and picked up the large bag and carried it to the

9

helicopter. Grass blew in concentric circles away from the helicopter.

Peter waited to the side, watching as they heaved the bag into the belly of the helicopter. The two Chinese turned and double-timed back through the grass to their original position next to the man who had stayed put.

Peter walked a few paces forward and stopped ten feet from the leader. He put the ammo can—filled with money and rubies—down in the grass.

One of the three Chinese bent and picked up the smaller bag. Through the scope he could see that the bag had been folded into a square a couple of feet across. The contents of the bag seemed to squirm beneath the gray-green covering, making it difficult for the Chinese to keep a solid grip on it as he handed it to the lead Chinese.

The first man moved back to the other two.

The lead Chinese held the body bag out toward Peter. Peter made no move to take the bag.

The Chinese shook the bag, making the contents move and slide. He laughed, and began throwing the bag up and down, shaking it as he caught it, the objects inside bulging and distorting the plastic. Peter stood hands folded across his chest, watching.

The Chinese threw the bag two handed at Peter's feet. He pointed down at the body bag, pointed at his slung AK, pointed at himself. The three Chinese behind him spread out, a five-yard interval between them.

He took a breath. Exhaled half of it. Put pressure on the trigger. Held.

Peter reached down in the grass and picked up the ammo can by the metal handle and threw the can underhand at the lead Chinese. The can struck the Chinese in the chest, knocking him a step backwards. His hand went to the slung AK, and as it did the crosshairs stabilized at the center of his chest and the rifle fired and the lead Chinese was down in the grass.

He shifted a fraction toward the other three and the rifle fired, and the scope settled, and the rifle fired, and the scope settled, and the rifle fired. As always, the rounds seemed to come more from his mind than from the rifle. Chest shots above the magazine pouches. One hundred sixty eight grain jacketed spiral boattails. Two thousand five hundred fifty feet per second. All of the Chinese were down. Only one, the second one, had been able to unsling his AK before the bullet punched him into rippling grass.

He took the rifle out of his shoulder and stood upright, scanning the far side of the valley with the binoculars. Nothing moved. All he could see was forest. There had to be others there. Peter was firing his 9mm down into the grass, moving quickly from man to man. Peter holstered the pistol and bent toward grass flattened by rotor wash and picked up the square body bag and the ammo can, and ran toward the helicopter. The helicopter was already up on its skids.

Holding the rifle in his left hand, he picked up the ruck and the radio with his right, and ducked under the branch and forced his way through leaves and branches, out from under the tree and through grass, stumbling and hurdling over the remnants of an old stone or concrete crypt that he hadn't seen in the grass, an image of a long, black snake raising its head forever etched in his mind as he jumped a recessed portion of the crypt.

Across the valley, the white Huey lifted from the grass and pivoted and, nose down a few degrees, tail up, headed straight for him. Forty yards out, it settled and slipped sideways toward him, skids dragging grass. *Shit hot pilot,* he thought. At least Peter had done that right. Rotor wash whipped and snapped at his fatigues, pressing against him as he charged toward the helicopter.

11

He threw his ruck and the radio ahead of him into the belly on top of the body bags, and handing the rifle to Peter staring open mouthed at something behind him, jumped in, twisting to sit with his ass in the doorway, feet on the skids as the Huey dipped and accelerated toward the end of the valley. The metal floor beneath him abruptly lifted, the g-forces like in a high speed elevator. Tree tops flashed beneath his feet. Blue-green tracers arched far behind into grass and trees on the hillside.

As they crested the saddle and immediately descended into the next valley, he hauled himself up into the seat across from Peter.

Peter handed him the rifle, shouting something, his voice lost in the wind coming through the open doorways.

"What?"

Peter grinned. "Face," he shouted.

He shook his head, and looked out the doorway. Looked down at the bags. The bags jiggled loosely on the vibrating floor.

The helicopter surged upward, headed for a safer altitude.

Face, he thought. What Peter meant was that selling dope to the barbarians and delivering their dead at the same time had not been enough for the Chinese. The Chinese had planned to shoot them, too. "If I throw the ammo can, light them up," had been Peter's instructions. "If I throw it, it means they are going to shoot us."

He watched the zipper on the small bag work its way open. The remains of a face, forehead and eye socket torn open, bone and tatters of gray flesh and clotted matter populated with colonies of squirming maggots pushed up out of the bag.

• • •

Two hours later, after he'd taken a shower and changed clothes, they sat on the veranda.

12

"Did you see those snakes?" Peter asked.

"What snakes?"

"Two of the biggest snakes I've ever seen were about ten yards behind you. Their heads were sticking up above the grass. I've never seen anything like it. Scared the shit out of me just looking at them."

"I think they live in that old grave I jumped across."

"Damn."

"Yeah."

"You must have spent the night right next to them."

"I reckon."

The sun felt good on his bare chest and legs and feet, the heat and the exposure to air drying out the usual assortment of bites and scratches and sores.

"You need to understand," Peter said. "They hate us. In their minds people like us have raped their country for centuries. Putting that head in there like that was their way of coping with the fact that they are business partners with people they despise. The head in the bag just wasn't enough face for the guy I threw the ammo can at–no pun intended."

Fucking Peter, he thought. No mention of the white helicopter or his Hawaiian shirt. Behind his eyelids the sun was orange and yellow, hot and clean on his face. From somewhere the sweet smell of flowers wafted across the veranda.

But underneath the smell of flowers and sun-baked veranda lingered the stench from the body bag. He could taste it at the back of his throat. And he knew that no amount of brushing his teeth or washing his body would be able to eradicate that smell from his memory. Not for a long time, anyway, and depending on how often he wanted to take it out and look at it, maybe never.

He'd thought they were doing it for the remains of somebody's son–and they were–but in the end the MIA remains had been secondary to the thing between Peter and the Chinese.

He wanted to blot the day out of his mind, wanted Peter's voice to go away, wanted to forget the head rising out of the bag like that–wanted only to concentrate on the sun and the heat.

He liked the heat. Liked to sweat. It made him feel clean.

After awhile, Peter's words, like everything else, went away. And in his mind only the snake watched.

Part I
Montana, 1987

Chapter 1
Winterkill

J ust inside the treeline Robert Lee and four men stood near two new brown-and-white trucks, BITTERROOT COUNTY SHERIFF'S DEPARTMENT lettered above white stars on the doors, TO PROTECT AND TO SERVE below the stars. The men watched as an old, faded-green International four-by-four trundled up the gravel road toward them.

Springs squeaking, engine rumbling, the International edged off the road and stopped behind the Sheriff's Department trucks.

Robert Lee left the group and walked toward the International.

The engine died, and the man inside hit the door with his shoulder. Hinges grated and the door opened a few inches.

"Damn, Tails. We heard you before we even saw you."

Ben Tails kicked the door all the way open and climbed down. "Don't be insulting my truck," he said. He slammed the door shut. "You know how sensitive it is."

"Yeah. Just like its owner."

"Yo, Tails!"

Ben Tails looked toward the four men clustered around the hood of the front truck; like Robert Lee, they were all wearing heavy wool shirts and trousers. A map was spread on the hood, two sides of the map held down by shotguns.

Ben grinned, and pointed at them. "Badges! Badges—"

15

"WE DON'T GOT TO SHOW YOU NO STINKIN' BADGES," they chorused.

"You fearless defenders of the public welfare play with that map a little more," Robert Lee said, "while I explain this to Ben." Ben could see that Robert Lee was packing a six-inch Smith and Wesson .44 magnum, full speed loaders in leather pouches. His boots were crusted with dried mud.

"Vacation's over, Tails!" one of the men called.

Robert Lee took off his sunglasses, and squinted up at Ben. "How you doing, Ben?"

"Fine. How you doing?"

"Well, someone was remarking a minute ago—Frank, I think it was—while we were listening to that tank—excuse me, that fine figure of a vehicle—come up the road, that we haven't seen much of you since—"

"Since the funeral."

"Now don't be getting pissed off again."

"I'm not getting pissed off. I'm just—" Ben looked away and made a gesture with his left hand, as if brushing something away. "Ahh. . . ."

Robert Lee leaned back against the fender of the International and folded his arms across his chest. He considered Ben for a moment. "I hear you are leaving us."

Ben looked at him. "Who told you that?"

"I'm the Sheriff. The Sheriff knows all."

"Yeah, right."

"George is on days off," Robert Lee said. "And I thought maybe you would give us a hand one last time before you depart for other climes." Robert Lee pushed off from the fender. "Come on over here. You'll like this." He walked around to the passenger side of his truck and opened the door and reached in and took a camouflage baseball cap off the seat. He handed it to Ben.

The cap was damp and sticky with dried mud and blood.

Ben stuck his fingers through two ragged holes in the bill. He handed the cap back. "Since it's not chewed, I assume that whoever was wearing it still has a head to put it on."

"The idiot who was wearing this could've lost his entire head and never known the difference." Robert Lee threw the cap back inside. "Says he hit it 'real good' at least twice."

He led Ben past the trucks to the edge of the trees and pointed down the valley toward an old abandoned homestead.

"See all those bushes and trees about three hundred meters to the left of the barn?" From where they stood, the collapsed barn and outbuildings looked like the scattered, bleached bones of a winter-killed animal.

"The old orchard, you mean?"

"Yeah. You used to grouse hunt down there, didn't you?"

"I used to hunt the creek on the other side of the barn." Ben had a sudden image of Evy in jeans and work boots and one of his gray sweatshirts, her black hair in a pony tail swinging back and forth as she came toward him. "I never hunted the orchard. Too many bears."

"Two hundred meters on the other side of that fallen-down barn is what's left of a barbed wire fence," Robert Lee said.

"Don't you ever do that again," she'd said, pissed off because he'd just shot a fool's hen she'd been stalking, the 158 grain hollow point from his .357 missing the head and exploding the body a few yards in front of her. It had been a stupid thing to do. One of those things he wished he could take back.

"It's another hundred meters past that to what's left of the orchard," Robert Lee said. "Looks pretty easy from up here, but the whole area is wet. In fact, it's a swamp. The brush and grass are so thick the bears have got tunnels going through it."

A grizzly charge in there would be as sudden as a grouse or a pheasant coming up out of grass, Ben thought. And maybe as close. Abruptly he was aware of the trees around them, the shush of pine needles moving in the wind.

His eyes quartered the old orchard and the open grassy slope between the orchard and the treeline.

Robert Lee said, "They stopped and asked at one of the places down below if it was okay to hunt pheasant. 'Sure. Help yourself. Lots of birds.' No one said anything about the bears because they figured you'd have to be blind, deaf, and dumb not to know they were in there. "

"You sure it was grizzlies?"

"A sow with two big cubs, and a big boar, near as Frank can tell."

"A lot of sign, that many bears."

"I went down there a while ago to check the situation out— that's when I found the hat. The stupid bastards were *walking* in fresh bear shit. Piles of it."

"This is no longer in my job description, Robert Lee."

Robert Lee smiled. "The locals say these particular bears live here all year, except July, when they head up the canyon to eat lady bugs. Sometimes they come up to the houses, look in the windows. The people hereabouts kind of like having them around."

Ben sighed. "So what happened?"

"About what you'd imagine. A pheasant went up out in the field, and the guy started blasting away. The bears jumped up and ran for the brush."

Ben tried to imagine four grizzlies rising up out of the grass.

"The other guy, he hears the shots, and looks over toward the orchard. Stands up. And I'll be damned. Lookee here. Four grizzlies beating feet about thirty five miles an hour straight at him."

"What's Frank say about that boar hanging around?"

"It's unusual. But he was definitely there. I saw the tracks myself. He's from a previous litter, maybe. One old guy I

18

talked to said he'd seen the boar following the other three around."

"I suppose the guy wearing that hat started shooting."

"Yeah. A shotgun. Bird loads. Which at that distance was about as useful as throwing rocks. The two cubs and the boar went by on either side, and the sow ran right over the top of him. Stopped just long enough to put his head in her mouth and slap him—he's got a few scratches and lacerations, but nothing serious. She wasn't trying to kill him. Just sort of wanted to say, stop shooting me and get the fuck out of my way."

"How many times did he say he hit her?"

"He says he fired seven rounds. Too many rounds in the gun, I know." Robert Lee reached down and pulled a shoot of grass from its stem, and put it in his mouth. "Says he hit her pointblank in the face and chest. Lots of blood; so probably."

He spit out a piece of the stem.

"Anyway, there he is. He's just experienced bear halitosis up close and personal, and he's got a scalp wound bleeding into his eyes. So what does he do? He panics and runs the wrong way. Ran right through the whole damn swamp, if you can believe it. Finally came out at a place about a mile the other side. Woman there says she heard him coming a long time before he got there."

"Reckon I'd be inclined to a little panic myself."

"I suppose." Robert Lee threw the grass shoot away. "I'm pissed because he was such a lucky fucker. Turns out the woman is a registered nurse. She patched up his cuts and scratches and called us. No ambulance needed."

"What about his buddy? What was he doing all this time?"

"Oh, his buddy is a real piece of work, his buddy is. He saw the bears jump up and take off at warp speed straight for his friend. Stood there for awhile listening to all the

19

bloodcurdling sounds coming from the bushes, and then ran back to the truck and locked himself in."

"He didn't go for help?"

"His buddy had the keys. And he was convinced by then that the keys were inside the digestive tract of a seriously irritated bear—we are not talking rocket scientists here, you understand. These guys were stupid enough to be hunting down there in the first place. He was sure the bears were coming to get him next; so he locked himself in the truck."

"Too bad they didn't."

Robert Lee laughed. "When we got there, he was still honking the horn—the battery was about gone, and it was the most anemic little beeping sound you ever heard."

"So what I hear you saying is that the bears were justified. The hunters were responsible for what happened. No one was seriously hurt or killed."

"That's about the size of it. And normally I'd say too fucking bad, and let the bear go. But she's hurt. Probably hurt bad. So we've got to make sure she's dead."

"Otherwise someone might get hurt and sue the ass off the County."

"There you go."

"Where are the boar and the cubs?"

"Probably up in the snow somewhere."

Ben Tails put his hands in his back pockets. He looked down toward the old homestead.

"Maybe she already bled to death," he said.

Robert Lee smiled and put his sunglasses back on.

"Nevah happen, Marine," he said. "We're not that lucky. Not in this life, anyway."

• • •

"Okay. It's Frank and me and Ben here," Robert Lee said. They were standing in front of the old homestead.

Desiccated cow pies littered the over-grazed, weed-infested ground.

"Backup team don't come in unless one of us calls for you."

Waist-high thistles sprouted here and there in the yard and out of broken, weathered boards on the steps and porch.

"No matter how much commotion you hear, don't come in unless one of us calls. It's going to be hard enough without you running around in there, too."

Everyone nodded. They all knew the drill, but it had to be said. When the shit hit the fan, it was amazing how many bad decisions could be made by otherwise intelligent, experienced people.

"Everything's going to get real crowded and tense in there. Most likely the best we'll be able to do is one man move a few steps at a time. Remember. No matter how thick it gets, keep in sight of at least one man at all times. Frank?"

"Make noise," Frank said. "Keep her moving. The more she moves, the more she bleeds. The more she bleeds, the sooner she dies. I don't got to tell you to holler 'bear' if you see her."

"Questions?" Robert Lee said. "Okay. Check your weapons. Take a piss. Beat your meat. I got to call the County and let them know we're going to be busy for awhile."

The group broke apart. Frank and Ben walked toward what was left of the fallen-down fence.

"What you been up to?" Frank asked. Frank was Evy's cousin, half-Indian, darker skinned than Evy. Same gray eyes.

"Not much. A little fishing now and then. You?"

"Same old same old. Write a few tickets. Bar fights, dog calls. You know."

"I see you found someone to take my place."

"You mean the guy who found you down at the river? Nah, you're still a deputy, far as I know. Robert Lee finagled another new position, is all."

21

"New trucks. New deputy. He must of caught the commissioners in bed with each other."

"It's some kind of government money. Law enforcement grant, or something. You know him. I can't never understand how he does it."

Ben put his hands in his back pockets and looked off toward the mountains. The cubs and the boar would be up near the snow line now, he thought. Afraid. Angry. "Might as well tell you now as later," he said. "I'm going away for awhile."

"Kind of thought you would. Back to Asia?"

"Yeah. That old guy, Jim—remember him? He offered me a job."

"Indian guy. Leaky waders. That one?"

"That's the one. He's got a company in Asia."

"Where you going this time?"

"Japan, I think."

"Japan? Damn, Ben. What are you going to do in Japan?"

"Not really sure." He glanced at Frank. "Checking out bad guys is all I know."

"Bad guys." Frank shook his head. "You told Manfred and Robert Lee yet?"

"Haven't had a chance to tell Manfred. Robert Lee is good friends with Jim, and he already knew."

They were silent for a long moment, gazing out at the field.

Ben shook his head. "Every time I turn and look at that old house, I keep expecting her to walk out onto the porch."

Frank looked down and scuffed at a dried-out cowpie. "We all miss her, Ben." The cowpie came apart. "Not as much as you, maybe. But we all miss her."

"I should have married her."

"Hell, that wouldn't have made no difference." Behind them Robert Lee was talking on the radio.

The bears had listened to the men, one on either side, come closer and closer, Ben thought.

"How you fixed for shotgun ammunition?" Frank asked.
"I could use a little more."

"One box be enough?"

"If it's not, we'll call for an air strike."

Frank smiled. "I'll be right back." He turned and headed across the weed and cowpie-littered yard.

Ben sat down against one of the few still standing fence posts. He placed the shotgun across his legs, barrel pointed toward the field. He leaned his head back against the post and closed his eyes, feeling the October sun against the side of his face.

It was a good place, this place, he thought. They'd had many good places, but this place with the bones of buildings and animals on its breath put her being dead in a context he could understand.

He was going away again. Maybe for a long time, this time. So that when he came back, she'd be just another set of memories boxed and bagged and put away in the proper compartment, like his memories of Vietnam and Asia. But right now, in this place, she was more than that. He could feel her here. It was good to feel her again.

A breeze ruffled dry grass behind him, whispered cool across the side of his face. He smelled grass and earth, gun oil.

The bear would have gone to ground by now, but the breeze would filter man smell through the grass and trees and get her moving again.

He tilted his head away from the sun, and opened his eyes and stared up at the sky, a huge blue bowl that became deeper the longer he looked at it. She had loved that sky, had said she couldn't live without it. Wouldn't go to Asia with him, not even for a vacation.

Her bones, this country.

Yours, too, he heard her say.

He'd better go help her, he thought. She's out back cleaning the grouse.

He stood and propped the shotgun against the post and walked across the dusty yard.

But when he walked around the corner of the house, she wasn't there. Of course, she wasn't there. What did he expect? Where she'd been was only bare ground, an empty water trough, a rusty hand pump.

Ice-cold water, shiny and clear, had come out of that spigot. But looking at it now, he had the feeling that working the handle would produce only rusty squeaks, the wheeze of pipe gone long dry.

He closed his eyes. Stood there feeling the sun.

Something about the pump and the trough was oddly comfortable.

He opened his eyes, and the ground was dry and the trough was empty, he could see that, and behind him, around the corner, were Robert Lee and Frank and the others, he knew that, too, but superimposed on all that was an image of the trough full of water, the ground around it muddied with matted feathers.

Evy knelt next to the trough, her sweatshirt on the pump handle, rinsing a cleaned grouse in the cold water, swishing it back and forth. With her free hand she brushed hair from her eyes. There was a smudge of blood on her cheek. She put the grouse in the styrofoam cooler.

"Want to fool around?"

"What?" Not really paying attention, putting the lid on the cooler.

"The Mighty Hunter wishes his woman to engage in another of her womanly duties."

Her gray eyes focused on his, irritated until she recognized his awkwardness.

She grinned. That slow grin. First with her eyes, then with her mouth.

He rested his face against the weathered boards of the abandoned house. Beyond the rusty pump and the empty trough, mountains dusted with snow stood etched against blue sky.

Cattle and mice and other critters had been in there before them, but through the busted-out windows and holes in the walls a breeze had brought the smell of grass and pine, a hint of apple.

"Come, Mighty Hunter," she'd said, and laughed, and grabbing him, pulled him shuffling, pants around his ankles, to an old table, the only piece of furniture left in the place.

With her free hand she brushed dust and dirt from the table, and then turned toward him, and lay back on the table. A dusty shaft of light coming through the far wall made a sash across her stomach and breasts. Behind the sunlight her eyes glittered like licked stones.

"Where's Tails?" he heard Robert Lee ask.

He straightened away from the wall as Robert Lee came around the corner behind him.

"There you are. What are you doing back here?

"Waiting for you to come and ask me what I'm doing back here."

"You ready?"

"I'm ready."

"Well, let's do it, then."

He turned and followed Robert Lee. But at the corner of the house, he glanced back at the old hand pump and the empty water trough and, as he did, caught a glimpse of her hair and the back of her neck as she bent over the trough. Only a glimpse, and only for an instant. And as he turned away to go and kill the bear, it was an old, rusty hand pump and an empty wooden water trough.

Only that and nothing more, he thought.

25

Chapter 2
Blood Trail

Splashes and drips of dried blood on trampled grass and leaves marked the beginning of the blood trail. Vibram-soled boots went in one direction, blood and bear prints in another. The marks were those of a bear with long, relatively straight claws, not the curled claws of a black bear.

Frank tracked. Ben and Robert Lee were spread to either side. A few scattered bushes and small stands of birch dotted the high grass.

"This isn't so bad," Ben said.

Robert Lee smiled. "You'll see," he said.

Eighty meters later, black, gummy mud and wet grass sucked at their boots. Thorn-filled bushes clung to pants and shirts, scratched hands and forearms.

Sunlight made the leaves bright green, but behind the leaves and in the deep grass the shadows were impenetrable, constantly moving, flickering, rustling in sudden breezes.

It wasn't afraid of them, Ben reminded himself. It knew people. Lived near people.

Probably knew more about people than people knew about it. Otherwise, it would have killed the hunter.

It knew every tree and bush, every dip and hollow. This was its home.

It was strong, intelligent. More dangerous than the predators he'd avoided in Asia. It was capable of a rage that would put it beyond caring about anything except taking them with it.

26

Bear tunnels meandered through grass and bushes, forcing Frank for long seconds to be out of sight as he crawled through sections of tunnel, following the blood trail.

Whole companies of grizzlies could hide in here, Ben thought. From up on the hillside the area had appeared level, but once into it they had discovered gullies and holes camouflaged by the high grass. Here and there bushes had been raked clean of berries to a height beyond his reach.

He kicked a clump of grass, and a cloud of gnats rose in a sooty puff. When he wiped his forehead, his hand came away speckled with bugs.

From the tracks, Frank judged the bear to be around six hundred pounds. A six hundred pound she-grizzly, hurt and dying, Ben thought. It would be a real mess trying to shoot it if it got to one of them. A blur of fur and mud and grass and whoever it was she'd got hold of.

You couldn't stand back and shoot. There was too much danger of hitting whoever it had hold of. Someone would have to stick a shotgun up its ass. Real *semper fi* bullshit that, like all *semper fi* bullshit, meant they'd all get hurt if it got hold of one of them. What was he doing here, anyway? He didn't need to be here. He was out of here in a few days.

He glanced at his watch. Forty minutes. They'd gone a whole hundred meters in forty minutes. Bleed to death, Bear. Bleed to death.

Crazy Frank crawling into another bear tunnel.

Water everywhere. Wet feet. Wet pants. Muck sticking to his boots. Decomposing vegetation. Rotted apples. Over-ripe berries. Bear stink. Clearings no more than twenty or thirty meters across. A grizzly could cover thirty meters almost before you could get a shot off.

Bleed to death in a clearing, Bear. Be nice and stay out of the bushes and trees, Bear.

Fat chance. Robert Lee was right. They weren't that lucky.

27

That kind of luck was reserved for idiots who shot at grizzlies with bird shot.

He felt this one in his bones.

Frank rose from the grass ten meters to his right front, sweat dripping from nose and chin. In front of him a wall of bushes and trees intruded into the clearing. "Now I know how those tunnel rats must've felt."

"No gooks with grenades and snakes in these tunnels," Robert Lee said.

"Yeah. Just a wounded grizzly bear." Sunlight reflected off leaves, made it impossible for them to see inside the wall of bushes and trees. Frank studied the ground. "Be advised, we're getting close."

"Just think of all the people who'll sleep better tonight because of what you're doing," Ben said.

"The only sleeping habits I'm affecting are my own. Man, I can't believe you let Robert Lee con you into doing this."

"Yeah, I had to talk real hard," Robert Lee said. Thigh deep in grass, he moved farther out into the clearing. From there he could see into another smaller clearing on the other side of the bushes Frank had to go through.

"Go ahead," Robert Lee said.

"Easy for you to say," Frank said, and stepped into the bushes.

They heard the rustle and shake of leaves, the splinter of green branches. Silence.

"Shit," Frank said from the other side. "Two bears been in here. And one of them is big. *Really* big."

"How recently?" Robert Lee asked.

"Hard to say with all this water. Couple of hours, maybe."

"Must've been the boar on his way up the hill," Robert Lee said.

"Yeah."

Ben licked his lips, and spit out gnats at the corner of his mouth. The bear was near; he could feel it. He pivoted his head back and forth in a forty-five degree arc, shotgun angled up, finger outside the trigger guard, keeping his eyes moving, trying not to see in the grass and shadows across the clearing what wasn't there.

"You on the other side?" Robert Lee called to Frank.

"Yeah."

"I'm coming through." He looked toward Ben.

Ben nodded, and Robert Lee moved forward into the bushes, and as he did, Ben felt his entire body flush, his stomach go hollow—all that before his brain registered movement. Movement not defined. Only the vague sense of a large mass easing through shadow and light.

"Bear!" he yelled, the shotgun into his shoulder, tracking back and forth across the area where he thought he'd seen movement. "Robert Lee's right! Twenty meters!"

Sunlight shivered across leaves on the other side of the clearing. He could feel it watching him, and in one of those vagaries of memory, triggered by a coincidence of sunlight and place and fear, he thought that this time it was him caught in the open, the utter unreasonableness of his being out in the open more terrifying than the knowledge that being out in the open meant he was dead.

He heard Frank crash forward through bushes: getting Robert Lee out of his field of fire.

His heart hammered. He wasn't caught in the open; out in the open was good. It was a bear, not a man with a gun.

The tops of the bushes moved. Wind, or something inside them, he couldn't be sure.

Sweat dripped off his eyebrow.

Come on, bear. Do it. Go for it.

It wasn't there anymore. He blinked sweat out of his eye.

He hadn't seen it or heard it, but he knew it wasn't there anymore. Fucking bears. He'd rather hunt a man with a gun.

29

That's what he'd been doing in that other clearing.

Watching bugs and spiders. A big, ugly-gray snake had crawled over the barrel of his rifle.

Nothing else had moved for hours. Only wind on leaves and in the grass.

One second there'd been empty clearing, and the next there'd been a stocky little Vietnamese in Tiger stripes and bush hat, and when he'd put the scope on him, he'd seen it in his eyes: the sick knowledge that he was dead because someone was there after all.

Maybe it hadn't been a bear. Maybe it was a big whitetail, a grouse going from branch to branch.

"Where is it now?" Robert Lee's voice from the other side of the bushes sounded small and distant.

"I don't know." His voice sounded puny as Robert Lee's.

He shifted his weight to make his thigh stop twitching.

Bears could do that. Make you think they were gone when they were still there. People couldn't. You always knew if people were still there. That NVA had known; he'd just stopped listening to himself.

"What?" Robert Lee shouted.

"I don't know." Better, his voice sounded better.

If that was a human being over there, then you were locked on, and nothing that person could do could make you lose that lock. That Vietnamese had been for real: it'd taken him all day to talk himself into believing the human being he was locked onto wasn't really there.

"You want us to come back over there?" Frank shouted.

"No. I'll come to you."

He licked his lips. He'd have to turn his back on where he'd seen the bear, then push through trees and bushes to get to the other side. If she charged then, the noise he'd be making would cover any sound she'd make coming across the clearing.

30

But he'd be out of luck, anyway, even if he heard her coming, because once into the bushes, he'd never be able to get turned around fast enough to do anything about it.

"How thick is this shit?"

"Couple of yards. Nothing big."

Fuckit, he thought, and turned and branches and thorns slapped, scratched at his face and neck. Muck and tangled grass sucked at his feet, tried to trip him. The shotgun caught on a branch, and he twisted it sideways, breaking the branch to free it. In his mind he saw the grizzly break cover. Shadows flickered with the sound of branches and leaves hitting him. And then he was out in bright sunlight, backing away from where he'd broken through, shotgun leveled.

The bushes showed nothing of his passage, only a thin, irregular line in the grass leading directly to him. Out of the corner of his eye, he saw Frank faced toward the bushes, shotgun into his shoulder.

"This sucks," Ben said.

"Ah, you love it," Robert Lee said. He was faced away from them, in the direction Ben had said the bear was moving.

Frank relaxed his shotgun. "Man, you came through there like you *was* the bear."

"It was moving like it's not hurt at all."

"Oh, that's just great," Robert Lee said. "A hurt bear that's decided it isn't hurt."

"You sure?" Frank asked.

"I'm sure."

"Well, there's a lot of blood. She ought to be dead or about dead already. But you know grizzlies."

"The other team'll be making noise," Robert Lee said. "That'll stop her from getting around behind us. Let's tighten the interval. Keep it no more than ten meters. Ben, you're the best shot; you try to stay in the middle. We'll crowd her while we've still got decent light–but not so much she'll get

31

pissed off enough to come after us. If it gets dark, we'll try again in the morning."

"What's this 'we' shit?" Ben said.

Robert Lee and Frank looked at him. "Sorry," Robert Lee said. "I meant Frank and me'll try in the morning."

Frank laughed, and shook his head, and turned and began following the blood trail.

Chapter 3
Reasons

Inside the birch stand blood glistened on white bark. "Look at this," Frank said. Coarse black hairs, like bristles from a cheap paint brush, were stuck in the blood. It was cooler in the trees, free of gnats, but the air was metallic with the smell of blood. Broken branches, like pieces of bloody bone, littered the grass.

The bear was close, very close, the blood told them that, and they now moved hardly aware of soggy boots and wet trousers, of pushing through waist-high bushes, of stooping low under branches too heavy to be shoved aside, focused only on reacting, fatigue purged by the steady drip of adrenaline.

She was hurt bad, the blood told them that, but teeth marks on tree and branch said she was angry and working herself into a rage. The teeth marks forced them to acknowledge what they'd known for a while now: in that place, against an animal like the one they were following, against the kind of madness such an animal could generate, they were at a disadvantage. Even with their weapons and their numbers they were at a disadvantage. Had they been predators other than human, they would have long ago broken off pursuit.

Ben edged through a bush too tall to see over, shotgun held waist high and in front of him, and found himself in a clearing of yellow grass. Thirty or forty meters on the other side of the clearing, the hump and shoulders, the head of a large, cinnamon-brown grizzly moved through thick grass.

"Bear!" he yelled, and the head of the bear swung toward him as if jerked with a rope. Its eyes met his, and it charged, disappearing immediately into a cut or gully he couldn't see.

And came up ten meters closer, chest and shoulders and head enormous, eyes black sparks.

The shotgun smacked his cheekbone. He chambered another round and fired. Chambered another round and Robert Lee and Frank fired and he fired.

The bear was down, out of sight, in another hole or cut, bawling and snorting.

It came up again. "More motivated, this time," Robert Lee later said. And they fired, a smooth, continuous, unthinking coordination of trigger pull and shotgun recoil and working the action, and trigger pull and shotgun recoil and working the action. "Like automatic weapons fire," Bill, the second bear team leader, would later say.

The bear went down again. All three shotguns were empty. It was still trying to move.

Ben smoothly reloaded, reaching into his pant pocket for rounds, one the first time, inserting it into the tube and jacking it immediately into the chamber, then a handful, one at a time into the tube, watching the bear, as Robert Lee with his .44 magnum, and Frank with his .357 aimed one-handed, both of them Camp Perry perfect, and carefully, in measured rhythm, emptied their revolvers into the massive animal less than ten meters away, the sound of their revolvers puny compared to the sound of the shotguns.

Each time a round hit, the bear flinched and rumbled.

Ben finished reloading, and Frank and Robert Lee with speed loaders reloaded their revolvers, shotguns held in the crook of their arms. They looked like British sportsmen out for a bird shoot on the moors, Ben thought.

Wordlessly the three of them fanned out, walking through the grass to within a few yards of the bear, weapons extended.

The barrel of Robert Lee's revolver trembled. He lowered it to his side, and took a deep breath, and raised it again. With a sound like boards being slapped together, the barrel kicked upwards, came down steady, kicked upwards again.

The bear was silent..

Robert Lee fired the remaining four rounds in rapid succession, the rounds slapping inert meat and fur.

The bear remained silent.

The skin of their faces was tight and shiny across cheekbone and forehead. Gradually they became aware of the ringing in their ears, the smell of cordite.

Robert Lee ejected the spent cartridges from his pistol, unsnapped another speed loader from his belt, and reloaded.

"Bear 1, Bear 2," a tiny voice from the radio on Robert Lee's belt said.

Robert Lee put the empty speed loader in his shirt pocket, and holstered the .44. He unsnapped and pulled the radio out.

"Bear 1."

"What's going on, Bear 1?"

"We've got her down. Everything's okay."

"Sounded like a war, and you guys weren't winning."

"Go on back and get the truck with the winch and bring it in as far as you can."

"10-4. One truck on the way."

"One of you take the other truck up the mountain, and direct the one with the winch toward us."

"10-4."

Ben headed toward a mound of grass, looking for a place to sit. Six hundred pounds, my ass, he thought. Half a ton was more like it. No way he was going to help drag half a ton of dead bear through mud and weeds. The Sheriff's

Department could handle that. Frank probably knew all along, just didn't want him and Robert Lee to get their bowels in an uproar over another four hundred pounds of bear.

Not that size made much difference. They would have gone after it regardless.

His skin felt tight and greasy. His cheek and shoulder throbbed from the shotgun recoil. Definitely going to be a few dreams about this one, he thought.

Killing something that wasn't bothering with him at all. Doing his duty. Serving and Protecting.

Well, that was a lie, wasn't it? He did it so he could see what was in its eyes. And, truth be told, that was why he and Evy hadn't gotten married. Why it probably never would have worked for them.

Don't need no cocaine; don't need no alcohol. A junky by any name.

And when the rush was gone, all he had to show for his trouble was the desire to take a nap. That, and a little gut ugly to remind himself of what he'd done. Evy had been right to be pissed off at him for blowing a grouse away like that.

He stopped for a moment and looked around. Robert Lee and Frank were bent over the grizzly. To his left bushes intruded into the high grass of the clearing, a spattering of bright red leaves on one of the bushes.

Man, was he tired. Tired of everything. He'd spent his life serving God and Country and the human race, and look at him. He looked up at the sky, her sky. Can you see me now, Evy? She'd cry if she could see how they'd massacred that bear. She'd felt toward grizzlies and other wild animals what most people feel toward religion.

He could see the shaft of sunlight across her body, dust motes in front of her eyes.

The leaves on the bushes in front of him glistened, and he

frowned, distracted by the strange red color, part of his mind thinking Evy and sunlight, part of his mind curious about the leaves and saying blight or fungus or *blood on the leaves,* and Evy reared up out of the grass, one eye bloodshot and almost dead, the other eye a mass of leaking red meat. And stretched, rising toward him, its mouth a rictus of dripping saliva and bloody fangs. His mind registered fur matted with blood and mud and tangled with branches, and he saw in minute detail where the eye had been. Felt his hand pull the action. Felt his finger depress the safety, as someone screamed, "Bear!" Felt the action come all the way back, a calm voice inside him saying, *never happen.* Felt his teeth clench, his neck and shoulders brace. Saw viscous blood and mucous stretch from blood yellow fangs to blood-red gums and teeth as the action chunked forward and the shotgun kicked in his hands, the blast ruffling through matted hair into the bushes behind, the shock of the pointblank miss instantly escalating his awareness to a freeze frame of reality—an impossibly huge moment filled with the horror of what was happening, and the terror of a dream he'd had hundreds of times: pulling the trigger and nothing happening.

Teeth and fangs snapped together, and the bear slowly eased sideways.

A shotgun not his boomed, and a choked roar rumbled up out of the grass.

He heard another round chambered and the shotgun again fired, the rumble more distant this time.

"You all right?" Frank shouted next to him.

Robert Lee appeared, his .44 extended toward the bear. Robert Lee fired.

A tiny rumble, but still a rumble.

"You okay?" Frank asked again. Robert Lee fired again.

The bear rumbled louder.

Frank chambered a round, aimed, fired.

37

Silence. Only the numbness in his ears and in his mind.

"One more time," Robert Lee said.

Later, they discovered that in both bears most of the shots had been killing shots, the slugs going nearly through the bodies.

Frank reached over and set the safety on Ben's shotgun. "You just used up about eight lives, my man."

"Bear 1, Bear 2."

Robert Lee took out the radio, and stared at it for a moment. Ben knew what he was thinking. The radio signal went to a repeater on one of the mountains. The repeater relayed the signal to other police radios and repeaters all over western Montana, and to any citizen with a scanner. He wasn't going to put out over the air that they'd just shot another grizzly—the right one, this time.

"It's okay, Bear 2. Come on up."

There was a long pause.

"10-4."

"I was just coming over to tell you we'd shot the wrong bear," Frank said to Ben. "Damned near shit my drawers when she raised up like that."

"Where'd the first one come from?" Robert Lee asked.

"Must be the boar. Hung around to protect her, I guess. Who knows?" Frank stared down at the carcass. "Grizzlies." He shook his head. "They get that chemical in their blood—"

He looked up at Ben. "You know what happened? She fainted. She lost so much blood that when she raised up and gathered herself like that, it drained her brain, and she fainted."

"You look like you've seen a ghost or something," Robert Lee said to Ben.

Ben laughed. A short harsh sound, vacant as the abandoned homestead.

Chapter 4
Ben Tails

Two leathery ranchers, worn and sweat-stained Stetsons tipped up on the back of their heads, stood at the end of the magnificent hardwood bar, their dark brown, heavy-veined hands at odds with the pale skin across their foreheads.

Manfred, the owner, and since grade school Ben's best friend, short and broad and crew-cut, absently wiped the counter with a white cloth. Manfred had been part of Robert Lee's Special Forces team in the later years of the Vietnam War.

A color TV mounted high in the corner across the room silently flickered sportscasters in red blazers talking into microphones against a background of green astro-turf. Above the door, a magnificent elk nearly a hundred years old, stared down at Arnold, retired and from California, passed out head down on the bar. Arnold's lips were pursed to the side, his cheek flattened against the scarred and carved bar top.

Other animal heads were mounted around the room. A pronghorn with a goofy grin. Another elk. Two deer, both whitetail. A goat with a withered, crooked horn. A benign grizzly dusty and moth-eaten and smaller than either of the two they'd shot that afternoon. The grizzly had been mounted back in the days before it became necessary to show bears snarling—back in the days when people knew bears were usually killed while eating berries or digging for bugs or just ambling along totally unaware they were about to have their day ruined by a high velocity rifle bullet.

Brown and cream linoleum squares, the two colors over the years become almost one, formica-topped metal tables, chromed chairs, red, plastic seats and backs, fluorescent lights, poker machines, the massive, ancient hardwood bar, Olympia, Bud, Rainier lights along the sides of the mirror, mounted animal heads—the bar was neither quaint nor seedy, was merely a bar that, if you were from there, retained pieces of every generation that had inhabited it. To strangers it seemed an abused relic of grander, more romantic times. But to Ben it was home and history, the juxtaposition of a shiny, new poker machine with the moth-eaten head of a grizzly killed a century before completely natural.

Robert Lee drained his beer. He held up two fingers. "Couple of shots, if you please, bartender."

Manfred brought two shot glasses of whiskey to the table. "You stink," he said to Robert Lee.

"So would you if you'd been doing what I been doing."

Manfred headed back for the bar.

"Fucking guy," Robert Lee said.

"You are a little ripe."

"We got the truck with the bears in it stuck, and it took the winch and the other truck and us pushing for damn near an hour to get it out." He picked up the shot glass. "Here's to those who do, and here's to those who don't. And to hell with those that don't."

"I'll drink to that."

Robert Lee took a sip of whiskey and put the glass down onto the table. "I got to apologize for something," he said.

"This'll be a first."

"How many times you heard me lecture new guys about never assume anything?"

"I'm not a new guy."

"First thing I tell new guys: never assume anything. Never. So I got to apologize–although I have to admit that since it's you it pains me to do so."

"We all assumed the same thing," Ben said. "Frank, too. Hell, you don't know enough about grizzlies to assume anything, let alone apologize for it. That's like me apologizing for grits, or something."

"Oh, oh. You shouldn't have said that," Manfred said from the bar.

"Yeah," Robert Lee said. "You should've seen Mr. Montana here. Eyes the size of dinner plates. Face about as white as that towel in your hand."

"It's true. My life went right before my very eyes."

The two ranchers at the far end of the bar stood and picked their change off the bar, leaving the coins, and headed for the back door. "Night, Manny," one called.

"You boys take care drivin' home."

"Hell for? Sheriff's sittin' right there, and he's already drank more'n us." The rickety, wooden screen door slapped shut behind their laughter.

"What's this? Pick on the Sheriff night?" Robert Lee said. "Just bring us the bottle, will you," he said to Manfred.

"What's the occasion?" Manfred asked.

"What do you think is the occasion? Getting rid of Ben is the occasion."

Manfred stared at Ben.

"Don't look at me like that," Ben said. "I would of told you sooner, but I didn't have a chance."

"Where are you going this time–as if I didn't know?"

"Back to the Land of the Little People."

"Laos? Thailand?"

"Japan."

"Japan? *Japan?* What in the name of God are you going to do in Japan that the Japanese can't do themselves?"

41

Ben sipped his whiskey.

"You know," Manfred said. "For someone who's supposed to be so smart, sometimes I think you're dumber than a box of rocks."

Ben lowered the shot glass to the tabletop and pushed it slowly back and forth across the formica.

"This ought to be good," Manfred said.

"You'll probably think I'm crazy."

"I *know* you're crazy," Manfred said.

"Remember Jim?" Ben said. "That old Indian guy. The fly fisherman."

Manfred's eyes narrowed. "What about him?"

"I'm going to work for him."

"You're going to work for him." There was a hardness in Manfred's eyes that Ben had not seen in a long time. "Well, I don't want to be telling you anything."

"But you're going to."

"I'm going to because I have to live with myself—such as I am."

Ben laughed. "You said it, not me."

"Do not be messing around with the Pumpkin Eater again."

"The Pumpkin Eater? What are you talking about? Who said anything about the Pumpkin Eater?"

"Unless he's dead—which somehow I doubt—if you go back over there, sooner or later you are going to meet up with him again. I know you, Ben. *We* know you. You go back over there and sure as God made little green apples, you'll start fucking around again."

"That was a long time ago, Manfred. If I never see him again, it'll be just fine with me. Anyway, he isn't what you think."

"He isn't what I think. Right. Robert Lee here is just the one gave him his name, is all."

"What are you talking about, gave him his name?"

42

"Old Robert Lee and Manfred, they still have a few war stories you don't know about, is what I'm talking about."

"Though it's not exactly our favorite story," Robert Lee said.

"If this is another one of your jokes," Ben said, "it isn't funny."

"We were in Laos," Robert Lee said. "Manfred and me and the rest of the team. We weren't supposed to be there, but there we were. If you were ever in Laos, you know that the Ho Chi Minh Trail in Laos wasn't a trail at all. It was a maze of big roads and little roads. By the time Manfred and me got there, they had some real righteous security protecting all those roads from people like us."

"Do tell," Ben said.

"We'd just popped an ambush." Robert Lee said. "Killed everyone. And we were getting ready to *didi*–you can't imagine what a hinky feeling it was standing out in the middle of a road in a place like that."

"Oh, I bet I can."

"And just like that," Robert Lee said, ignoring the sarcasm in Ben's voice, "the Pumpkin Eater and a team of Hmong stepped out of the bushes." He shook his head. "I still don't know how they did it, because we were pretty good. I mean, we're here, aren't we? But they did. Scared me so much it took two days for my balls to drop. It was flat amazing nobody got shot."

"Looked like a bunch of hippie gooks," Manfred said. "Long haired. Pony tails, some of them. Ammunition and grenades and knives everywhere, but hardly any water or food."

"So the Pumpkin Eater," Robert Lee said. "Only his name wasn't the Pumpkin Eater then. It was Peter something-or-other the third–he waltzes up to me, and says, 'No need to hurry. There are other teams above and below us.' I couldn't believe it. We stood in the middle of that road, both of us trying to out cool the other, and shot the shit about how he used to be in the Marines, and about how it was a lot more fun working for the CIA. Be your own boss, he said. Make a lot of money."

Robert Lee lifted his glass to take a drink, but set it back down. "Understand, this conversation is taking place in the middle of deepest, darkest gook land. We'd just sent about fifty gooks to the Great Buddha In The Sky, and we're still wired from that—and from him and his motley crew suddenly appearing like they were beamed down or something—and he's standing there talking like he just got off the back nine. I look around. And what do I see? His guys are cutting heads off. Tossing them in a big pile in the middle of the road.

"'What *are* you doing?' I ask.

"'Halloween,' he says, like that was some kind of reasonable answer—"

Ben laughed.

"After they cut off the heads, they sawed off the tops," Manfred said. "Then they scooped out the insides."

"I could not believe this was happening," Robert Lee said. "I mean, they were *prepared.* They even had these little surgical saws—shiny little stainless steel things that he said a friend had flown in from Singapore."

"One of his Air America buddies," Ben said.

"Whatever. All I know is there we were out in the middle of this road, an assembly line of hippie-gook-pirates, or whatever they were, cutting off heads, hollowing them out, and the Pumpkin Eater—only his name wasn't the Pumpkin Eater then—is trying to recruit me. Be all you can be, that kind of thing. And he digs into his ruck and hauls out a bunch of big, fat candles, and his men proceed to put candles in each head, and then with commo wire they hang the heads in the trees." Robert Lee glanced over at Manfred. "Manfred likes this story. Don't you, Manfred?"

"I *hate* this story. They were soldiers, too."

"Hung them all the way to this big plain," Robert Lee said. "That night we could see some of them from the hill we were on. I can *still* see them. Green and glowing in the night scope."

"Trick or treat," Ben said.

"Oh, yeah. Trick or treat. Tell him about the treat, Manfred."

"They ate some of the brains," Manfred said. "Him, too."

"Peter. Peter. Pumpkin Eater," Ben said.

Robert Lee nodded. "That's exactly what I said."

"You ever ask him about it—his nickname?" Manfred asked.

"He said it was all part of what he'd been hired to do," Ben said. "Gave me one of his lectures on the value of a good myth."

"That's him all right," Manfred said. "Eating brains and talking about myths."

"Myself, I don't believe I'd ever want to fuck with him," Robert Lee said.

"Not even," Manfred said.

"I have no intention of *seeing* him, let alone—do you two know something I don't?"

"What do you mean?" Robert Lee asked.

"Why are we talking about what we're talking about? What's it got to do with anything now?"

"We're talking about it because we'd like to know why you want to go back over there," Manfred said. "And I figure that with Evy gone and all, he might be the reason."

"Why would you think that?"

"Because Japan for damn sure ain't here."

Ben leaned forward. "Let me tell you where here is," he said. "Here is no matter where I go or what I do, I'm reminded of her. And it's pissing me off, Manfred. Seriously pissing me off."

"Yeah?"

"Yeah."

45

"Well, I don't know about Robert Lee, but personally I don't feel sorry for you at all."

"It's like I've got rattlesnakes in my head sometimes," Ben said.

"You've had snakes in your head since you were a kid."

"It's no joke, Manfred. It's making me mean. I don't want to end up someone like the Pumpkin Eater."

"You go off mean and pissed off, and you *will* end up like him," Manfred said.

Ben prodded his glass across the formica.

"Luck," Robert Lee said. "That's all it is. Fate. Destiny. Beginning. Ending. Those are just words citizens use to make themselves feel better. You start thinking it's any thing besides luck, and you're just playing with yourself. Mental masturbation."

Ben grunted.

"He's right, Ben."

"You bet your ass, I'm right," Robert Lee said. "Sometimes we forget who we are, and how we got here. These days, we're so full of war stories and bullshit citizen words, we think we were in a movie or something."

Ben's eyes focused on him.

"You ever look in the mirror?" Robert Lee said. "'Course you have. But I bet you don't see what the citizens see."

"And what might that be?"

"They see The Guy From Around Here. That even sounds like a movie, doesn't it? Lean, mean Ben. All grin, ugly as sin. A war scar like a dueling scar in an old German war movie. Don't be giving me that look, asshole. The kids, they see a big, friendly old dog with a badge. Their mothers get all wet and juicy thinking about what a dashing and romantic and tragic figure you are. And you love it. So don't be giving me that look. You're just like the rest of us: you been talking about it so long you've forgotten what it really is."

"Oh, I see," Ben said. "And when reality once again reared its ugly head, I just went all to pieces, is that it?"

Robert Lee scratched at his chest. "You know what I'm talking about."

"Yeah. I know what you're talking about."

"What am I talking about?"

"What goes around comes around."

"That's right. That's exactly what I'm talking about. Except that when you say it, you make it sound like it was all your fault."

"Maybe it was."

"Oh, bullshit. It didn't have anything to do with you. Her dying was bad luck. That's all. Bad luck. Sometimes you're lucky; sometimes you're not. You know that if anyone does."

"Damn, Manfred," Ben said. "I think maybe he got elected God instead of Sheriff."

Manfred laughed.

"There's no going back," Robert Lee said.

"It's not like that. It's a job."

"Then why not Mexico, or Europe—any place but Asia?" Manfred asked.

"Because I know Asia; I speak a language. In fact, it's kind of like the job here—only I don't have to find the bad guys. All I have to do is check them out."

"Yeah?" Manfred said. "And exactly how are you going to go about doing that?"

Ben shrugged. "It'll be sort of like working undercover Narcs. I'll have a regular nine-to-five—selling motorcycles—but what I'll really be doing is worming my way into the good graces of bad guys to see if the bad guys are really as bad as everyone says."

"And you're working for who exactly?" Robert Lee asked. "A company, the government, what?"

"A trading company. Raven International Trading Company, Ltd. The import/export stuff pays the bills. But what Raven really does is take care of problems that governments for one reason or another don't want to or can't handle."

"Problems." Manfred shook his head. "You *are* an idiot you know that."

"Think of Raven as a subcontractor," Ben said to Robert Lee. "It's been in existence, in one form or another, since the Korean War. But according to Jim business really picked up, and it came into its own, during the last years of the Vietnam War and through the Carter Administration–when because of politics, the CIA, State Department, and other agencies and departments were forced to do more and more subcontracting."

"Deniability," Robert Lee said.

"Something like that."

Robert Lee looked at Manfred and then back at Ben. "So how long has it been since you were last in Asia?" he asked. "Four-five years?"

"Five years," Manfred said. "And things'll be just as screwed up as ever," he said to Ben.

"I'm going crazy here, Manfred."

"Bullshit. You're just looking for an excuse, is all."

"You think that's it, huh?"

"Well, it's a thought," Manfred said. "And if it wasn't, you wouldn't be looking at me like that."

Robert Lee scratched at his chest. "Damn bears had fleas."

"I saw where you got those fleas," Manfred said. "And it wasn't no bear."

"From your mother probably. I threw his mother in jail again," he said to Ben. "That's why he's so grouchy tonight. She was only in for an hour before the judge himself came down and bailed her out, but to listen to this idiot you'd think I kept her in for a week and beat her with a rubber hose every day."

48

"A person's home is their castle," Manfred said. "This country is founded on that principle. What she does in her own house is her business."

"Not if she's beating one of her boy friends to death with a tennis racket, it isn't."

Ben laughed.

"That's right," Robert Lee said. "Laugh. You two been springing people from the County jail since you were in high school—since you were *born* probably. My crime statistics would drop in half if it weren't for your relatives."

"I still say if she wants to beat some old fart to death with a tennis racket, that's her business as long as she's in her own home," Manfred said.

"Christ. You're like a dog with a bone."

Ben stared blankly at the moth-eaten heads on the wall. Luck. He'd been real lucky today. Evy hadn't been lucky at all. It just is. There it is. Bless me, father, for I have sinned. When? How often? How *much?*

"Hey," Robert Lee said. "Yo." He raised his glass. "Here's to the bears. May we die as well."

Ben looked at him.

"The bears. We're drinking to the bears."

"I'll drink to that."

"Light-hearted soul that you've become, I figured you would."

Ben raised his glass to the moth-eaten grizzly on the wall. "To dead bears, wherever you are."

They drained their glasses. "Whew," Robert Lee said. "All this macho, tossing down a shot of whiskey is supposed to get easier. Hey, barkeep. How about some burgers."

"Forget it. The last time you two got drunk in here, you barfed burgers all over the floor."

"We did that?"

"*You* did that."

"Come on. I haven't eaten since breakfast."

"The kitchen's closed. In fact," Manfred stood and stretched, "the bar's closed. Hey, Arnold," he shouted, walking toward Arnold. "Wake up. Time to go home."

Arnold mumbled. His cheek slid along the surface of the bar. He sat up elbows on the bar, head hanging down between his shoulder blades.

"Go on. Git. Before I call that lovely wife of yours to come and get you."

Arnold twisted slowly on the stool. Hesitated.

"E.T. go home," Manfred said.

Arnold stood.

"That's it. You got it."

Arnold walked unsteadily to the door.

"Open the door, Arnold. Sometimes he forgets to open the door."

Arnold opened the door. Hesitated.

"Go home, Arnold."

Arnold shuffled out, and Manfred locked the door behind him. Through the plate glass door and windows they watched him cross the street.

"That wife of his is ugly enough to stop a truck," Manfred said. "She comes in here and just plain gives him hell in front of God and everyone. But you say anything bad about her to him, or about him to her, and you'll get your head bit off."

"Their only child was studying piano in Vienna, four or five years ago." Robert Lee scratched his chest. "She went on a sightseeing tour to Germany and was killed when some terrorists blew up a disco she was at. That's how come they moved out here."

Manfred stared at him for a moment. "Great," he said. "Now I feel like a real asshole. Why didn't you tell me that before?"

"I don't know. So you could feel like an asshole, I guess."

They watched Arnold tack his way unsteadily out into the

50

field across the street–watched him until he disappeared into the darkness on the other side of the railroad tracks.

Manfred pulled the blind over the door.

"I've never heard of one that old coming back like that," Ben said to Robert Lee.

"Might as well ask why the wind blows," Robert Lee said, refilling their glasses. "You can put collars on them, track them with satellites. Dissect them. Bisect them. And all you can say after you've done all that is that they're as unpredictable as people–and you knew that before you even began."

"Or maybe as predictable."

"There you go."

"I could never understand why you want to be Sheriff."

"The pay."

"Oh, sure. The pay."

"All the beautiful women."

"I've seen your beautiful women," Manfred said. "Most of them belong up there on the wall with the rest of the stuffed animals."

"You haven't seen them all."

"Thanks for the warning." Manfred flipped a switch on the far wall, and the neon beer signs over the bar and in the windows went out.

"We're just like those bears we killed today," Ben said.

Manfred and Robert Lee looked at each other. "It's called changing the conversation,"

Manfred said. "He's real good at it."

"You said the locals said the bears would sometimes come up to the windows and look in," Ben said to Robert Lee. "Well, we're like that. We go up to windows and we look inside, and we see people doing what normal people do, and we know we aren't the same. They know it, too. They're fascinated with us. Sometimes they're even afraid of us. But the really strange thing is that we feel the same about them."

"Did this just come to you?" Robert Lee asked. "I mean, were you just sitting there and like a bolt from the sky it just came to you?"

"We sit here and watch Arnold stagger off home across the field. And we feel sorry for him. That's the only difference between us and the bears. Sometimes we feel sorry. Not very often, but sometimes. We say we do what we do to help people—or because it's right, or because we're good at it. But that's all bullshit. We do it because it's the only way we know of to feel connected. It's how we look through the window."

"This is why I'm Sheriff?"

"No. You're a special case. All your talk about words not mattering, but you believe them."

"Ah, yes. Dignity and Justice. To Protect and Serve. Semper Fi, all that good shit."

Ben smiled at him. "Tell me you didn't hate to see something like that reduced to a ratty bag of fur and blood. Even a bear has a right to expect something better than that."

"That's a double-edged knife you're waving around there," Manfred said.

"It's not her dying that's making me leave, Manfred. It's remembering her when she was alive. And that's the truth."

Manfred turned from the till and looked at him.

"Always so fucking smart," he said. "Is that why you're going back to Never-never Land: to seek more wisdom?"

"Here's a thought for you," Robert Lee said to Ben. "Who do you think that old guy, Jim, is?"

"An old guy?"

"An old guy, huh? You think maybe because he's part Indian and because he's old and wears leaky waders and got a gimpy leg, he's your friendly old uncle or something?"

"I think he's just like you and me and Manfred, only older, is all."

"We saw him once in Nam," Robert Lee said. "Didn't we,

52

Manfred? He was dressed like he was going golfing. As you may recall, that's how the spooks dressed in those days. We saw him again in Laos, and he looked like an anthropologist on a field trip."

"So?"

"So don't let those leaky waders and those hand-tied flies fool you."

"If I don't like it, or if it gets strange, I can always get on a plane and come back. "

"And if frogs had wings, they'd fly," Manfred said, putting a row of long-necked beers on the bar.

"What's that supposed to mean?"

"It means we know you," Manfred said.

"You going to bring those beers over here, or are you going to piddle around behind that bar for the rest of the night?" Robert Lee said to Manfred.

"I have to admit it feels weird to be going back," Ben said.

"Bring a glass, too," Robert Lee said to Manfred. "Damn. Sometimes I can't believe you call yourself a bartender."

"I know nearly anyone walks in this bar," Ben said.

"I can't *ever* believe you call yourself a sheriff."

"I'm related to half of them—are you guys listening to me?"

"You said bring a glass. This is a glass."

"My great uncle shot that elk over the door."

"It's a beer glass."

Ben's fist hit the table. Whiskey jumped and splashed, and Robert Lee caught the bottle of Bushmills as it fell over.

"Are you two listening?"

"Sure," Robert Lee said. "We're listening. Aren't we, Manfred?"

"Absolutely."

"I'm trying to tell you guys something here."

"He's trying to tell us something here," Manfred explained

to Robert Lee. He sat down. "What are you trying to tell us?" he asked Ben.

"I'm trying to tell you that this place has become a bad case of claustrophobia for me. I feel like I'm melting into the environment or something."

"Melting's pretty serious," Robert Lee said to Manfred.

"Yeah. Imagine what he's doing to the environment."

"I'm leaving because I know everyone and every place around here so well, pretty soon I won't even know I'm here," Ben said. "That's why I'm leaving."

"You didn't look so bored this afternoon," Robert Lee said.

"You know what I mean."

"Made you remember who you are, though, didn't it?"

Ben laughed without humor. "Oh, yeah. It did that."

"You might want to ask yourself what anyone in Japan wants with someone like you," Manfred said.

"I don't think anyone particularly wants anything with me."

"You had two rounds into him, and almost on your third before Frank and I even started shooting," Robert Lee said.

"You were still in the bushes."

"We were right next to you. And we all saw it at the same time. But before Frank and I could do anything about it, you'd already shot it twice. Like you'd read its mind, or something."

"Well, there's no grizzly bears where I'm going."

"Yeah," Manfred said. "Only Pumpkin Eaters, *yakuza,* and wrestlers the size of whales."

"I'm too old now for the kind of shit you're talking about," Ben said to Robert Lee.

"I saw how old and slow you were today."

"That's different."

"No. That's the point," Manfred said. "And you just got done saying it when you were comparing us to bears. The fact is, most of us are dead, in prison, or too fat and too long

54

away from it to ever do what you and Frank and Robert Lee did today with those bears."

"Manfred, he met me. He liked me. He feels sorry for me because of Evy. I'll probably hate it and be back next week."

Robert Lee raised his hands. "I give up." He dropped his hands flat onto the table. "Manfred?"

"Robert Lee?"

"It's time to celebrate."

"What are we celebrating, Oh Great Chief of the County, and Violator of Basic Constitutional Rights."

"We are celebrating, Oh Son of a Crazy German Refugee, that with this idiot gone life can finally get back to normal around here."

"Normal?" Manfred looked at Ben. "That'll be the day."

Chapter 5
Running Dogs

F ish heads and rice for you, from now on," Manfred
said. Remnants of sausage and eggs and hash browns
lay on the plates in front of them.

At the other end of the restaurant, floor to ceiling windows
looked out across runways and fields to a horizon of clean
blue sky and dark blue mountains.

"I still don't see how you can keep going back over there.
They'd all seem like Vietnamese to me."

"You seem to like the Hmong just fine," Ben said.

"The Hmong I knew are either dead or over here."

Ben yawned, stretching his arms behind his head and
arching his back.

"I need more coffee," Manfred said.

A waitress they hadn't seen before came out of the back
carrying a full pot of coffee. They watched as she poured
coffee for a family of five at a table next to the windows.

"When's the first time you ever thought about going to
Asia?" Manfred asked. "I don't ever remember talking abut
Asia when we were kids."

Ben shrugged. "I don't know. Talking with some of my
grandmother's people when I was a little kid, I guess." The
waitress was working her way closer, pouring coffee and
joking with a group of suits waiting for a flight. She was older
than she'd first appeared, but trim and fit in a tight-fitting
brown dress and small, white apron.

"What's a bunch of Tribal Members got to do with Asia?"

"They all served in Asia–in the Pacific or in Korea. The idea of American Indians fighting Asians–I don't know, I guess it always fascinated me. I remember they talked a lot about the Japanese. How brave and stupid their soldiers had been. The women." He held up his cup so the waitress could see it.

"Don't do that," Manfred said.

"Don't do what?"

The waitress reached around Manfred and poured coffee in Ben's cup.

"Good morning, gentlemen. You, too, Manfred."

"Well, hey," Manfred said. "Look who's here."

She poured coffee into Manfred's cup. "What brings you down here, Manfred?"

"Just getting rid of some of the local riff-raff."

She smiled at Ben. "You don't look like riff-raff to me. You look like the famous Ben Tails I've heard so much about." She transferred the coffee pot to her left hand, wiped her right on her apron, and extended her hand to Ben. "Mickey," she said. Her grip was warm and firm.

"How do," he said.

"I could probably get sick right after the Delta flight comes in," she said to Manfred.

"Well, I wouldn't want you to–"

"He's being shy," Ben said.

"Shy! *Him?* Hey, don't let his aw-shucks, gee-whiz act fool you. One o'clock," she said to Manfred. She winked at Ben. "Always nice meeting a member of the local riff-raff." She moved over to the next table. "How are you folks today?"

"This always happens," Manfred muttered. "Every time I'm with one of you assholes, this happens."

"You still think I'm making a mistake, don't you–going to Japan, I mean?"

"Maybe. But, look . . . never mind what I said before. That old guy, Jim, he's okay. I've known him for a while–since the last time you were in Asia–and you're right, he's a lot like us."

"Now if I only had a clue as to what 'like us' means."

Manfred considered Ben for a moment. "Tell me again what it is you're going to be doing."

Ben took a drink of coffee and set the cup back down on the table. "I'm going to work for a company–Raven Trading. Raven is a blanket company for a bunch of smaller, also mostly trading companies. The smaller company that will be my cover is called Speed Works. My job at Speed Works will be to import and sell Harley Davidson motorcycles, parts, and equipment."

"And Jim is the boss of all this?"

"I don't know how much of the day-to-day stuff Jim is involved in. I think they've got other people who take care of the business side of things. Raven is controlled by a Board of Directors: Jim. Someone in Thailand. Someone in Singapore. Someone in Japan. And–small world–a Chinese guy it turns out I know from way back."

"From your Pumpkin Eater days?"

"Yeah."

"So let me get this straight. There are all these legitimate companies–little companies like Speed Whatever–and through them Raven gets the money to pay people like you to do whatever it is you are really going to be doing?"

"Basically, yeah."

"So why do you think they need someone like you?"

"What do you mean, like me? I'm perfect. I worked undercover narcs for what? Two years and change. I know a lot of places and people in Asia. I speak an Asian language. Hell, the DEA even tried to recruit me to work in Hong Kong."

"And what did you tell *them*?"

Ben picked up his cup and took a drink. "That's different."

"You told them no because you knew there was no way the Chinese—the Triads, especially—would not know who you were and who you were working for."

"I didn't want to end up food for the sharks just so the Chinese drug lords could make a point to the DEA—but that's different."

"How is it different?"

"It's completely different. I'll be working undercover, sure, but only at the behest of whatever country it is that has the problem—and only at the request of a U.S. government agency or department. I don't have to find the bad guys. All the background work has already been done." He moved the coffee cup back and forth on the table cloth. "It's not Mission Impossible, Manfred. I make sure the person I'm investigating is as bad as everyone says, and I make sure the locals don't have ulterior motives—revenge, unfair business competition, that kind of thing. It's a simple job."

"Yeah, right. If it's so simple, and if they are all Americans, why not just deport their ass? Or let them rot in a foreign jail. Why sic someone like you on them?"

"Because most of them have done things so rank we don't want them back. We don't want them in the system—any system. Jim didn't say it, but obviously the negative publicity could do serious damage to American interests. These are really bad people, Manfred. We're not talking white-collar crime, here."

"So what happens to these people after you've done your investigating."

"The locals do whatever they want with them."

"Kill them, you mean."

Ben shrugged.

"And you're okay with that?"

"Are you kidding? Sociopaths, psychopaths, serial killers, terrorists—I was made to take down these kinds of people."

"Take down?"

"You know what I mean."

"You were made to do a lot of things, Ben."

Ben snorted. "Right."

"Look," Manfred said. "A minute ago, you wanted to know what 'like us' meant. Well, I'm from Germany; you're from here." He gestured toward the windows. "But we both belong to those mountains out the window there. That's part of it."

He leaned forward and reached smoothly back and brushed his jacket open and Ben heard the thumb break snap open, and Manfred pulled a revolver from a holster behind his hip. "But this is the biggest part of it."

He put the revolver down on the table. The revolver was a well-oiled and cleaned four-inch Smith and Wesson .357, bluing worn at places along the barrel and cylinder where it had been pulled from and pushed into holsters, the walnut grips scratched and darkened with use. Manfred carried it because Robert Lee had made him a deputy sheriff. The County gave him medical benefits, but he was paid only when Robert Lee called him in for special assignments.

"This is what it all finally boils down to," Manfred said. "People like me and you and Robert Lee pointing one of these things at people just like you and me and Robert Lee."

He nudged the pistol with his index finger.

"Look around. In front of God and everyone. In the middle of an airport restaurant full of citizens, I pulled out a gun and set it on the table, and no one in here except us is even seeing it—or, if they are seeing it, are admitting what they're seeing."

He nudged the pistol again.

"Now, we can sit here and look at it. We can admire it. We can call it good or evil or anything in between. In fact, we can say anything we want about it because right now it's just

60

sitting there–kind of like a rattlesnake sunning itself on a rock."

He slid his hand around the grips, his finger slipping inside the trigger guard, onto the trigger. He took his hand from the pistol, waited a moment, and then again slipped his hand around the pistol grips, his finger on the trigger.

"Feel that?"

Ben frowned.

"I'll do it again. Watch. Pretty amazing, huh?"

Manfred sat back. "You were wrong about the grizzlies, Ben. Whatever we are, we aren't grizzlies. Grizzlies are bears." He leaned forward and picked up the pistol and slid it back into the holster and snapped the thumb break closed.

"What are we, then?"

Manfred shrugged. "How do I know? I'm your friend, not your guru. Rattlesnakes, maybe. We catch rats and other critters that no one wants."

"I yam what I yam, said Popeye the Sailor Man."

"Not Popeye," Manfred said. "Mr. Slide."

Ben's eyes narrowed.

Manfred grinned. "Mr. Slide. He slide in; he slide out. He slide on his belly like a snake. Evy and me, we used to talk sometimes. A cup of coffee, or something."

Ben looked toward the windows.

"Old Mr. Slide, he killed a lot of people, he did," Manfred said.

"Is that what you told her?"

"I told her you were Mr. Slide over there, but here you were just an old boy come home from the war. I told her that coming back was kind of like shedding skins."

"Well, that's bullshit."

"Of course it is. A rattlesnake is still a rattlesnake no matter how many times it sheds its skin.

Ben looked at him. "What'd she say to that?"

61

"I didn't say any of that to her. I figured someday she'd figure it out for herself, if she already hadn't. And then it'd be between you and her, and none of my business."

Ben looked out the window. Far out on the runway an airplane taxied toward him. "Mr. Slide," Manfred said. "That's why they need someone like you."

Chapter 6
Bitterroots

Intense yellow light clarified folds and ridges, even tiny crevices in the Mission Mountains far below. Flathead Lake was a flat expanse of gold stretching toward Canada.

The plane banked the other way, and directly below out the window at his elbow the mountains were different, their jagged peaks like whitecaps in an angry sea. Streamers of snow trailed from the highest peaks. He knew what it would be like to be on those ridges. The snow would feel like sand in a sandstorm.

"Would you care for something to drink, sir?" Middle-aged and blonde, he automatically noted. Under the makeup there were crow's feet at the corners of her eyes and mouth.

"No, thanks."

She moved forward to the next passenger. "Would you care for something to drink, sir?"

He smiled. Women.

One morning he'd opened his eyes to Evy's face suspended inches above his own.

"Do you think I'm getting wrinkles?"

"I can't breathe."

"Be honest, Ben. Am I getting wrinkles?"

"Yes."

"Really?" Her eyes were so healthy, the whites had a bluish tinge.

"I like your wrinkles. They give you character."

"Character is just another way of saying I'm not attractive any more."

"You'd be even more attractive if you'd get off my chest."

"Be honest, Ben. I'm becoming less attractive, aren't I?"

"Sit a little lower. I'll show you how less attractive I think you are."

"Am I handsome?"

"What kind of question is *that?*"

"Am I?"

"What's wrong with handsome?"

She swung off him and sat on the edge of the bed. "I knew it. *Shit.*"

She stood and glared down at him, and turned and stomped out of the room. "Aghhh!" she yelled from the living room, and something crashed against the wall.

Some men had called a woman she rode horses with "handsome," and she'd overheard them. Years of riding, hiking, fishing, hunting, being active outdoors in all kinds of weather, had matured and weathered her friend's beauty. "Now that's a handsome woman," one of the men had said, and Evy had thought they were talking about her.

His smile faded as an image of Evy's dead eyes flashed through his mind.

He turned his head and looked at the yellow light and the mountains on the other side of the plane. The Missions had been Evy's mountains. She'd been born at the base of them, had lived most of her life around them. The light made them proud, like a woman showing herself, worn ridges, crevices, and all.

There's nothing wrong with being handsome, Evy, he thought.

The Bitterroots with their twisted ridges, and dark, dead-end valleys, were the antithesis of Evy's mountains. The Bitterroots were his mountains.

There'd been a time when, because of Evy, he would have

talked Robert Lee and Frank into waiting until the next morning to find that bear. He would have done it for Evy, and not because it was the natural thing in him to do. Hunting that bear, there had been moments when, for the first time in a long time, he'd felt like all his pieces had come back together—as if he'd hidden pieces of himself, and then forgotten where he'd hid them.

Probably they would have become just another couple, with all the misunderstandings and disappointments that he'd seen between married friends—maybe even they would have ended up in a relationship like some he'd seen at family disturbances.

Well, no use thinking about it now. She was dead. For a time things had been different, and now they weren't. No answers in Asia. He knew that. She'd be just as dead there. But he'd look anyway. Get away for a while. If nothing else, maybe there would be a little adrenaline.

He leaned back against the headrest and closed his eyes.

How many times as a kid had he watched an airplane climb overhead toward another world and wished he could be on that plane looking down at himself—a tiny figure receding to not even a speck in the vast panorama of mountains.

He turned his head and opened his eyes. The light on the other side of the plane was already fading to darkness.

Part II
Japan, Three Years
Later

Chapter 1
The Slide On In

Ｎew and huge and white, the complex of apartment buildings loomed like science fiction. Two sides of each building were constructed with apartments staggered on top of apartments, like blocks in the side of a pyramid, the roof of each apartment serving as a verandah for the apartment above. Many of the balconies and verandahs were crowded with potted plants and trees. The complex reminded Ben of a painting of the Hanging Gardens of Babylon that he'd seen in a catechism book when he was a kid.

Modern Japan, he thought. The history and culture he'd expected paved over with apartment and factory complexes. Massive green girders and huge, gray one-legged stanchions supporting expressways five or six stories above streets jammed with cars and trucks in the daytime, deserted at night.

Carlos was right. This place was ripe. All it would take was a little corporate organization and marketing skill. The police were already running around like little Dutch boys trying to stick their fingers in the holes in the dike—and Carlos and his people were doing their best to help make sure there were too many holes, not enough fingers.

Even after nearly three years, he couldn't get used to walking down empty sidewalks.

Evy used to ask him about Asia, and he'd tell her about

crowded sidewalks, villages surrounded by rice paddies. Ancient graves. People everywhere, he'd say. Asia had held him for nearly eight years after he'd gotten out of the Marines—a little more than ten years if you counted his time in the Nam. But that Asia was gone as if it had never existed. Sometimes he'd wake up in the morning and look out the window and if not for the *tatami* mats he wouldn't be sure what country he was in, the cities looked so much alike anymore.

Maybe if he'd stayed, or had come back after a year like he'd first intended, the changes would have been gradual and he wouldn't have noticed so much. But he hadn't come back after a year. He'd rediscovered Montana, and then he'd met Evy. "I want you to meet someone," Frank had said—and that was all she wrote, the end of that story. He'd looked into her eyes, and he'd known he'd never return to Asia.

Except here he was.

Maybe his problem with this place was that he kept trying to make Japan be like other places in Asia. Bitching to himself about the sidewalks, when probably the sidewalks had always been empty—made for show, and for whoever had the brick-and-tile monopoly.

The Japanese had probably from day one been tense and silent and in love with uniforms. High school students in black. Kindergarten students in matching knickers, hats, and stiff, shiny, red leather packs that looked like Flash Gordon jet packs. Salarymen in dark blue or gray suits. Construction workers in khaki. The men directing traffic at building sites in blue shirts and trousers, bloused boots, white puttees, white helmets, whistles, braid, the whole nine yards. Elevator girls with silly little hats and white gloves. Even the Yakuza wore matching suits—and matching haircuts and matching tattoos—and drove matching cars.

What could you say about a place where the gangsters dressed so that everyone knew they were gangsters?

He began to bounce a little as he walked. Talking to himself now. Working on it.

The Motorcycle Man.

Asia be changed. Asia be one big factory. But you be ninety-nine, and you still know how to slide on in. It be empty sidewalk, then you be empty sidewalk. It be bad air, then you be polluted and everywhere. The Slide On In. Asia taught it to you.

Snakes, you be a snake. Leeches, you be a leech. Mosquitoes, you be a mosquito.

He smiled to himself, the Motorcycle Man. Coming at you, Carlos, my man. Time to pay the piper, grim the reaper.

Science Fiction, that's what the cityscape seemed, he thought. All concrete and dark glass. But behind the glass and concrete, below the girders and stanchions, gray, decayed apartment buildings and houses. A maze of airless, narrow streets. Moldy futons draped over balconies and open window sills. Hanging wash. Sullen children. Dogs of all shapes and ugliness. Well fed cats.

And him. Walking down this street. Forty something now. *Ain't going to live to be forty.* How many times had he heard that? And how many times had it almost come true? A certified survivor, that's what he was, certified by the number forty.

What he really was was a certified anomaly, who couldn't even get himself killed while he was young and spry, like nearly everyone else he knew had. A certified statistical oddity walking down a street in the City of Nagoya, in the country of Japan, on the planet Nippon.

He turned onto a bigger street. Golf Ball Street, the *gaijin* called it, a canyon of concrete and glass and steel. Four lanes solid with traffic, the street divided by narrow islands, big, round metal balls made up of many small lights perched at intervals along the islands. The big, round, metal balls looked like giant golf balls on spindly, metal tees.

Office ladies anonymous in blue and white uniforms hurried past. Housewives stylish in heels and dresses, faces made up to perfection—masks, if you looked closely; they didn't look nearly so good when bidding bye-bye to hubby-san in the morning. Suits everywhere hurrying to meetings or to dinner with other suits—suits hurrying because suits were supposed to hurry. But despite the bustle, a cold place without the spontaneity and color and emotion of other Asian places and people. The Japanese have forgotten their past, he thought, not for the first time. Face, like the makeup the housewives wore, was merely a mask to the Japanese.

Whoa, ho. The Motorcycle Man be getting poetic.

More likely they hadn't forgotten a thing, were in fact infatuated with the past—not realizing, but maybe understanding, that looking at the past too much or too long was a kind of insanity. Maybe that's why they loved violence and suicide and any movie with death and violence and horror in it.

When you coupled all that with their infatuation with things Disney cute, what you got was a whole lot of people with neuroses growing fast and thick as the mold on the tile in his bathroom.

But, hey, different strokes for different folks. America wasn't so different.

Trouble was, if you looked long enough at the kinds of things the Japanese loved to dwell on, pretty soon you started seeing what was behind them. And, believe it, that was a whole different ball of wax. Most people, especially Americans, couldn't stand to even glimpse death, let alone get a solid look at what was behind it.

He'd looked, though. Hadn't wanted to. But there it was. Opened his eyes and, Hello, dere, Mr. Slide. How you like the view from here? Looking at it had been kind of like one of those Egyptian curses: open this, and your soul will shrivel to the size of a black, disgusting pea. Flick it with your fingernail, and it'll turn to ash.

It hadn't made him crazy—well, not yet, anyway—but then he'd been better prepared than most. A tad antisocial, maybe, Carlos, my man who has checked me out but doesn't know that I know he has checked me out.

Carlos Wolfgang Montoya. Now, what could you expect from a man with a name like that? He grinned, using his grin to snag eyes, hold them longer than they wanted to be held. You cute, honey, but lookee here, lookee here.

He laughed out loud. Booga, Booga. Meat-eating *gaijin* on the loose.

Damn, he hated cities. Any city.

His grandmother's people, Plains Indians, had believed that the further men get from nature, the less human they become. Well, a city, any city, was about as far from nature as it was possible to get and still remain alive and breathing.

Rows of *bonsai* in big ceramic pots stood behind the amber, smoked-glass windows of a hotel. What would his grandmother's people think of a place that celebrates crippled trees as an art form? The only beautiful *bonsai* he'd ever seen was at the treeline, high in the mountains of Montana. Tough, little trees warped by altitude and wind and cold. A man could relate to that kind of bonsai. Japanese *bonsai* reminded him of the old Chinese custom of binding feet.

Japan: most of its people, their space, creativity—life itself—truncated, bent out of shape, like *bonsai.*

So what was he doing here?

Be satisfied in your own mind. Or walk. Any doubts, any doubts

70

*at all, even the smallest, take a hike. I demand that, Benjamin. You
are no good to me if you cannot live with yourself.*

I'm satisfied, Mr. Jim. I'm satisfied. Carlos is wanting to do
what they say he's wanting to do. But it feels like bullshit,
political bullshit, and that's the worst kind. That's why I'd
like to take a walk on this one.

Twice in Taiwan, he'd been satisfied, and once with Huang
in Thailand, he'd been more than satisfied. In fact, he'd been
so satisfied in Thailand that he'd done the deed himself—
he'd been the assassin that he'd told Manfred he would not
be.

Where was Huang when he needed him?

He'd walked into Jim's apartment in Bangkok, and there
drinking tea by the window was Huang looking the same,
exactly the same, as if Phnom Penh and Long Tieng had been
yesterday, instead of a lifetime ago. It had seriously spooked
him. It was like seeing a ghost. Except this ghost was all gristle
and bone and had eyes like winter water on the Blackfoot.

The other cup of tea steaming on the window ledge had
said it all. No one had told Huang he was coming. He'd just
known. That would be enough to raise the hair on the back
of anyone's neck. It was coincidence enough working for a
company that Huang was a big part of, but what was really
weird was that it had been fifteen years since he'd last seen
Huang, and Huang hadn't aged a bit.

He stopped at a stoplight, conscious of the people around
him. Time to put on the cammo, he thought. Time to become
the Motorcycle Man, crude, lewd, and tattooed.

Be de doper when you de nark. Be de elk when you de-
Oh, my.

Who says Japanese women don't have legs? Long, black
hair. Black dress. Lipstick like blood. Single strand of pearls
expensive and real and just to make you wonder what she

would be like with only the nylons and the heels and the pearls.

The woman's eyes met his, and slid away, focusing on a point somewhere between the middle of the street and infinity.

Oh, man. Cold. Cold to the bone. No smile. Not even a sneer. No thanks-for-looking-but-no-thanks. Just one of those since-I-can't-see-you-you-must-not-be-there looks. All that time and effort to give men a hardon so she could disappear them. He grinned and waggled his fingers at her. Hello, darlin'.

In the envelope now.

Carlos had to think he was more show than go. Mr. Motorcycle a shadow of his former self. Wired just enough for Carlos to believe that with proper tutelage—Carlos' tutelage, of course—Mr. Motorcycle could be revitalized, made into executive material—Carlos' idea of executive material, of course.

He didn't want to do it this time. It was righteous, he knew that, but—

Don't think about it. Get rid of the "friends" bullshit. Get some adrenaline into it.

Carlos was trying to *bonsai* him, that's what he was trying to do.

There you go. Getting *bonsaied* would be enough to piss anyone off. Carlos was trying to *bonsai* the Motorcycle Man. Fuck with his mind like the Frenchman had.

Ah, but Carlos was not the Frenchman. Not even close.

It was going to be interesting to see how the Nips handled it. A lot of posturing for posterity, he supposed. They were good at that. All macho and mean, and then, as they booted Carlos' ass out of the country, they'd probably bow and say how sorry they were. *Sumimasen,* but get the fuck out, and don't ever, never come back. *Gomen nasai.*

He turned the corner by the Hilton, a new, absolutely

without personality glass-and-brick rectangle. The doormen, as usual, looked embarrassed to be in top hats and tails. Who wouldn't. Three Mercedes, a white Bentley, a Toyota Century. All the Century needed was a cannon to make it the perfect Soviet-mobile.

Russians come here they'd be jealous of more than cars, he thought. Japan was everything the old Soviet Union had tried to be, the corruption the envy of every good commissar, the cops so intertwined with the Yakuza, the Yakuza so intertwined with politicians and big corporations, it was impossible to see where one began and the other left off. Everything organized, everything a bureaucracy of some sort.

The real problem with people like Carlos, when you cut right through it, was that Carlos represented something disorganized, something that not even Yakuza commissars could control.

He didn't understand why Jim had him on this. If it weren't for the fact that Carlos deserved a boot in the ass, he'd take a walk, and let the Japanese take care of their own garbage. For sure, Carlos did not fit the brief.

Just do it, he thought. Get it over with. It was probably something as simple as a favor for a favor. That was pretty much how Asia worked, and if anyone knew how things worked in Asia, it was Jim.

Danny's authentic, made-by-Mitsubishi American jeep was parked up on the sidewalk. Mud tires. Gold reversed rims, the logo, *Another Country* painted on the doors.

Another Country, like the jeep, was authentic American; and like the jeep it was designed for Japanese, not Americans. Authentic American atmosphere. Authentic Tex-Mex food. Authentic Japanese prices. Danny was very Japanese about making money.

He entered the tiny foyer and ignoring the elevator took the stairs down a narrow, twisting concrete stairwell not much wider than his shoulders, his leather jacket scraping rough concrete walls. The stairwell smelled of damp and mold. Down the stairs to a small landing, elevator on one side, big shiny hardwood door on the other.

The hardwood door opened onto a small passageway leading to another big, shiny hardwood door. Floor-to-ceiling glass covered one side of the passageway. A giant terrarium covered with sand and five-foot high cactus in clay pots was on the other side of the glass. Bold, Mexican-Indian-Aztec-whatever designs covered the other wall, the designs matching the heavy bass of the sound system on the other side of the second door.

He put his fingertips against the door, feeling more than hearing the vibration of music and conversation. He always paused before opening the second door. Opening the second door was like stepping into another dimension. Alice in Wonderland, the rabbit leading him past the Hilton and the white Bentley and the doormen in top hats and tails, down the street to the tricked out Jeep. Down the winding stairwell. Through the first door. Past the cactus and paintings.

He pulled the door open, the sudden sound and heat a physical blow. Behind him he could feel cold and mold, sterile cactus and glass, pagan art. In front of him heat and *gaijin* shrieks, music with a big bass beat. A subterranean world of mirrors and people, shiny hardwood bar, cologne mixed with the smell of chili and tacos and cigarette smoke. Japanese in suits and dresses, cuff links, necklaces. Foreigners in jeans and polo shirts and L. L. Bean fall clothing. People shouting, laughing, their teeth displayed as if for auction. Shelves of keep-bottles glittered in front of the bar mirror. Black ceiling, black pipes, black ventilation flumes. Rustic wood beams suspended by long, black metal bolts, baskets hanging from the beams. The smell of ribs and bourbon, tortilla chips. All of it a figment of Danny's imagination.

The city was huge, but there were only a few thousand foreigners in the whole city. Sooner or later most of them came to Danny's.

Yuppies from California-Indiana-New York-Texas teaching English as a Second Language—whatever that was. Hi, I teach at. Where do you teach at? How much do you make? Aren't the Japanese—choose one—hopeless/decadent/wonderful/stupid/amazing/the scourge of the earth?

MBAs from Harvard-Yale-Illinois State, learning to speak *Nihongo*, convinced that Japanese efficiency and marketing skills are a myth. MBAs like Visigoths waiting to sack and pillage.

Young California or Vancouver women taking a night off from the clubs they worked. *Dancers, entertainers,* they called themselves. They reminded him of Montana girls he'd grown up with who'd gone up to Alaska when the pipeline was being built. Four or five years in Alaska and they'd come back rich, retired, hard as nails. Street smart, people smart, some of them just plain smart, they knew the world was going to get a piece of you one way or another, their intellectual abilities consciously retarded in the felt belief that the more their intellects developed, the more they removed themselves from being alive. He could relate to such women. Intellectual to them, and to him, was just another term for cynical, sarcastic wit that only illustrates in a more bitter way what anyone who hasn't been *bonsai'd* already knows: body bags and old age.

Yessir, he thought. Just your basic small town full of small town people playing small town games, vicious or otherwise, nearly all of them expending impressive amounts of energy in single-minded pursuit of making money and verbally beating up on the people who were paying them a whole lot more than they'd ever make back where they came from. In here to get drunk and be shrill and to impress each other the way they thought they impressed the Japanese.

Manfred would laugh. Out of the frying pan into the fire, he'd say.

The pathetic thing was that these days the whole of Asia was full of places and people like this. These days there was no real difference between the natives and the foreigners and the foreign ways the natives claimed to disdain. These days the natives did what they damn well pleased not because it was better or traditional, but simply because they could.

Which was why–*exactly why*–he was here: one way or another, with or without them, the Japanese were going to do exactly what they wanted to do. They'd been very clear about that. No smiles. No sucking of teeth. None of the usual bowing and grinning and acting like junior Confucians. We'll do it with you; or we'll do it without you. We want your *hanko*, your stamp, but with or without it, we are going to put a hurt on this dude, and then we are going to kick his ass out of the country.

At least that was the situation according to Jim.

Unfortunately, after nearly three years of observing how things got done here, he was pretty sure that this time Jim was wrong. When push came to shove, the Japanese were going to wimp out.

"Busy," Danny shouted at him, and paused at a table of Japanese suits–expensive suits, expensive paisley ties, expensive bottle of 12-year-old Wild Turkey–and said something in Japanese that made them laugh. Danny turned and rolled his eyes at Ben, and pushed his way through the Dutch doors into the kitchen. A few seconds later, he backed out carrying an order of nachos grande, bowls of chili.

"There's room around the end of the bar," he said, maneuvering the tray of food into the crowd.

Ben shouldered his way toward the other side of the bar.

The bar ran most of the length of the room, the end third constructed so that people could sit on stools or stand along both sides. It was the only bar he'd found in Japan tall enough for him to comfortably stand next to. Not exactly Manfred's place, but what the hey, when in Japan . . . .

Danny came around behind him. "You want a beer?" Red work shirt, turquoise bolo tie, blue and green and black wavy-striped vest. An ex-steelworker from Nebraska who'd somehow found his way to Japan, and then, even more improbably, had promoted Japanese backers for the bar. Slicked-back hair. Pony tail. Earring. Ex-boxer. Kendo. Karate. Shiatzu, the Chinese art of healing by touch.

"You bet."

"Tecate, okay?"

"Sure." Danny in Nip Land, Ben thought. Danny the Rabbit in Tex-Mex-L.A.-Bad Dude-Bad News clothes. All he needed was a big pocket watch for his vest. Right this way, folks. Down this stairway, through the door, past the cactus, past my own, personal pagan art, through the door, and, hello, what'll it be? A rusty can of Tecate for five dollars? A bowl of chili for eight? Table charge goes up if there's live music—and there *will* be live music.

"Seen Carlos yet?"

Danny glanced at the big, antique clock with no hands on the wall next to the cash register. "Not yet." He slid a Tecate toward Ben. "On the house."

"What's the occasion?"

"No occasion. Just better business practice."

Ben laughed.

"Yeah," Danny said. "It's getting so hard, I'm thinking of trading my jeep for a Mercedes."

"You think handing out free beer is going to get you a Mercedes?"

"The Japanese see a big, mean-looking *gaijin* like you drinking Tecate, they want one, too.

Ben took a long drink, nearly draining the can. "Tell you what," he said. "Long as you're using me for free advertisement, how about I put you onto a Harley instead of you driving that made-by-Mitsubishi hunk of junk? Improve your image. The heartbeat of America, all that good stuff."

"Let me explain something to you, *Senor.* You see all these *gaijin* in here?" He handed Ben another beer. "They don't spend worth a damn. Beer is all. Some nachos. A bowl of chili. I only put up with them and their cheap ways because they attract Japanese who want to be *International*–excuse me, *Global*–and Global to them means *gaijin.*"

"Well, that's exactly what I'm saying. *Gaijin* ride Harleys. Riding a Harley'll make you even more Global."

"You still don't understand the psychology, do you? The Jeep is part of the bar, and because the bar is part of Japan, therefore, the Jeep is Japanese. Even if the Jeep was a real made-in-America jeep, it would still be Japanese by association. Follow me?"

"No."

"Well, look at it this way, then. The *image* of the jeep is American, and the *image* of the bar is American, but in fact this bar is Japanese. And all that makes it *International.* I could probably get by with a real American Jeep, or something like a Mercedes–a Mercedes would say this place is successful–but a Harley? A Harley would be tacky. It's *too* American. Understand what I'm saying? A Harley doesn't say International; it says American."

"I'll give it to you below cost."

"See this lime? The day I start riding a Harley around Nagoya will be the day you start putting lime in your beer."

"Give me that lime."

Danny laughed, and threw the slice of lime into a plastic

garbage can under the bar. "Spoken like a true American businessman."

There was a commotion at the door, and a group of Japanese, seven or eight well-dressed men and women, came in.

"Excuse me," Danny said, edging behind and past Ben. "I think part of my retirement plan just arrived."

Ben watched him hurry through the people clustered around the bar to the group that had just come in. The group parted, giving Danny access to a lantern-jawed, bulletheaded Japanese dressed in a sharkskin suit.

The man bowed; Danny bowed; the people around them bowed. The man laughed and said something; Danny laughed and said something; everyone around them laughed and said something. Danny and the man shook hands. A diamond pinkie ring and a solid gold bracelet inlaid with rare stones gleamed.

Flash that in the States, Ben thought, and you wouldn't just lose the bracelet; you'd lose your entire arm. Maybe that's why they're all bowing. They're bowing to all that jewelry.

A woman dressed in a dark dress edged her way into the group and bowed to the man. He looked surprised and delighted all at the same time—too surprised and delighted, Ben thought—and bowed twice to her, up and down, up and down, like an energetic wind-up toy in a sharkskin suit.

She laughed; he laughed.

Ben laughed. How does Danny keep this shit straight, he thought.

She bowed again—classy, sexy, about what you'd expect, and the man bowed. Both of them bowing as if they were connected by an elastic band, the man clearly determined to get in the last bow. A new exercise craze, Ben thought. Aerobic bowing.

Laughing, she gestured toward the back of the room, the gesture itself almost a bow.

Maybe all the bowing was their way of being witty, Ben thought. Some kind of code done with the whole body. What they were really saying was something like, You lookin' hot tonight, babe. Why, thank you, Mr. Dude in a Sharkskin Suit. You lookin' streamlined yourself.

The woman led the man and his people to a table in the back corner, next to the mirrored wall, Danny with his pony tail and bizarre clothing bringing up the rear, order pad at the ready.

At the table, the bulletheaded man indicated where he wanted people seated, his gestures polite, not imperious, though clearly he could be as imperious as he wanted to be. The woman sat to his right, both of them facing the room.

Must be old money, Ben thought. Old money meant old connections. It must be something like that because the whole place was ready to kiss his ass. Some of the yuppies looked as if they were in the presence of royalty. The MBAs looked like sharks about to embark on a feeding frenzy. The guy seemed not such a bad guy, though, just rich and keeping some kind of weird face.

Ben took a drink of beer. On the other hand, the guy *was* rich, real rich, and one thing being a cop had taught him was that most rich folks reverted to type. Fuck with them and their wonderful manners disappeared right before your very eyes.

The man leaned toward the woman and said something. The woman smiled and nodded, and looked up at Danny and said something.

Danny wrote on his order pad.

The man said something else. She looked questioningly at the people around the table.

Everyone smiled. The smiles didn't get bigger or smaller;

they just stayed in place—which meant that whatever it was must be real expensive, he thought. She smiled up at Danny.

Danny nodded and wrote.

And then she looked toward Ben and smiled again, and even though she was obviously too far away to pick his face out of the crowd and was smiling a smile that was merely a Japanese reflex, directed at no one in particular, he nevertheless returned the smile and as he smiled the room abruptly focused, the people, the furnishings, the colors and tints and details clear and discrete. For a moment, while she smiled at him, he was just Ben, not Mr. Slide, not the Motorcycle Man, just himself without the baggage of memories and skills. He shut his eyes. When he opened them, the room was its noisy, crowded, hazy self, and the woman was unreachable—an educated, upper-class Japanese woman at the other end of the bar, as alien to him and his experience as he was to her and her experience. He felt this. But what he thought was that she looked a little like the one he'd seen on the street—except that the woman on the street had been all flash, and this one would rip your heart out and feed it to you while you stood there grinning like an idiot begging for more.

The guy, his smile a tad too polite and earnest—a clue to the people around him—said something to Danny, and Danny turned and read labels from a row of bottles at the end of the bar, the expensive end of the bar.

The guy must be outdoing himself this time, Ben thought, because the people around the table, even Danny, had gotten real nonchalant. Danny was writing the order down as if the guy had just ordered coffee and home fries.

What a place. What a weird, awful place Asia was getting to be. In Japan it cost fifty thousand dollars for a full-dress Harley Davidson FLH and leathers. Fifty thousand dollars for a motorcycle. And in Taiwan he'd gone to a party at a woman's apartment where the German toilet fixtures were more expensive than the Harley Davidson FLH in Japan. The fact that he could compare German toilet fixtures in Taiwan to American motorcycles in Japan was bizarre enough. The prices were insane. The universe was out of tilt.

He drained his beer. And underneath it all, he thought, festering, like maggots in an open wound, were nightmares these people could not even begin to understand—and, worse, would not understand even when those nightmares started knocking at their doors.

But, hey, do the Motorcycle Man care? With his fingers he lightly tapped a rhythm on the bar, keeping time to the music, a band he didn't recognize. Rap rhythms with lots of saxophone—a dynamite saxophone. He liked saxophone.

A group of Americans and Brits on the other side of the bar kept glancing his way, one or two at a time, looking quickly away or smiling vaguely whenever his eyes met theirs. They didn't know what to make of him. He didn't look like a teacher or a businessman, and he was too old for it to be an act.

He could see himself in the mirrored wall at the other end of the room, a head taller than the people around him, his too-long hair pulled back in a pony tail, the scars on his forehead visible even from there—tiny white streaks running out of his hairline down to the corner of his left eye.

He grinned at his image in the mirror. The image grinned back.

Maybe he'd let his hair grow a little longer, cultivate braids like some of the not-so-Native American tribal members back home were doing now that it was neat to have Indian blood.

Nah, he thought. He already stood out enough.

Some good times in here, he thought. That night he'd gotten it off the ground with Carlos, it had been him and Danny and Paco Wang the half Chinese, half Mexican cook, Carlos and a bunch of girls from Canada, the sound system *cranked.* Satrianni at eight million decibels. Carlos and two girls at one end of the bar feeding their noses. Him and Danny blasted on expensive scotch. Three of the girls drinking margaritas straight out of pitchers, one to each girl. Los Lobos and Healey, Vaya Con Dios and Aretha. Carlos looking like a bear on roller skates whenever he danced, too big even for the nearly empty room; the women like sleek deer. In the middle of the bar, Paco Wang totaled to the point of incoherence on bourbon and cocaine. Four o'clock that morning, Carlos had decided he was executive material.

A product, Ben. That is all. Supply and demand. A business. Nothing more. The rest is all politics."

Politics? Allow me to introduce myself, Carlos, my man. Allow me to introduce myself.

Danny put a shot glass of whiskey in front of him.

"What's this?"

"A shot of thousand-dollar scotch."

"I knew that."

"Until this very minute, you didn't even know such a thing *existed.*"

"A complimentary shot of thousand-dollar-a-bottle scotch?"

"It's compliments of the gentleman in the back there, the one I met at the door."

"This tastes like scotch."

"You can't imagine how relieved I am to hear that."

"Tell him I'm impressed, even though I think his jewelry is a tad ostentatious."

"It's supposed to be."

"He wants a deal on a Harley, doesn't he? In his heart he lusts for a full-dress FLH—saddlebags, reflectors, whip antennas, the whole works."

"That's probably it, all right."

"Well, I'm a man of principle. Tell him it will take a lot more than a shot of ridiculously expensive scotch."

"Two?"

83

"Two would probably do it."

Danny poured another shot.

"Unless, of course, I could get three."

Danny put the lid on the bottle. "I think it's got something to do with how big and destitute you look."

"Well, sure. You can't go to the zoo without feeding the animals. Who's his babe?"

"His 'babe,' as you call her–" Danny put the bottle on a shelf above the cash register. "–is just another example of the finer things in life that *gaijin* peasants like you and I will never be able to afford."

"She's for sale? You sure could have fooled me."

"She's definitely *not* for sale." Danny began cleaning up the area behind the bar, throwing bits of lime and bottle caps and cans into the plastic trash can. "And that's the most expensive kind."

"What's she to him, then?"

"She's the daughter of a friend or something–I don't know who, so don't ask. But I'd say some kind of serious weight from the looks of it."

"Define serious weight."

"Serious weight is serious weight." Danny wiped his hands on a bar towel.

"I probably ought to hit you on your pointy head for a remark like that–but since this is the mysterious Orient, I'll assume you're just being inscrutable."

"All I'm saying is, what these people do is what they do."

"Ah, so."

"You know what I'm talking about. It's not so different here than in the States."

"I have one question."

Danny smiled. "You always have one question."

"Does she know I don't practice safe sex?"

Danny laughed and shook his head.

"Oh, I see. You think maybe she's a little out of my social stratum."

"The closest thing you've got to a social stratum is a social scrotum."

"Really? Is that something I should worry about? I mean, does it, like, you know, make it difficult to seat me at *functions?"*

"For you it might be something to worry about. For the rest of us it's something to be thankful for. She's a talent. A photographer."

"Well, there you go. I just happen to have a collection of rarely seen Harley Davidson art. She'd probably like to come over and peruse it."

"Why don't you ask her?"

"And how would I go about that, do you suppose?"

"You can go about it any way *you* want to go about it."

"You're trying to tell me something, aren't you? Well, go ahead. I can take it. I'm tough. I'm global. I ride a Harley when I'm not riding my Yamaha."

Danny laughed. He walked up and down the bar, rearranging drinks, putting new paper coasters under glasses and bottles. He came back to Ben.

"Look at her," he said.

"Not wearing anything under that dress, is she?"

"Now look at yourself in the mirror. And remember that the lighting in here is supposed to make people look their best."

"Agh! Who's that?"

"See what I mean?

"Man, I got to talk to you about improving your clientele."

"Another beer?"

"Do I get another shot of thousand dollar scotch, too?"

Danny took the bottle down from above the cash register, unscrewed the lid, and poured another shot. He set the bottle on the bar, reached into the refrigerator below the bar and put an unopened Tecate next to the shot glass.

"She ever come in here before?"

"She had lunch in here with a couple of *gaijin*, the other day."

"See there. I'm a *gaijin*, aren't I?"

"These *gaijin* wore suits."

"I wore a suit once."

"They had manicures and expensive haircuts."

"I wore a suit once."

"I think they graduated from the same school your buddy Carlos graduated from."

"All right! My kind of guys."

"Yeah, the spade was probably your brother."

Ben felt his stomach twist. He popped the top on the Tecate. "A spade? What kind of a spade?"

"What do you mean, what kind of spade? A spade. Excuse me." Danny moved down the bar to refill drinks and take orders.

Ben looked down at the shot of scotch. The amber liquid matched nicely the tans and browns of the hardwood strips in the bar.

Across the bar a *gaijin* woman, her denim jacket unzipped, exposing a lacy, black bra that barely covered the bottom half of her breasts, perfect alabaster skin showing above and below the bra, was looking at him. Teased, medium-length brown hair. Heart-shaped face. Lips a permanent pout. She laughed at something the man she was with said, and took off her jacket, twisting a little from side to side as she did.

The black-lace bra and her alabaster skin made him look away.

There was movement near the door. The bullet-headed man bowing to Danny and to his entourage, some of whom were staying.

The woman, the photographer, was standing to one side, smiling, waiting for the man and Danny to finish their goodbyes. Japanese women do that smile better than anyone, Ben thought. It was a smile that meant nothing; meant everything. Meant whatever they wanted it to mean, but only they would ever know what that was. The only person he knew who did it better was Huang.

The guy bowed, and she bowed, and he bowed, and then they both bowed. Someone opened the door, and the man turned toward his audience, and as he did, his eyes met Ben's, and he nodded, and then, smiling hugely and waving a little wave to no one in particular, like a politician after a speech, he turned and went through the door, the woman following him out.

A politician's twitch, he thought, that was all. He'd seen Ben staring over the top of everyone, and he'd nodded. His nod had been nothing more than the woman's smile had been when she'd seemed to be smiling at him from across the room. A Japanese reflex, nothing more.

The door opened and the woman came back in. Her eyes met his and slid away, her lips parting in a smile as she excused her way through the crowd.

Thousand dollar scotch, he thought. Do it to you every time. A million dollar woman looks at you, and you think she's looking at you because you're a thousand dollar man.

Well, what the hell, he thought. Nothing ventured, nothing gained. Ben Tails might be a little shy, but the Motorcycle Man damn sure wasn't.

He turned and began to edge his way through the crowd, forcing his way through groups standing between people seated on stools at the bar and people seated at tables against the far wall, winking at the woman wearing the black-lace bra as he went by, letting his size do most of the work, gently guiding people to either side when they didn't see him, or

87

were too drunk to care. It seemed as if every *gaijin* in the place was either shouting or grinning maniacally or being morose and boring to some cute little Japanese girl who understood about every tenth word, and every Japanese was doing his or her best to look rich and arrogant and about like you'd expect them to look in a bar full of barbarians.

She was even better looking up close than he'd thought she'd be, the blue silk dress more like expensive lingerie than like a dress, her thick black hair woven into a single braid draped over her shoulder.

She looked up, and in the mirrored wall behind her he glimpsed the stretch and flex of fine back muscles moving beneath dark silk. Her wide-spaced eyes were perfect almonds, warm and questioning. He hadn't expected that— her eyes.

"Hi," he said.

"Excuse me?" A thin gold necklace glinted at her throat.

"Do you mind if I sit here for a minute?" Her lips were like those on women in old Japanese paintings, delicate and swollen at the same time. Her eyebrows were heavy black strokes from a calligrapher's brush, their thickness and length attractive but slightly out of place with her Chinese eyes and lips and high forehead. Probably a little Ainu there, he thought, a *samurai* in the woodpile somewhere.

"I'm sorry, but I'm expecting friends." Her English was more than just good. The accent was American. East Coast someplace, he thought.

"Just for a minute." He pulled back a chair and sat down. "I'm waiting for someone, too."

She sat back, and folded her arms underneath her breasts, her nipples clearly defined by thin silk.

He smiled. "I saw you sitting here all alone and—"

"Surely you can do better than that?"

He grimaced and shook his head. "I never do this," he said.

"Never do what?"

"I never just walk up and sit down and start talking like this."

"Oh?"

"Your English is great," he said.

"Thank you," she said sarcastically. "I'm from Boston."

"I saw you at the entrance," he said. "Only a Japanese could smile and bow like that."

She uncrossed her arms, and put her hands around her drink. Her fingers were long and slim, the nails light pink and not too long. "Or a Chinese," she said.

"You're not Chinese."

She raised her chin the way a Chinese would.

He smiled.

She inclined her head the way a Chinese would.

He laughed.

"Why are you laughing?"

"Among those who cannot be taught," he said in Mandarin, *"are women—"*

"And monkeys," she said in English. She leaned forward, her breasts sliding beneath the silk. "In Japanese we say *o-usotsuki.*"

"Sorry. I don't speak much Japanese."

"It means bullshit."

He winced. "Walked into that one, didn't I?"

She sat back, her eyes tracing the scars on his forehead, checking out his hair, his clothes.

Listing his pedigree, writing his résumé, he thought. And he had no problem with that, except that despite his Motorcycle Man camouflage she looked as if she might be getting most of it right. He felt heat on the back of his neck. Time to leave.

89

She frowned. "Have we met before? There's something familiar about you."

"No. You're just confused by my appearance."

"What do you mean?"

"In real life I'm not like this."

"I don't understand."

"In real life I'm worse."

She smiled. "Maybe it's because you're so American."

"There you go."

"Big. Strong."

"Aw, shucks, ma'm."

"Rough."

"Only on the outside, ma'm. Only on the outside."

"Wearing out."

He cleared his throat. "I prefer comfortable as an old shoe."

"Oh, I'm sorry," she said, sounding not sorry at all. "I didn't mean to offend."

"That's okay. My self-esteem will never be the same. But that's okay."

She smiled. "Your self-esteem seems to be doing just fine."

He stuck out his hand. "Ben."

"Kei." Her grip was warm and firm.

"Where are you from, Kei?"

"Where are you from, Ben?"

"I'm from Montana, Kei."

"What do you do in Japan, Ben? You can let go of my hand now, Ben."

He grinned, and released her hand. "I sell motorcycles. What do you do?"

"What do you think of Japan, Ben?"

"What is this? A Berlitz lesson? Would you like a drink?"

"No, thank you, Ben. I have one."

Los Lobos came up on the sound system, and he had to shout. "Kei? Just Kei?"

She waited until the volume was turned down. "I used to have a last name. But now that I'm a success, I'm just Kei."

"Ah, an *artiste*. What do you do?"

"I take pictures." She smiled. "What about you? Do you have any talents?"

"Only for putting my foot in my mouth."

She considered him for a moment, a tiny frown between her eyes. "Would you mind if I took your picture, sometime?"

"Like for a Centerfold, you mean. Rough, worn out American men who inhabit Japanese bars—that kind of thing?"

She smiled. "No. Nothing like that."

He liked her smile, even if he couldn't read it, and he liked her voice, and for sure he liked her body. But what he didn't like, beside her condescension, was her eyes. He didn't like them at all. They'd been soft and warm when he first looked at them, but now they reminded him of eyes he'd seen in Cambodia. "Let me get this straight. You want to take a picture of my face?"

"Not just your face. I mean, it depends on the picture. But, clothed, yes."

"Even my mother doesn't want a picture of my face." Never mind, he thought, that he'd never known his mother.

"You're afraid." It was both a statement and a challenge.

"Kei, you can't imagine how much courage it took just to get myself to come over here and talk to you."

She picked up her drink. Watching her pick up the drink, he could almost feel her skin beneath its silken covering. She put the drink on the table. "You're not a very honest person, are you?" she asked.

"Would you like to go for a ride on a motorcycle?"

She frowned. "Is that your idea of being honest?"

"We could skip the motorcycle ride."

Her frown deepened. "Now you're just being rude."

"How do you know I'm not being honest?"

"Because I'm not very honest, either."

"Is that why you're drinking tea?"

"I don't understand."

"I know other women who speak English and Japanese and Chinese, and who also drink tea in bars."

"Are you implying that—"

"I'm not implying anything, Kei-with-no-last-name. I'm just saying that I've met other women in other bars who speak many languages and who drink tea."

Her smile told him how wrong he was.

"If I only knew, huh?" Shit, he thought, he really was being an asshole tonight. The Motorcycle Man, for sure.

"How could you, Ben-whom-I've-not-asked-for-a-last-name? You're an American."

"Oh, ho," he said, and someone, Danny or one of the bartenders, cranked the sound system up. Los Lobos too loud to talk over.

He closed his mouth and stared at her.

She stared back, her eyes unreadable.

"Louder," someone yelled, and the sound dropped several levels.

"The places he has been; the things he has done," she sang.

"You like this song?"

"I like Mexico."

"This song is about L.A."

She leaned back, her eyes locked with his. *"She hopes for heaven, while for her there's just hell,"* she sang.

He had to look away. Light reflected off perfect rows of I.W. Harper behind the bar. A rich Japanese woman singing about an L.A. barrio girl, he thought. That wasn't bothering him so much as the feeling he had that by watching her sing he was being given a glimpse of something he didn't want to see—as if he'd twisted it, not her, even though he had no idea what it was that had been twisted. The way she was singing

92

made him feel sad and shabby, and he didn't know why. Maybe it was because he was tired of this place. More likely it was because he knew that a rich, good-looking Japanese woman had about as much control of her life as did a girl from an L.A. barrio. Through a shift in the crowd at the entrance, he saw Carlos talking to someone. *'Bout time*, he thought.

"I've got to go," he said. He shoved his chair back and stood.

She nodded, still quietly singing the words to the song.

Next to him at the bar were Japanese in black leather pants and black leather jackets with padded shoulders. Through an alley in the crowd he could see the woman with the black lace bra watching him from the other end of the bar, her pale skin and black lace bra again reminding him of the old woman who had answered the door wearing a black lace bra and nothing else except varicose veins and blood to her elbows, her husband downstairs in the family room on a black leather Barca Lounger, legs sprawled, arms limp to the side, head lolled back on soft black leather, throat grinning hugely at Jay Leno on the Sears console. Soft, black, expensive leather, like the leather the Japanese were wearing this year.

At the station, under harsh fluorescent light, the blue, ropy veins had made her legs look like skinned snakes.

"If you change your mind."

He looked down into warm, almond eyes. She was offering her *meishi*, her business card, to him.

"Change my mind about what?"

"About sitting for me—letting me take your picture."

He took her card and put it in the inside pocket of his jacket. "We'll see."

She smiled, and waggled the fingers of her right hand up at him. "Bye, bye, Ben."

He smiled crookedly and turned and began forcing his way

93

toward Carlos. The last thing he needed in his life right now was a Japanese photographer, an *artiste* rich and condescending and suffering from acute cultural schizophrenia. Take his picture. *His* picture, for Christ's sake.

Carlos was talking to a middle-aged Japanese with gleaming, slick-backed hair. The Japanese was wearing an over-sized black leather jacket with padded shoulders. Even with the padded shoulders, he looked less than half Carlos' size.

Carlos turned the Japanese man in Ben's direction, and pointed at him. Ben forced his way toward them. Carlos was wearing a baggy, gray suit with padded shoulders. A salmon-colored T-shirt. No chains, no earrings, sleeves pulled to his elbows.

"What's this?" Ben said. "Your Miami Mice look? You look like a house with the drapes on the outside."

"Benjamin. Glad you could make it. I was just telling Mr. Yoshida here about you. Mr. Yoshida, Benjamin Tails."

Mr. Yoshida half-bowed. Short, pudgy. Middle-aged and trying to hide it. Carlos sure could find them, Ben thought.

"As you can see, Mr. Yoshida, were I not so fat, Benjamin would be nearly as big as am I. I was just telling Mr. Yoshida the other day that I am not much larger than average," he said to Ben.

"Yeah. Not much larger than your average barn."

"But as you can also see, Mr. Yoshida, Benjamin is nowhere near as handsome as am I." Carlos' blue eyes sparkled with humor. "Benjamin, Mr. Yoshida used to be in law enforcement, too."

"No kidding?" He smiled at Mr. Yoshida. Decadent little fuck, he thought. Bag man was more like it.

Yoshida's eyes were like little black marbles.

"That's pretty amazing," Ben said.

Yoshida's stare turned to undisguised contempt.

"I must be going," he said to Carlos.

"Going? But Yoshida-san, you just got here. At least stay and have one drink with us."

"I'm sorry, but I have business. *Amazing business,*" he said to Ben.

"For better human life," Ben said, mimicking a popular television commercial.

"Well, if you must go." Carlos put his arm around Yoshida's shoulders and squeezed, and the padded shoulders of Yoshida's leather jacket crumpled up around his ears. Carlos squeezed harder. "Don't forget, Yoshida-san. Tomorrow. My office. Be there or be square." Yoshida struggled free, and straightened his jacket, a sickly grin on his face.

"Tomorrow," he said and bowed. He turned and made his way toward the door.

Both men watched him until he went out the door.

"Pompous little fuck," Ben said.

Carlos put his arm around Ben's shoulders and drew him close. "Benjamin. Benjamin. What am I going to do with you, Benjamin?"

"You're going to let go of me, that's what you're going to do." Carlos' fat was like the fat on a bear. He could feel a strength far beyond his own.

"This is a people business, Benjamin. Image is important." He released Ben. "We cannot afford to be in a bad mood. You understand what I am saying?"

"I understand that Mr. Yoshida is mean as a rattlesnake."

"Of course, he is mean. He is supposed to be mean. He is also connected. And in this country that is more important than being mean."

"He's an asshole."

Carlos smiled, a wide, wonderful grin full of dimples and perfect white teeth. "We are going to make a great team, you and I, Benjamin."

"No, we're not."

95

Carlos raised his eyebrows. "Oh?"

The Motorcycle Man looked away. "I've been thinking about it. The States, maybe. But not Japan. Who knows what these people are thinking, let alone doing."

"What people are we talking about exactly, Ben?"

"People like your Mr. Yoshida."

Carlos laughed. "I believe you are afraid."

"You bet your ass, I'm afraid. I'm always afraid. What do you think I've been talking to you about for the last month?"

"I know a little about fear, too."

"I'm not talking about being shot at, Carlos. I'm talking about these people will feed you to the sharks so fast you won't believe it. You're messing with their rice bowl. You're messing with their face. And they won't be having any of that. These aren't a bunch of beaner cowboys with Mac 10's you're dealing with. These are the people who had the balls to bomb Pearl Harbor."

"Benjamin, Benjamin."

"Your drink, sir," Danny said.

Carlos looked at him. "Ah, Danny." He took a small beer glass half filled with amber liquid from Danny. "What is this?" He sniffed at it.

"It's for Ben."

"For Ben?"

"It's the new house brand. I wanted him to try it."

Carlos took a sip. "House brand indeed. A bottle of 'house brand' for me and my friend Benjamin."

Danny looked at Ben. "Uh. . . ."

"It's a hundred and fifty thousand yen a bottle," Ben said.

"Wonderful! Make it two bottles. One for each of us."

Danny laughed. "You want that now, or when hell freezes over?"

Carlos withdrew a long, slender wallet from the inside

pocket of his coat and handed a platinum American Express card to Danny. "Now will be fine."

"Well, all right! A *gaijin* who spends money. Two bottles of the bar's best coming right up."

Carlos put his wallet back into his coat.

"I'm impressed," Ben said.

"You are not. You could care less. If you cared, I would not buy it."

"Oh, that makes a lot of sense."

"Let us just say it is my way of saying that it is not the money."

"Speak for yourself, *esse.*"

Carlos smiled. "I'm not your *esse.*"

"Let me get this straight: you are paying a stupid amount for a bottle of whiskey just so I know that you know that neither one of us gives a rat's ass about money?"

"That and the fact that it is excellent whiskey."

"I'm a motorcycle salesman, and you're Pancho fucking Villa, and we don't care about money?"

"You know, Benjamin, sometimes, you can actually piss me off."

"What's wrong, *esse?* You don't like being called Pancho?"

"I do not like being called *esse,* and I do not like being called Pancho. I am not from some L.A. barrio." He leaned close to Ben. "And we might as well get something straight right now. I suffered the fools at Harvard in silence because I had to. But you, I do not have to suffer at all."

Ben took the glass of scotch from Carlos.

"What are you laughing at?" Carlos asked.

"Tough guys don't say anything, *esse.* They just do it."

Carlos waggled his finger at Ben.

"Yeah, yeah," Ben said. "Have a drink. Here take this one. It's pretty good."

"What is evil to you, Benjamin? A powder that people put

up their sinuses? An ego that sends young men to die in war? That allows factories to produce pollutants? That lets babies starve because their parents have the wrong ideology? Tell me, Benjamin. Tell me what the worst evil is."

"I give up."

"Killing our enemies. That is the worst evil."

"You read that in a book somewhere."

"Listen, I am trying to be serious. When we kill our enemies, it makes us hunger for more enemies. And the more enemies we kill, the more hungry we become." Carlos smiled. "And I see in your eyes that you know exactly what I am talking about. So, please, no more bullshit about Asia. No more bullshit about money. No more bullshit about all the helpless people who cannot control their desire to put powder up their noses."

"I sell American motorcycles to rich Nips, Carlos. That's all I do."

"I know you, Benjamin. I know you."

"You don't know shit, *esse*. That's what you know."

"Do you want to know what I know about you?"

"No."

"I quote: 'A misfit who probably sees himself more a mercenary than a law enforcement officer. Too much war. Too much death. With a personal loss that has probably severed whatever connections remain to the society he was raised in.' Our consultant, incidentally, advises a number of big-city police departments in the U.S."

"Lots of probablys, I noticed."

Carlos smiled. "He characterized you as antisocial—a dangerous personality. But a Marine sniper with classified kills on his record pretty much defines a dangerous personality, don't you think? He recommended that you not be employed in any law enforcement capacity."

"The shrink thought I wanted to be a cop?"

"He has no idea who he is really consulting for."

"Lucky for society I'm just a motorcycle salesman."

Carlos chuckled. "I love it when you do that."

"When I do what?"

"Ssssss." Carlos made an weaving motion with his hand. "Into the grass."

"Let me put this to you as plain as I can, Carlos. You have surely got me mixed up with–"

Carlos held up his hand. "Please. You are not angry, Ben. Not really. Anger is just something you use to hide behind."

Ben was silent.

"Besides." Carlos chuckled. "There are eight years not accounted for."

"Eight years?"

"There is no need to play games with me, Ben."

"Who's playing games? It's news to me that I don't know about eight years of my life."

"A lot can happen in eight years."

"Yeah, or nothing can happen in eight years."

"In that case, the shrink would be right."

Ben sipped his whiskey, watching Carlos over the glass. Carlos' eyes were cold.

"What did you do with those eight years, Ben? A minute ago you said all I had to do was ask."

Ben put the glass down and shook his head. He let his gaze take on a far away look.

"Rumor has it that you and some very bad news nigger were helping some guy named V.P. take opium to market," Carlos said.

"Some *guy* named V.P.?"

"So maybe I know–"

"Some *guy* named V.P.?"

"–more about those eight years than you think I do."

Ben laughed. "You don't know squat from diddly, that's what you know."

"But you cannot be sure."

"Oh, yes I can."

"How?"

"Nearly everyone from those days is dead—and even you and all your money that you don't care about can't get the dead to talk."

"Ah, nearly everyone, you said."

"And those that aren't, even I wouldn't know how to find them." In his mind Ben saw the extra cup of tea steaming on the polished teak window sill. He smiled to himself. Even if Carlos found Huang, he would probably think Huang was the janitor, or something. His smile faded as in his mind he saw a beat-to-hell C-47 come out of nowhere and pass overhead no more that ten feet above shattered palms. He saw that C-47 in his sleep the way some people see sheep jumping a fence. Over and over, the beat-to-hell C-47 passing overhead, gone each time before he was sure it had even been there, the echo of its stuttering engine like the echo of a dream he could never quite remember. He looked down at the drink in his hand. He did not want to do this.

He looked up at Carlos. "You want to know what it was, *esse?* It was eight years of people dead. People dying. People getting rich. And it fucked me up." He smiled his tough-guy-vulnerable-just-for-this-very-special-moment-smile. "So give it a rest, okay?"

Carlos grinned his wonderful white, dimpled grin, and slapped him on the back. "I asked; you answered. That is good enough for me. Let us talk about fear for minute."

"Why is it every time we start drinking, you want to talk about something like death or fear? Let's talk about women for once."

100

"Fear is the thing by which we judge all people like you and me, do you not agree?"

"No. I do not agree."

"Because, unlike sin, unlike any other emotion we have been taught, fear carries no shame. Real fear, I mean."

"Oh, *real* fear."

"Real fear is never shameful, Benjamin."

"Congratulations. That's the first intelligent thing you've said all night."

"You are starting to piss me off, Benjamin."

"Well, give me a break. You read all that in a book somewhere."

"And what if I did? How many people understand it?"

"How many people besides us understand fear?"

"Yes."

"Well, let me see. The entire population of Cambodia. Everyone listening to the doctor give them the bad news. Gee, I don't know, half the population of the world, maybe."

"I'm serious."

"You're not serious. You're talking out your ass."

"We are unique, Ben."

"Yeah, we're about as unique as the common cold." Ben put his drink on the bar. "Look, I understand what you're saying. You think I ought to throw in with you because you think working with you will get my juices flowing again. You think working with you will make me stop feeling guilty about all the crap in my life that the Catholic Church told me I ought to feel guilty about."

"It is truly amazing how articulate and logical you can be sometimes."

"Yeah. Well. Sweet talk me all you want, but I are not going to do it. I agree with a lot of what you say, but those eight, very-much-accounted-for years, thank you, taught me a lot about Asia. And these particular Asians, so perfectly represented by your Mr. Yoshida, are going to jump in your shit. And I do not, repeat, *do not,* want to be around when they do."

"Sorry," Danny said, setting two bottles on the bar. "It got a little busy down at the other end." He dropped ice cubes into glasses and poured scotch over the ice. "How's it going with the lady?" he asked Ben. "I saw you talking to her."

"The lady and I walk to the beat of a different drummer," Ben said.

"What lady?" Carlos asked.

"Danny nodded toward the other end of the room. "In the back. Last table."

"The woman with the three men?"

"Yeah."

"One of the men is a nigger?"

Ben felt a sudden tingle start at the back of his neck, felt his stomach go hollow, a flushed, sick feeling leaking hot into his limbs. In his mind he heard Robert Lee say, *I wouldn't want to fuck with him.*

"That's the one," Danny said.

Slowly, deliberately, Ben forced himself to turn toward the mirrored wall at the back of the room.

In the mirror there was the woman, Kei, and two well-dressed white men, one short and stocky and with the kind of glasses that change shades, the other tall and slender and dark tanned. Late thirties both of them, the smaller one going bald. Government, Ben thought. The tall one looked like a case officer.

The crowd at the bar shifted, and in the mirror looking directly at him was an ebony skull, its eyes hidden deep in shadowed eye sockets, skin stretched tight and shiny across high cheekbones, a trick of size and light and height juxtaposing his own face just above and to the right, his scars and the dent in his forehead clearly visible.

The Pumpkin Eater grinned, his teeth dead white in the opaque light, neck muscles clearly defined, close-cropped hair and impeccably tailored suit contrasted with himself shabby and mean-looking above the crowd at the opposite end of the bar.

Three people–two Japanese men in suits, and a Japanese woman in black skirt and too-big leather jacket–moved away from the bar toward the door, obscuring his view, and when the mirror again cleared, there was just the woman, Kei, and the two white Americans. It had been so sudden, as sudden as that C-47 roaring past overhead, and knowing his own state of mind, Carlos and all, Ben was not sure what he'd seen, or why he'd seen it, because there was nowhere for the Pumpkin Eater to go. And for an instant he felt panic, the same panic he'd felt that time the cobra had gone to ground. He scanned the crowd, trying to convince himself that it had been only a vision brought on by the woman and the whiskey and Carlos dredging up the past.

Sweat slid down his neck.

He'd known since he'd gotten on the plane in Montana that it was going to happen sooner or later, and whether he'd imagined it, or whether it was real and the Pumpkin Eater was here, didn't matter. What mattered was now he knew how he'd react. And he didn't like the way he'd reacted. He didn't like it at all. It was the same way he'd felt when he'd seen shadow and sunlight shift and become grizzly. And thinking about the bear, he knew that what he'd seen in the mirror really was the Pumpkin Eater. It hadn't been his imagination. Peter was here, and he wasn't a grizzly slinking through the trees. He was here and he was exactly like that cobra he'd seen rise like a nightmare periscope above the tall grass.

Searching the shifting crowd for those eyes, for that

impeccably tailored gray suit, he saw in his mind the cobra spread its hood. Heard it growl.

Carlos nudged Ben with his shoulder. "Not bad," he said, and Ben, not even remotely the Motorcycle Man now, almost hit him in the throat. *Go for Peter right now,* screamed through him. *Go over the bar and get him.* He wanted to feel bone and cartilage and gristle give beneath his fists.

"Whoa," Carlos said. "Whoa. Whoa. Whoa. What did I say?"

He couldn't. Carlos. A huge wheel of logic and reason and kill, made even more terrifying by the realization that the image in the mirror probably knew it all—knew why he was there—ran through his mind. The door was closing, and he hadn't seen who'd gone through it.

"What?" he said to Carlos.

"I said, I'm sorry if I offended you."

If Peter had been here, was here somewhere, then Carlos was no longer important. Had never been important. Was not even an issue.

Carlos looked at him, concern etched in furrows across his forehead.

Ben put his drink on the bar. Calm down, he thought. Peter wasn't here for him. If he was, he never would have shown himself like that. Carlos wasn't the real issue. Whatever the real issue was, Carlos was only the ante. "What do you say we get out of here," he said. "Go somewhere and talk." And he smiled, not caring about the puzzled look on Carlos' face.

Smiled because he hadn't felt that good in a long time.

Chapter 2
Good Men Never Do Bad

The street, four lanes on both sides, was a bleak, empty expanse of pavement bordered by concrete sidewalks, concrete buildings, and cinder block fences. What little color it had to begin with was bleached flat by light from halogen street lamps. Taxis now and then crossed distant intersections, their single-minded hurry reminding Ben of rodents crossing open spaces.

"I should walk more often," Carlos said. He patted his stomach. "Get rid of some of this."

In the distance, they could hear the high-pitched whine and roar of motorcycles over-revving, and the even more distant sound of police sirens following the motorcycles. *"Bosozoku,"* Carlos said.

"Yeah."

"What would you do with people like that in the States?"

"Throw their ass in jail."

"That's all?"

"That's more than they do here."

"No. I'm serious. You were a cop. A bunch of barbarians are running amok with motorcycles. What would you do?"

"Well, some of the bikes are stolen. That's felony theft–you do understand what a felony is, don't you?"

Carlos laughed.

"Selling drugs is a felony," Ben said. "You go to prison for selling drugs."

"Not if you have my lawyers, you don't. What else could you get them for?"

"What are you getting at?"

"I'm getting at how ineffectual the Japanese police are. I mean, consider, Ben, police in this country drive around with their emergency lights on to let the citizens know they are on duty. What do they do if there is a real emergency? They use bicycles; that is what they do. My God, they actually *escort* the *bosozoku* around the city."

"This is Japan, Carlos. Things are different here. There's a place up ahead. You want to go in there?"

At the end of the next block they could see advertised by large red lanterns the social equivalent of a bar in Montana. A place where mostly neighborhood people, and mostly men, could meet and drink and eat. The atmosphere was usually warm and friendly, even rough at times, the emphasis as much on food as on drink: grilled fish, tiny wooden skewers of pork and chicken and leek, cold potato salad, tofu steak, *sake*, beer, whiskey.

"Now that I am moving, the cold air feels good," Carlos said.

"I know a place down by the port," Ben said. "But it's a forty-fifty minute walk."

"We can always find a taxi and go back to Danny's."

"Nah," Ben said.

"It's not another of those dives you insist on frequenting, is it?"

"It has a certain ambience, if that's what you mean."

Carlos put his arm around Ben's shoulders and squeezed. "Work with me, Ben. Work with me."

Using both hands Ben pried Carlos' arm from around his shoulder. "They've got a saying here about nails, Carlos. The nail that stands up is the one that gets pounded down. And your snowy-white dope is standing you up in a big way."

Carlos shrugged. "No pain, no gain."

Ben reached out and grabbed his arm, stopping him. "Look,"

he said, letting his voice be his real voice, not the Motorcycle Man's. He released Carlos' arm. "I'm warning you. Sell your shit in the States. Sell it in Canada. Sell it in Europe. Africa. The North Pole, I don't care. But do not sell it here."

Carlos laughed. "Everybody wants drugs, Ben. Everybody."

Ben sighed. "You're not listening."

"You are the one who is not listening."

They both paused, as ahead, at the end of the block, two policemen walked their bicycles across the intersection. The two policemen stopped on the other side and looked back toward them.

"I'm telling you as a friend, Carlos."

"It's a business, Ben. Merely a business. America was *built* on fortunes begun with drug money. Railroads were financed with opium money from China—from Chinese who were making even more off the opium trade than were the foreigners who were delivering the opium. It's going to be the same for the Japanese. They are going to make a lot more money off our product than are we."

"Look at what drugs are doing to America, Carlos."

"Ah, America." Carlos made a cross with his index fingers. "Out. Out. Demon drugs." He chuckled, and put his hands in his pockets. "One man's relaxation is another man's medicine is another man's ticket to hell. We could say that about a lot of things, couldn't we? Even sex. A certain percentage of the population are *determined* to be losers, Benjamin. They will find a way, with or without us. So do not lay that look-at-America bullshit on me."

Ben was silent.

"Well?"

"Whether or not I agree with you is beside the point. This is Japan."

"These people are not people?"

"This place—even the Japanese themselves no longer

understand this place, Carlos. A lot of wrong things are at work here. I can't explain it."

They reached the intersection where the two cops had crossed. To his left, in the direction the police had gone, Ben could see the faint black and white of a police car parked in the entrance to a small lane.

"You sell motorcycles, don't you?" Carlos asked.

Ben stopped. "See, that's the problem. Just because you and I react to the *bosozoku* like the bunch of little assholes they are, we think that naturally the Japanese react the same way. The cops must be weak and stupid—otherwise they'd do something about the *bosozoku*, right? Wrong. Because—are you listening?"

"I'm listening."

"This is Japan."

Carlos grunted.

"We look at this place," Ben said. "And we see decadence and corruption. Money everywhere. And we say, Yo! This is the place. But what we don't see is what motivates these people."

"You give these people too much credit, Ben. These people still think the world is flat. There is no control here."

"Even if you're right—and you are not—then that only makes them more dangerous and unpredictable."

"Have I ever said this was without risk? Part of the attraction is supposed to be the risk. I thought we agreed on that at least." They walked past the entrance to a tiny lane. A uniformed policeman with a bicycle was standing just inside the lane.

Carlos nodded. "Good evening, officer."

The policeman stared without expression.

"Mr. Personality," Carlos said, when they were past the lane. "Doesn't it ever bother you, Vietnam and all—don't you ever get the urge to—"

"I learned a long time ago that the gooks, as the stupid among us used to call them, take care of business as well as we do, Carlos. To them our size only makes us better targets."

"But you get the urge?"

"No. I never get the urge."

"Never, Ben?"

"If I did, I wouldn't be here."

"You know what your problem is, Ben?"

"Yeah. You."

"You have lost your self respect; that is your problem."

Ben looked at him.

Carlos chuckled. "You are a good man, Ben."

"And good men never do bad?"

"I never said *that.*"

Ben stopped. "Look. Let's be real for a minute, okay?"

Carlos turned back toward him.

"Remember what you said about fear?" Ben asked. "I knew as soon as you said it that you'd read it in a book, or heard it from someone else. You know how I knew?"

"How, Ben? How do you know so much?"

"Because you talk about it too much, that's how. And when you talk about it, you give it exactly the same weight you give all your other bullshit."

Carlos walked back toward him. "Perhaps you imagine that I am some jolly fat man?"

"You are going to get your ass handed to you," Ben said.

"These people are fools."

"The people you are dealing with are *not* fools, Carlos. They don't care about being Catholic. They don't care about sin. All they care about is face. Ah, fuck it," he said, resigned suddenly to the whole thing. He put his hands into his jacket pockets.

"We are affiliated with many Asians, Ben."

"Yoshida is nothing."

Carlos chuckled. "For Better Human Life. I liked that."

"Carlos, some of these people have been mean and nasty since long before Cortez or Balboa or any Jesuit fanatic ever imagined sailing off to the New World to rape and pillage and save souls and father your sorry ass."

"The face you are so worried about, Benjamin, is nothing more than a matter of negotiation and money. If we do it right, and if the money is right, then everyone gains face. But even if we mess it up, well, as you say, we are *gaijin.* The authorities will bow and smile and tell us they no longer require our presence, and that will be that until we try again. And since they will never admit that this country has a drug problem, we *will* try again." He chuckled. "These people are their own worst enemy, Ben. We cannot lose even if we lose."

"The cops here are not like any cops you've ever dealt with."

"What have the cops got to do with the price of rice, Benjamin? They are different in every country—and they are always the same."

"The police here can bust your door down any time they want, hold you as long as they want."

"In other countries they do more than that."

"The prosecutor decides who to prosecute, how much to prosecute, what kind of sentence should be passed. Never mind the system on paper. The prosecutor *tells* the judge what kind of sentence you should have."

"Yes." Carlos said. "A most effective system. As you may have noticed, we have wandered about a major city for some time with nary a mugger or rapist in sight."

"*No one* is in sight, Carlos."

"Benjamin, if these people do not feel the need for civil liberties, then that is their problem. It has no bearing on our task. Anything is possible here; you know that. If this place has a religion, it's money. Anything and anyone can be bought."

"Now there's a quaint thought."

"The police are tied to the Yakuza."

"Everything is tied to the Yakuza, Carlos. The Yakuza and the police hold this place together."

"Well, finally."

"Oh, I see. You know a couple of Yakuza who know a couple of police, and you think that's all there is to it."

Carlos chuckled. "You have hit the nail on the head."

"The cops a long time ago made a deal with the devil," Ben said. "Organized crime for disorganized crime. Corruption is not sanctioned the way you think."

"You're contradicting yourself," Carlos said.

"No, I'm not. It's the system that is contradictory. And the system is showing signs of unraveling. Disorganization is creeping in. And there is nothing that makes these people more nervous than disorganization. They're control freaks. To them a *gaijin* is inherently disorganized; that's why they keep us in our *gaijin* box. But you. You represent chaos to these people."

"I'm getting cold again."

"You scare these people, Carlos." Thirty meters ahead, two men dressed in khaki jackets and pants came around a corner, laughing and joking, arms around each other's shoulders.

"Look at these guys," Carlos said.

The two men looked like construction workers on their way home from a night of cheap whiskey and karaoke, Ben thought. On their way home from a *Snack,* a club where the price has more to do with how much a man wants to be mothered than with how much he wants to get laid. Their construction uniforms were neat and clean, creases still in the pant legs.

"Who are these men, Ben?" The two workers were no longer

111

laughing. Behind them, on both sides of the street, pairs of uniformed police appeared out of lanes and streets. Two police cars, their red top lights on, pulled into the middle of the nearest intersection, blocking it. One of the construction workers dropped slightly behind the other. Ben stepped away from Carlos.

"What is happening here, Ben? Speak to me, Ben." Carlos whirled—much faster than a man of his bulk had any right to—flowing without hesitation into a martial arts movement, half-karate, half something else, the movement compacting him into a squat, solid mass.

The trail man stepped off the sidewalk into the street.

Carlos rotated toward him, and in one seamless movement the lead man pivoted and swung backhand a black baton of some kind down into the middle of Carlos' forehead. The force of the blow drove Carlos' head down solid into his shoulders, his body instantly became that special kind of heavy, his ass collapsing almost to the ground, limp hands slapping wetly onto the sidewalk, knees and ankles impossibly flexed, upright only because his balance had been perfect.

Ben knew from the sound of the hit that Carlos was dead— knew from the sound that it wasn't a baton at all, was instead an iron or steel pipe leaded and wrapped with black tape.

The man in khaki waited a beat for Carlos to settle, and then, in quick succession, once to either side, as if knighting him, broke both collar bones.

Ben turned to run and, as he turned, was shoved hard. Skin scraped from the palm of his hand as he hit and rolled, somewhere in the roll seeing more than one person standing over him—seeing next to Carlos the other man in khaki, the one who had stepped into the street, swing two handed another black baton at Carlos. Swing as if he were swinging a baseball bat.

He heard the baton connect with Carlos' skull, the sound

like the sound of a hand ax splitting open the chest of a fresh-killed elk, and he pushed off the pavement, and from high behind his right thigh was kicked back down, skin tearing off both palms. "Motherfuckers," he said, and was kicked again, landing awkwardly onto his hip this time. To his left, he saw Carlos topple backwards.

Two of the largest Japanese he had ever seen were standing over him, their faces in shadow. Black or dark blue, loose-fitting suits, white shirts, ties, the padded shoulders of the suits giving them an impossible breadth of shoulder, their nearly shaved heads and thick necks nevertheless in proportion to the shoulders. He moved crablike backwards on hands and feet, aware of the reek of urine and human feces coming from the direction of Carlos.

The two men watched him.

He got to his feet and backed away. They were both taller than him. Carlos was on his back, knees bent, legs sprawled open, feet flat on the sidewalk, as if his shoes had been nailed to the concrete. The two men in khaki were looking down at Carlos.

Three uniformed police stood watching from the middle of the intersection.

Carlos' suit coat was open, his stomach impossibly flat, ribs jutting beneath the salmon-colored shirt.

The two big men abruptly split away from each other, in unison, as if they had been given a command, and shuffled forward, crouched slightly, their hands moving lazily, their slow shuffle forward and the movement of their hands benign, as if to reassure him that they meant no harm. He knew that if one of those hands got hold of him, his jacket or anywhere, he'd have no chance. They were *judoka,* and they were playing with him—someone was playing with him. He could see a black wire and ear piece on the one on the right.

113

The two men in khaki had left Carlos and were coming toward him, one behind the other along the sidewalk.

Carlos was dead, and he was next. Some bullshit excuse to Jim the next day.

He moved backwards. The two *judoka* were herding him toward the sidewalk and the steel shutters of a shop. Relax, their hands said.

The two men in khaki began thumping their lengths of pipe in measured taps along a concrete wall. *Tunk.* Coming to get you. *Tunk. Tunk.* The psychology of it all was pissing him off.

He glanced back. At least six uniformed police were at the other end of the street. A figure, a suit, was coming diagonal from behind him across the street.

He heard the scrape of shoe on pavement, as the man on his left, his big hands, reached for him. Like all good athletes, the man made it look easy, a big, slow shark reaching casually for his jacket.

Ben stepped one step back, and as he did, time slowed. He set. Watched the big man make the adjustment. Waited for those fingers to reach for him, and when they did, put a solid left into the man's smile. There was no memory of throwing the left, only the vague memory of knuckles hitting.

He stepped back. Set. Waited for the adjustment–slower this time–and hit him again as hard as he could with a right to the heart, the clarity and smoothness of it wonderful. He moved sideways, changing his lead, stacking the two *judoka* one behind the other, the two with the pipes behind them.

The man behind him was not hurrying. They weren't going to shoot him; if they were going to shoot him, they would already have shot him. He'd hit the big man as hard as he could, and he was a heavyweight and could hit as hard as a pro, but all the man had done was grunt and lose his smile. Carlos' head and shoulders were in shadow, his legs open and awkward. *"Probably beat on him a little," Jim had said. "Just enough to let him know they are serious."*

The four men had stopped and were watching him.

Peter had been at Danny's. *Get yourself under control. Let the good times roll.* Peter singing that the first time they'd been on a mission together.

He took off his jacket.

You only live but once. And when you're dead, you're done. The Pumpkin Eater singing Ray Charles while they watched about fifty Hmong across the valley get their asses blown to hell.

He pulled the folding Paul knife from his back pocket and opened it with both hands, the click of the locking mechanism crisp and clean in the silence of the street. Someone probably had a scope on him right now. They'd have to shoot him. He wasn't going to let them beat him to death. He held the Paul knife tight in the palm of his hand, index finger along the squared back of the blade. The blade was only two and a half inches, but he'd dressed out elk with it. The man he'd hit now knew he was fast enough to cut him anywhere he wanted.

"For Better Human Life," a voice said from behind.

Ben half-turned. Yoshida, dressed in dark gray suit, white shirt and paisley tie, hair washed and blow dried and combed with a part on the left, stood fifteen meters back. He barked a command in Japanese, and the four men in front of Ben snapped to attention.

"You can put the knife away, Mr. Tails. I think we have made our point." He said something in Japanese to the four men, and the four men bowed in unison. The two in khaki began walking toward the uniformed police at the intersection. The other two turned toward each other.

"I should have known."

"Ah, but how could you?"

Ben pushed the button on the locking mechanism and folded the blade into the handle and put the knife into the front

115

pocket of his jeans. He pulled on his jacket. "Not about you. About this."

Yoshida smiled. "A foreigner was robbed and killed. A rare occurrence in this country. Alas, one that happens now and again."

"And if I'd killed one of your cops?" Ben felt tired suddenly, sick and weak–the after affects of the adrenaline, he knew. His right thigh and buttock where he'd been kicked began to twitch uncontrollably. He tightened his muscles to stop the twitching.

Yoshida laughed. "Not likely. But in the event, this is Japan. Explanations are often not required." No one was making any effort to do something with the body; it was alone on the sidewalk, the salmon colored shirt garish against the grays and blacks of the street.

"Where did you learn your English, Mr. Yoshida?"

"Sato. Captain Sato."

"You killed him."

"Yes, we did. We killed him."

"Nobody said anything about killing him."

"Nobody asked."

"Oh, I bet someone did."

Sato strolled toward him, hands clasped behind his back. "Do you know that during the Second World War we had factories here and in Manchuria and in Taiwan that produced enough heroin tablets to addict most of the population of China? We did. It was our pacification program, and it worked most efficiently. We have great respect for drugs, Mr. Tails."

"Scotland Yard, I bet."

"Excuse me? Oh, my accent. Yes. One year. And before that four years at Cambridge."

Ben moved closer to Sato, knowing he was going to do something, not sure what it might be. The physical movement of his body felt real enough. He felt the ache where he'd

116

been kicked, a burning in the palms of his hands. But all that was detached, not really there. "It had nothing to do with drugs," he heard himself say, his voice calm and matter-of-fact.

Sato raised one eyebrow, and the way he did it Ben knew it was something he practiced in the mirror.

"You had a parabolic or a laser on us, and you heard us talking, and you lost it, didn't you? It wasn't planned." He forced himself to focus more closely on the man in front of him.

"You are a guest in this country, Mr. Tails. It would behoove you to behave like one."

"Do you know that American condom companies make condoms in two sizes only?"

Sato's eyes narrowed.

"Japanese and everyone else," Ben said.

"This would be a good time for you to leave, Mr. Tails."

"You motherfucker."

"He is an example."

"Really?" Ben reached out and flipped the ends of Sato's tie.

"Don't be a fool, Mr. Tails."

Ben tugged gently on the ends of the tie. "See, what I think is that it was some petty little humiliation. A laugh. A look. A word like *gook.*"

"Leave now!"

"Killing him and kicking me around the street is really all about the size of your dick."

"Leave now, or I will summon my–"

Ben grabbed Sato by the throat, lifting him up onto his toes, forcing his head back, chin up, pivoting so that Sato's back was toward the two *judoka.* "I'll break his neck," he said, the tone of his voice, if not the words, freezing the two men where they were. If anyone knew how to break a man's neck, they did.

He tightened his grip, feeling his fingers bite into cords of muscle, the hard gristle of throat beneath his palm. He looked into Sato's eyes. "Maybe I'll break it anyway."

Sato's hands pawed at his arm and wrist.

Ben shook him. "That would really fuck up your day, wouldn't it?"

Sato's hands fluttered.

Ben pulled Sato's face closer to his own. *Real evil, Ben. Real evil,* Carlos had said. He half threw, half shoved Sato backwards toward the two big men. The one he'd punched caught him.

Behind them, on the other side of the street, Carlos lay on the sidewalk, legs splayed open, his salmon-colored shirt pastel in the bleached light.

A man neither more nor less good than himself, Ben thought. A man who had done bad. *Real evil, Ben.* A man killed by an evil little fuck people were going to say had done good.

Sato was retching and coughing, bent over between the two men. The two men stood stolid as cartoon Russians.

Ben turned and walked away. Fuck it, he thought. Don't mean nothin'.

Don't mean a fucking thing.

But he knew that it did. Knew that when he least expected or wanted it, it would be there. A memory pale as a fish rising to the surface of a dark pool in the Blackfoot—a memory pale as a salmon-colored shirt on a gray street in Nagoya, Japan.

Chapter 3
Flesh Wounds

Early morning light filtered through bamboo curtains, onto Ben dressed only in a pair of gray gym trunks, lying on the *tatami*, bandaged hands laced behind his head.

A stereo in the other *tatami* room, a small refrigerator and a two-burner stove in the kitchen, and a washing machine half the size of a standard American washer in the bathroom were the only furnishings in the apartment. Even the *shoji*–sliding doors made of wood and paper–had been removed in an effort to make the apartment as spacious and as empty as possible.

He liked to lie on the *tatami* and feel the hard, tightly woven grass against his bare skin. Liked to look at it, the color of wheat stalks. It would be nice to have a room like this back in Montana.

Before he'd come here, he had it in his mind that most Japanese had beautiful little gardens, rocks and plants and water perfectly arranged and raked so as to give a feeling of space and harmony. But his apartment, and all the apartments around it, had no terrific little gardens–had instead concrete balconies that overlooked a scraggly park where people brought their dogs in the early morning and in the evening after dark.

He stared at the patterns and whorls in the wood ceiling. A breeze chill against his chest and arms rattled the bamboo.

119

The Japanese claimed that if you stared at your little garden long enough, sooner or later you'd see inside that garden. And then, if you could see inside that garden, sooner or later you'd see into the garden of the heart—your soul, as it were. And if you could see into your soul, then sooner or later you'd see the Supreme Garden, the Supreme Garden being— well, what was the Supreme Garden, anyway? Buddha? Jesus? Famous Amos Chocolate Chip Cookies? All this lying around on *tatami* staring at bamboo curtains, all this sooner or latering about gardens—the fact was, all that was no more than a lot of romantic drivel fostered by a bunch of *gaijin* who wore sandals with their suits and ties.

For months he'd stared at real gardens wherever he could find them. Real rocks. Real sand. Real pools of water. Ancient shrines and temples. And felt nothing. Not a thing. Except that once. And that was a graveyard, not a garden, and it had been a buzz, that was all. The hair on the back of his neck had stood on end, and he'd gotten a few goose bumps. Big deal. He felt more than that in places he knew in Montana. For sure, it wasn't exactly what you'd call enlightenment.

He closed his eyes, and the Pumpkin Eater mottled gray and black with camouflage, a shotgun slung barrel down across his back, stood among the gravestones.

He bolted upright, on his feet before he was conscious of moving. His heart pounded. A sour, metallic taste filled his mouth, the adrenaline gray and shaky as the light coming through the bamboo.

Peter in camouflage among the stones. *Samurai* death. Vietnamese death. Khmer death. Carlos dead in an alien place filled with alien stones. He was sweating. Jesus. The image had been so powerful that the residue of it was still there at the periphery of his vision.

Bamboo curtains rattled. Light bounced and flickered on the *tatami.*

When he'd stood among the gravestones, the hair had raised on the back of his neck, and he'd felt kill like carbonation in his blood—an old familiar feeling that should have told him then that something was coming. But he'd told himself—let himself believe—that he was reacting only to the *Samurai* buried there. He eased back down onto the *tatami,* feeling the cool, pliant surface on his back and on the underside of his legs and arms. He spread his arms straight out to the sides, ankles together. Sweat slid down his temple, tickled the inside of his ear.

He'd been behaving like an idiot these past six months. Touchy-feely bullshit. Trying to get the Frenchman out of his system. But when he'd walked through that red *torii,* among those old gravestones, he'd known right then, same as if someone had walked up and told him, that things weren't right.

He'd known, too, that he'd never be able to look inside anything. Not him. Someone else, maybe, but not him. Standing among those old stones he'd felt the edge of it, what someone else might be able to see, and he'd known right then, only he had been too stubborn to admit it, that he couldn't stay sane, not even half sane, and look at the all of it. Months of walking around Japan, pissing and moaning and feeling sorry for himself. Blaming the way he felt, who he was, on what Asia had become. And how accurate was he about even that? His perceptions hopelessly biased by his wanting to be something noble. A warrior. A *Samurai.* It was enough to make you puke.

Howdy, all you *Samurai.* How you doing? I'm you, you're me, bad dudes all of us, you bet. Been this way forever. I've got the kills to prove it.

And one of them is lying on a street in Nagoya, Japan.

No. Look at it straight. Not just a kill. Carlos.

Damn. This was about the worst he'd ever felt in his life.

121

Worse even than when Evy had died. Worse even than when he'd shot those Marines. And on top of everything the Pumpkin Eater was here and haunting him.

When he was seventeen years old, he had been a warrior. Thirty years old he'd still been a warrior. And now here he was. Here he fucking was. Middle-aged and lying on the floor in an empty apartment in Japan. He shut his eyes.

Seventeen years old. No bamboo then, not even a hint.

Seventeen years old and standing inside a stand of spruce, Asia still a year and a half away, a big doe bounding and plowing through snow, up the slope toward him. Slowing to a walk, wheezing through bushes twenty yards below, tongue hanging out the side of her mouth. At the bottom of the slope, other deer ran, white and gray haunches bouncing and flashing through bushes and between trees.

Chest heaving, leg and haunch muscles trembling, the doe stopped, white showing around her eyes, and leaped silently away as farther down the ridge three dogs spread in a line came panting and grinning, bounding through the snow toward her.

He'd raised his rifle and shot two of them. He hadn't even thought about it. He'd just shot them. *Bam.* Cycle the bolt. *Bam.* A pure moment, if ever there was a pure moment, the rounds hitting like they'd come out of his mind.

The third dog he'd tracked to a meandering line of dog prints leading down an old logging road, the only tracks in the unblemished snow. Two switchbacks below—maybe a hundred yards in a straight line—a big yellow Labrador-cross of some kind plodded head down through the snow in the center of the road. Someone had probably dumped it on the edge of the woods the spring before—not enough guts to kill it themselves; too red-necked or otherwise stupid to take it to the pound—and it had survived and grown not into some kid's dog, but into a killer that killed deer for the sheer fun of killing, a killer that could kill a rabid skunk or rodent, and become rabid itself.

He'd taken his time, sat down against a stump, legs crossed in what he'd later learn was a modified version of the sitting position, left elbow resting on left shin, right elbow solid into the bend of the right knee, and shot it behind the head, the big yellow dog slammed face down, legs sprawled comically to the sides like a cartoon dog run over by a truck, the sound of the shot fading across mountains gone silent.

He'd watched as a gray skiff of snow moved diagonally across the little valley, the trees and bushes on the opposing slope black and harsh against the snow and the cold. And in that moment, a moment as lonely as he would ever again be in his life, he'd learned that a life, any life, so taken, carries a judgment.

The trees and the mountains and the leaden sky had looked upon his actions, and their judgment had been harsh. The first two killings were one thing, they'd said. It was the third by which he had been judged: a big yellow Labrador-cross of some kind plodding head down along a snow-covered logging road.

And now, years later, it was Carlos, big, amiable Carlos with a grin that nobody could resist. Carlos as alone on a gray street in Japan as that big yellow dog had been in the middle of a snow-covered logging road in Montana.

This time it felt like maybe it was his turn to plod down that snow-covered road.

The woman last night in Danny's. Kei-with-the-no-family name. She'd seen what he was, all right: a big, mean, slow-witted Labrador-cross of some kind. She had as much as said so.

He took a deep breath and let it slowly out. He'd damn well better get real, or it *would* be him on that road. He'd had no business talking to Carlos like that. The time for talking had long passed. But he had. And now the universe was out of kilter. Most definitely out of whack. He'd best get his head out of his ass most rickey-tick, or someone–Peter, maybe– was going to hand it to him.

Time leaked, someone had said. And it was true that feeling alive was sometimes a function of time, Evy and all that, but it wasn't time that leaked. It was your mind that leaked. Every once in a while that seventeen-year-old, or Evy, or those Marines leaked out and looked around. And that was okay; that was normal. But if he wanted to some day go back to his land in Montana and build a cabin with *tatami* on the floor, he best be keeping all that under control.

What had happened to that seventeen-year-old was that somewhere along the trail the clean energy of youth had mutated into a craving for life on the edge of extinction; an adrenaline-laden existence both worse-than/better-than fear. And he'd better accept all that– accept who and what he was–and quit screwing around, because if he kept screwing around with a lot of sooner or latering, someone like Captain Sato was going to feed him to the sharks for real.

Carlos had recognized that the Motorcycle Man was a disguise. Too bad he hadn't been able to see what was under the disguise. He'd known about Evy, but he hadn't been able to understand–was too romantic to understand–that Evy had been only a temporary derailment. Carlos had understood that Evy dying had weirded him out, but he had not under- stood that Ben Tails had shed that particular skin in favor of another, more familiar skin–one that he had begun to grow when he was seventeen and listening to the sound of a perfect shot fade across mountains gone silent.

It was all weird now, he thought. His intellectual abilities warped into strange tangents and introspections. Gardens- of-the-heart bullshit. Gravestones. *Samurai.* The other side of the world, the wrong side of the road. Ashamed of himself–

and that was a first. All the things he'd done, he'd never felt shame. Regret more than once. Disgust. Anger. Mental and physical pain. But never shame.

He sat up, legs crossed Indian fashion. The bamboo curtains ticked and rustled, busy in the silence of the room. Despite the coolness of the breeze and the room and the *tatami,* a sheen of sweat oiled his chest and arms, his mind only now letting him hear the sound of the grunt the second man had made swinging the taped pipe into the side of Carlos' head— a soft grunt, confusing to him at the time because it was like the sound a man sometimes will make when he takes a killing wound, and he'd thought for an instant it was Carlos making the sound.

The Khmer did it like that, he thought. They would swing hoes and axes. . . . Oh, man.

It mattered not that he had not known it was going to go down that way. What mattered was that, like dogs chasing a deer, the Japanese had made brutal sport of Carlos. And he had been an accessory to it; he had led Carlos to the killing ground. Real evil is killing our enemies; you said that, Carlos. But you weren't my enemy. You weren't even an enemy of this country. Not really. And killing you was about as evil as it gets.

Something somewhere had gotten bent out of shape, he thought. Sato, maybe. But now that he had a little distance, it felt like more than just Sato.

It had felt wrong all night, especially after he'd seen Peter. He'd ignored his feelings because it hadn't seemed like much— a beating was all.

The Frenchman had been killed, it was true, but it had been understood from the beginning that if he concurred, there would be no choice but to kill the Frenchman. Legal had not been an option with the Frenchman. And with the other two that he'd worked on, there had been no doubt whatsoever about the things they'd been doing. No doubt whatsoever about letting the locals do whatever they wanted with them. Carlos had not been in the same league with those three, especially not with someone like the Frenchman. Not even remotely in the same league. Even a beating was pushing it in Carlos' case.

Killing the Frenchman had been a serious favor to the world. And even though he was supposed to leave the killing or whatever was decided to the locals, he'd done the Frenchman himself. And he'd do it again.

The Frenchman. With the Frenchman, he'd finally understood why Jim had hired someone like him.

He still couldn't get the Frenchman's voice explaining the drawings out of his mind. *Anatomically correct, monsieur.* Had someone like that ever been a human being?

Jim's briefing had said it all: The Frenchman had walked the Street Without Joy long before American Marines had walked it. The Frenchman had spent five years with the GCMA, *Groupement de Commandos Mixtes*, French NCOs parachuted into mountain villages to lead mountain tribes against the Viet Minh. If the tribe liked the NCO, they would follow him; if they didn't, he was never heard from again. Sink or swim.

Unlike the Americans who had followed in their footsteps, the GCMA were there for the duration, left to stay because by then they had become compatible with the mountains and jungle, the food and water and customs. They were there until they were killed or wounded or went mad, living with the tribes, harvesting opium, fighting the Viet Minh. The Frenchman claimed that the GCMA units paid for themselves through the sale of opium.

The Frenchman was still in the mountains at the time of the cease fire after Dien Bien Phu and, like all those other members of the GCMA still in the mountains, was abandoned. No attempt had been made to get him out.

He'd never met anyone as bent as the Frenchman.

The Frenchman made it out only because he'd been operating on the Laos/Cambodia border.

He collected his back pay and worked his way to the U.S. where he'd met and married an American woman in Indiana. The Frenchman became a U.S. citizen. A U.S. citizen interested in animal sacrifice, strange occult practices, and philosophies part Western, part Asian. Mad monks. The Inquisition. Moors. True Believers. Jesuits. The Kami, the ubiquitous spirits that hill people believe inhabit everything, rocks, trees, water, air.

Soldier. Assassin. Torturer. The Frenchman had been adept with nearly every weapon used in Southeast Asia. A hypnotist with an IQ of one-sixty something, the Frenchman had scared him in ways that nothing or no one else could.

According to Jim, the Frenchman had been used for assassinations in Vietnam—flown out of an Air Force base in the Midwest to Vietnam, where he'd do his thing, and then be flown back to Indiana. Sometimes he wasn't gone more than a few days. *"Monsieur, I want to tell you. Indiana is the most boring place on the face of the earth. Corn. Corn everywhere you look. In the mountains of Laos we would grow first a crop of the corn because it makes the soil better for the poppy. But Indiana corn—Monsieur, in Indiana the people they even look like the corn. Even they talk like the corn. Even they rustle like the corn."*

Rustle?

"Yes, Monsieur, people rustle. Do you not know that? The Hmong taught me that. The Hmong say people rustle like the dried skins of the garlic when they are very very afraid and know they are going to die."

The Frenchman.

"Ah, but, Monsieur, the children, the children of America. They

are beautiful and they are fat and they do not rustle. They are like the flower, the beautiful flower, and when you cut the flower, the narcotic it weeps from the cut, does it not?"

The Frenchman.

"Would you like to see my drawings, monsieur?"

Drawings of children dismembered, the Frenchman's version of cut flowers. Boys, mostly. Tiny penises chopped off and stuffed in mouths without lips. *"So you can see the teeth, Monsieur. I only call you Monsieur because I know you like that. It helps if I am sinister, does it not?"* Children flayed. Girls with stomachs ripped open, legs and arms cut off, sawn off, ripped off, everything rendered in detail and with a true artist's touch. Each picture an obscene rictus of terror and pain. *"Anatomically correct, monsieur. Anatomically correct."*

The Frenchman left Indiana and went back to Asia a citizen of the United States of America. The Indiana police were getting too close, he said. Oh, they'd never be able to take him to court, not on anything significant, but they were close enough that some corn-fed redneck might want to murder him. *"Murder, Monsieur,"* and he had laughed the darkest laugh Ben had ever heard.

The Frenchman had recognized something in him. In his warped mind he had somehow made Ben if not a kindred spirit, at least someone he thought could truly understand. Showing and telling, admitting everything. *"Why not, Monsieur? Maybe you are sent by your government. I think perhaps you are. But what can the Americans do, eh? There are only my drawings. And of them, can you in truth say they are any more horrible than the works of many celebrated masters? Of course not. And these lovely children . . . . Monsieur, as you can see—I call you Monsieur, and I speak like this, because I know you like it—they do not have the birthmarks or the identifying features. They are only of my imagination, are they not?"* And he would laugh his dark laugh.

128

The bamboo curtains rattled. The bamboo and the light flickering like that reminded him of the way moonlight had flickered on the ground in the sugarcane field.

The sugarcane field would always be there, too, just as the big old yellow dog would always be there. Just as the laugh and the drawings and the Frenchman's eyes would always be there. Right there, always there.

Light flickered.

He closed his eyes.

Sugarcane leaves shivered like long shards of metal in the moonlight.

The Frenchman, small and slight, professorial in his black, horn-rimmed glasses, knelt ankles crossed, hands tied behind his back, the white plastic wire ties clearly visible. Moonlight silvered the dark curly fringe of hair around his nearly bald head.

Huang and Sergeant P., a Thai cop that Huang had vouched for, had made a clearing around the kneeling figure, their long cane knives glinting in and out of the moonlight, clumps of cane shaking with the solid, sharp chunk of each stroke. Their grunts as they worked were like noises made by the cane. The air had been humid with the smell of fresh-cut sugar cane, the rancid smell of the Frenchman cutting through it all.

The three of them, Huang and Sergeant P. and he, hadn't talked much about it, but looking back on it he realized they'd all three wanted to make some kind of ceremony out of it–an unspoken attempt to overcome, or to at least neutralize, the incredible malignancy that was the Frenchman.

When Huang and the Thai sergeant had finished making the clearing, the three of them had stood for a long time looking down at the kneeling figure–waiting, perhaps, for some kind of response.

But the Frenchman had been silent and withdrawn, out of their reach, not even looking at them. Without doing or saying anything the Frenchman had managed to warp what he was and what they were doing into something tangible—into something for him to gain evil pleasure from—and it had angered Ben, and he'd taken Sergeant P's issue .45 and stepped into the moonlight and shot the kneeling figure in the back of the head where the bald spot met the fringe, the muzzle flash a flare of yellow-orange energy that kicked the slight figure face down between rows of sugar cane stubble.

He'd stood for a moment looking at the body, and it hadn't been enough, a simple bullet to the back of the head, and he'd become angry again, and fired the rest of the magazine into the head, screaming then at the Frenchman, trying with the bullets to drive the head deeper into the earth.

All he'd really done was drive it deeper into his mind.

Real evil. Carlos' idea of evil had been real enough, but it wasn't even half the evil that had been the Frenchman.

He rubbed his face with both hands, scrubbing away the memories.

He regretted what he had become not because of the good or evil of it, and not because he would never again feel what he'd felt when he was seventeen, and not because he would never again be what he'd been with Evy, and not because his mind sometime leaked. He regretted what he had become because he would never be able to see past it.

He smiled at the bamboo curtain. Well, that was bullshit, too, if ever there was. He was doing it again. Sliding away, as Carlos had said. If he wanted to, he could see past it, all right. It was there, plain as day. If he wanted to, he could look inside his small and nasty and withered garden. Fact was, he didn't want to. He didn't want to because he was afraid that if he did, he might find another monster like the Frenchman.

He lay back onto the *tatami*, hands behind his head, and stretched. He was back in Asia. And lying here on this *tatami*, it seemed as if he'd never left. A weird matrix of solitude and violence and death that looped from the mountains of Montana to the mountains of Vietnam and Cambodia to the mountains of Laos and Yunan and the Golden Triangle, from the Street Without Joy to a street in Nagoya, Japan, from jungle boots on his feet to a gold sheriff's star on his chest, from a woman named Shia Ling to a woman named Evy, from the Pumpkin Eater and Huang to Manfred and Robert Lee and back to the Pumpkin Eater and Huang. Caught in it. Playing in it. The real twined inseparably with the surreal, perspectives, values, meanings distorted, warped depending on which way the matrix was rotated: the oh-so-real Frenchman mixed with the mythical seventeen-year-old. Ben Tails skittering along grids of anger and adrenaline and loss. Cynical, mean Ben Tails. This way because it was the only way he knew of to cope with being afraid: after all these years and so much bad blood, there was no way Peter had just happened to wander his impeccably-attired self into Danny's place on the very evening the Japanese cops had decided to lose their cool, not to mention their reason, and murder a man. Murder his friend.

He stood and stretched. *Et tu,* motherfucker. His knees and elbows and the palms of his hands were sore and scabbed over, his thigh bruised and tight where he had been kicked.

Got to keep a proper perspective, he thought. He was no sorry-assed dog dragging down a logging road. Not yet, he wasn't, and never. If the dog had kept coming, it would have gotten away, past him and over the ridge and down into the bushes and trees before he could have worked the bolt one more time.

He stretched again, smiling at the possibility, but in mid-stretch saw the movement, heard the rattle and swish of bamboo against window sill and—something about the change in the texture of sound and light—was inexplicably aware that he was at that moment at the edge of his past. He could continue to live in the past if he wanted to. The past was known and, if not comfortable, at least it was something that had boundaries. He could quit this job and go back to Montana and live in the past with no penalty other than the penalties already levied.

But also in that moment he recognized that the past had become little more than the flicker of shadow and light on the *tatami.* His arms dropped to his sides. He didn't know how he knew, but he knew now that the past had only been flesh wounds.

There would be no going back until it was over.

Chapter 4
Cherry Blossoms

Beneath the curved, wooden walk bridge, clumps of cherry blossoms, bits of styrofoam caught in their midst, pinwheeled gently past a teddy bear lying face down in the shallows. Scattered among the weeds and in the milky-green water above the teddy bear were white plastic grocery bags, faded beer cans, tiny health drink bottles. The plastic grocery bags looked like giant white mushrooms. Upstream the skeletal remains of a stolen bicycle protruded from the middle of the river.

Wind gusted, streamers of blossoms scudding into leaden sky.

From the top of the curved walk bridge, he could see over the tops of the trees that lined the riverbanks. Masses of white, delicate blossoms stretched toward a horizon of gray sky and white and gray concrete buildings. Wind ruffled his hair, pressed his nylon running suit against his side. Blossoms scattered across the water and stuck like snow to latticed-concrete riverbanks.

He leaned forward elbows on the wooden guardrail. The teddy bear was sprawled ass up in that exposed, vulnerable way that corpses sometimes have. Not human, that teddy bear, but a corpse, nonetheless. Someone had thrown it into the river and killed it as surely as taped lengths of pipe had killed Carlos; as surely as rounds from Peter's AK had killed that Hmong kid.

133

Real fear has no shame. Carlos had said that, or read it somewhere, and even though Carlos hadn't understood it, he'd been half right. There might not be shame for the one experiencing the fear, but there is for the survivors and for those responsible. Even the Frenchman had felt shame for the fear he had caused, had in fact reveled in that shame.

It must have been some gross humiliation, or some set of humiliations, more than anything else, that had made the Frenchman into what he had become. To know you were going to die not of natural causes but at the hands of, or because of, another human being must be the greatest humiliation of all. The Frenchman had experienced that kind of humiliation more than once. Sato probably at least suspected it.

Far more dangerous than a born psychopath was someone like the Frenchman—someone whose humiliations could be relieved only by creating fear in others. Blood was not important to monsters like the Frenchman. Mutilations were merely technique. What *anatomically correct, Monsieur,* really meant was, admire my technique. Blood and pain were only the means to an end. Fear and humiliation were that end.

Near as he could tell, almost everyone had it in them. People like the Frenchman and Sato were rare only in that circumstance and experience had conspired in ways that defied probability.

The sound of wind in the trees again reminded him of the Hmong kid, the rushing sound of his body sledding down the steep slope like the sound of a mountain stream heard through distant trees.

He looked up. The sky was beginning to lighten, the shrubs and grass under the trees and in the shallow water around the teddy bear taking on a tropical luminescence—a special light and humidity appropriate to his thoughts, the air thick not with the scent of cherry blossoms but with the memory of rotting vegetation and fear and suffocating, tough, resilient grass. The invisible touch of cherry blossoms alighting on his face reminded him of spider webs. The rustle and snap of wind against his running suit was a little like the sound the grass had made—except that the sound the grass made had a delay, and whenever he stopped, it had sounded as if someone was following him. Someone with an AK-47.

Two high school girls in matching uniforms and pigtails and black leather briefcases passed behind him, their footsteps light on the wooden boards.

Below, barely seen beneath a skein of blossoms, a white and orange and black carp nosed the teddy bear.

He smiled to himself. Gray sky. Rain. Cherry blossoms. A river filled with murdered teddy bears and bicycles. Ugly water and even uglier fish—it was as if someone had looked down on him and said, You want to feel bad? Here, feel bad. All it lacked was some Catholic music. A little Handel would be perfect.

"No trout in that river," a familiar voice said.

Ben straightened and turned toward the figure at the end of the bridge. Jim was peering over his wire-rimmed reading glasses at a small, wooden sign bolted to a concrete, made-to-look-like-wood post at the end of the bridge. Short. Grizzled. Jeans and worn cowboy boots. Long-sleeved Pendleton shirt. His clothes and his high cheekbones and dark skin always made Ben think of an old paddy farmer dressed up like a cowboy.

"Former Beautiful Place," Jim read. He glanced over his glasses at the river and the trees. "A place where artists and poets and people of all sorts would come to admire the beauty of this place."

"We come under the heading of 'all sorts'," Ben said.

"Surely this sign belongs somewhere else."

"'Former' is the operative word."

135

With one hand Jim pulled off his glasses, folded them, and put them in his shirt pocket.

What an act, Ben thought. Someone's friendly uncle. Big ears, big nose. Creased face. Late 50's, he looked like, despite the creases, but he had to be in his 60's. Still so obviously healthy it was disgusting. Only his nose, the large, curved beak of a true Native American, prevented him from passing himself off as an Asian.

"You ought to try suspenders and lace-up boots," Ben said.

"You think that would work?"

"You bet."

"Are you coming down here, or am I coming up there?"

"Might as well come up and enjoy the view. The gang that's been following me around all morning has probably got the whole world wired by now, anyway."

Jim walked, limping slightly, up the bridge. Strode was more like it, Ben thought. Jim always walked as if he were exploring new territory. Even with the limp, he would be a hard man to outwalk in the mountains. "How are you, Ben?" The size and strength of his hand, like his stride and his grin, always a surprise.

"Still here, I guess."

"Out jogging, are you?"

"Got to stay svelte."

Jim chuckled. "In that suit you look about as svelte as a Mack truck."

"It's the only one I could find big enough."

"I don't believe I've ever seen a powder blue and passionate pink jogging suit before. At least the cars won't have any trouble seeing you."

"They killed him," Ben said.

Jim winced. "I had no idea they were going to do that."

"Beat him to death."

Jim's eyes reminded Ben of the eyes of paddy farmers he'd

walked past in Vietnam, the emotion way down deep, easy to miss if you didn't know what to look for. "I understand he put up a fight."

"Is that the story?"

"They say a big man, strong as only a *gaijin* his size could be, trained in the martial arts."

"He was dead after the first hit. I doubt he even saw it coming."

"I see."

"Of course, I have no idea what passes for a fight around here."

"Tell me exactly what happened."

Ben shrugged. "They sent two guys dressed as construction workers down the street toward us. They were clean and pressed and he saw—or at least felt—that it was wrong. But since they were so obvious, and there were only two of them, I don't think he was particularly worried. When they got close, he assumed a position—some kind of kung fu, or something. They split up, one guy to the street. He turned toward the guy in the street, and when he did the other guy hit him in the forehead with a taped length of pipe. It was over faster than I just told it."

Jim's eyes narrowed.

"Except they kept hitting him," Ben said. "The one in the street looked like he was swinging for the bleachers."

"But no fight?"

"He was one of the strongest men I've ever met. He worked out every day at a pretty good *dojo*. If he would have had a chance to put up a fight, there would have been hurt cops."

Jim sighed. He turned and leaned forward elbows on the railing.

"The only reason he made any move at all was because he sensed I wasn't with him."

Jim straightened away from the railing. "What the hell is *that?*"

"What the hell is what?"

"Down there in the water."

"A teddy bear."

"By golly, it is. For a moment, I thought it was a child." He glanced sideways at Ben.

"Don't look at me. I didn't put it there."

"What are you doing here, Ben?"

Ben shrugged. "I was out for a jog, and I stopped to admire the view."

"You know what I mean."

"Oh, you mean here, as in Japan." He smiled. "I'm selling motorcycles."

Jim crossed his arms. "Sold any?"

"Sure. Lots. It's the easiest thing I've ever done. I'm a natural. I go into the office. Shuck and jive for awhile. The secretary puts a pile of orders on my desk–Sato shop or Tanaka shop or Yamamoto shop or somebody shop wants FLHs or Softails or whatever. I sign the orders." He looked away from Jim's eyes. "Then I go jogging or I go eat or I go chase women or," he looked at Jim, "I go get someone beat to death–what is this? Am I speaking to an audience, or what?"

"No. No audience. They're gone now."

"Well, what do you want me to say then?"

"I want you to tell me what you're doing."

"Until you got here, I was checking out the cherry blossoms."

"I see. If I didn't know better, I'd think you were being obtuse."

"It's a cultural event."

"What is? Looking at cherry blossoms, or being obtuse?"

"Both."

Jim smiled. "Well, it never hurts to look at cherry blossoms."

He turned and put both hands on the railing. "My old grandmother–Assiniboine, she was, bless her soul–she used to say that a little melancholy now and then was good for you." The skin at the edges of his eyes was creased with humor, but his eyes, when they glanced at Ben, were like chips of mica. They reminded Ben of the eyes of his grandmother's people when they told stories about the Reservation.

"It never hurts to contemplate the brevity of it all, she'd say–though, I don't know what she would have thought of beautiful blossoms that produce only sour, withered fruit."

"Why did they kill him, Jim?"

"Well, now. I believe I just answered that question."

Ben frowned. Below, the white and orange and black carp had been joined by another, bigger, solid-orange carp. Both carp were nosing around the teddy bear's right leg.

"Two people died in Osaka," Jim said. "They say it was Carlos' dope that killed them. They say they found nearly a ton of it in a warehouse in Kobe."

"Oh, that's bullshit! He wasn't in business yet. And even if he had been, he never would have stashed that much in one place."

"They had an informant."

"An informant?"

"Someone who worked for him," Jim said.

"What'd they do? Stick bamboo slivers up his ass?"

"Ben, let me ask you something. What would have happened if you and Robert Lee had caught these people in the States?"

Ben was silent.

"When all was said and done, after all your time and energy, after all the taxpayer's money spent, Carlos and his people would have gotten maybe a year or two in prison. *If* you had

139

a gung-ho prosecuting attorney. *If* you had a sympathetic judge and jury."

"This isn't the States."

"Well, that's exactly what I'm saying. This isn't the States. The Japanese look at the problem a little differently."

"Why didn't they just beat on him a little and deport him like they said they were going to?"

"In Montana if someone beat a dope dealer to death, you and Robert Lee would be down at Manfred's bar drinking toasts to whoever had done it. You'd be making jokes about it."

"Carlos hadn't sold any dope yet."

"Not here, he hadn't."

Ben looked down at the river. A clump of cherry blossoms broke off from the blossoms washed up against the side of the teddy bear, and floated out into the current, exposing more carp nibbling at the underside of the leg

"They mean Carlos to be an example, Ben."

"Oh, right. As if people like him pay any attention to examples."

"Well, if you were them, wouldn't you at least make the effort?"

"Not that kind of effort."

"Ben, you have a natural, instinctive loyalty, and that's good. It's part of the empathy you must form in order to do your job. But look at it from the Japanese point of view. At first they publicized their drug busts, put foreigners in jail. Hell, they even put Paul McCartney in jail once. When that had no effect, they simply deported—"

"In return for their own being quietly sent home from the States," Ben said. "So that mama-san and papa-san and, most especially, Japan won't lose face because some rich, spoiled, little Japanese doper bastard is in an American prison getting butt-fucked by half the prison population. It's politics," he said. "That's all it is. And you told me we try to stay out of politics."

"I said we clean up messes that governments, for a variety of reasons, cannot. I said your job is to investigate—to get as close as possible to whomever you are investigating.

"Now, you indicated that Carlos was everything the Japanese said he was, did you not? Action was agreed upon. Just a moment. Let me finish. The fact that the action taken was not the action agreed upon is not your problem. It's mine.

"I don't like this any more than you do, but for a long time now this system has worked. In fact, it has worked with far more certainty, and with far more justice, than has our own legal system. It is never a perfect world, Ben. You know that, if anyone does. Sometimes things go wrong, and this is one of those times.

"Carlos was the genius behind a very large and very dangerous drug cartel. He frightened the Japanese, and because he did, we had no control over their response."

"Then let them do it without us."

"We are merely doing a job that must be done, Ben."

"Yeah? Well, tell me, then, what do we do in the States when some Yakuza asshole falls through the cracks in the system? Do we beat him to death with lead pipes?"

"Look, Ben. Make no mistake. Maybe Carlos didn't carve up babies, like the Frenchman did, but he was ruthless. You liked him, felt an affinity for him, but when that kind of ruthlessness and intelligence is coupled with more money than is in many national treasuries, all bets are off."

"So what happens now?"

"Well, obviously our work in this country has been concluded for the time being."

Ben gazed without expression out at the trees and blossoms, the gray, concrete city beyond. "The jackal and the kite have a healthy appetite," he murmured to himself.

"I beg your pardon?"

"Kipling."

"Ah. . . ."

He looked at Jim. "And the next line is, 'And you'll never see your soldiers any more.'"

"It's not like that, Ben."

"No? Well what is it like then? Carlos wasn't meant to be an example. Don't give me that. The Japanese know as well as we do that it is not possible to make examples out of people like Carlos. This whole thing has been way out of line from the beginning—and I'd damn sure appreciate it if you'd tell me what the hell is really going on."

Jim stared out at the river. The creases at the corners of his eyes made his eyes look ancient and wise.

"The first guy hit him across the forehead," Ben said. "He was probably dead right then. Then the same guy broke his collarbones. Then the other guy hit him alongside the head like he was swinging for the bleachers. Busted his head open like a melon."

Jim's mouth was a thin, hard line.

"And while all that was happening to Carlos," Ben went on, "two of the biggest Japanese I've ever seen were taking turns drop kicking me across the pavement."

"I want to hear your version of that."

"What's their version."

"What you'd imagine."

"They hit him. They hit me. I went down. They hit him some more. I went down again. They were just playing with me, but I didn't know that then. I figured I was next. They let me up, and I hit one of them a couple of times. It had about as much effect as hitting this bridge. So I pulled a knife. Sato or whatever his name is stepped in. We had a conversation. I went home."

"Captain Sato has a severely bruised neck, I'm told."

142

"Well, *Gomen nasai.* Carlos has a severely dented brain pan."

"They're frightened," Jim said. "And well they should be. No matter how much money they make, their world seems to be going to hell in a handbasket. The quality of life gets more and more expensive, but it doesn't get better. The younger generations don't have the drive the old guys my age had. The economy is ready to tank. Other Asian countries are wolves at the door."

Listening to him, Ben had an image of Jim in his patched and forever leaking wadders standing knee-deep in the Blackfoot. Jim turned from the railing, his face without expression.

"What are you saying?" Ben asked.

"I'm saying it's time to earn your keep, Benjamin."

Ben stared at him.

Jim winked. "It's easy for us, you and me, Ben, to stand here and feel noble and righteously outraged, to condemn this country and its people for doing to themselves exactly the same thing we've done many times and in many places to ourselves. How many Former Beautiful Places do we have? You think this city is bad, and it is, but look at our cities. You've talked to cops. In many places going on shift is like saddling up to go outside the wire.

"The Japanese are not blind to, nor are they stupid about, these things, Ben. To them our institutions are in decline. Never mind how strong our military, to them our days are numbered. They want to be around and healthy when we self-destruct."

"And drugs are supposed to be responsible for our demise, is that it?"

"You don't believe it, and I don't believe it. But you have to admit it doesn't seem so farfetched when viewed from here. More than a few of the folks back home—folks who ought to know—believe it is a better than even chance that

143

we have finally dug ourselves into a hole we can't get out of unless we change a few of our institutions. Hell, imagine you are running this country. Blaming us is not only convenient; it's accurate as well."

The sky was darkening again, beginning to threaten rain, the greens and browns of trees and bushes made pastel by the waning light. Ben could smell leaves and grass humid beneath the trees. "Cherry blossoms were the symbol for the *Samurai*," he said. "Because they blossom strong and beautiful and die scattered by the wind before they have a chance to grow old and wither."

"I didn't know that."

"It's bullshit," Ben said. "Same as you're trying to feed me."

Jim smiled. "Our purview, as I said, is to help clean up messes and dangers that can't be reasonably cleaned up by our government or the government of the country we are operating in. Drugs are now deemed to present that kind of mess, that kind of danger."

"Last night was out of control."

"The arrangement is obviously not perfect. Next time it might be another killer of children. The decisions and methods won't be so difficult, then. But for now it's drugs." A white egret floated down the river, landing in the shallows near the bicycle.

"People kill what they can," Jim said. "It's as simple and as complicated as that. Cambodia. China. Ethiopia. Europe. The Ukraine. The Assyrians. The Mongols. SS, KGB, *Kempeitai*. The U.S. Army used blankets infected with smallpox against my grandmother's people. Remember the first time we met?" He chuckled. "I was so anxious to begin fishing, I couldn't wait until the next town to get a license. I looked up and there you were sitting on the hood of a patrol car. Uniform. Badge. Sunglasses. The whole nine yards. Well, I thought, these are going to be some very expensive fish. But they

144

weren't. You believed me when I said I fully intended to get a license at the first town I came to but couldn't help myself, the day and the river and all." He smiled.

"Later, after I'd bought my license, and we were having dinner together with the formidable and lovely Evy—who could have seen us sitting there at a table covered with fine linen, drinking a decent California wine, laughing and telling fish stories . . . who could have seen us like that and imagined that not so long before you had been kneeling in the road to Thailand." He turned toward Ben, his eyes brittle. "Hands laced behind your head, certain one of those Khmer kids was going to pull the trigger."

Ben felt the hair on the back of his neck rise. Below, in the river, the carp had moved away from the teddy bear, and were waiting, a great swarm of them, fat and ugly and sluggish in the milky water.

"The guy next to you wet himself," Jim said. "And it was cause for great hilarity among the Khmer—someone wetting himself like that."

Ben's hands tightened on the railing.

Jim considered Ben for a moment. "You see those carp down there, Ben? The Khmer Rouge and people like them are like those carp down there. Feeding is their principal reason for living. Once they start to feed they can't stop." He straightened away from the railing and his eyes and the way his weathered skin was stretched tight across his cheekbones reminded Ben of old black and white photographs of Crow warriors.

"Who told you?"

The skin creased at Jim's eyes and at the corners of his mouth. "The man who wet himself told me."

Ben was surprised. He'd thought maybe Huang had told him. "Where'd you find him?"

"Unlikely as it may seem, he's now teaching Asian languages at a large American university."

"Really. How's his Cambodian?"

"Why didn't they kill you, Ben, the Khmer Rouge?"

"It didn't seem like a real good time to ask."

"The man I spoke to said they were going down the line and when they got to you, one of the older men tipped your straw cowboy hat off, and when he saw your face, your forehead and the scars, he stopped laughing, and they all stopped laughing. He said one of them cocked his weapon and put it to your forehead, and no one laughed when he did it. Their mood had changed completely."

Huang had put out the word, Ben thought. Huang wouldn't admit it, because then Ben would owe him, but that had been the only possible answer. When they'd knocked off his hat and seen the scars, they'd recognized him. A near thing. A very near thing. He'd always figured that Huang must have had connections with the Chinese who had been supplying the Khmer at the time.

"It wasn't Huang, Ben. Don't look so surprised. Of course I know Huang. I've spent a lot of my adult life traipsing around the mountains and villages of Indo-China. It would be most unlikely for me not to have met a man like Huang."

"Who was it then?"

"It wasn't a who. They probably thought you were some kind of spirit. A *kami*. A devil disguised as a foreigner."

Ben spit into the water, and the carp converged on his spit in a sudden roil of many-colored fish, and then just as abruptly resumed their languid, oily movement. The spit floated away untouched.

"You knew about me long before I caught you fishing without a license, didn't you?"

Jim smiled. "I'm always looking for people like you."

"That's not an answer."

"No, it's not. Have you heard from Manfred recently?"

"No."

"You ought to send him a picture of you dressed in that suit, all these cherry blossoms in the background."

"No, thank you."

Jim smiled and extended his hand toward Ben. "I want you to stick around for awhile, Ben, but you need not go in to work." He shook Ben's hand, his grip hard and dry. "Take a little R and R. Find yourself a girl. I'll see you soon."

He turned and walked down the curve of the wooden walk bridge, his gait and his clothes and his handshake reminding Ben of some of the ranchers that came into Manfred's place.

At the bottom of the walk bridge, without turning around, Jim raised his hand in farewell.

Ben raised his hand, but Jim was already gone, disappeared into the gloom beneath the blossoms. He was alone with the wind and the approaching darkness.

Jim had given him speeches. Background stuff they'd talked about before he'd even come to Japan. Jim had talked about Huang as if Huang was not a Board member of Raven—as if Huang had never made the three of them tea in Jim's apartment in Bangkok. Wait for Huang, he had meant.

Somewhere on the roof of one of the distant buildings, someone was listening and watching.

Jim had talked about drugs. He'd reminded Ben of Ben's experience with the Khmer Rouge. But what he had not talked about was what was really going on. By talking about the Khmer Rouge, Jim was telling him that there was more to this than what had happened to Carlos. Jim had steered the conversation in directions expected by their listeners. But threaded through the conversation was another message: there are people out there who wish Raven ill, and these people are lethal in the same way that the Khmer Rouge are lethal.

The breeze was picking up, the air abruptly fresh and whole, free of the dank, heavy smells of the river. Find yourself a woman, Jim had said. Use the woman, he'd meant. Ben took a deep breath, filling his lungs with oxygen. He felt the invisible touch of cherry blossoms.

What woman?

Chapter 5
Point of Contact

Ben opened his eyes. The chrome handle on the refrigerator was metallic in the moonlight. Random edges of silverware glinted like fresh shrapnel. He closed his eyes. The corpse bounced, vibrating on the floor of the helicopter, right leg gone at the knee, bone white and obscene, shredded skin and cloth flapping wetly in the wind blowing through the open doorway.

The pilot turned toward him, and it was Manfred. "Ottis and Aretha," Manfred said, which was a strange thing for Manfred to say because Manfred liked Country and Western.

"The Mamas and the Papas," he replied.

Manfred pulled down the sun visor on his flight helmet and pointed out the open doorway. Below, the Missions were lit with a perfect golden light.

He groaned and turned on his side, his feet and legs twitching much as a dog asleep on the floor will twitch in its sleep. His eyes opened and then closed.

Hundreds of corpses waxen and clean as the body he'd pulled out of the Blackfoot watched without emotion something behind him. He turned and saw himself running through grass flattened by rotor wash, screaming as the helicopter vaulted into the air above him. He fled through slate-grey mist, down an alley in the jungle, where bodies thrown soddenly down crept white and puckered.

He woke, and frowned. The thin mat felt soft, over stuffed, immensely comfortable. Outside the window the plants next door glinted silver in the moonlight. He closed his eyes, was gone again.

Shadows of dancing cane moved across one hand splayed into moonlight, the smell of gunpowder acrid against the fertile humidity of the cane. Dark tendrils crept from the head, and he squeezed the trigger, feeling the .45 recoil again and again into the web of his hand as the phone rang.

He opened his eyes, immediately disappointed to be awake, and struggled to sit up, the stink of his sweat and of the whiskey he'd been drinking permeating the air.

The phone rang.

He rubbed the stubble on the side of his face, the dreams not remembered, but the residue of them still with him. He kicked the tangle of sheets and blankets away from his legs and feet, and rolled over onto his knees and hands, and pushed off with his hands, groping above his head for the wooden track that the *shoji* normally fit into. He pulled himself upright.

The phone rang.

"Fuck off," he croaked. His body felt hot, bloated, the taste of whiskey and spicy rice crackers wrapped in dried seaweed rancid in his mouth. He needed water. Lots of water. Ice-cold water.

The phone rang.

He moved from the divider to the wall to the next room, the kitchen, toward the phone in the entrance way, knowing by the hour that it must be Manfred calling to tell him how wonderful spring was going to be. He picked up the receiver. "Fuck you and the horse you rode in on," he rasped.

The line was silent, free of white noise.

"Hello?" he said, and heard a laugh, deep, melodious, familiar as his dreams. "Long time no see, Mr. Slide."

"Peter."

150

"I wanted to say hello, buy you a drink, a taco or something. But you looked like you were busy."

"What do you want?"

Peter clicked his tongue. *"Heaven does not hear a forced oath,"* he said in elegant Mandarin.

"Go away, Peter. Just go away."

"Hey, you know, it be good, *real good* to hear your voice again, Mr. Slide."

"Start your nigger shit, and you won't be hearing it for long."

"When I saw you, I said to myself. Whoa, there he is. But I have to tell you, man. I wasn't sure. You aren't the lean, mean, fighting Marine I used to know."

"Long time passing."

"Hell, it was only yesterday. You know that."

Ben sat on the hardwood floor and leaned back against the wall. The cold floor and wall felt good against his over-heated skin. "What do you want, Peter?"

"I want to know what you're thinking about when you're out jogging, or standing around on quaint little bridges, surveying the cherry blossoms."

Ben was silent.

Peter coughed. "Uh . . . Look, man. I didn't call to give you a ration. Maybe this isn't the time, but I heard you lost a good woman, and–"

"You're right. This isn't the time."

"Yeah, well. You know. . . . "

Ben picked up the phone and rolled to his feet and carried it into the kitchen. He turned on the tap and let it run.

"Have you seen Huang lately?" Peter asked.

"Why would I see Huang?" He cradled the receiver against his shoulder and picked up a glass and sniffed at it.

Peter chuckled. "You be working for Raven now."

Ben filled the glass and drained it, feeling the water cool all the way to his belly. He refilled the glass.

"Been drinking, huh?"

Ben drained the glass again. It felt almost as good the second time.

"I heard you were in Thailand not too long ago. You and Huang working with my old buddy, Sergeant P. The three of you taking care of some business the State Department wanted no part of."

Ben refilled the glass.

"What it is," Peter said, and the way he said it, Ben knew it was the Pumpkin Eater who was talking, "is you are here, and I am here, and we've got to do something about that."

Ben drank half the glass and threw the rest into the sink. "Why?"

"Because Mr. Slide, he still thinks I'm a bad man, that's why."

"Mr. Slide isn't here."

"Oh, no? Maybe you put on a little meat, but you still looked pretty slick when you popped that big motherfucker right over the heart. Surprised even me, and I know you."

Ben was silent.

"You looked pretty lonely out there," Peter said.

He heard Peter's voice, his mind registered the words, but it was as if they were coming from a great distance.

"Hello?"

"I'm here."

"I said, you looked pretty lonely out there."

"What do you want, Peter?"

"You still think I'm a bad man, don't you?"

Ben laughed, and the laugh was a catalyst that finally shifted him fully awake and sober, a transition as subtle and as abrupt as seeing a shoot of bamboo change from green bamboo shoot to green bamboo viper. Peter's voice and the knowledge that Peter had been there watching, had seen it all, Carlos sprawled on the sidewalk, him rolling around in the street, all that mixed and combined in his mind and in his stomach to resurrect a thick, darkly sensual past, a clarity so savage that for a long moment he didn't know where he was or with whom he was talking.

He felt the rictus of his smile, and shivered–not with cold, but with the adrenaline in his blood. He could see Peter plain as if he was there in front of him, *a black major seated behind a battered metal desk, cheekbones and forehead highlighted by the lantern light. Eye sockets and mouth pools of blackness darker even than his black skin.*

"You haven't changed," he said into the phone. Water dripped from the tap, the sound reminding him of *the tedious sound of sweat, his and the black Major's, tapping onto the wooden pallets.*

"Well?"

"Sir?"

"Think you can handle it?"

"I don't know."

"I don't know, sir."

"How do you know I haven't changed?" the Pumpkin Eater asked.

Ben smiled. "You want to watch what you say on this line," he said.

The major tilted his chair so that his face from just above his mouth was in shadow. "You don't like niggers, sergeant?" he asked, his teeth unnaturally white in the light.

Peter chuckled.

"No niggers where I come from, sir."

"No niggers where you come from! Where you from, sergeant? Mars?"

"Montana, sir."

"What I said. Mars."

The phone was silent.

Water dripped from the tap.

"I'd appreciate it," Peter said, "if you'd remember that there's not much that I've done that you haven't done, too."

"I hear you shot a gook snuffy at eight hundred meters. Drilled the sucker."

"In fact, we did a lot of it together."

"I've been looking for someone like you for a long time."

Ben looked at the moonlight coming through the window. "Not everything," he said.

"Man, all the people you aced, and you still remember that one fucking kid."

"What kid?"

"Don't give me that shit. Don't even be giving me that shit."

"Oh, *that* kid."

"Those NVA were there to find us, and to kill us. There was a whole fucking company of them."

"You called me at four o'clock in the morning because you've still got that on your mind?"

"You were my responsibility. Those Hmong weren't. The gooks would have killed us both, and what possible good would that have done?"

"It sounds like it would have let you sleep better."

Peter was silent. He chuckled. "Yeah, it's on my mind. One of those things. I bet you got things like that on your mind, too."

"Like I said, you want to watch what you say on this line."

"Man, I *know* who is on this line. And I don't give a damn. Now what does that tell you."

"I give up. What does that tell me?"

"It tells you to go to coffee shop ChaCha tomorrow at 1500 hours, that's what it tells you."

"Why would I want to do something like that?"

"Because I said so."

"Heaven does not hear a forced oath," Ben said in Mandarin.

Peter laughed. "Your Mandarin still sucks," he said and hung up.

Chapter 6
Appetites

S mall, wooden crates stamped CEYLON TEA were stacked inside the window of coffee shop Cha Cha. Ben opened the door and a tiny bell rang, and as he stepped inside, a woman behind the counter, cute in green polo shirt and gray apron, her hair cut long in front so that jet-black wings of hair framed her face, smiled and said, *"Irasshaimase."*

Red tile floor—real tile, not linoleum. Framed, glass-covered prints colorful on the walls—toucans and parrots and other jungle birds he didn't recognize. Two couples sat at the back of the room. A man and a woman were at the counter. Rock music from a very good sound system: Boz Skaggs. *Cool Running.*

Huang sat at a small, wood table next to the stacked tea crates. Blue work shirt. Tan trousers. Grizzled hair close cropped. He looks like a Japanese fisherman, Ben thought. A cup of coffee and a partially eaten bowl of what looked like vanilla ice cream were on the table in front of him.

Ben smiled at the woman and pointed toward Huang and walked over to him, conscious of the fact that everyone in the shop was watching. He pulled out a chair and sat down. *"Hao jiow bu jian nin,"* he said in Mandarin, long time no see, using the polite form of you to emphasize his sarcasm.

155

Eyes nearly crossed, frowning with concentration, Huang took a dainty sip of coffee, his eyes and the delicacy of his movements at odds with his thick, blunt fingers and the thin scar that began at his hairline and trailed down the right side of his face, into a dent just below the junction of jaw and ear. He gently placed the coffee cup onto the saucer. His callused hands made the cup and saucer appear even more fragile than they already were.

Ben waved the shop owner back. The couple at the counter were watching him out of the corner of their eyes.

"You are very American today," Huang said. His eyes reminded Ben of Jim's eyes.

Ben studied him for a moment, trying to read his expression. The people at the back of the room stood to leave. University students, he could tell by their attitudes toward each other. The two women walked to the cash register to pay; the two boys waited at the door.

Huang smiled at his ice cream.

The voices at the cash register were quiet and polite, nearly formal. The people in the shop could feel the tension between him and Huang, Ben thought, and, being Japanese, had retreated into excessive politeness. The tiny bell tinkled as the four students went out. He watched as they walked past the window, their conversation suddenly animated.

Huang spooned ice cream into his mouth and slowly pulled the spoon out, ice cream still on it. Playing with it like a kid, Ben thought. One of the toughest men he'd ever met. All gristle and bone and scar tissue, when he had his shirt off. A man who knew things before they happened. And look at him: a kid smiling around a spoon of ice cream.

Huang put the spoon down next to the bowl. "Silence can sometimes be like water—"

"Yeah. You can drown in it."

Huang nudged the spoon closer to the bowl of ice cream.

He leaned back and crossed his arms and smiled. "When I was a child, I could not have imagined even one spoonful of ice cream. I could not have imagined a cup of this coffee."

Ben felt the back of his neck redden. He did not need another lecture on privations endured during the Great Revolution. "What are you doing here, Huang? You hate this country. You hate these people. And what has Peter got to do with me meeting you here?"

Huang's smile stayed, but his eyes dilated.

"Oh, excuse my rudeness," Ben said. "Please finish your ice cream."

"You Americans," Huang said. "You think you have sacrificed. But all you have done is exhaust appetites."

"This from a man eating a bowl of ice cream, drinking a cup of imported coffee."

"You and Peter," Huang said in Mandarin. "You two think only of your own small wounds."

"So this meeting is about me and Peter."

"Peter is working for me."

"What?"

"Peter is working for me."

"Peter is working for Raven?"

"No. Peter is working for me."

The couple at the counter stood and prepared to leave.

"We are speaking Mandarin," Ben said. "And that is making the people in here nervous."

"That is not what is making them nervous."

"You are angry."

"*We* are angry."

"We are friends," Ben said. "We have been friends for a long time."

"Yes. We are friends. That is why I am here."

Ben opened his mouth to speak, and then thought better of it.

The bell tinkled and the couple went out the door, voices noisy as soon as they reached the sidewalk, and the shop was abruptly empty, the woman shopkeeper busy behind the counter. Ben could feel what had happened to Carlos and the phone call from Peter permeate the air between them. Friends or not, he thought, fuck you and your scar. Fuck your cold black eyes and your Chinese smile. He despised that Chinese conceit: five thousand years of history and culture, every damn one of them would tell you. Five thousand years of constantly reinventing the wheel was more like it.

"So tell me, Huang *pengyou,* friend Huang. How much difference besides age and ice cream between you and me and Peter?"

"You two are only yourself."

"Oh, and you are what?"

Huang smiled. "I am Chinese."

Ben laughed, a quick blurt of humorless sound, and quickly held up his hand. The scar was stretched tight against Huang's forehead. "No offense," Ben said in English.

"Peter lives in Shiamen now," Huang said. "He has a Chinese wife–a beautiful woman, educated in Shiamen and in Japan. They have a child and are expecting another."

"My condolences to his wife and child."

Huang sighed and looked out the window, unconsciously rubbing the side of his forehead where the scar disappeared into his hair. "The world has become a very small place, Ben. Every day there are fewer of us, even as there are more of those we fight against." He turned toward Ben. "In former times, people like the Frenchman remained largely unsatisfied. But today such people are finding ways to acquire the education and the means that it takes to exercise themselves in relative safety."

"Peter was there when they killed Carlos; did you know that?"

"He was as surprised as were you. If he would have tried to intervene, perhaps both of you would have been killed."

"But he was there."

"Yes. He was there."

"Why?"

Huang shrugged.

"Is that why you are here?" Ben asked. "To tell me that you don't know why he was there?"

"I am here in part to tell you that this thing between you and Peter must wait. You must put it out of your mind for now." He smiled. "I am also here to tell you that the woman you are to meet will be along shortly."

Ben sat back against the chair. On the other side of the window, cars and people went by. Japanese dressed in the latest fashions from Europe and America and Tokyo. Uniformed kids on black bicycles. All of it a blur. What was Huang telling him? He held up his hands so that Huang could see his bandaged palms. "Carlos is dead. You are here. Peter is here. A Japanese named Sato–"

"Captain Sato is a very dangerous man."

"I realize that."

"As is Peter."

Ben laughed, a short bark of sound devoid of humor.

"Yes, you understand that Peter is dangerous," Huang said. "But you do not understand why."

"He is mad, that's why."

"He believes in his own death, Ben. That's all. He is not mad."

"Peter doesn't believe in anything except Peter. I should have killed him when I had the chance."

Huang's brittle eyes weighed Ben.

"I am not like Peter, Huang. Don't look at me like that. Besides, you would have shot me."

The skin at the edges of Huang's eyes crinkled with humor.

159

"Chin Shi Huang Di, the first Emperor of China, built a huge tomb to house himself when he died. Are you familiar with it?"

"Of course."

"We are like those warriors Chin Shi Huang Di cast to protect himself in the after life."

"How very noble of us."

Huang smiled. "I do not mean to imply that we are noble—or even that our intentions are noble. Only that we are who we are." He stood, as always the fluid economy of his movements startling. "Peter is more complex than you imagine."

"Not hardly likely."

"As a representative of the company you work for, I am instructing you to leave him alone."

Ben considered him for a moment. "Jim asked you to meet me here?"

"Yes."

"Why?"

"We want you to find out what Sato is up to."

"Sato?"

Huang's callused hand closed momentarily on Ben's shoulder. "Thank you for the sugar cane field, *Lao* Ben."

Ben frowned up at him.

"Talk to the woman," Huang said. "Go with her."

Ben watched him walk to the register. Watched him deposit the exact change on the counter. It was a mystery to him how Huang did that. He'd never seen him count money at a restaurant, but he always had the exact amount ready.

Huang paused at the door. *"Shao shin,"* he said to Ben, be careful. And then he was gone, and when Ben turned to the woman to ask for a hot towel and a cup of coffee, she was watching him with the eyes of someone who knows what they are looking at.

Chapter 7
Running Dog

"Would you like more coffee?" the woman asked. Her English was precise, the accent more in her tone than in her pronunciation. "I am making a fresh pot." The slant of her eyes was slightly reversed, the ends of her eyes lower rather than higher. The reverse slant somehow made her face appear more Japanese. Little Winnie the Pooh bears dangled from her ears.

"Please."

He watched her go to fetch the coffee, her movements behind the counter fluid and economical. She seemed more an athlete than a shopkeeper.

He stood and walked to the counter and watched as she poured coffee from a brass and glass coffee press. The way she held the press reminded him of a tea ceremony. She smiled politely, her gaze fixed on what she was doing, her awareness of him standing there without the tension that his size and appearance usually generated.

"Sorry to trouble you," he said in Mandarin. "Is there a bathroom?"

"Yeou—" she began in Mandarin. She looked up at him, smiling. *"Gomen nasai."*

"Toilet," he said in English.

"Ah. . . . " She carefully set the coffee press on the counter and pointed to a small black-and-white sign over a small doorway at the far end of the shop. "There."

161

"Domo."

"Bu shie," she said in Mandarin; don't mention it.

This was getting really weird, he thought, as he walked to the rest room. He was beginning to feel like a bear in a cage, surrounded by people who expected him to perform some trick. He kept telling himself that Jim and Huang knew what they were doing, but he was getting the feeling that they didn't. Everyone was watching him, even the woman behind him. Why, he had no idea. All he knew was that it was not part of his job description.

His great grandmother's people had included a society of warriors called the Dogs. The Dogs fought rearguard actions, sacrificing themselves if need be so that the tribe could survive. Well, he was not a Dog. He hadn't signed on for that kind of shit. Running dog. Stalking horse. Bait. Whatever you called it, he wanted no part of it. Maybe it was time to go home. Go fishing with Robert Lee. Teach him how to fish his secret hole.

The bathroom was spotless. Tile floor. Small sink and mirror. Western-style toilet. A small vase filled with fresh, yellow flowers was on top the toilet tank. In the mirror he could see the bandages on his hands.

No Running Dog, maybe. But admit it. The second time he'd been kicked down, he'd felt it had been time to die. Those two *judoka* and the sound of leaded pipe tinking off the concrete wall had put him on a different plane entirely. He bent forward hands on either side of the sink and looked at himself in the mirror. What would the Dogs have thought of someone like him?

He smiled at his image in the mirror. No way he was going to run tail between his legs back to Montana. No way in hell. Not after the Frenchman. Not after Carlos.

He pushed off from the sink. Fuck 'em if they couldn't take a joke.

162

When he came out of the bathroom, the two men he'd seen with Peter at *Another Country* were seated at a table against the wall. Both men were looking at him. The woman—two glasses of water and several plastic-wrapped hot towels on a tray on the counter next to her—was also watching him, her hands at her sides.

The tall one was smiling. Both men had aviator sunglasses pushed up on their heads. The tall one, his blond hair cut long at the back, short in front and at the sides, had a pale-yellow sweater loose around his neck and shoulders. Light-green polo shirt. Jeans. The other man was short, stocky, dark complexioned, with the shoulders and neck of a body builder, receding hair close cropped. He was wearing a long-sleeved denim shirt buttoned at the wrist, some kind of academy ring on his hand. A vibrant-colored toucan looked down from a print on the wall behind them. The woman was watching him, not the two men.

He sighed and walked to their table.

"Mr. Tails—" the blond man began.

Ben held up his bandaged hand. "I don't want to hear it."

"We'd like to talk to—"

"You know who I work for, right?"

"Yes, but—"

"Talk to them, then. Don't talk to me."

The blond man's smile widened. He opened his mouth to say something.

"I'm trying to be polite," Ben said.

The other man's face darkened. Ben could see the anger in his eyes.

"Just leave," Ben said to him.

"You're making a mistake," the blond man said.

Ben shrugged. "I'll get over it." Where do they find these people, he thought. It seemed like everywhere he went in Asia, he ran into people like these two. Good little Intelligence

Community bureaucrats on the outside, mean as snakes on the inside. CIA, DEA, NSA, FBI–it didn't matter who they belonged to; they were all the same. Clever and cunning and condescending, willing to sacrifice anyone or anything to whatever bent notion of career enhancement they subscribed to at the moment, their philosophy a lethal mix of realpolitik, manifest destiny, Mormon or Jesuit fervor. The idea that the end justifies the means elevated to an entire way of life. Sociopaths, most of them. Some of them were worse than the people he was tasked to investigate.

The body builder stood up.

Ben smiled and raised his eyebrows. The Japanese cops loved it when *gaijin* fought. As long as no one was killed or seriously injured, there wasn't a cop in the country who would haul them in for beating on each other. "Yes?" he said.

The blond man stood also. "Some other time, then," he said, his movement as smooth and as relaxed as his voice. "But until then, Mr. Tails, please know that we only have your best interests at heart."

"I'll bet."

"What he really means," the other one said, "is that you best be paying attention. The big boys are playing now."

"Wow. The Big Boys."

The blond man threw three thousand-yen notes on the table and pushed the other man toward the door.

"Domo arrigato gozaimashita," the woman said and bowed. "Thank you for coming," she said in English, as they went out the door. "Please come again."

Ben shook his head. This was so fucked up, nothing would surprise him now.

The woman popped open a plastic-wrapped hot towel and handed it to him. Customers were always given a hot towel when they came out of the rest room. He wiped his hands with the towel and placed it on the tray. "Big Boys," he explained.

"Hai. Big Boys."

He smiled and started toward the table at the window but stopped and looked back at her. Her smile and her dress said she was a coffee shop manager, but the intelligence and alertness and humor in her brown eyes said something else.

"Kei will be here shortly," she said, making no attempt to hide the quality of her English.

"Would you like your coffee now? Or would you like to wait until she gets here?"

Chapter 8
Caribbean Queen

Through the window, above the stack of tea crates, he saw her coming down the block on the other side of the street. She stepped between parked cars, hesitated a moment, and then crossed light on her feet through a break in the traffic, long black braid swinging, a smile and a slight inclination of her head and neck for the people in the cars. She was wearing a designer T-shirt–light cotton or silk from the way the breeze and her movement made it cling. The T-shirt was several sizes too big, tucked into beltless chinos tight at the waist, loose and baggy at the leg.

The way she moved, free and easy and without apparent conceit, made him smile, made him forget why he was there. For a moment, one of those inconsequential moments that inexplicably remain forever vivid, he was nothing more than a man seated relaxed in a coffee shop, watching through the window a pretty woman brighten the day and the people around her as she hurried across a street.

Her clothes and the way she moved made him think of old Fred Astaire and Gene Kelly movies–never mind that he'd never seen a Fred Astaire and Gene Kelly movie.

Cheeks flushed, eyes moist and eager, she barged through the door.

"Sensei!" she said. *"O-hisashiburi!"*

Startled, the woman at the counter looked up, her surprise clearly feigned. *"Kei-chan!"* She hurried around the counter, and the two women embraced, their affection for each other devoid of any Japanese pretend. The woman held Kei at arms' length. *"Hisashiburi, Kei-chan,"* she said, it's been a long time.

Kei bowed her head. *"Gomen-ne,"* she said, and started to say something else but, raising her head, caught sight of Ben seated by the window. Her smile faded, the sparkle in her eyes replaced by a look that Ben could not decipher. She squeezed the other woman's arms and smiled, her smile rueful. Business first, Ben thought. Business being the big, ugly *gaijin* seated by the window.

She released the woman's arms and turned toward Ben. Her eyes were cool and appraising as she walked toward him. What would it be like, he wondered, to have a woman like her come through the door the way she had, cheeks flushed, eyes eager to see him. He almost laughed out loud. Not in this lifetime, he thought–and the way he was going, not in the next, either.

He stood, the fact that he was standing an even bigger surprise to him than had been his smile when he'd watched her cross the street. An old Billy Ocean song popped into his mind. *Caribbean Queen.* He could feel an awkward electricity between them–a polarity of difference that changed her smile from neutral to quizzical, frown lines appearing between her eyes. "Mr. Tails. I'm sorry. I didn't see you sitting there."

"I'm early," he said, thinking, *Oh, man.* Thick black hair. Heavy eyebrows. Wide-spaced almond eyes. Small nose. Oval face. Perfect lips. Vaguely he realized that taken individually the components of her face did not match. A little more of anything and she would have looked awkward, homely even. But taken as a whole she was one of the most striking women he'd ever seen. In a room full of women more beautiful than her, she'd be the one you'd remember. A Caribbean Queen, for sure. But then he remembered how quickly her eyes had changed when he'd first met her–changed into eyes like those of the Khmer Rouge.

"Kumi and I are old friends. We have not seen each other for quite some time," she said.

"You called her *sensei?*"

"Yes." She turned her head to grin at the woman. "Coffee, please, *Sensei.*"

"Hai." The woman bowed, her voice and the deep bow mocking Kei's request.

"It's sort of a joke," Kei said. "Kumi is my *sensei*–my Aikido *sensei,* actually–but she is also my cousin. We have been friends forever." She gestured toward his chair. "Please sit. There is no need to be so polite." She pulled out the chair opposite his and sat, hitching herself around to get comfortable.

He slowly lowered himself into his chair. Near as he could tell she wasn't wearing much makeup. Lipstick. Some eyelash darkener. Tiny jade studs at her earlobs. A large, functional watch with leather band. No rings. No necklace. He smiled to himself. No visible scars, marks, or tattoos.

"Kumi was my father's assistant. She is very accomplished. But now she is married and has two children who take up most of her time–two boys. My heroes."

"How does she find time to run this place?"

"Oh, she doesn't usually work here. I mean, she is–we are– the owners." She paused, and smiled. "I'm sorry, I'm running on, and you must wonder why we are meeting like this."

Ben leaned back, the bamboo wicker in the chair creaking against his weight. "I didn't know until I saw you crossing the street that we were," he said, thinking never mind that he had not a clue as to what was going on. Never mind that she must have known who he was when he met her in *Another Country,* it was a fine feeling just being at the same table with a creature like her–and since fine feelings these days were most definitely at a premium, he might as well enjoy it while he could.

She had a knack for making him feel big and slow and awkward, it was true, but he didn't think it was intentional. She was simply being whoever she was. He knew in his bones that people were going to die before this was over. Maybe him, too. But for now, it was a fine feeling sitting there with her.

"Why are you staring at me like that?" she asked.

"What?"

"Why are you looking at me like that?"

"Like what?"

"Like you are a bug collector, and I am some new species you've never seen before."

He grinned. "You're kind of a shock to the system, that's all." Damn, he sure hoped she wasn't just a messenger. "Sorry."

She frowned. "What happened to your hands?"

"In addition to a talent for putting my foot in my mouth, I have an even greater talent for tripping over my own feet. I was out jogging, and stumbled, and found out there are lots of sharp little stones in the pavement along the river."

"I see," she said.

"Not to change the subject, but how did you know my last name?"

"My uncle told me."

"Your uncle?"

"My father's youngest brother. You saw me with him at *Another Country*."

"Big guy. Big jewelry?"

She smiled. "Yes."

"I thought maybe he was an *Oya-bun*," he said. An *oya-bun* was a Yakuza don.

She winced. "Anything but. He is what you would call a—" She frowned, searching for the words in English.

"A wheeler-dealer?"

She shook her head. "No, that's not right. A mover and a shaker?" She smiled. "My uncle makes money, influences people. He runs the financial side."

"The financial side of what?"

"Oh, of the family, of course." She clasped her hands on her lap. "Mr. Tails, I am here because my father wishes to speak with you. But before we meet with him, you need to understand a few things about my father, and about my family."

"Do you know what happened last night?" he asked.

Her eyes darted from one side of his face to the other. "Yes, I know."

"Did your family have something to do with it?"

Her eyes widened. "Of course not."

"How about your uncle? When he was at the club, did he know what was going to go down?"

"Go down?"

"Going to happen."

Her eyes narrowed. "No."

The fingers of his right hand unconsciously drummed the table top. The other woman—Kumi, he thought Kei had said her name was—quietly placed cups and saucers in front of them. A bowl of sugar cubes. Spoons. A tiny pitcher of cream. She poured coffee, careful to leave at least a third of the cup empty. As she turned to go, Kei lightly grasped her arm for a second. *"Domo,"* she said.

Wordlessly the woman retreated back to the counter.

Ben poured cream into his coffee, picked up a spoon, slowly stirred.

"My family is like a corporation," Kei said. "Everyone has his or her place. And that place is determined by talent, aptitude, desire. My uncle, for example, showed a great talent for things financial. As a result, the family saw to it that he received the best education possible–London, Harvard, Singapore. His older brother–a man of little talent and ambition, but a good man and a hard worker–functions as the family chauffeur."

He put the spoon to the side and picked up the cup. The handle was small and awkward in his hand. He sipped his coffee, watching her over the rim of the cup.

"My father is the head of the family," she said. "Think of him as the CEO–a CEO who listens very carefully to the rest of the family. My father also helped to found the company that employs you–Raven International."

He gently placed the cup into the saucer.

"Collectively and, in some cases, individually, my family is not without influence."

This is truly fucked, he thought. So far out of his depth, he didn't have a clue to what she was telling him.

"Please tell me what you are feeling," she said.

"Feeling or thinking?"

"Feeling."

"I used to have this dream," he said. "I'm point, and we're creeping down a trail. I've got a real bad feeling about what's ahead. I turn around and there's no one behind me. I look down and I no longer have a weapon. All I can do is stand there and wait for it to happen."

"Did something like that really happen?"

He smiled. "No."

"In your dream, should you be on the trail?"

"No, I shouldn't be on the trail–any trail."

"You have no weapon?"

"None."

"And you are alone."

"Yes."

171

"You are on a trail, but you should not be on a trail. You are alone when you thought you were not. There is danger ahead. You have no weapon." She paused. "You are feeling vulnerable and perhaps . . . what? Expendable?"

He smiled. "People like me are always expendable. It's part of our basic design."

"And you are unhappy with that?"

"No, ma'm. I surely am not. As Popeye the Sailor Man said: I yam what I yam."

She sat back and crossed her arms across her chest, her almond eyes assessing him.

He raised his eyebrows. She was way too intelligent to play games with. "And you?" he asked. "What is your place in your family?"

She reached to put sugar in her coffee. "I am my father's assistant—the same position Kumi held." Her fingers were long and slim. "My father is old and sometimes infirm, and since my mother died, he does not like to travel. Basically, I am his eyes and ears to the world that exists beyond the small city he lives in." She put two cubes in her coffee, added cream. "Many people come to visit my father. He holds no formal position in government or industry, but many who hold such positions often come to seek his counsel." She stirred her coffee.

"He is a powerful man, your father?"

"Yes, he is."

"And he wants to talk to me?"

"Yes."

"Why?"

She put the spoon on the saucer and with both hands picked up the cup and took a sip. She set the cup down, the cup slightly tipped up on the edge of the indentation in the saucer. "I think I'll let him explain that." For some reason the fact that she'd set the cup slightly askew made him feel better.

She smiled at him. "If you'll excuse me, I need to make a few phone calls to arrange our transportation. It takes about three hours by Shinkansen and express train. You'll want to stop by your apartment and get whatever is necessary for an overnight stay."

"Where are we going?"

"A little city called Ohmihachiman."

"Near Lake Biwa?"

She stood. "You've been there?"

"A motorcycle trip. There's a great coffee shop that a couple of hundred years ago used to be a *sake* factory."

She smiled, the first genuine smile since she'd seen him. "You really have been there! I'll just be a minute."

He watched her walk to the counter. The bounce in her step, the sheer athleticism of her movement, was the same as it had been when he'd watched her cross the street. Why is it, he thought, not for the first time, that life is always at its best when you know it is about to turn to shit.

He picked up his cup and took a sip, abruptly aware of the complex taste and texture and aroma of the coffee. Rays of sunlight filtered into the room between the stacked tea crates. The palms of his hands throbbed.

There was no going back now, he thought. Intentional or not, she had made certain of that.

173

Chapter 9
Marine

The doors hissed shut, and the Shinkansen began its effortless glide out of the station, clusters of people and kiosks, other trains loading or unloading people passing at an accelerating rate past the window, the bland, fluorescent interior of the train station quickly giving way to an elevated view of the city. Here and there huge, steeply pitched traditional tile roofs marked temples and shrines. At night the city was less harsh, a forest of colorful neon blurring past the window. He liked traveling at night on the Shinkansen. But it was the middle of the day now, and the city was seen for what it was: a massive manufacturing and retail complex designed with business and manufacturing convenience, not people, in mind. From the windows of the elevated train, it was a bleak, man-made landscape, modern architecture with its flagrant use of polarized glass and stainless steel interspersed with older, strictly utilitarian cubes of gray and dingy white.

"Would you like something to snack on?" Kei asked. "Something to drink?"

"No, thank you."

She was sitting across and one seat over from him, next to the aisle. The car was nearly empty, only the two of them, and maybe eight or nine other passengers scattered around

174

the compartment. She crossed one leg over the other and he could see bare ankle between shoe and the hem of her trousers, a blue vein beneath her tanned, flawless skin. She leaned forward and with her right hand reached behind her neck and pulled her braid forward over her shoulder and breast, the thick braid falling nearly to her waist. She smiled. "You have not asked any questions."

He looked out the window. Rice paddies were beginning to slide past. The sky was gray and overcast, blue mountains on the horizon.

"My father has long been a part of Raven International; he is very upset about what happened to the man, Carlos," she said.

"Your father has control over such things?"

"My father approved of your investigation of Carlos Montoya. But since Captain Sato—who is normally the liaison between the National Police and Raven—did not ask for advice, my father knew nothing of what had actually been planned."

He turned his head toward her.

"My father is a man of honor, Mr. Tails. He was a Captain in the Imperial Navy."

"During the War?"

"Yes."

"What does his being a Captain in the Imperial Navy have to do with anything?"

"It has to do with the fact that my father well understands Japanese—tendencies."

"Tendencies." Anger shivered his spine. "Carlos was killed by *tendencies?"*

"My father is as upset as are you."

"Oh, I don't think so."

"He—" She smiled. "You can decide for yourself." She

175

uncrossed her legs and stood. She looked down at him. "Can I get you something while I'm up?"

"I'm fine. Thanks."

She moved out into the aisle to the rear of the car.

He sighed and put his seat back, resting his head on the clean white cloth of the headrest. He'd offended her. She was probably back in the ladies' room cursing him. He smiled to himself. Cursing him in English or Mandarin; he couldn't imagine her cursing in Japanese. He looked out the window. Gray, concrete telephone poles whizzed past. In the distance, rice shoots sprouted green in windowpanes of gray water. A large mound forested with bamboo and huge old-growth pine and cedar squatted alone in the midst of rice paddies. A temple or shrine of some kind, he thought.

She didn't understand. On one level he wanted to know the who and why of Carlos' murder—wanted to know why the Pumpkin Eater had been there. Wanted to know why those two government assholes wanted to talk to him. Wanted to know why Jim and Huang had placed him in the middle of whatever it was that they'd placed him in the middle of. But on another level—the level he'd be operating on if push came to shove—he didn't give a damn about any of that. Right now he felt vulnerable. Expendable, like he'd tried to explain to her in the coffee shop. And that was all that counted. That's what she didn't understand: his feeling that he was on his own.

Clearly something was coming to a head. Captain Sato and whoever Sato represented were involved. Kei and her family were involved. At least two of the local CIA and State Department types were involved. For some reason, Raven had placed him in the middle of a constantly mutating and demonstrably lethal mix of people and agendas: Jim. Him. Carlos. Huang. The Pumpkin Eater. Sato. The two government assholes. Kei. Her uncle. Her father.

The chemistry of whatever was coming down had been precipitated by politics. Carlos' death had been merely the catalyst.

He squinted out at the rice paddies. He could feel this one in his bones. He might even get dead this time.

He studied his reflection in the window.

And now, thanks to what had happened, and contrary to what he'd said to Peter, Mr. Slide was here, too.

Is that what Jim and Huang had in mind? To resurrect Mr. Slide? Could they know him that well? Know him well enough to know that it would probably take a combination of the past–Huang and Peter–and the present–the murder of Carlos–to shift him that far?

Maybe. But he didn't think so. That would be too complicated. Too unpredictable. More likely, it was a case of boxes within boxes. His gut told him that Carlos had been the catalyst all right, but the catalyst for something that had too many people with too many agendas in it to be under anyone's control. As life had ended for that figure sprawled alone and betrayed on a gray Nagoya street, whatever it was that had been precipitated had already escalated out of anyone's control. He'd felt it then, and he could feel it even stronger now. The killing had tripped a switch–had inserted into the equation an energy that could not be predicted or controlled.

His own choices were simple: he could go back to Montana, or he could stay and trust his instincts and reflexes to get him through. The death of Carlos told him all he needed to know: if he stayed, it was going to get real.

Outside the window, beyond rice paddies and isolated hillocks of bamboo, rays of gray light filtered through the overcast onto blue mountains.

He sighed. If he let it, the scenery always reminded him of

another time—of other paddies and other mountains. He felt a rush of heat in his stomach. Of Mr. Slide, alone on a ridge. . . .

• • •

The ville—until just a few minutes ago an idyllic picture of thatched huts and ramshackle sheds—was about 350 meters straight out across rice paddies green with ripening rice, and maybe 35 meters below where he had his hide inside a stand of bamboo. Even from where he was, he could hear the woman. An unending series of faint, high-pitched sounds—short, truncated, exhausted screams that reminded him of the sounds gut-shot deer sometimes make. A black, seriously ugly pig nosed around the edges of the common area, impervious to the sounds the woman was making.

On the far side of the ville was an old graveyard, the stones gray and moldy and leaning every which way, like the stones in old, Civil War graveyards he'd seen in North Carolina. A stream, ten or twelve feet wide, meandered along one side of the village and out into the valley. Bushes and stands of bamboo and low, broad-leafed palms bordered the stream. Taller palms and larger trees, grapefruit and banana, probably, grew in and around the ville.

Most of the valley floor consisted of rice paddies and villages. Veins of water bordered by thick foliage connected the villages. Some of the villages were bigger, some smaller, but nearly all were a copy of the one the sounds were coming from.

Small gusts of wind swept haphazard across the paddies, bending rice shoots in scattered waves that seemed more a product of the sounds the woman was making than of wind. On the other side of the valley the bombed-out ruins of a Catholic Church shone gray-white against green, jungled mountainside.

The other side of the valley was Indian Country, and no fucking doubt about that. Last night, he'd watched as strings of lights, made hazy and diffused by moisture in the air and by the lenses on Chinese-made flashlights and lanterns, moved erratically across far foothills: groups of NVA moving secure in the knowledge that the monsoon had grounded American air.

Platoon-sized contingents of U.S. Marines spotted on easily defended high points—rock outcroppings for the most part—controlled the side of the valley he was on.

The village below him was well out of range of Marine mortars, and out of sight—thanks to the finger ridge he was on—of any Marine strong point. The ridge stuck out half a mile into the valley, a peninsula in a sea of green rice and yellow grass.

At night the NVA went where they pleased. But during the day squad-sized Marine patrols would traverse the foothills and valley edges, checking out the villages that dotted this side of the valley floor, looking for any excuse to call in air or artillery.

It had taken him two days to walk in. Last night, an hour before the evening monsoon, he'd set up in a grove of bamboo at the top of the ridge, and wrapped in his poncho sat out the mosquitoes and the rain, sleeping a few minutes at a time as sheets of rain and wind swept through the bamboo. An hour before first light, he'd gone into his routine, a routine he never varied: Broke down his weapon. Used a silicon-embedded cloth he'd purchased at a sporting-goods store in Okinawa to wipe the surfaces. Ran a clean patch down the bore. Reassembled the weapon. Removed and wiped the rounds and reloaded the eight magazines the black Major had made him bring. Ate some rice and *nuoc-mam*—he was actually starting to like *nuoc-mam*. Had a drink of water. Took out the old, faded-yellow, plastic tobacco pouch his grandfather had

179

used and poured a spoonful or so of black, sandbag ash into his hand. Added a little water. Mixed the ash into a paste, and applied it in streaks and smudges to his face and arms and hands, the back of his neck. Stowed his gear, making sure it was tight and quiet.

And then, his routine finished, he'd moved out of the bamboo, down around the military crest, into a heavier, taller stand of bamboo. A wide cut in a waist-high ridge of rock just outside the bamboo gave him a field of fire that covered all approaches to the ville and, at the same time, allowed him to keep the flash suppressor well back inside the cut so that the muzzle flash would be well hidden from anyone down in the valley. The hill fell away steep on the other side of the rocks; there was no tall grass in front of the rocks to stop him from using the prone position.

He'd taped a thick piece of C-rat cardboard across the top of the lenses on his binoculars so that the morning sun could not reflect off the lenses, and then he'd waited. He was used to waiting. Most of his time in the bush was spent waiting. Just him and the mosquitoes and the ants and whatever creepy crawly happened along.

Mosquitoes didn't like him much—too much ribo-something in his liver, according to the doc—so he didn't bother with bug juice. But ants were not nearly so choosy, and he'd sat until just before sunrise putting up with the ants, wiping them from face and neck and hands. Leeches were nasty. Snakes were an adrenaline rush nearly as bad as an ambush. And there were legions of yet-to-be-discovered bugs and spiders that could fuck you up, make you sick, even dead. But it was the ants that he hated. No matter where you were, no matter where you stopped, the ants always found you. Black. Red. Brown. Big ants. Little ants. VC ants, every one of them. Some with mandibles you could see. All of them mean as hell.

The morning sky had been clear and blue and bright,

sunlight hitting a mass of giant white cumulus clouds beyond the mountains on the other side of the valley. Ground fog had crept from the forest below, spreading into fields of grass and rice, turning the air under the bamboo heavy and wet and cold, clogged with the smell of decay—the forever rot and regeneration of forest, the evil sewer smell of paddy and village.

He'd felt them before he had seen or heard or smelled them, a sense that something lethal was near. Shadow figures seen and then not seen through the leaves and branches of the bamboo. Woodland issue camouflage, face paint, bush hats. Twenty meters to his left, exactly where he would have crossed the ridge if he had been leading the squad. Intervals of about fifteen meters. No tinks. No rattles. No coughs. Lean, mean Marines. His people. Only the alien swipe of cloth against leaf and grass to mark their passage. The soft knacking sound of bamboo and grass coming straight again.

Twelve in all. One man short, if he hadn't missed one.

Forty-five minutes later, they had reappeared below, easing out of the forest, waist deep in ground fog and grass, their interval lengthened to twenty-five meters, a single, staggered file headed toward the village. He'd recounted. Twelve men. A squad leader and three fire teams, one team a man short. Exactly as the black Major had said it would be. One radio. One blooper. No sixty. Shotgun at point. Shotgun at rear, M-16 slung across the ruck of the rear shotgun. Through the binoculars he could see they were heavy on ammo and grenades, light on everything else. M-16 magazines taped together, two men with ass packs, lean rucks on the rest, the RTO carrying the radio, a PRC-25, in his ruck, the three-foot antenna pulled down over his shoulder and taped or tied to his doggy strap, four bandoleers on the blooper man—way more than usual. Probably three fleshette rounds and 3 HE rounds in each blooper bandoleer. Buckshot and fleshette rounds for the shotguns. Twenty one-inch long, finned metal darts the size of finishing nails to each shotgun fleshette round. Each man carried an incendiary grenade in addition to the usual HE. The RTO and the squad leader carried smoke.

"The UCMJ does not and never has worked in these cases," the General had explained. "The Uniform Code of Military Justice might work for a peace-time military, but it for damn sure does not work in combat-related situations." He'd paused and glared at Ben. "And I'll be God Damned if there is going to be a Marine Corps version of My Lai on my watch. Do you understand me, Sergeant?"

"Yes, sir." What else could he say? How else do you reply to a general? Especially one lean and starched and pissed off, ribbons up the wazoo.

In the distant ville the woman was finally silent. *Combat-related situations*. Roger that, General, sir.

"In any other war, if Marines had done what these people have been doing, they would have been shot out of hand," the General's black Major, no ribbons, but clearly bad news, had added. "Marine lawyers are calling it 'The Mere Gook Rule.' Those convicted of atrocities earn at most four years in the brig."

"Do you think that is right, Sergeant?" the General asked.

"No, sir."

"Have a seat, Sergeant," the black Major said.

He'd been at parade rest, but instead of taking a seat, he'd come to attention, eyes on the fake-wood paneling on the far wall of the General's trailer. "Sir. The Sergeant is a Marine, sir."

He felt the General's eyes on him. "What *the hell* do you mean by that, Sergeant?"

"My mission is to kill the enemy, sir."

"Go on."

"Sir. I use my skills to protect Marines, sir."

"No one is ordering you to shoot Marines," the black Major said.

Ben lowered his eyes, staring directly into those of the Major. The Major was maybe ten years older, skin so dark it gleamed, the pupils of his eyes darker even than his skin. Aquiline nose. Small, close-to-the-head ears. Boot haircut. Small, cruel mouth. Bad news, no doubt about it.

"Your orders are to go alone into the bush," the Major said. "To be at a place later to be named, at a time later to be determined. *Your orders are to observe.* The Marines in question will have opportunity to be where they should not be. If they do not show up in a reasonable amount of time—say, within three days of your arrival at the place to be named—you are ordered to extract yourself."

"Yes, *sir.*"

The black Major stared at him. Ben couldn't read his eyes—but there was something there. "You are further *ordered* to use your discretion in deciding a remedy appropriate to the actions of the Marines in question. *Do you understand?*"

"Yes, *sir.*"

"You are one of the best we have, Sergeant," the General said. "There is no paper on this, and there will be none. Whatever your decision and subsequent actions, all of this is between you and the Major and myself. No one else. Do you understand?"

"Yes, *sir.*"

"Their sleeves will be rolled down to hide scars or tattoos," the Major had later told him, and through the binoculars he could see that despite the heat their sleeves were indeed rolled down. "Big, hairy, red-faced Americans all look alike to the Vietnamese, especially to those who live in villages, but scars and tattoos are easy to remember."

The Mere Gook Rule. He'd thought of his grandmother's ancestors, as he'd watched through the binoculars four

183

Marines move rapidly ahead of the file, slogging and splashing through paddy water and muck to the side of the ville. Two men to the snaggle-toothed graveyard at the rear. Another man hurried to the right front of the ville, to the edge of the stream—security against anyone leaving or entering from the side that bordered the stream.

The rest of the squad paused—checking the ville out—and then quickly entered the now deserted village, slipping between hooches and sheds. He knew for sure that this was not the ville the OP had tasked them to visit. The ville they were supposed to inspect was to his right, a couple of klicks out in the valley on the other side of the ridge—at least five or six klicks from the village they were in.

Two figures, a bareheaded old man wearing black pajamas, and a middle-aged woman, conical straw hat, white blouse tight at the waist, baggy, black pajama bottoms, had come out of a hooch and walked to the center of the common area. Two Marines—the squad leader and one of the shotguns—weapons pointed at the old man and the woman, had walked across the open area toward them and, from maybe a meter away, and probably without saying a word, the squad leader had fired a short burst from his M-16 into the woman's stomach.

Even before the M-16 had fired he'd felt bile rise, burn his chest and throat.

Combat-related situations.

The woman had fallen to her side on the ground, and curled into a fetal position, and began making those high-pitched, keening sounds.

The pig was skittish at the corner of one of the hooches. Marines were entering several of the hooches.

A group of five black-clad figures, two with white blouses and long hair and conical hats at their backs, broke from the rear of one of the farthest hooches. An unarmed man in black

184

pajamas ran from the rear of the hut nearest the stream and disappeared into brush and bamboo at water's edge.

The distinctive sound of M-16s on full auto reached him, the deep thud of a shotgun, and the figures that had run out the rear in the direction of the graveyard were down in the grass and among the weathered stones. Three of them, two men and a woman, sprawled together. Another, a man, was face down, ass up, arms sprawled behind him as if taking an ungainly dive into the grass. The other woman was on her back in the grass, white blouse flowered red at throat and upper chest. A man was feebly trying to crawl back toward the ville.

A Marine rose up from behind a tombstone and threw something and dropped back down and a dirty gray-brown spray of dust and grass and shrapnel blossomed next to the crawling man, the hard, flat sound reaching Ben a moment later.

He moved the binoculars and the old man in the center of the ville was on his back, his body at a forty-five degree angle to that of the woman, one leg at an impossible angle to the side, as if it belonged not to him but to someone lying underneath him. The old man had been shot in the face more than once. The face had no definition, not even in the 7X50 Nikons.

Nothing moved.

The two Marines in the center of the ville stared down at the two bodies.

Chickens wandered between hooches.

The pig headed toward the bodies in the center.

He took his eyes away from the binoculars. To his right, way down at the far end of the valley, a black, impenetrable wall, an afternoon monsoon storm, was slowly advancing toward him.

Sick had seeped into his muscles and in his mind he'd seen

three dogs spread in a line, grinning as they ran, bounding through powder snow toward a wide-eyed, exhausted doe. The bright, technicolor greens of forest, the blue sky and clean, white clouds had faded to pastels. And in that moment– a moment that completed the metamorphosis begun when he'd executed that big, yellow dog plodding down a snow-covered logging road–he'd felt the anger that would forever be a part of him. Anger at whoever or whatever had put him there in that place at that time. And under the anger, warping it, a sense of loss as black and as consuming as the monsoon coming toward him on the horizon.

The village was just another dirt-poor village in Vietnam. The valley was dotted with villages exactly like it. For all he'd known, the entire fucking continent was filled with villages like it. But through some grotesque whim of place and time evil had visited that particular village at that particular time, and had done so in the guise of a squad of Marines–young men who, until only a short time ago, were as like him as the villages in the valley below were like each other.

Evil had visited that village and, in doing so, had visited him, leaving him with no choice–except one that in some form and to some degree required him to exercise more evil in order to do good. The General and the black Major had foreseen this. Had counted on it. That was what he had seen in the Major's eyes.

He raised the binoculars.

In the village a woman naked from the waist up ran out of a hut and breasts flailing, arms abruptly thrust out to the side, skidded face down in the dust and mud, her head and long dark hair hitting the haunches of the pig nuzzling at the body of the headman's wife. The pig lurched forward. Red like the meatball on a Japanese flag expanded from a spot below her left shoulder blade. Fleshette round. One of the shotguns.

"They've been taking only gold and silver, maybe a few rubies if they're lucky," the Major had said. "The Vietnamese don't trust currency. They torture the locations of their stashes out of them. They even bring pliers to pull teeth with gold fillings." The Major paused, studying Ben. "When it's all over, they call in air or artillery to clean up the mess. To the pilots and gun crews it's just another set of coordinates. One less NVA ville to set booby traps or ambushes. One less ville to aid and abet the enemy."

The enemy.

"Only good gook is a dead gook," the Major said. "That kind of thing."

That kind of thing.

The two Marines in the graveyard stood and advanced toward the hooches. The other two, on the near side, were already somewhere in the trees or in the ville. He could hear the sporadic stutter of rifle fire, the deep boom of a shotgun. Two men had a woman down on the ground between a hut and the stream. One man stood and kicked her in the head and then bent and ripped her blouse open.

He gently laid the binoculars down on the ground to the right of the rifle, and picked up the rifle, and dialed in the scope for 350 meters. Judging from the grass and trees there was no wind, just small breezes now and then.

The Major had given him the M-14, an Army 3X9 ART telescope mounted on an assembly fitted into the groove and screw recess on the left side of the receiver. The Major had insisted that he carry the M-14 instead of the Remington because he would be alone and might need more firepower than that offered by the bolt-action Remington. Accurized and glass-bedded by Marine Corps armorers, parts stamped MM to prove it, the M-14 had shot a four-inch group at 500

187

meters. The Army scope was basically the same Redfield scope he had on his Remington. The 14 used a twenty-round magazine, and was fitted with a full-auto selector switch. At the Major's insistence, he'd brought eight, loaded magazines and ten boxes, twenty rounds to a box, of 7.62 match-grade ammunition.

Each round was one hundred sixty-eight grains of full-metal jacketed spiral boattail. Muzzle velocity two thousand five hundred fifty feet per second.

The scope had range-finding reference wires in the reticle, but he kept it dialed to the full nine power, confident in his ability to estimate distance.

He flipped the butt plate open and slipped his left arm into the sling and eased down onto the ground, rifle firm into his shoulder, the open butt plate resting on top his shoulder, helping to ensure that the rifle would not slip, the rotation of his body into the prone position forcing the sling tight, both elbows on the ground, left elbow well under the rifle, cheek on top his right thumb, the rifle as steady and as solid as if he had it rested on top of a sandbag. The ground had felt unaccountably soft. Instead of the usual rush of adrenaline, he'd felt sleepy—real sleepy. He'd wanted to close his eyes and his mind and sleep. Just for a minute.

Instead, he'd wiped an ant off his cheek and forced himself to look through the scope, searching for the RTO. Saw the antenna fastened to the doggy strap. Saw one side of the unnaturally square ruck. Pushed the safety off with the top of his trigger finger and, at the same time, took a breath and released half of it, the sleepy feeling abruptly gone. He put pressure on the trigger. Waited for the RTO to turn away.

The rifle fired, the round striking the ruck and the radio inside the ruck center mass, the full-metal jacketed boattail continuing through the RTO, pushing him up against the wall of the hooch he'd been about to enter. He waited a beat for the scope and the radioman to steady, and the rifle again fired, the round striking the radio, further ruining the radio and killing the RTO at the same time.

In the scope, the RTO was slumped face against the hooch, bent backward at the waist, legs sprawled behind in the dirt, as if he had been broken in half at the waist.

When the first round had fired, the quiet of his hide had disintegrated. The stock recoiling into his shoulder had replaced the unfamiliar lethargy with a familiar clarity, the dank smells around him overpowered by the stink of cordite. He'd made his decision, and he'd acted on it, and from the instant the first round left the barrel he was in the zone, his mind and his body concerned only with what he did best.

Squirming with knees and feet and elbows sideways against bamboo and damp leaves, he shifted the sight picture to the two men with the woman. One man knelt knees pinning the woman's arms to the ground behind her head.

He exhaled slightly, and the rifle fired, the bullet striking the man center mass between the open folds of his flak vest. He took a breath, and partially exhaled, shifting as he did to the man between the woman's legs, and the rifle fired, the man hit in the side. A heart-lung shot. Lucky shot.

He scanned the center of the village, but only the pig and the three bodies in the middle and the radioman sprawled against the wall of the hooch were visible. He crabbed sideways to the right, using his left elbow cranked tight into the sling as the pivot point, and the crosshairs found a kneeling Marine aiming an M-16 over the top of one of the gravestones toward the ville. He took a breath. Exhaled. The crosshairs found the base of the helmet, and the rifle went off, and the man fell sideways into the grass. His M-16 teetered on top of the ancient gravestone.

Four down. He scanned the village.

A Marine with a shotgun, no helmet, appeared barely seen

189

inside and to the side of the doorway of the hut the woman who had been shotgunned had run from. He exhaled. Held. Waited. A face appeared in the light, mouth open in a shout, and the crosshairs settled center mass and the rifle fired. A camouflage-clad leg and jungle boot slowly retracted into the shadows. The crosshairs settled on the shadow above the leg, and the rifle again fired.

He swept the village. Nothing moved. The pig was down, trying to get up, its side a mass of gore, head flopping around in the dirt. Someone had panicked and had shot at whatever moved—the pig, in this case. They would be looking for a gun at ground level, a spider trap maybe, aware only that there had been gunfire and that some of them were down. Because of their own sporadic fire, and because he'd selected targets not close to each other, they still would not know it was a sniper, and that already five men and the radio were down.

Moments passed. His ears were ringing, but he didn't think there had been any more shooting in the village. Hard to tell, though, because shots fired inside the huts would be muffled. He leaned to the left and removed the rifle from his shoulder, keeping his left hand in the sling. With his right hand he reached down and unsnapped a magazine pouch and took out a full magazine and placed it on a rock in front and to the side of the magazine in the rifle. Next time he fired, they'd be looking for a muzzle flash. They wouldn't see it. He was buried too far back in the bamboo and rocks. He put the butt of the rifle back in his shoulder and rotated his body back into a tight, solid prone position.

A figure darted among the gravestones, running toward the M-16 still balanced on top a gravestone, and knelt in the grass and then, as he acquired a sight picture, stood and ran toward the hooches, the crosshairs steady when the rifle fired, the jolt of thumb against cheekbone barely felt, the round seeming to come more from his mind than from the rifle. The Marine was face up on his back, only a few feet from a leaning, tilted gravestone–the last stone before the village. He fired again. The body didn't move.

Six. They'd know now that a sniper was up on one of the hillsides.

They also knew by now that their radio was gone and they could not call for air or artillery.

They were in a ville out of sight of or contact with their OP. They were in a place they weren't supposed to be. And the place they weren't supposed to be was on the edge of deepest, darkest Indian Country. Shit out of luck is what they were. They could stay hidden in the ville–which was no option at all because, 1. the natives would definitely be getting restless and, 2. they naturally assumed that he was an NVA sniper and, as such, would be calling or sending for reinforcements. Since the NVA, when they came, always came in strength, a platoon at least, their ass was grass unless they got out of that ville most ricky-tick.

To reach the hillside, they'd be forced to run across at least three hundred meters of open paddy and grassland. Waist-high grass. Six inches of paddy water. Another eight inches or so of muck.

Their only choice was to go for the stream. The cover along the stream was patchy in places, but in others it was thick bush and bamboo and broad-leafed plants. From where they were it would look as if there was good cover. But from where he lay looking down on them, the foliage along the stream offered little concealment. They'd be silhouetted against the water, and the brush would only serve to make them move slower. Sooner or later, he'd have a shot.

Two men ran across the center of the ville between hooches before he could get a shot off. Two others were at the bodies where the girl had been. The rifle fired, but the man must

191

have moved. Bursts of automatic weapons fire–M-16s–came from the village. He lowered his head behind the rock formation, but no rounds cracked overhead or through bamboo or bush. They weren't shooting at him. They were shooting as many people as they could before they left.

He raised his head and reached over and retrieved the binoculars, wiping a black ant from the right eye piece. He scanned the village. A hooch under a big tree next to a paddy was beginning to burn, white, sooty smoke boiling out of the thatch roof. Barely glimpsed figures moved quick through trees and bamboo next to the stream. He put the binoculars to the side and again fit the rifle into his shoulder, squirming to the left to get the scope in front of the lead man.

He waited for the lead man to stop and kneel inside a cluster of bushes on the stream bank, and shot him in the hip, the round knocking him off the embankment into the water.

Seven.

One man was helping another half-run, half-walk through trees and grass and bush. Both men fell to the ground under a small tree and he shot the wounded man in the back, waited for the scope to steady, and shot the other in the body. Waited for the scope, and shot him again.

Nine.

He slowly scanned back and forth, from village to about two hundred meters downstream. The other three had gone to ground or into the stream.

He relaxed away from the scope, wiped sweat from his eyebrows and forehead. The hooch in the ville was really burning now, red-orange flames shooting up into the smoke and into the branches of the big tree. The thatched roof of the neighboring hooch was beginning to smoke.

Movement from above the ville caught his eye, whatever it was barely seen through the smoke of the burning hooch. Keeping the rifle in his shoulder, with his right hand he picked up the binoculars, looking over the top of the rifle to see what it was.

Two files of NVA regulars were moving fast toward the village. One file was strung out on a trail on the far side of the stream. The other file double-timed along a trail on the near side that ran at the edge of the foliage next to the paddies. Loose brown and faded-green uniforms. Bush hats. Web gear. Extra magazines in chest pouches that went from waist to upper chest. At least two RPD machine guns. Mortar tube. Mortar baseplate. Several with RPGs. A couple of what looked to be U.S.-issue M-79 grenade launchers, bandoleers of blooper rounds criss-crossing the chests of the men carrying the M-79s. That lone figure in black pajamas that he'd seen run from the ville must have either run into them or run to get them. Most of a company from the looks of it. Typical NVA. Risk a company to kill a few Marines.

Lead elements on the village side of the stream spread in fire-team sized groups out into the paddies, keeping good interval, fifteen to twenty meters between individuals, fifty or sixty meters between teams, the teams leapfrogging toward the village. No FNGs from the North, that was for sure. No wasted motion. No whistles. No nervous fire. Moving fast.

Villagers were suddenly everywhere in the ville. Ants in an anthill. Running around trying to put out the fire. Several were bent over the Vietnamese bodies. Kids stripped dead Marines of anything useful. An old woman knelt in the dirt, her arms cradling the head of the woman who had been shotgunned, the old woman's raw, red, beetle-nut stained mouth raised toward the sky.

The file of NVA had already reached a point on the other side of the stream opposite the village and had sited an RPD to cover that side of the ville and downstream.

The Marines were a hundred to two hundred meters downstream. They probably had no idea the Calvary had

193

arrived. Twitchy as hell, they'd be hoping to stay put until dark. Fat chance.

Lead NVA elements entered the village, filtering between hooches, materializing out of the smoke to mix with villagers. A group of kids and an old man with a long, thin goatee, were pointing in the direction the Marines had gone. Two NVA, one with a radio that looked like a PRC-25, were listening to the old man. Other NVA were examining the dead RTO; two others dragged a Marine body by the feet from a hooch. Others, their weapons slung, began helping villagers fight fire.

The NVA next to the radioman spoke at length into the handset and handed the handset back to the radioman. He began shouting, gesturing toward the other end of the ville.

NVA on the other side of the stream began leapfrogging downstream, keeping the RPD in the center of their movement. Groups of two or three men left the village and began sweeping through the grass and bush along the stream bank, moving a group at a time toward where the Marines had gone to ground.

He reached his finger to the front of the trigger guard and pulled the safety on. The North Vietnamese Army was about to finish what he'd started.

The sound of an M-16 firing full auto swept across paddies, joined almost immediately by sustained AK and RPD fire.

Using the binoculars, he scanned the area. He could see NVA kneeling next to trees and bushes. Grenades exploded between front NVA elements, abrupt spurts of dirt and shredded foliage, the sound reaching him an instant later.

The NVA on the far side of the stream had fixed the Marine positions and were pouring sustained fire into the area, while NVA on the near side moved closer, some throwing grenades, the sound of the explosions deeper than those of American-made grenades. Rats in a trap, he thought.

Firing ceased on the far side of the stream, and he watched as small uniformed figures ran through the Marine positions, the sound of AK and M-16 fire rising in volume for a few, brief seconds, ending abruptly. Punctuated by a few, short bursts of AK fire.

He watched two soldiers fire down into the grass. Watched as another group pulled a Marine upright, the side of his head and face red with blood, his camouflage utilities shredded and ragged on his right side.

The soldiers on the far side of the stream began wading the stream, mixing with those on the near side looking at American bodies. A small group were having their picture taken with a body that had been pulled from the stream. Dead and wounded NVA were being carried back to the ville. Several, hands shielding their eyes, were looking down the valley and up at the sky above the ridgelines. Wondering when the air would show up, he thought.

"One last thing," the General had said. "I don't care how you do it, but you make damn sure the Viets know it's us. There is no way we want Charlie claiming it was them that got justice done."

Justice? Fuck you, General, sir.

He watched as the wounded Marine was dragged toward the center of the ville. The burning hooches had been reduced to a few smoldering timbers. Several groups of villagers and soldiers were still throwing water on the thatched roofs of the hooches nearest the two that had burned. One side of the big tree had been reduced to blackened branches, but the tree itself had not caught fire.

The bodies in the center of the village had been taken away, and the officer, his radioman still next to him, was addressing a small cluster of villagers. The officer paused and turned as two soldiers, AKs slung across their backs, dragged the wounded Marine into the center of the ville and threw him to the ground between the villagers and the officer. Villagers started forward, but the officer said something and they stopped.

The Marine pushed himself up off the ground onto all fours, too exhausted or too hurt or both to climb to his feet. His head was almost touching the ground, shoulder blades prominent.

Most of the NVA had already formed up and were beating feet in a long strung-out file from the back end of the village along the trail that ran at the edge of the trees and brush next to the rice paddies. Wounded and dead were on ready-made stretchers made of poles and what looked like ponchos, two men to each body.

Holding his AK with both arms extended, the officer stepped toward the Marine and fired a short burst into the back of his head, the AK recoiling back and up.

He unsafed the M-14. Exhaled. The crosshairs settled on the officer's chest, and the rifle recoiled back into his shoulder. He moved the scope to the soldier who had been standing behind the officer, barely aware of the jolt of the stock against thumb and cheekbone, the recoil into his shoulder, as the rifle fired. The crosshairs moved back to the officer, down now on the ground, the top of his head facing directly toward him.

I don't care how you do it, but you make damn sure the Viets know it's us.

He took his time and shot the officer through the top of the head.

Damn sure.

Rolling onto his left shoulder, he ejected the magazine, inserted another, fully loaded magazine, and put the stock back into his shoulder and rolled upright, squirming to the side to acquire the column moving away from him.

The rifle fired the instant the crosshairs settled on a man, and fired again as they settled on another man, a litter carrier. A man turned back to see what was happening, and the rifle fired, and then, even though his every action at the time must have been clear and precise, in his memory the rest of it was a blur. The scope acquired a target, and the rifle fired, and the scope acquired, and the rifle fired, again and again and again, until abruptly there were no more uniformed figures to be seen. An RPD began firing into the trees well off to his left, blue-green tracers zipping across green paddies, disappearing into the trees.

He scattered three quick rounds into the area the tracers were coming from, and then rolled onto his side and ejected the magazine, unsnapped another magazine pouch, and inserted a fresh magazine into the rifle. He placed the rifle on the ground, the end of the barrel on top of a rock. Removed boxes of ammunition from another pouch and opened the boxes and quickly crammed rounds into the used magazines. He put the magazines and loose ammunition back into ammo pouches, crushing the boxes around the loose rounds so they would not rattle. Fastened the pouches. Put the binoculars in his ruck and, still on the ground, struggled into the ruck.

He lifted the rifle and, careful to keep the end of the barrel and the scope off the ground and free of vegetation, he backed into the bamboo and, turning on his stomach, crawled using elbows and knees and the sides of his boots through bamboo and grass and spider webs, across the ridge and, pulling with his elbows and pushing with the sides of his knees and the edges of his boots, slid down a slope of high grass. In his mind he saw NVA soldiers crest the ridge behind him.

Inside the trees, out of breath, heart pounding, he slowly stood and watched the ridgeline and the long, grass-covered slope he'd just traversed, the feeling that someone was close behind him gone as soon as he stood and looked back. Not good to go low, but he'd stirred up an anthill, that was for sure, and if they sent people after him, they'd be looking for him near the top of the ridge. They wouldn't expect him to go down a long, open, grass-covered slope.

He turned and began the long hump to the pickup point, his ears still ringing, cheekbone slightly numb, the barrel of the M-14 still hot to the touch.

Twenty-one years old, and stinking of cordite and sweat. Only two and a half years removed from the teenager who'd shot those dogs as they ran grinning up a snow-covered ridge. Mr. Slide, now. Giver of death. Suffused with death. Him. A sick miasma surrounding him, gray as the ground fog beginning to appear. Dark, gnarled, vine-covered trees and broad-leafed plants grew green and slick out of the ground fog. All of it—the jungle, him—reeking of death and decay.

That was the closest he'd ever come to losing it. The forest, its shadows and great trees, had seemed for the first time an evil, haunted place. He'd felt its dark recesses watching him. For a long time, he'd sat against a tree, not really thinking, trying to let what had happened and what he'd done sort itself out in his mind. Tiny rays of sunlight had played far above as breezes moving across the forest canopy stirred branches and leaves. After a while, he'd stood, and in standing the teenager had been forever gone. In his place, Mr. Slide moved silent through shadow and ground fog, his mind and body tuned to smells and sounds, subtle changes in light and air. Moved alone through the forest, the Death Factory, ancient and green and alive, heavy with the stench of death and rot. Understanding in a felt way that killing those Marines was not so much a weight to be carried as it was a crazing of his soul, each round fired a rent in the fabric of his being. Justice to him then—and to him now—weak sustenance.

• • •

Outside the window of the Shinkansen, he watched as another Asian landscape slid by.

The first concrete and glass buildings of a small city came into view, a haphazard arrangement of narrow streets and gray and white rectangular buildings moving past the window. The doors and balconies and windows, even the railings all seemed identical. Neon signs unlit and skeletal cluttered the fronts and tops of the buildings nearest the station.

As the Shinkansen coasted through the station, clusters of people abruptly appeared on concrete platforms. Men in suits, reading papers or standing stoically, ignored the train as it hissed past. Old ladies weighted down with shopping bags and umbrellas. A knot of blue-uniformed schoolgirls, each with identical black briefcases. The train gently accelerated and the people on the platform blurred, and then they were out of the station, accelerating harder, the view quickly changing from city to country. Large, two-story farm houses sat among neat paddies, the houses roofed with traditional tile but built also with sliding glass doors and windows. Blunt-nosed trucks, most of them white, were parked in front or to the side of some of the houses.

The right thing to do, shooting those Marines? At that moment and in that place, it had not been a question of right or wrong. Just as there had been no choice when he'd shot the dogs chasing that deer, there'd been no choice when he'd shot those Marines.

Listening to the General and to his black Major, he'd been certain that he would not, could not, kill fellow Marines. He was there, and those Marines were there, because they had volunteered to serve their country. In his family, serving in the military was what all able-bodied males did before they went on to university or to job and family. It was how they

199

paid their dues for the chance to be citizens of the best damn country on the planet. Most of those Marines he'd killed—maybe all of them—had gone to Vietnam believing exactly as he had.

He'd volunteered, and they'd volunteered, young and bright and committed, most of them athletes, nearly all of them high school or college graduates, and like a slick, green bamboo viper invisible against the branches and leaves, Vietnam had reached up and bitten them before they'd even known it was there.

It hadn't taken him, or any of them, long to become disillusioned with the war. He believed then, as he believed now, that they had served not in the best interests of their people or of their country. They had served as instruments in the service of malevolent men, politicians and soldiers and businessmen alike. It had been a uniquely American blend of racism and hypocrisy and greed that had conspired to put him and that squad of Marines and those villagers and their North Vietnamese protectors in that place at that time.

He'd stayed in Vietnam not because he wanted to but because he had to. By the time his first tour was up, he'd been forced to balance his ability and his experience against the ability and experience of the man who would take his place. Likely as not, that man would have been an FNG, a Fucking New Guy. His decision to stay had been equated in terms of enemy he could kill, versus the number of enemy the FNG could kill. He'd figured that for every two or three NVA or Vietcong he killed, a Marine lived or was not seriously wounded. By the time his first tour was up, he was no longer there to serve his country; he was there to protect his fellow Marines. The arithmetic had given him no choice.

His first operation had been on Route One, the Street Without Joy, and how appropriate was that name for what was to happen. One day he'd been a lean, mean, full-of-himself Marine. A kid from Montana. A teenager who could hunt and track and shoot. And the next he'd stepped from a helicopter onto the Street Without Joy. He'd been walking that street ever since. By shooting those Marines, he'd sentenced himself to walk it forever.

Mei yeou guanshi, as the Chinese said, there was nothing to be done about it now. What was done was done.

All things considered, he'd do it again. Not shooting would have been worse. It mattered not that he'd understood those Marines, who they were and where they'd come from and how they'd come to be what they were when they entered that village. To lie there and watch them completely destroy that village, to watch them kill everyone and everything in it, men, women, children, old, young, pigs, chickens, to watch them kill every living thing for gold and silver and to assuage that black thing in their guts and in their minds–to lie there and watch all that and do nothing would have condemned him right along with them.

His anger had been directed not so much at the Marines he was watching as it had been directed at his country and his people and his God for putting him and them in that place at that time. His anger had been a function of the certain knowledge that the instant he squeezed off that first round, there would be no return, no way back to who and what he'd been up to that moment. What he had not realized, until it was all over and he was standing inside the forest, was that by executing those Marines, he had placed himself not only outside the society he'd been born to, but also outside the society of warriors to which he felt he belonged.

Among his grandmother's ancestors, the Dogs had been respected. Loners out of necessity more than choice. Accomplished warriors willing to sacrifice themselves if the situation demanded so that the tribe could live on. Lonely men, no doubt, who lived always with that bittersweet clarity known only to warriors. The sour taste of fear, the stink of death always at the edge of their consciousness. Not an easy existence, but at least the Dogs had had themselves—the camaraderie and understanding of men like themselves. Until that ville, he'd always seen being a sniper akin to being a member of that small society of Plains warriors. Afterwards, he knew that he had made himself an outcast even among them.

He sighed, watching the Japanese countryside go by.

As much as possible he spent his remaining time in the Corps in the bush. He was never alone in the bush. In the bush he was part of the food chain. Whatever genetic connection he had to Blackfeet or French or German or Mongol warriors, a childhood spent in the mountains of Montana and then in the mountains of Southeast Asia had nurtured that genetic connection, made him into Mr. Slide, a man at home only in the bush. He hadn't realized it at the time, but watching that Marine shoot the woman in the stomach, he'd begun shedding skins—a process that had been complete by the time he'd crawled away from his hide. On the other side of the ridge, moving through forest and ground fog, he had morphed into a new, more attuned, and even deadlier version of what he had been before.

It had been a dark coalescence of fates, his and theirs—the villagers and the Marines and the NVA—that's all. Just as the dogs he'd shot might have grown to be good-natured pets had they not been abandoned to die or to fend for themselves, so too might the members of that squad have grown to be reasonable and productive members of society had they not been placed in circumstances that had turned them feral. It had been his personal fate then, and it was his fate now, to be at the conjunction of those who had turned feral and those whom the feral preyed upon. The wheel had started with those dogs, and it was a wheel he couldn't seem to get off, no matter where he went or what he did.

Truth be told, he'd enjoyed it—the new version of Mr. Slide. He knew he would never again take on such a mission. And he knew there was no way he would, or could, make the Marine Corps a career. But for the rest of his tour, until he again met the black major, he'd done everything he could to go out alone.

Mr. Slide, they had called him. Spooked by the way someone his size could move through the bush. Spooked most of all by the fact that he liked to go out alone.

He smiled wryly at his reflection in the window. Looking back on it, it was amazing that the bush or the NVA or just plain old bad luck hadn't caught up with him. A snake. A liver fluke. A stray round. A booby trap. The bush had a multitude of ways to kill you.

He hadn't cared. Back then death was always with him anyway. Only in the bush had he felt alive. A Death Monster creeping the Death Factory.

And then Peter had come along.

Peter. Peter. Not yet the Pumpkin Eater.

The General's black Major.

Dawn and he'd come back through the wire after two days of an uneventful training creep with a Force Recon team, all but one of them an FNG. The powers-that-be had decided in yet another testament to their vast reservoir of experience and common sense to acquaint Force Recon with sniper tactics—never mind that the last thing a Recon team wanted to do was call attention to itself. Recon fired only when they had no other choice; he fired whenever he had a reasonable chance of not being caught.

But by then the war was about over, anyway, at least for the Marine Corps, and he was short and no longer gave a rat's ass what his Country or his Corps thought or did. After

203

two years and change in Vietnam, he was faced with the fact that it would soon be over, Vietnam, and he would be going home.

Someone on the perimeter had told him he was wanted in the Recon Commander's tent, and he'd parked his grody gear and his rifle with the Gunny, knowing that the Gunny would not let anyone touch the rifle. Grabbed a couple of cans of Orange Crush from the Recon cooler. Opened both with a church key tied to a string tacked to a wooden beam. Belched a great satisfying belch—a noise that he could never make outside the wire—and threw the empty in the shit can next to the Gunny's desk, and carried the other with him to the Recon Commander's tent.

He'd entered the tent without announcing himself and the tent had been empty except for the General's black Major sitting behind the Recon Commander's beat-to-shit metal desk still on a platform of wooden pallets at the rear of the tent. The sides of the tent had been rolled up, and the light coming in under the rolled up sides caused the upper portion of the tent and the Major from the chest up to seem in shadow. He'd never been in the tent when it wasn't cluttered with the Recon Commander's gear: his rack, and his reel-to-reel TEAC, the rickety, homemade bulletin boards with all kinds of shit tacked to them that nobody read. The bare, dirt floor made the tent seem much wider and longer than it really was.

"Sergeant Ben Tails. Have a seat."

"No."

"No?"

"No. I will not take another mission from you."

The Major laughed and leaned forward, his face from the middle of his forehead down lit by the light coming in under the tent flaps, his hands clasped on the desk in front of him.

"And what sort of mission might that be, Sergeant? Babysitting Force Recon?"

"The Major knows what I am referring to."

"No, Sergeant. The Major does not know what you are referring to. As far as the Major is concerned, the only mission you have ever been on is the one you just got back from. Are we clear on that?"

"Yes, sir."

"Then have a seat." With his right hand the Major gestured to a metal folding chair also still on pallets to one side and in front of the desk.

Ben walked slowly to the chair and sat down.

"Relax. Drink your soda."

Ben took a drink. The soda tasted too sweet and carbonated. He glanced around the tent.

"This base is history, Sergeant. Recon is out of here in two days. They'll come and get this desk as soon as we're done here."

"Yes, sir."

"Probably spend a lot of taxpayer money to ship it all the way back to the States, just so they can shit can it there."

Ben was silent.

"Word has it you are leaving the Marine Corps, Sergeant."

"Yes, sir."

"What are your plans?"

Ben shrugged. "University."

"No girl back home?"

"No, sir."

"Family?"

"Lots of relatives."

"A traffic accident, wasn't it?"

"Sir?"

"Your parents."

"I Drive Highway 93, Pray For Me," Ben said.

The Major arched his brows. "That's the highway they were killed on?"

"Yes, sir."

"Raised by your grandfather." The Major leaned back, his face in shadow. "How's he doing?"

"Passed, sir."

"No hurry to get back to Idaho, then?"

"Montana."

"Montana, *sir.*"

Ben raised the can of Orange Crush to his mouth and tilted his head back and drained the soda, watching the Major around the can. He crushed the can with one hand and dropped it next to his chair, a dull *tunk* when the can hit the wooden pallet.

The Major leaned forward into the light, his eyes laughing at Ben. "Salty, are we?" Blisters of sweat beaded the Major's wrists and forearms.

"What do you want, Major?"

The Major reached up and with his left hand grabbed the tip of his collar, bending the material, thumb behind so that the insignia sewn onto the collar tip was toward Ben.

"See this?"

"I see it."

"This is my rank." He released the collar and dropped his hand back to the desk. "I'll make Lt. Colonel someday. Colonel if I'm lucky, and if I kiss enough ass. But I'll never make General."

Ben watched him.

"Do you know why I'll never make General?"

"Only one color in the Corps, Major."

The Major laughed. "Marine Green."

"That's it."

"Uh-huh. And if frogs had wings they'd fly. They tell me you keep to yourself. Read a lot."

Ben was silent. He hadn't seen it very many times. But he'd seen it. Most officers put in their time in country, had their tickets punched, and were out of there. The Major had been around for a while—maybe a good long while. Skin black and shiny as polished glass. Patrician features. Ivy-league education. An athlete probably. It was plain that Vietnam had stripped him of most of that. Maybe he would have been promoted if he hadn't stayed in-country so long. He could tell by his eyes that he didn't like being looked at.

"What is it you read, Sergeant? Hong Kong fuck books? *Playboy?* Louis L'Amour, maybe? All you guys from Idaho must read Louis L'Amour."

Ben felt his neck and ears flush, the hair on the back of his neck stiffen.

"Am I pissing you off, Sergeant? Insulting your intelligence?"

"No, sir."

The Major studied him for a moment, his face and eyes unreadable. "It's rare to encounter a man of your talents who also reads Malraux and Conrad."

"What do you want, *sir?*"

The Major sat back, his face again in shadow, fingers of his right hand tapping the desktop.

"Where do you get your books, Sergeant?"

"A friend."

"A friend in Kuala Lumpur, maybe?" The Major smiled. "Tall. Willowy. Chastely but tastefully dressed. A university student. An orphan who lives in a dormitory run by Catholic nuns—Catholic nuns, I like that. She has dormitory curfew but she still managed to spend most of two nights with you walking the streets of Kuala Lumpur. The two of you sat for hours on a bench in a park, talking. *Talking!*" He shook his head. "You keep that shit up, Sergeant, you'll ruin your image."

Ben felt something inside switch on, like it did when he

207

stepped outside the wire. He smelled himself, the rank, moldy, animal smell of body and bush mixed with the Major's aftershave and the starch wilting in his nice, clean utilities. The musty smell of sun on canvas. The clank and tink of gear being moved. Distant laughter. Cynical laughter.

A breeze hissed across the canvas above his head. The air inside the tent was still and humid.

He should have known she was too good to be true. Not quite beautiful—and more attractive for that. Intellectual. Always challenging him to put his thoughts into words. The sexual tension between them serving only to intensify whatever it was they were talking about. Talking to her, writing to her, he'd felt clean, stimulated by ideas and thoughts, instead of by fear and adrenaline and animal reflexes—

The Major was looking at him like he'd just caught him beating his meat.

"You didn't think we were going to let someone who had done the deeds you've done wander drunk and disorderly and—for all we knew—with diarrhea of the mouth about the streets of Kuala Lumpur or Bangkok or wherever the hell you decided to go on R and R, did you?"

"I don't remember anyone like her when I took my thirty days."

"When you extended your tour the last time? You went back home to Montana. Back there it's your word against however your government wants to spin it." The Major smiled. "Look. Don't let it get you down. Whatever your relationship with her, trust me when I say that it was—is—real. I know her well, and for her, you quickly became more than just an assignment." He paused, studying Ben. "Look. Think about it. You know. I know. The General knows. The General told you there would be no paper trail, and there is none. But, here's the thing; there are a lot of other people who know, too. A whole fucking village of them—or what's

208

left of it. An entire NVA company—or what's left of it. And anything you say—anything you *ever* say—drunk or sober. When you are feeling maudlin. When you are feeling full of brag. Or when you are feeling full of whatever it is that leads you to read Malraux and talk instead of fuck all night with a seriously sexy Chinese woman—" He paused. "Are you getting the picture, Sergeant?"

"Yes."

"Anything you *ever* say in Asia about the things you've done is sooner or later going to get back to your friends in the North Vietnamese Army—and from them maybe to their Chinese and Russian advisors. I don't think you want that to happen, do you?"

"We talked about a lot of things, but never about what I do."

"Hell, I know that. I'm not here to lecture you. And I for damn sure am not here to send you on another mission." His teeth shone bone white in the shadow. "Go ahead. Ask me why I'm here."

"Why are you here, sir?"

"I'm here because I want to hire you."

The doors at the head of the compartment whisked open and a chubby, smiling young woman pushed a wheeled cart laden with *bentos* and cans of juice and beer and sweet coffee and a thermos of hot water through the doorway, and with great energy announced, *"Obento wa ikaga desu ka. Beeru ni kan juice. Kohi wa ikaga desu ka,"* and bowed and proceeded down the aisle. She stopped the cart almost immediately and handed a *bento* to a hand reaching out into the aisle.

When she got to him, he bought a can of UBC coffee, even though he knew it would be too sweet with milk and sugar.

"Xie-Xie," he said, and she smiled, recognizing the Chinese for thank you, thinking the *gaijin* believed he was speaking

Japanese. Too polite or too well schooled to correct him. *"Arigato gozaimashita,"* she said, and giggled, and moved on.

He popped the tab and took a sip. Luke warm and too sweet, but it beat drinking green tea. He hated green tea.

In hindsight, it had been typical Peter. When he'd walked into that tent empty but for desk and chair and the General's black Major, he'd known something was up. The last thing he'd expected was to have the Major explain about Shia Ling.

Shia Ling. Shia Ling had later taught him how to drink Oloong tea. Really good Oloong tea. He put the can of UBC coffee on the window ledge.

He couldn't remember now how he'd met her. Some place casual. A store or a shop, probably. "Call me Rebecca," she'd insisted. "It's easier for Americans." Rebecca. A name totally unsuited to her—perhaps by design. He'd called her Shia Ling because that was what she'd said was her Chinese name.

The General's black Major.

Peter.

Laying all that on him, and then offering to hire him. Reaching across the desk to shake his hand, introducing himself not as a Marine officer, but as a person. Peter the Snake Oil salesman. Soon to be the Pumpkin Eater. "The Green Machine doesn't know it yet, Ben, but I am *out* of here in two weeks. Hell, I'm shorter than you are."

He hadn't said anything, unable to keep up with the sudden shift in conversation.

"You thought maybe I was the General's boy. His black dog robber. A black Major instead of a white lieutenant." He smiled. "A lot of people think that."

He hadn't thought that at all. He'd assumed that the black Major was anything but a dog robber. The General's Man For All Occasions—especially those that had no paper trail.

Bad news for sure, the Major, that's what he'd thought all along. And, boy, had he been right.

"I know all about you, Ben. So let me tell you about me. I've been in Southeast Asia since '66. Platoon Commander. Company Commander. Couple of months in the hospital in Japan. Most of my time in the Corps has been spent here or in Laos or in Cambodia or Thailand or Taiwan. I've got more time in the bush than you do. Ran ops with Mung, Hmong, Cambodes. Wounded five times, if that counts." He paused, his smile thin. "I would have gone in your place except that, one, I'm a good shot but not in your league and, two, the General didn't think it politic to have a black man—an officer at that—light up a squad of white Marines."

It had been hot under the tent, and the Major's face glistened. Sweat ran down his jaw and neck, darkened the collar of his utilities.

"I'm from Cornell—the town, not the university. My father is a surgeon of some note. He teaches at Cornell, occasionally at Johns Hopkins. I ended up at the Naval Academy, chose the Corps." His eyes glittered. "You've seen pieces of Vietnam. Drank root beer in Kuala Lumpur. Me, I've seen a lot more than that—and I want to see more. I love it here. The cultures. The people. The cities—" His pupils expanded. "What?"

"Hire me to do what?"

"Well, what do you suppose?"

"Thanks, but no thanks."

Peter sat back, his eyes absorbed by the shadows, and for a long moment they had sat there like that. Peter relaxed, hands behind his head. Ben sitting upright, tired and wanting to wash, take his grody clothes off and air out the usual collection of sores and bites. Sweat tickled the back of his ear, ran down his ribs. He could smell the crushed can at his feet.

"You aren't done with this part of the world," Peter said. "And you know it."

211

Ben remained silent.

"You've had some shit details, no doubt about it. One in particular. But you extended your tour in spite of it." Peter leaned forward, face coming into the light. "What it is, Ben, is that people like us we live on death. We've been living on death since the Green Machine grabbed our sorry, naïve asses and sent us to this place. It doesn't matter what we did or what we were before we got to where we are right now. Right here. Me and you. Sitting in this miserable fucking tent. In this miserable fucking excuse for a war." He smiled thinly, his eyes black and shiny and unblinking. "None of the before matters. My family. The Naval Academy. Your family. Jesuit high school. None of it matters. This place, this war, peeled us like we were onions."

He sat back, face and head again in shadow. "This war isn't over, you know. Excuse the pun, but not by a long shot. We may have been wrong—hell, we *were* wrong to be here. But here we are, and in the process we've managed to make it wrong to *not* be here. We've put a lot of people in a position where they have no choice but to fight."

"Ben Tails. Peace Corps Sniper. Is that what you had in mind?"

Peter laughed and raised his hands in surrender. He dropped his hands back to the desk, his eyes shrewd. "People to meet, Ben. Places to go. Things to do. Asia. The Orient.

Adventure. Excitement. Women. Money. A little of what you've been doing, but most of it will simply be helping to, ah, to facilitate the exchange of goods and services."

Ben laughed, a sudden bark of derision.

"What?" Peter asked.

"Work for the spooks and die; that's the word going around the Special Forces guys."

"You won't be working for spooks."

"Yeah. I'll be working for you. But who will you be working for?"

"Work *with* me, then."

"You and who else?"

"Hell, I don't know, Ben. Does it matter? Believe me, there's no lack of work. We'll be able to pick and choose. We don't like it, we'll walk. Forget the spooks. Think of us as entrepreneurs."

"Right."

"I'm serious. The spooks play their games, but they lost control of this part of the world years ago. Before Vietnam, even."

Ben frowned. He'd never met a man so hard to read. Part of him said the man in front of him was a warrior with a warrior's sensibility and honor, but another part of him said there was too much complexity. Too many boxes within boxes. Brains or worms behind those eyes, it was impossible to say. For sure, he didn't think there was much the Major was not capable of.

He could hear the tedious sound of sweat spattering onto wood.

The Major's utilities were dark with sweat at the neck and under the arms. His face glistened. "The new spooks don't understand diddly about Asia, Ben. The old guys are almost all gone. Most of the new guys don't even speak an Asian language."

"Neither do I."

"Well, we'll fix that, don't worry. Look," he said. "Bottom line is it's like I said. We've grown up on it, what you feel when you go alone into the bush. And now it's gotten to the point that for people like us it's mother's milk—no matter how sour it sometimes tastes. There's nothing for us back home. Not yet, anyway."

Ben looked down. The colors of the bent and twisted Orange

Crush can looked vulgar in the sunlight. He reached down and picked up the can and put it on the desk.

"I know you, Ben. I knew you when we first met—and you knew me."

Ben grimaced.

"Well, who do you think you are, Ben? Some kind of noble savage running around the forests and fields of Vietnam? The Last of the Mohicans, or some such shit. You've been reading too much; that's your problem. This is Vietnam. It's not about right and wrong. It's not about a heart of darkness. It's not even about principles. And it's sure not about honor, duty, country."

"What is it about then?"

The Pumpkin Eater leaned forward, eyes glittering. "You want to know what it's all about?"

"Yeah. I do."

"I don't have a clue. I only know what it's not." A thick vein pulsed at the side of his temple. "Bottom line. You're not just a shooter. You've got a brain. I need someone with a brain. Someone I can count on. Someone with your experience."

"Someone without principles, you mean."

"Principles are not an issue. In a few months you'll understand that."

Ben stood.

"Think about it," Peter said, looking up at him. "If you don't like it, you can always catch the next bird out."

Ben stepped off the pallet, and Peter shoved his chair back and stood. "End your enlistment in Okinawa. I'll arrange it. Fly to Taipei. Stay at the Mandarin. I'll hook up with you in a week or two."

Outside the tent, Ben stripped off his skivvy shirt. A breeze began to dry the sweat. But instead of cooling, the breeze against his wet, oily skin had made him feel scaly. Desiccated. The heat of his body contained by the dried sweat.

• • •

The broad valley was shrinking, mountains moving rapidly toward the train as it slid past pre-war wooden houses and sheds and small, irregular-shaped paddies. Grass and forest encroached on dirt paths that meandered between forest and paddies.

He'd left the Marines and gone to Taipei and Shia Ling had been there to meet him—Shia Ling and her three children and her husband. He smiled at the memory. For two weeks, she and her family had taken him under their wing. Put him in an apartment. Enrolled him in a language program at *Shi Dah*. Showed him Taipei. Some of the restaurants and stores. The Palace Museum. Even lined him up with a tutor—old Ma *Laoshi*, tough as any Marine Corps drill instructor.

He hadn't known it then but Shia Ling and her husband worked for Huang. The last he'd heard they were living in Shiamen, which, come to think of it, was where Huang had said Peter was now living. The kids must be about grown by now. Damn. He hadn't thought of them for a long time. Truly, what a long, strange trip it had been. Except that back then it hadn't been strange at all. Back then what must have seemed strange to most people had been just life for him. Things happened—had happened—that was all. One thing led to another. And until he had gone back to Montana, he hadn't stopped long enough to consider the fact that maybe the directions his life had taken were anything other than normal.

Taipei had been good to him. A refuge from the rest of Southeast Asia. He'd wandered the streets at night, sometimes talking with the soldiers and Marines guarding strategic points around the city. His favorite place had been the Museum.

215

There was an ancient sculpture of a bird-like creature in an exhibit on the bottom level, and he would spend an hour or so every time he visited the Museum staring at the creature. The creature had a power over him that he could not define, only feel. Other pieces in the Museum also affected him, but none in the way and to the extent that did that ancient sculpture. He'd plotted ways to steal it.

Peter introduced him to a dojo, and that, too, became an escape. A few years later, he'd been accepted to another dojo— one that had never before included a Westerner.

He grimaced. That had all ended after his last foray to Laos and Cambodia. The old *sensei* had taken one look at him, shaken his head, and wandered off. No one had said anything; there was no need.

He'd left the dojo, and he'd never gone back. Not to the dojo. Not to Taipei. Not to the creature on the bottom floor of the Museum. He'd left everything—his paintings, his pottery collection, furniture, clothes, even his bank account—and gone back to Montana.

And found himself a stranger in his own land. Five thousand dollars and his grandfather's old house and five-hundred acres, give or take, of trees and meadows and mountain, and a beat-to-hell old International four-by-four to his name. Blood thinned by more than a decade spent in tropical environments. The mountains and forests of Montana too open and with too many people to be comfortable. He'd be drunk in a bar and he'd begin a joke in English and finish it in Mandarin and not know what he'd done until he'd see the faces around him.

He'd fixed up the old house. New roof. New wiring. Learned how to do things as he went along. Painted it inside and out. Installed indoor plumbing. A furnace. A new porch.

And sold it along with five acres, keeping the other four

hundred and ninety five acres for himself. He'd rented one of Manfred's apartments.

And somehow convinced himself that if not happy at least he was at peace. As full of bullshit and jokes as the rest of the good old boys who'd meet for coffee every morning at Marie's Café. Taking life a day at a time, until one day—a clean, beautiful spring day, nearly a month before the start of fishing season. Bearded. Pony tailed. The old International grumbling and rattling down a gravel road, headed for a fishing hole not yet clouded by spring runoff. Cold beer in the cooler on the seat next to him. He smiled out the window of the Shinkansen. A spring day perfect as only a spring day in Montana could be. So engrossed in feeling good that he hadn't noticed the Sheriff's car slip up behind him until the siren squawked.

He'd pulled over and the new Sheriff—Robert Lee, only he hadn't know him then because Robert Lee had been gone to the FBI Academy when he had returned from Asia; had only heard about him from Manfred—clean shaven and spiffy in a new uniform, had come up to the window.

"Howdy."

"Howdy to you, too."

"You probably wonder why I stopped you."

"Nope."

"Nope?"

"You probably think I'm a nefarious criminal masquerading as a fisherman or something."

"Nefarious?"

"Either that or my tags have expired."

"You are Ben Tails, that's who you are. Manfred has told me all about you, and notorious would be a better fit than nefarious." He stuck his hand in the window for Ben to shake. "Robert Lee."

"Howdy, Sheriff Robert Lee. I've heard about you, too."

"I'm looking for a few good men."

"Now where have I heard that before?"

"The pay sucks. The hours suck. You can never please any of the people any of the time." Robert Lee had stepped back and looked at the side of the truck. "But looking at you in this poster child for a moving vehicle violation, I figure you'd be perfect for the job."

He'd become a deputy. Shaved off his beard, cut his hair, and surprised himself by being good at it. A while later he'd met Evy. And then Evy had died. And here he was: looking out the window of a Japanese bullet train, waiting for a woman who bothered him more than even Evy had bothered him, on his way to God only knew what.

The train slowed as it entered a tight pass in the mountains, the mountainside abruptly close and green with thick, scrubby foliage. Across from him, Kei settled into her seat. She crossed her legs and smiled at him.

"We'll be changing trains at the next stop," she said.

Chapter 10
Ohmihachiman

The taxi turned into a narrow, paved lane barely wide enough for the taxi. High wooden walls topped with long, narrow roofs of gray or blue tile, and the sides and backs of white stucco or wood-sided buildings lined both sides of the lane. Here and there low, sliding wood doors marked entrances. Only the pavement and the gray concrete power poles prevented the lane from being a scene out of the Japan of two or three hundred years ago.

"This part of the city has been preserved as a historical site," Kei said. She was seated next to him, behind the driver.

The interior of the taxi was spotless. Snow-white cloth covers, instead of the usual plastic, covered the seats. The driver was old and thin, with a straggling moustache and wispy white goatee. Most taxi drivers wore shirt and tie or a uniform of some kind, but their driver was wearing a tan, lightweight jacket. Most taxi drivers wore gloves, but he wore none.

"The buildings you see are centuries old," she said. "Our family house is more than two-hundred years old—as old as the United States."

A small, portly, gray-haired man a block or so ahead stood alone in the otherwise empty lane.

The lane made Ben uncomfortable. The walls and buildings lining both sides were too high to easily climb. Entranceways were built to within a few feet of the edge of the pavement.

Even as slow as they were going, if someone stepped through an entranceway into the lane, there would be no chance for the taxi to stop in time.

He noticed that most of the entranceways were built low so that even a short person would have to bend forward to enter—a throwback to a time when *samurai* would be vulnerable for the time it took to bend and step over the threshold.

The taxi stopped a few meters from the man. He was standing to the side of an open entranceway.

"Thank you, uncle," Kei said in Japanese to the driver. "We'll get out here," she said in English to Ben.

He opened the door and they climbed out. As soon as he shut the door, the taxi moved away, leaving him and Kei and the portly, gray-haired man standing alone in the lane.

"Mr. Tails," the man said. Late seventies, Ben guessed. Hair parted to the left and brushed up in front, a big smile on his round, bespectacled face. "My name is Mitsunari Ishida." He bowed. "I am honored that you could visit on such short notice." His English was precise, with a slight British accent—the English of someone fluent in the language but not accustomed to speaking it. He extended his hand toward Ben.

"Thank you," Ben said, careful of the frail hand in his. "I am honored to be here." He had long ago learned that most Japanese men were uncomfortable shaking hands. Most offered handshakes that were limp at best, and he'd inadvertently hurt more than a few before he'd adjusted. Mr. Ishida's handshake was firm; there just wasn't much strength in his hand.

"Please." Mr. Ishida gestured toward the entrance. "After you."

"Watch your head," Kei said. He could hear the laughter in her voice, and he had a mental picture of himself stooping low, a big *gaijin* taking up the entire doorway.

Inside it was another world, the narrow, claustrophobic lane difficult to reconcile with the openness and spaciousness of the compound. A stone walkway led between gnarled pines trimmed like giant *bonsai*, across a graveled yard landscaped with small boulders and meticulously trimmed shrubs, to a long, single-storied house. The house was white stucco with a traditional gray-tile roof. Behind the house he could see the upper story of a much taller structure—an old warehouse, perhaps—the gabled end of the building topped with a steep, tiled roof, the broad wall latticed with dark, wood beams. At the peak and at the tail ends of the roof were stone figures weathered and pitted. Tall bamboo rose above and to the sides of the larger structure.

He stepped to the side as Mr. Ishida and then Kei came through the entranceway. The door rattled loosely as Kei slid it shut.

The walkway was intersected by other walkways that led through shrubs and trees to other, smaller buildings. From somewhere he could hear the tinkle of water. A pool stocked with carp, he thought. He reckoned the compound took up at least three acres—an unbelievable amount of space inside a Japanese city. He had a mental image of his grandfather's old house: kitchen, living room, two bedrooms, an outhouse out back. "This is beautiful," he said.

"At one time, this city was devoted to commerce," Mr. Ishida said. "Canals connected it to Lake Biwa. It was much safer in those days to transport goods by water than to risk the roads. A castle on a nearby hill protected the canals and the merchant compounds below. This is the last of those compounds. The large building that you see to the rear of the main house is what is left of a series of large warehouses."

"Your family were merchants then?"

Mr. Ishida smiled. "My father's family were merchants and, later, doctors and engineers, even an architect. Kei's mother's

221

side of the family are descendents of *samurai.* That is where Kei gets her height."

Let's hear it for the *samurai,* Ben thought.

"Kei's mother was an accomplished poet and artist. It is from her that Kei gets her talent for photography." He smiled a father's smile at Kei. "And her temper."

"I understand you were in the Navy during the War?"

"During the war every able-bodied male was in the military, Mr. Tails. I was lucky. I experienced no combat during the War, only the bombing. In fact, I did not go abroad until after the War. But come," he said. "You must be tired from the journey. Kei, will you please show Mr. Tails to the guest quarters. After you freshen up, we will have tea," he said to Ben. "I hope you do not mind, but I have invited someone to join us."

"Of course not. Thank you for asking."

"I think perhaps you have already met." Behind his glasses Mr. Ishida's eyes were unreadable. "His name is Sato. Captain Sato."

Chapter 11
Tea Time

Kei led him along a serpentine stone walkway, past a well-tended Japanese garden. The fresh rake lines in the sand curved gently around rocks and along mossy borders. From outside the guesthouse appeared a small, traditional Japanese house.

She slid open the latticed wood and glass door. A long, wood-floored hallway stretched from the *genkan*, the entranceway, to the far end of the house. Sliding *shoji* screen doors lined both sides of the hallway.

"You have a choice," she said, slipping off her shoes and stepping up onto the hardwood floor. Pairs of light-yellow slippers were arrayed on the floor. She stepped into a pair and walked down the hallway, sliding open doors on both sides of the hallway.

He kicked off his shoes and stepped up onto the floor. All of the slippers were too small for his *gaijin* feet. Sunlight lit the *tatami* floor in the room to his right. A low table surrounded by flat pillows sat in the center of the room. The room on the other side was a carpeted Western-style living room filled with tan and brown, comfortable-looking couches and chairs, a glass coffee table. A modern home entertainment center took up the far wall, its doors open to reveal a large television and a bank of receivers and stereo equipment. Through a door at the far end of the living room he glimpsed a western-style bed and dresser.

"You have the house to yourself," she said. "There is a small kitchen off the living room. You'll find it well stocked. Please help yourself."

There were two toilet rooms at the end of the hall, one with a Western-style toilet complete with heated, padded seat. A complicated-looking control module was mounted on the wall next to the toilet.

"Whoa," he said. "Beam me up, Scotty."

She laughed.

Two other doors opened to the bathrooms, one with a vanity and mirror and sink and an American-made tub/shower combination complete with sliding glass doors; the other a typical Japanese bathroom with inch-square, blue-green tiles on floor and walls, white tile on the ceiling, large drain in the middle of the floor. The *furo*, the hot tub, looked large enough even for him. A tiny stool and a stack of plastic basins were placed in front of a hand-held shower and a large mirror mounted at waist height above the floor. Shower. Wash. Soak. Repeat the process as many times as you liked. Splash water all over; you were supposed to. If he ever built a house in Montana, it would have a Japanese-style bathroom.

Kei was back down the hall at the entrance to the *tatami* room. "Your bag is in this room," she said. "But if you'd rather sleep on a bed with a mattress, please feel free to move to the other bedroom. You'll find towels and toiletries in the small closet between the bathing rooms." She was backlit by sunlight coming through the doorway to the *tatami* room, and he couldn't make out her eyes or the expression on her face. It felt curiously intimate to be alone with her in the house.

"If you'd like to use the facilities," she said, "I'll wait for you in the living room."

"Is this tea thing formal?"

"No. It's just tea."

"Just tea?" he said.

"Yes."

He still could not make out her features, but he could feel her looking at him. She made no move to leave.

"Just tea," he said again.

"Yes."

"With Captain Sato."

She was silent.

"Do you know Sato, Kei?"

"Yes, I know him." Her voice was quiet.

"Do you mind if I ask how you know him?"

"How I know him is not germane."

"Not *germane?*"

"It was a long time—a little more than ten years ago. We did *omiai.*"

He knew that *Omiai* meant a date or a series of dates arranged by a professional matchmaker. Most marriages were the result of *omiai*. Three dates and you were serious.

"Once," she said.

"I see." The fact that the relationship had not progressed beyond the first date told him that probably it had been Kei who had rejected Sato, not the other way around.

"No. I don't think you do," she said. "You must be very careful of him."

"Oh? And why is that?"

"It is complicated."

He was silent.

"My country is in trouble, Mr. Tails. I'm sure you know this. Education. The economy. Politics. Nothing seems to work very well these days, and it is getting worse, not better. Captain Sato is a member of a group of young Japanese Police and Military officers who are talking about taking things into their own hands. Change is necessary, but their reasons are the wrong reasons, and their methods would be disastrous."

225

She came closer to him, her eyes luminous in the shadow of her face. "But much more important to you is the fact that you broke his face." She spoke the *you broke his face* in Mandarin. "Do you understand?" she said, also in Mandarin.

He understood all right. In Japan—in most of Asia—men such as Sato lived by face. They had no sense of the Western concept of sin. Only of face. There was no equivalent in Western cultures. Loss of face, sure. But she had deliberately used Mandarin to emphasize the fact that he'd done much more than cause Sato to merely lose face. He'd "broken" his face. He had a sudden image of Carlos with his arm around Sato, Sato's leather coat bunched up around his ears.

He felt her hand soft on his arm. "My father understands," she said, "But my father has become old and somewhat reclusive, and it sometimes seems to him as if all his hard work has been for nothing. To him, despite their obvious faults, Sato and his group are young, energetic, idealistic. He remembers himself when he was their age."

"He agrees with them?"

"No. It's not like that. My father is the last one who wants history to repeat itself." Her hand left his arm. "He hopes to channel Sato's group toward something more productive."

"Fat chance."

"I agree. But I have little say in the matter."

"Your father strikes me as a wise man."

She nodded. "He is. But you must not antagonize Sato. No matter how rude and overbearing, you must not react to his rudeness. My father is a Board member of Raven. And as such there is no question that he will back you. But please remember that he is also Japanese."

"Why am I here? Can you tell me that?"

"I don't know why you are here. I haven't had a chance to talk with my father. Always before it was Uncle Jim or Huang *xian-sheng* who came."

226

"*Uncle* Jim," he said.

She smiled. "Yes, Uncle Jim."

"You know Jim?"

She laughed. "Only for as long as I can remember. When I was at school in Boston, he would take my father and me on fishing trips to upstate New York. He taught us both how to fly fish."

There was a commotion from the direction of the front gate. Loud voices. A harsh, imperious laugh that he would recognize anywhere.

"The guests have arrived," he said. "Are you going to be all right?"

"Of course."

"Are you sure?"

"Did Uncle Jim ever tell you about Mr. Slide?"

She frowned. "Mr. Slide? I don't think so."

He smiled and gestured toward the door. "Tea time," he said.

Chapter 12
Face

The floor of the main house *genkan*, like the guesthouse *genkan*, was concrete. The blond hardwood floor of the main house was raised about a foot above the concrete. A large, reddish, earth-colored urn filled with umbrellas stood in one corner. A variety of men's shoes, all black, were lined neatly in pairs at the base of the step up to the hardwood floor, all pointed back toward the doorway. Tan slippers, several gaps in the line, were arrayed on the edge of the hardwood floor. One pair was noticeably larger than the others.

He stepped out of his shoes and up onto the hardwood floor. "Let me guess," he said, stepping into the extra-large pair of slippers.

Kei moved past him down the hallway. "This way, please," she said, her voice formal. She slid back a *shoji* door, and gestured him inside and, an unaccustomed nervousness in the pit of his stomach—the way he'd felt when as a kid he had to stand in front of the class and give a speech or a report—he bent his head to clear the doorframe and stepped into an unexpectedly large *tatami* room. Sliding paper screens diffused sunlight coming through the windows.

At the far end of the room Mr. Ishida and Sato and a tall, slim, handsome man in Self Defense Forces uniform rose from around a polished, dark-hardwood table low to the floor.

Exposed beams stained the same light-blond color as the hardwood floor in the hallway outlined the corners and ceiling and were placed every ten feet or so to break up the white walls. Scrolls of different length and width were scattered about the walls.

Behind Sato the wall was recessed into a *tokonoma*, a large, paneled niche containing a long scroll depicting a scene out of old Japan—people sitting under cherry blossoms. A clay pot, the *koro*, a pot for scent, was placed in front of the scroll. Mr. Ishida sat to Sato's right, the man in SDF uniform to his left. A pillow had been placed on the floor across the table from Sato.

"Please join us, Mr. Tails," Mr. Ishida said.

This sucks already, Ben thought, smiling as he crossed the floor to the table. His back would be to the door. The host or the guest of honor normally sat with his back to the *tokonoma*. The host was supposed to sit across from the guest, where the pillow had been left for him.

"You know Captain Sato, I believe."

Sato inclined his head in the merest of bows, a sneer nearly breaking through his smile. Sato and Mr. Ishida were wearing suit and tie. Light gray for Mr. Ishida; blue for Sato. A blue and yellow striped school tie for Sato; dark maroon silk for Mr. Ishida.

"And this is Major Ishii."

The Major was a vain man, Ben thought. Short hair permed just enough to give it a slight wave. A touch of gray at the temples. Broad shoulders, but no real muscle, his features and hair more Western than Japanese. A poster boy for the SDF.

"So nice to meet you," the Major said. He made no move to shake hands. His face was without expression; his eyes filled with contempt.

"Major."

"Please. Please sit down everyone," Mr. Ishida said.

"Perhaps we should move to the other room," Sato said to Mr. Ishida in Japanese. "No doubt sitting on the floor is uncomfortable for the *gaijin*."

Mr. Ishida smiled and, his voice gentle, said in Japanese, "We will speak English today, Sato-san. My daughter will translate should I need help."

"Thank you for your concern," Ben said in English to Sato. "But this is fine." He made his smile warm, thinking, Mr. Slide, he slide in; he slide out. Until he figured out what this little tete-a-tete was about, he would be the big, good-natured American. A little doofus, and, like all Americans, incapable of holding a grudge.

He waited for Mr. Ishida to sit and then quickly sat before the other two could. He crossed his legs Indian fashion: your basic U.S. Marine Corps sitting position—a position he could maintain for hours if need be.

"This room is great," he said to Mr. Ishida. *"Amazing,"* he said to Sato. "I'd love to have a room like this back home," he said to the Major.

The Major stared at him—a biologist examining a new bug.

Someone shuffled quickly across the *tatami* behind him, and Kei knelt between her father and him. She placed a large, square, black and red lacquered tray on the floor behind him and from it took ceramic teacups with matching lids and placed them on the table. She put a cup in front of her father, then one in front of him, and then reached across the table to put cups in front of Sato and the Major. He could see that Sato did not like the fact that she had breached Japanese etiquette by serving her father first, Sato and the Major last.

"Dozo," Mr. Ishida said.

The three men reached for their teacups. Ben removed the lid on his and inhaled the smell. Green tea. He hated green tea. He smiled at everyone and took a drink. The better the grade, the worse it tasted, and this was a pretty good grade. He carefully placed his teacup on the table and gently replaced the lid. Looking down at the teacup, he folded his hands in his lap, smiling at nothing in particular.

Kei stirred and from the tray on the floor behind him took a ceramic teapot that matched the cups. "More tea?" she asked.

He held his hand over his cup. "I'm fine," he said. "Thank you."

She stood and walked around the table and knelt between Sato and the Major and refilled their cups. He saw a look that he could not decipher pass between her and her father.

He winked at Sato.

Mr. Ishida turned to him. "Mr. Tails, I have asked Captain Sato and Major Ishii to join us today in the hope that we can restore the relationship pioneered by Raven International— by Mr. Jim and myself so many years ago."

"I'm afraid, sir, that I can only speak for myself."

Mr. Ishida smiled, his eyes behind his spectacles sharp and probing. "Before Jim-san departed for the United States, he made it clear that you may speak for him."

Ben stared at him. He felt Sato and the Major looking at him. Returned to the States? Not to somewhere else in East or Southeast Asia? He felt the hairs prick at the back of his neck. "To be frank, Mr. Ishida, I'm a little out of my depth with all this."

Sato snorted.

Kei knelt between Ben and her father and began to translate everything in a low voice. There were to be no misunderstandings, no excuses later offered because of language, Ben realized.

Mr. Ishida bowed his head slightly. "Perhaps you underestimate yourself."

"With all due respect, sir. I don't think so."

231

Sato laughed—a humorless sound that said there was no way Ben could underestimate himself. Ben was careful not to look at him.

Mr. Ishida smiled. "Be that as it may, Jim-san has indicated his trust. It is important that you speak for him, especially since I have—how do you say?—a conflict of interest in this matter."

Ben stared down at his teacup for a moment. Thanks a fucking lot, Jim, he thought. He picked up the cup and examined it more closely. It was handmade and very old, the workmanship exquisite. So thin and strong he thought that it would perhaps ring like fine crystal if he flicked it with his fingertip. He carefully placed the cup on the table. Something was haywire or Jim would be there. Well, if they wanted a bull in the china shop, it was on their heads, not his.

He looked up at Sato, letting a little of it leak out. "Then, perhaps this *gentleman* could explain why he had a man murdered, instead of merely deported, as had been agreed." Sato's face flushed. "Our understanding was that the man would not be seriously harmed," Ben said.

Sato's fist hit the table, stopping Kei's murmured translation. The cups and their lids jumped and rattled. Ben held his cup off the tabletop.

In Japanese Sato said to Mr. Ishida: "This is Japan. I do not have to explain anything to this *gaijin*. The man in question represented a serious threat to Japan."

Ben glanced at Mr. Ishida. Mr. Ishida was staring down at the table, his face blank.

"The *man's* name," Ben said to Sato, "was Carlos Montoya."

"You Americans," Sato said in English, his voice ugly. "You are like rats eating at the foundation of the world. You take no responsibility for your actions. You do not even *acknowledge* obligations that attend your wealth and power. You are a disease."

The Major smirked.

Careful to keep his voice mild, Ben said, "The Japanese police murdered a citizen of the United States of America."

"Yes. And if more like him come to this country, they will meet the same fate."

Ben smiled what he hoped was a Japanese smile. "If you felt so strongly, why did you ask us to investigate?"

"We did not ask you to do anything," the Major said.

"Men like you–men who are answerable to no one–have controlled the destiny of this country for too long," Sato said. "Men like you have turned our young men into drones incapable of any fight, except the fight to be a drone." He turned his head toward Mr. Ishida. "Ishida-san, look at what is happening to our country because of men like this."

Ben realized that Sato was using him as an excuse to say what he wanted to say to Mr. Ishida. Mr. Ishida must have known from the moment Sato's fist hit the table that Sato was here to deliver a scripted message.

"We are become a nation of worker ants," Sato said to Mr. Ishida. "Neurotic. Spineless. Without honor or principle. *On* and *giri* have been warped, made meaningless. We have no face. And all because America will not accept the responsibility and obligation of its wealth and power." He glared at Ben. "Khomeini was right. They are the Great Satan. Their wealth spawns hypocrisy and a sick competition for material goods. We can no longer work with men like this man here."

"Don't be shy," Ben said. He felt Kei's hand pinch hard the skin behind his kidney. "Tell us what you really think."

Sato stared at him for a moment. He glanced at the Major, and they both rose to their feet.

Ben stood also. The message had been not in what they

had said but in how they had said it.

Sato said in Japanese to Mr. Ishida's bowed head, "Today we talk with you." He glanced at Ben and said in English, "Tomorrow perhaps not."

At the doorway Sato turned and looked at Ben. "Personally," he said in English, his small eyes flat and without expression, "I look forward to tomorrow." He turned and left the room.

Ben heard them putting on their shoes. The sound of the door sliding open, and not closing. Sato's voice on the walkway, the arrogance in it. The Major's laugh. The outer gate banged open, and a car started up in the street. Car doors opened and closed, and a car motored slowly away, down the lane.

He turned toward Mr. Ishida. Mr. Ishida was staring without expression at the table. Kei looked up at him, her eyes hot, shiny with tears of anger and humiliation.

He wasn't sure if he should sit down and say something, or if he should just leave, collect his bag, and get the hell out of Dodge. Sato probably had those two big *judoka* waiting for him. Now that he'd met the Major, he'd bet the smaller guys with leaded pipes were SDF.

"Please sit down, Mr. Tails," Mr. Ishida said. He sighed and looked up. "Kei-chan, could we have some tea, please. He smiled at Ben. "Black tea. I don't think Mr. Tails has yet acquired a taste for green tea."

Ben sat. He watched as Kei gathered the teacups and saucers and placed them on the tray. She picked up the tray and stood and quickly left the room.

"Their bark is worse than their bite," Mr. Ishida said. "Isn't that what you Americans say?"

"I don't know. It sounded like a declaration of war to me."

"Their words were meant for me. Did you understand that?"

"Yes. By speaking to me, he allowed you to keep face."

Mr. Ishida smiled. "Jim-san told me you understand these things."

"But by speaking that way and with those words, he was speaking to me as much as he was speaking to you. He is letting his personal feelings affect his judgement."

Mr. Ishida regarded him for a moment. His eyes communicated nothing. Exactly like Jim, Ben thought. Or Huang. But where Jim and Huang were creased and weathered, all gristle and bone, Mr. Ishida was soft, portly, a scholar. And like most scholars and priests, only his gray, almost-white hair, and a few age spots on his face and hands indicated his true age. Nevertheless, despite their physical differences, he'd be a fool to think that Ishida was any less than Jim and Huang. The three of them were like peas in a pod. He wondered if Sato and Ishii knew what they had taken a bite out of.

"Sato and I have a history," Ben said.

"Yes, and I am afraid that my daughter has added to that history."

"Your daughter?"

Mr. Ishida smiled. "You remind me so much of Jim-san when he was your age."

Ben frowned. Mr. Ishida's grasp of the English language was much more sophisticated than he'd thought.

"Have you studied our history, Mr. Tails?"

"A little."

"Some of our young men today are much like the young men of my day."

"You mean Sato and the Major?"

"Captain Sato and his friends believe that Japan is an American creation."

"Well, it's hard to argue with that."

"Yes. On the surface. But in truth, we Japanese have no one to blame but ourselves for our present condition." Mr. Ishida smiled. "Men like Captain Sato take the mythical past–

235

the Japan of old–to be a fact. They refuse to recognize the myth."

"Every country must have people like Sato, Mr. Ishida."

"Humanity is like a generator, Mr. Tails. And like all generators, humanity must have a . . . what is the word? . . . polarity. Yes, a polarity. What you call good and evil, those are the poles of our existence. We are at our strongest when caught between the two. The weakest among us–men like Captain Sato and Major Ishii–do not understand that the conflict between the two poles is what brings out the best in us."

"By weak, you mean dangerous."

"Yes, that is what I mean."

"In the case of Captain Sato, just how dangerous is dangerous–if you don't mind my asking?"

Mr. Ishida smiled. "I have heard from Jim-san that you spent some time in Cambodia during the latter years of the Vietnam Conflict."

"I did."

"The Khmer Rouge were nothing new in human history, Mr. Tails. Like some of our soldiers in Nanjing during the Second World War, the Khmer Rouge continued to kill long after their goals had been reached. You see, in the course of waging war, they had discovered new appetites, and in order to satisfy those appetites, they created enemies where before there were none. And then after they had killed those new enemies, they discovered that the killing had only increased their appetite for enemies." He smiled. "Can you understand what I am trying to say? My English is so poor."

"Your English is great. And I understand." And he did. Sato and Ishii would have fit perfectly with those demented little fucks that had made him kneel in the dust on the road to Thailand. "But as far as I am concerned, whether such

236

people are created or are born the way they are doesn't much matter. All that matters is that they are what they are."

"Ah," Mr. Ishida said. " But it does matter if our institutions are responsible for creating such people." He smiled. "Today, America sets the standards by which the world must live. But it is the nature of America to be in a constant state of change. This fact is merely life to most Americans. But to much of the world this constant state of change is unnatural. You must understand that outside of America and a few European countries, most people are raised to be essentially reactionary. And like all reactionaries, when threatened with change their instinct is not so much to govern as it is to compel."

Ben smiled. "An unhealthy situation."

"Yes, Mr. Tails. That is exactly what it is. Unhealthy. Especially for Japan."

"Is that why I'm here, then?"

"You and others like you, Mr. Tails, represent the generation that will follow men like Jim-san and myself."

"I don't understand."

"There is always a point of contact between cultures and peoples," Mr. Ishida said. "Not the contact between heads of State or heads of business, I don't mean that. Such people are always out for something they want. They use people like us to get it for them. Of course, we understand this. There is nothing unusual about it. We go along with it because our reasons are not their reasons. No, the point of contact that I speak of transcends national and economic boundaries." Mr. Ishida smiled. "I am told that these ideas are not unknown to you?"

"In the world you speak of, I am a soldier, Mr. Ishida. Nothing more."

"Let me put it another way then: the most important contacts between peoples are those contacts that allow us to adapt to each other on a personal level."

Ben frowned. "The company I work for, and that you help direct, operates outside national concepts of law and order. Isn't there as much danger inherent in something like Raven as there is in people who are, as you say, essentially reactionary in their thought and intent?"

"Indeed there is, Mr. Tails. Indeed there is. But the danger in an organization such as Raven lies not in the wish to compel or to govern, but in the fact that after a while, as you Americans say, it knows where too many bodies are buried. That knowledge can be a source of great power, especially if placed in the hands of men like Captain Sato and Major Ishii."

"Can I ask you a question?"

"Of course."

"Why am I here? I understand what you are saying, but as I said, I am just a soldier."

"You are here, and Jim-san is not, because some of our young men are attempting to borrow a page from the American book."

Ben raised his eyebrows.

"The idea is to provoke *gaijin* to fight *gaijin*," Mr. Ishida said. "It is the Guam Doctrine in reverse."

Ben was silent. The Guam Doctrine had been Nixon's rationalization for a policy that aimed to get Asians to fight Asians. The Hmong who fought for the United States lost nearly every male between the ages of fourteen and forty. The Khmer Rouge flourished. He understood the Guam Doctrine perfectly. Sato was trying to get the two assholes he'd met at Coffee Shop ChaCha to fight Jim. But the target was not Jim. The target was Raven—the secrets and connections and wealth that Raven possessed. That's what Mr. Ishida was trying to tell him. Nothing else made sense.

Sato and his Japanese buddies wanted Raven; the two American assholes, the "big boys," wanted Raven.

"I have another question," Ben said. "I hope you won't take offense."

"Please."

"Am I right in assuming that you hoped Sato would one day take over some of your responsibilities?"

Mr. Ishida's eyes glinted with amusement. He chuckled. "No. Not Sato, Mr. Tails. My daughter, Kei."

Chapter 13
Stretched

"Good evening," Kei said. She was wearing dark slacks and a white blouse and an old, unbuttoned, ratty-looking sweater, the sleeves pulled up to her elbows. She looked scrubbed, healthy, her hair freshly washed and braided. Her eyes held no hint of what had transpired with Sato and the major that afternoon.

"Good evening." The same pair of oversized slippers was pointed heels toward him on the raised hardwood floor. He stepped up onto the raised hardwood floor and slid his feet into the slippers.

"We will be joining my father for dinner in his living quarters. My uncle has been delayed in Nagoya and will not be here until later."

"Great. I'm tired of meeting people."

"This way," she said, and turned and led him down the long, broad hallway, doors open on either side to reveal spacious *tatami* rooms, including the one in which they had met Sato and the Major. At the far end of the hallway, the top third of the doorway was partially obscured by a dark-blue cloth hung above the doorway.

"Watch your head,' she said, moving to the side to let him enter first.

He raised the cloth, ducked low and stepped into a much

older house. He could smell an underlying dampness—mold in places he could not see. There was a large *tatami* room in front of him, the *tatami* old and worn, almost brown. Dark, rough-hewn posts about eight inches in diameter held up the ceiling. All of the wood in the room was stained dark brown, nearly black. The stucco walls had aged to yellow-gold, cracks showing here and there.

He smelled cooking food, but underneath the smell of cooking food he caught a whiff of something unpleasant and at the same time familiar. His grandfather's house had not had an indoor toilet, and he'd grown up using an outhouse. He knew that many old houses in Japan—including, apparently, this one—still had what amounted to an indoor outhouse.

Mr. Ishida, dressed casually in gray slacks and checked gray and white sweater, was standing next to a large *kotatsu*—a table with a heating element mounted to the underside. When it was cold—and it must get very cold in this part of the house, Ben thought, especially when it snowed—the *kotatsu* would be draped with a heavy quilt, a removable, hardwood top placed over the quilt, and people would sit covered to the waist, their legs and feet under the heat element. Sitting under a *kotatsu* in the winter always made him fall asleep.

"Please come in, Mr. Tails."

There were slippers lined up just outside the *tatami.*

"It's okay," Kei said. "Keep your slippers on."

"Yes. Yes. It is quite all right," Mr. Ishida said. "Please come in."

To Mr. Ishida's right, large *shoji* doors were opened part way to reveal yet another *tatami* room. As he crossed the floor to the table, Ben realized that all the rooms were connected by large, sliding doors. If all the doors were opened, most of the rest of the house would become one large room.

The corner of the room to the left of Mr. Ishida was devoted to a dark-paneled cove filled with a large, ornate family altar, candles and incense sticks in bowls and pictures of departed ancestors haphazard on the altar.

Framed, glass-covered calligraphy lined the top of the walls, each frame a couple of feet long and a foot or so wide, attached by wires so that the frames tilted out from the ceiling, making it easy to look up from wherever you were sitting to read the calligraphy.

"This part of the house must be very old," Ben said.

Mr. Ishida gestured Ben to the side of the table facing the *shoji* doors and the rest of the house. "Yes," he said. "Very old."

"My grandparents died when my father was in high school," Kei said. "Both of them. A sickness of some sort. My father was left to raise his brothers and sisters. This was the house they lived in then."

Ben waited for Mr. Ishida to sit before lowering himself to the pillow.

"It was wartime," Mr. Ishida said. "Not yet with the United States, but in Korea and Manchukuo. There was no help to be had. Everyone was working in war industries."

"It must have been difficult."

"We thought so." Mr. Ishida smiled. "But looking back on it, it was one of the best times of my life."

"When I was a child, my father always made Sunday breakfast," Kei said. She took a seat across from her father, next to Ben.

"After high school, you went to university?" Ben asked Mr. Ishida.

"Yes. Kyoto University. Engineering. After university, I entered the Naval Academy at Iwakuni. Do you know Iwakuni?"

"It's near the U.S. Marine base."

"So. So. You were a Marine."

Ben heard a door slide open and the quick sound of feet shuffling across *tatami* and a middle-aged woman wearing a tan, nondescript dress and a white apron elbowed open the connecting doors and carrying a tray ladened with Yeibisu beer and crackers and Pon juice–mandarin orange juice–came into the room. She put the tray on the table and bowed to Ben.

Both Kei and Mr. Ishida smiled. "This is my sister, Ikuyo," Kei said. "Ikuyo, this is Mr. Tails."

"Pleased to meet you, I'm sure," the woman said in heavily accented English. She extended her hand.

Ben half rose, realizing as he did that she was a very short woman. Her face, despite her age, was cover-girl cute, short hair parted in the middle and permed curly out to the sides. She shook his hand vigorously, her hand small but her grip strong.

"Howdy," she said. "Howdy, howdy, howdy."

"Well . . . howdy," he said, still half crouched. She released his hand and turned and hurried out of the room. He slowly relaxed down onto the pillow.

Mr. Ishida was smiling and shaking his head. Kei was laughing. "You should see the look on your face," she said. Using an old-fashioned church key she uncapped a bottle of beer.

She poured beer into three small glasses, holding the long, brown bottle with both hands, one hand grasping the base, the other gently cupping the long neck.

"Ikuyo will cook for us this evening," Mr. Ishida said. "She is an excellent cook." He picked up his glass, and Ben quickly picked up his. "Welcome to our house, Mr. Tails." Mr. Ishida raised his glass. *"Kampai."*

"Kampai," Ben and Kei echoed.

Mr. Ishida drained his glass. "Ahh," he said, and Kei quickly refilled their glasses.

Ben felt his shoulders relax. He glanced up at the framed calligraphy. The calligraphy was very good. He could read most of the characters in Mandarin, but the meaning was in Japanese, not Chinese, and way beyond his modest Japanese.

"Are you surprised?" Mr. Ishida asked.

"Everything else is so new and modern. The guest house even has a toilet seat that I'm afraid to use . . . "

"But this part of the house is old and worn."

"And all the more comfortable for that," Ben said.

Kei rolled her eyes and set a small dish of spicy crackers and peanuts in front of him.

"I live here because I take comfort from the company of my ancestors." Mr. Ishida drank from his glass and set it down. "But I also live here because it is a constant reminder to me of who I am." Kei topped off his glass, and then put the bottle to the side.

"I understand," Ben said.

"Yes. Jim-san said that you do."

"Hand me the bottle," Ben said to Kei and, taking the bottle from her, waited for her to pick up her glass so he could fill it.

"*Domo,*" she said.

"Have you known Jim for a long time?" he asked Mr. Ishida.

"Yes. Since the Korean War."

"And Huang?"

"I first met Huang-*xiansheng* about the same time you must have met him. Jim-*san* introduced us."

They were silent for a moment, Ben studying his glass of beer, Mr. Ishida and Kei waiting patiently.

"My assignments up to now have been very. . . ," Ben began, not sure if he should speak his thoughts out loud. "Specific."

Mr. Ishida nodded, and Kei picked up the bottle of beer. "More beer?" she asked.

"Please."

He watched the amber liquid bubble as she topped up his glass. "If I understand correctly," he said to Mr. Ishida. "Raven grew out of a sort of loose-knit, good-old-boy network. You and Jim and others like you built it mainly on personal relations with each other and with people in your respective governments."

Mr. Ishida nodded. "In the beginning most of us were employed by our governments. Occasionally, we encountered problems that could be solved only by going outside the charter of whatever agency or department we worked for. In those days, it was not difficult to—how do you say it? To not go by the book. As long as we were successful, and as long as whatever action was taken was kept quiet, it was possible to go not by the book." He smiled. "But as time went on and the world became smaller and at the same time more legalistic and our bureaucracies became much larger, what had been infrequent became almost constant. During the last years of the Vietnam War, and through the 70s, your intelligence services—especially the CIA—purged most of the people who had made up the old OSS and the early CIA, and then promptly lost many of the best new people due to ideological differences stemming from the Vietnam War—and from the fallout from Watergate, and from the Carter Administration's attitude toward intelligence services in general. The need for an organization like Raven became acute. Some of us severed our official ties and, like Jim-san, we began working for our respective governments on a contract basis. Today, the relationships remain cordial, as well as casual—as well as they should. We have worked for decades with many of the people who have risen to positions of power within our governments."

"But times have again changed," Ben said. "Is that what this is about?"

Mr. Ishida smiled at Kei.

"It's not so much that times have changed," Kei said. "As it is that the world has become much smaller. On one hand, our institutions, especially our bureaucracies, remain nationalistic, but on the other hand, our economies and cultures have mutated into global cultures and economies. Because of these pressures, there is a need for what has always been a loose-knit entity—Raven International—to become a more coherent organization."

"What do you mean by coherent?" Ben asked.

"Focused is perhaps a better word," she said. "What we are trying to focus Raven on is the fact that in today's world sociopathic and psychopathic individuals and organizations—especially terrorist organizations—are proliferating in the no-man's land that exists between the real world—the Global World—and government institutions and bureaucracies. Like never before in history, these individuals and organizations have learned how to function in multi-cultural, multi-social, multi-lingual environments. They have prospered and grown by understanding and manipulating the gap between obsolete, nationalistic, overly legalistic societies and the reality of a rapidly evolving global society and economy."

"And you think a handful of good-'ol-boys, even men like Jim and Huang and your father here, can control that?"

"Do not underestimate the influence of a few good men and women," Mr. Ishida said. "The influence of a single person, at the right time, in the right place cannot be over-estimated."

Ben shook his head. "Look," he said. "I'm sorry. What you both are saying is interesting. Maybe Jim asked you to explain it to me. But I am not much of a thinker. My role is to be a nuts-and-bolts guy. Life for me happens on a more, ah, a more immediate level."

Mr. Ishida laughed. "Jim-san did not say you could be so diplomatic."

"I am not trying to be diplomatic, sir. I am trying to understand why I am here."

"Just so," Mr. Ishida said. He turned to Kei. "More beer, please, Kei-chan."

"Two glasses, Papa," she said in Japanese.

"Tonight can be an exception. Tomorrow I will have none."

"You know it doesn't work that way," she said in English. But she uncapped another bottle and filled his glass. She glanced at Ben. "He's not supposed to drink more than two glasses a day."

"Do you like *sake*?" Mr. Ishida asked Ben.

"It depends," Ben said. "I don't much like it cold or sweet."

"Yes. *Sake* is like a woman in that regard."

"Papa!"

Ben smiled.

"My father does not have much tolerance for alcohol," she said.

"Your father is an old man," Mr. Ishida said, "who spends most of his days in this house. You should feel sorry for him."

"And because I feel sorry for you, I should give you all the beer you want? Despite what the doctors say?"

"Do you know how I spend most of my time, Mr. Tails?"

"No, sir. I have no idea."

"Pondering the fate of humanity, do you suppose—as this conversation would seem to suggest?"

"Well, you seem to have given it some thought, that's for sure."

Mr. Ishida smiled. "I spend most of my time remembering what it was to be your age." He peered over the top of his glasses at Ben. "You know, you are a strange man, Ben-san."

"Papa!"

"With all due respect, sir. So are you."

Mr. Ishida blinked, and then laughed—a long, cheerful, spontaneous laugh that made his eyes squint and his cheeks turn ruddy. Wheezing slightly, he removed his glasses and took a rolled hand towel from the tray and unwrapped it and wiped his face and eyes. "Ahh," he said. Chuckling to himself, he put his glasses back on, and smiled at Ben. "But we are not the same, are we, Ben-san?"

In his mind Ben heard Huang say, *I am Chinese.* "You are Japanese," he said.

"No. No." Mr. Ishida made a shooing motion with his hand. "I don't mean like that. I mean some men fight, but most do not."

"Fight or flee," Ben said.

"Yes. That's it. Most—myself included—will flee if given the chance, is that not so?"

Ben was silent, wondering where this was going.

"My daughter, Kei, for example. In the face of aggressive behavior, her sisters were always like little rabbits. But not Kei."

"No more beer, Papa."

"Yes. I will wait for the *sake*."

"And no *sake*."

"See what I mean, Ben-san?"

"She's a stubborn one all right."

Kei's eyes flashed at him. And he realized that Mr. Ishida was not joking about her; Mr. Ishida was telling him about her.

"I'm confused," he said to Mr. Ishida.

"Fate has in the past placed you in circumstances, Ben-san, where you have used your abilities to help protect the innocent."

"You make it sound heroic."

"And so it is."

Ben shook his head. He looked at Kei.

"But heroic only to those of us whose instinct it is to flee."

The good humor of a moment ago was gone from Mr. Ishida's eyes. "No matter how heroic or honorable their deeds, men like you live for the hunt, is that not so, Mr. Tails? It is that generator we spoke about. On the one hand you serve and you protect, but on the other hand you feed off the danger. You are stretched, as few are, between the poles of human existence. The clarity that you achieve is a clarity that men such as myself can only imagine."

"I'm a psychopath with honorable intentions, you mean."

Mr. Ishida laughed. "I do not mean to imply anything of the sort. As a matter of fact, your sense of right and wrong, good and evil, is much more developed, much more accurate than most."

"How do you know that?"

"I know because otherwise you would not be working for Raven."

Ben smiled.

"The fact that you are charged by the hunt is a healthy quality," Mr. Ishida said.

"It is not the hunt that bothers me," Ben said.

Mr. Ishida nodded, and Ben realized that Mr. Ishida was not tipsy. Nor was he in any way a doddering-old-man. He was merely using the alcohol as an excuse to be blunt.

"If what you do did not bother you," Mr. Ishida said, "there would be no difference between you and the people you hunt."

"Investigate, you mean."

"No, I mean hunt."

Ben considered him for a long moment. "So who do you want me to hunt?" he asked.

"The American military has recovered from the after-affects of Vietnam, but your intelligence agencies, especially the CIA, and some of the Federal law enforcement agencies, such as the DEA and the FBI, have not." Mr. Ishida sighed. "There are others beside Captain Sato and his friends who see what Raven International does and what it knows as a potential source of power and money."

"I don't understand."

"Captain Sato and his people seem to have created an alliance with renegade elements in your law enforcement and intelligence communities—men hired during those lean, post-Vietnam years. Men who are now in danger of being displaced by the recent change in American attitudes and values—changes that have provoked a marked effort to improve the quality of people assuming positions of responsibility in your law enforcement and intelligence communities. Both Captain Sato and the Americans with whom he has forged an alliance want to take over Raven so that they can continue to exercise a modicum of power and influence." He paused. "But make no mistake, neither Sato nor his American allies are without their ideals. Both, I am afraid, have—how do you say?—bigger fish to fry. And it is this latter quality that makes them so unpredictably dangerous."

"But Raven—the real Raven—is so loose and scattered," Ben said. "It depends on personal relationships that have matured over many years. How could anyone from outside Raven use it as a source of power and money?"

"Perhaps," Kei said, "it has become a case of, as the Chinese say, 'I would rather betray the whole world than let the world betray me.'"

Ben looked at her. She smiled sweetly at him.

"Her mother was the same way," Mr. Ishida said.

Wordlessly Kei picked up their glasses and dishes and placed them on the tray. She placed damp, rolled towels on lacquered holders in front of them, and then stood and picked up the tray. "I will go help Ikuyo," she said and, ignoring Ben, turned and slid the door open with her elbow and left the room.

"I have no talent where women are concerned," Ben said. "None."

"With that one it would not matter. She is stronger than any son I could have wished for. The best of both sides of the family. But sometimes she is too strong, too spirited." He peered over his glasses at Ben.

"Oh, I agree," Ben said.

Mr. Ishida laughed and unrolled another towel and wiped his face and hands. He placed the towel on the table.

"This is my home, Mr. Tails. This compound represents my family. Jim-san and Huang-*xiansheng*–despite our differences, we long ago learned how to function as a family." He picked up the lacquered tray in front of Ben and offered the towel on it to Ben. "We will have dinner," he said. "And at dinner we will not discuss anything of substance. I have said all that I have to say tonight in that regard. Later, my daughter, Kei, will take you to see the local festival."

Ben took the towel from the lacquered tray. "Thank you," he said.

Mr. Ishida nodded. "Welcome to our family, Mr. Tails."

Chapter 14
Playmates

We seek our playmates
Waking them . . .
Before it is morning

−Rabindranath Tagore

Ben stepped through the open entranceway and slid the door shut behind him. The lane was silent, empty for as far as he could see in either direction. Kei had changed to jeans and running shoes, a white t-shirt under a green, cotton jacket. Her hair was in a ponytail that reached most of the way down her back. It was the first time he'd seen her without the braid.

She turned one ear toward him. Her earrings were miniature dream catchers. "A gift from Jim-san," she said. "I forget which tribe."

"They look good on you."

"Thank you. You look like a coach."

He was wearing jeans and an old pair of cross trainers and a dark maroon University of Montana sweatshirt. He smiled, embarrassed, and she took his arm and they began walking down the lane. Fifty meters ahead at the junction of another, even smaller lane, a gas-vapor streetlight blinked on and slowly began to brighten. Farther down the lane other lights began to blink on. Above the walls and buildings white clouds streaked a deep-blue sky. The evening air was an unsettling combination of fragrant blossoms and diesel exhaust.

"I never went to university," he said. "I just like the grizzly bear paw print." There was a small, gold paw print above the left breast on his sweat shirt.

"Never?"

"Well, I studied Mandarin at a university in Taipei. But no degree, or anything like that."

"Why not?"

He shrugged. "I don't know. By the time I went back home—after Vietnam, and all—I guess I figured anything I wanted to know was in a library somewhere. I didn't need some professor to hold my hand."

He could feel her smile. "The cowboy way," she said.

"You'd be surprised how well-read some cowboys are."

Two old women bent and hunchbacked in kimonos exited a doorway a block ahead and turned and hurried down the lane, sandals slapping. Three middle-aged women appeared at an intersection ahead of the old women. They waited for the old women to catch up. There was a flurry of bowing and good evenings, and then they all turned and headed down the lane, their short, quick steps and their chatter reminding him of a gaggle of ducks. "Tell me about this festival," he said.

"Originally it was to celebrate spring planting. People from surrounding villages meet at the Shrine we are going to. Each village builds a large, straw float that represents the animal that belongs to the present year. This is the year of the Horse. The floats are carried by groups of extremely inebriated men. Once they reach the Shrine grounds, the floats are set on fire. There will be a lot of people. I've been told that it is sort of like a county fair in your country."

He turned to look back the way they'd come. The lane behind them was empty, shadows deepening at entranceways and behind concrete utility poles.

"What is it?" she asked.

"I'm not used to so much quiet," he said.

"Well, don't worry. There will be plenty of noise at the festival."

He turned back to her, and they continued down the lane. "Your father is a dangerous man," he said.

"Oh? Why do you say that?"

"What he says sounds reasonable. And I am beginning to understand why I am here. But it is one thing to sit around on *tatami* and drink *sake* or beer and intellectualize, and another thing to deal with people like Sato in real life."

"Don't you think he knows that?"

"What he knows is not the point. What makes him dangerous is that his words tend to obscure how lethal men like Captain Sato and Major Ishii really are."

"My father is well protected. You need not worry about him."

"Worry about *him*? Hey, I'm not worried about him. I'm worried about *me*."

She laughed. "Don't worry, coach," she said, tightening her grip on his arm. "I'll protect you."

The lane ended at a busy street alive with people and families headed for the festival. A huge brown horse bobbed above the heads of people a block ahead. There was a lot of commotion around it, shouts and laughter and heads milling every which way, as it disappeared around the corner.

Something plucked at his sleeve and he looked down at a little boy staring big-eyed up at him. "Hello," said the little boy.

"Hello, yourself."

"Hello."

"What are you, an echo?"

The little boy frowned. "Hello!" he shouted, and turned and rushed back through the people behind them.

"What was that all about?" Ben asked.

"Not many foreigners come here these days. He wanted to talk with you. But hello was all he could manage."

"Cute little guy," Ben said. A man had stopped fifty meters back and was looking in a darkened shop window. The sign above the door said sewing supplies in Chinese characters.

Clumsy, he thought. He smiled at Kei. But clumsy or not, he would not have noticed if not for the boy.

They turned the corner where the giant horse had disappeared. The entire street was a stream of people headed for a wide, short bridge. Beyond the bridge, he could see stone or concrete pillars topped with squat statues. Cedars towered above temples and shrines. And above the cedars, the dark mass of a steep mountain—probably the mountain that the castle had been built on.

As they began to cross, he saw that the bridge spanned a large canal. Dirt paths, round, irregular stones set into each path, ran along each side of the canal. Next to the paths were stone retaining walls, trees and wide walkways of rough-hewn stone on top the retaining walls.

He edged his way through the crowd to the concrete-and-wood railing. The water in the canal was smooth. Here and there small, narrow, wooden boats were tethered to posts sticking out of the water. The houses and storage buildings that lined the walkways were mostly white with tile roofs, the trees and bushes old and well tended. He tried to imagine what it must have been like several hundred years ago, the stone walkways and dirt paths alive with people, the canal clogged with boats. Life hadn't gotten better, he thought, that was for sure.

He turned from the railing. He'd lost Kei, and now another,

even larger, but much cruder rendition of a horse was forcing its way across the bridge. The horse was made of bundles of straw—rice straw, he assumed—and was sitting on a large platform made of small logs. Logs extending out from all four sides served as large carrying handles by which the platform could be carried on the shoulders and arms of a small mob of brightly-clad men.

As the horse drew near, he could see that the men were dressed in khaki pants and blue-and-white *happi* coats, cotton jackets with large, loose sleeves, and *hachimaki*, a red sash with large, black Chinese characters worn across the forehead and tied in back. The men were shouting and chanting. Their *happi* coats, normally held closed with a sash belt, were open, exposing bare chests slick with sweat. The platform tilted and rocked. Some of the voices sounded hysterical. Abruptly he realized that all of the men had their faces made up into garish caricatures of women—*geishas*? He laughed out loud. It was like watching a platoon of seriously inebriated Little Richard clones shout and screech and struggle to keep the platform and the Horse aloft.

"Hey, Gaijin!" one of the men shouted. Under the *happi* coat, his arms and neck and upper chest were soft as a woman's. He left the roiling mass of chanting, straining, falling, shouting men and forced his way in front of Ben. "How it hanging, baby?" he shouted, his eyes feverish and not quite focused. "Gimme five." Swaying, he raised his hand.

Ben slapped his palm. "Hang in there, buddy."

The man turned and reeled back to his friends. Ben wondered how many men would end up on a slab or in the emergency room before the night was over. Under the garish makeup and the frantic, macho shouting and shoving and lifting, it was obvious that most of the men were soft from jobs that required little physical effort. For some of them the alcohol and the physical exertion required to carry something as heavy as the platform and the effigy of a horse had to be a sure ticket to heart attack or stroke. Many were flushed an unhealthy-looking shade of red that extended from face and neck to chest.

Japan, he thought. A hundred years ago, the platforms made of logs would have been carried by men accustomed to long hours spent working in fields and forest, or toting goods into warehouses along the canal. Well muscled men, they must have been, like the men he'd seen in the paddies of Southeast Asia, some of them with perhaps the heart and stamina of the Hmong he'd fought with in Laos.

Those long ago Japanese men of strength and stamina, now reduced to . . . what? To men made up to look like women? He wasn't sure what these men had been reduced to because, despite their poor physical condition, it was clear that the energy and will to fight were still there. No doubt before the night was over, some of them would keel over from heat prostration or alcohol poisoning or heart failure. But he suspected that the men carrying the platforms expected that. In fact, they probably considered it an acceptable price to pay for an opportunity to generate and vent a little of the energy and aggression of old. Watching them, he could well understand how a Sato or an Ishii could appeal to them.

He turned and let the stream of people carry him into the Shrine/Temple grounds. Once inside, he saw that the street continued through the temples and shrines to the base of the mountain. The main Shrine complex was on the right, behind a chest-high wall of boulders fitted together and hewn flat on top. Large buildings with ornate, pagoda-like roofs were festooned with lanterns and streamers of all sorts. Tall, thin banners flapped from long poles set in the ground. Portable booths, like the booths at fairs back home, sold souvenirs and food. He smelled sweet corn on the cob and *mochi* balls—

257

glutinous rice balls dipped in a sweet concoction of soy sauce and sugar—roasting over charcoal.

To the left was a large open area filled with people. A variety of horse effigies were scattered among the crowd, one of them already engulfed in flames. Sparks from the fire whirled up into dark sky.

He laughed, unaware that he had laughed out loud. The kids must love this, he thought. The night and the temples and shrines with their ghosts and their stories. Fire licking up into darkness. Weird, drunken men chanting and singing and fighting. Demons unleashed. He still wasn't sure why he was here, but who cared. This was fun.

"What are you laughing at," Kei said from next to him.

"Look at the kids," he said. "Look at their eyes. Where's your camera?"

"I've been taking pictures of people at this festival since I was a child. I was worried you might be offended by the men."

"They are different, that's for sure."

"Were you shocked when you first saw them?"

"Obviously you've never partied with cowboys or with Marines."

She laughed, and wrapped her arm in his.

"What happens now?" he asked.

"They'll burn the floats, and then there will be fireworks. After the fireworks, a lot of people will hang around buying food and talking. Others will pray and leave money at the various shrines. There will be some fights. A few men will be taken away in ambulances. Eventually, everyone will go home or to a restaurant or, in the case of the drunk men, to a *Snack*."

More of the horses and their platforms began to burn. People were grouped tight around the fires, less tight the further away they were—as if the flames were magnets, and the people were bits of metal. Kei slid her hand into his and pulled him toward one of the bonfires. The feel of her hand in his, its blend of softness and strength, reminded him of Evy, and he realized with surprise that this was the first time he'd held hands with a woman since Evy had died. Strange, the things that triggered memories, he thought. Music. Smells. The feel of a woman's hand.

What would Evy have thought of all this, he wondered, and looking around, trying to see it through her eyes, he saw a figure waving off to his right near a huge tree—a dark figure dressed in dark clothes, the light from one of the fires reflecting off his ebony skin.

He released her hand. Peter, Peter, Pumpkin Eater. You motherfucker, he thought. He'd half expected something like this: Peter come out to play—to fuck with his mind.

"Ben!" he heard Kei shout, and he turned and saw her near the bonfire and beyond the bonfire near the entrance Sato's two *judoka,* their size and bulk as out of place as he must be himself.

"Ben!" she called again, and this time he heard panic in her voice and saw that one of the small men who had killed Carlos had her by the arm, her other arm bent up behind her back. The small man was trying to push her in the direction of the two *judoka.*

He shoved people to the side, conscious only of what was hidden at the small of the man's back, beneath his loose shirt, and the other small man was abruptly in front of him, crouched, his grin a cruel rictus of pleasure, a length of pipe in his hands. Behind the man facing him, the other man and Kei fell to the ground, and in their place was only the huge bonfire. He made as if to move to his left, toward where Kei and the other man had fallen to the ground, and when the man shifted to block his path, he sprinted toward him and, as the pipe swung toward his ribs, was inside the swing, using his momentum and his mass to shove the man, hitting and

259

lifting him toward the fire. The man disappeared into the fire. One second he was there, and then he wasn't. For the people nearby it was if the fire had reached out and pulled him in, his passage marked only by a sudden burst of sparks spiraling up into the darkness.

Ben glimpsed people around him, mouths open—what their eyes had seen not yet fully processed by their brains. A dead spot in the festivities, he thought, part of his mind, as he turned toward where Kei and the other man had fallen, amused by the pun, another part incredulous that he'd think such a thought at a time like this.

Kei had fallen to the side forcing the man to fall with her. The man had hold of her arm and her hair and was dragging her to her feet. Ben stepped forward and hit him as hard as he could with his fist where the neck connected with the skull, driving him face forward over Kei, a black, kinky-hair wig jumping off his head. Boot-camp short, his real hair. A soldier, Ben thought, the wig to make him look like a Yakuza.

He reached down and with his left hand grabbed the man by the belt and pulled him off Kei. People were beginning to scream and move. He reached under the shirt with his right hand and pulled a short-barreled automatic from a belt holster. A Beretta .45, he knew immediately—knew because Robert Lee had one, and he'd spent an afternoon with Robert Lee firing it at the police range. Eight rounds in the magazine, plus one if a round had been cycled into the chamber and the magazine ejected and another round loaded into the magazine. Ambidextrous safety. All this going through his mind in an instant. He turned and as he did pushed the safety off with his thumb, looking for the tree and Peter. Peter was the real danger. And saw him standing on something, trying to see what was happening, probably with no idea that the small man had been armed. He brought the .45 up, sighting over the crowd, and the pistol recoiled, most of the boom absorbed by the commotion around him, and Peter was down. Hit in the side or the arm, he wasn't sure which. Not dead maybe, but for sure out of the action. Another wounded grizzly that could be dealt with later. With his thumb he flicked the safety back down and stuck the Beretta behind his belt at the small of his back.

Kei shoved him away. "Run! Go to my father's house. They won't hurt me now. Run!" She shoved him again. "Go!"

He turned and ran, shoving his way through people, into a group of drunks, faces that were so humorous a few minutes ago now sickly, their too-bright and too-black eyes leering as he shoved sweaty bodies and grasping hands away.

He broke out of the crowd and saw that he was near the tree Peter had been standing next to. He pulled the automatic from his belt and thumbed off the safety. *Get this over right now,* he thought. He ran crouched past the tree and turned and made a u-turn back toward it—making sure Peter, and not him, would be silhouetted by the fire.

"Ah, shit! Ah, God damn it!" he heard from the side of the tree.

Peter was sitting propped against the tree, trying to use his belt as a tourniquet above his left bicep. His left arm hung limp, shiny with blood darker than his skin. Glistening bits of bone showed at the elbow.

"Stupid fuck," he muttered, panting. "I'm here . . . to help."

"Sure you are."

Peter started and glared up at him, his eyes stark white in the light from the fires. "Unh," he grunted, and pulled the belt tighter. "Best be getting your shit together, Marine. Get out . . . of here."

The two small men had been serious about killing him, Ben thought. They were going to kill him like they'd killed Carlos; he'd seen it in the eyes of the first one. The cops would claim that a *gaijin* had gotten into a fight with some

261

Yakuza. And taking into consideration that many festival participants were too drunk and too high on aggression to know what they were doing, blame would be suitably apportioned—most of it the *gaijin's* fault for being there in the first place.

Why had Peter been waving to get his attention? Trying to distract him while the others got into position? From where he was Peter wouldn't have been able to see the two small men.

Not in that crowd. And the two *judoka* hadn't yet spotted him and Kei—at least not until he'd fired at Peter.

"Huang says you have a wife. Kids."

"You've ruined my arm."

"You're lucky it was a big, fat, slow .45."

"Help me up. I've got to get out of here."

Ben pointed the .45 at him. "Now you know how that Hmong kid felt."

Wordless Peter looked up at him, and for a moment his eyes were bald with fear. But only for a moment, and then they were merely resigned.

Ben knew he should do it—knew he should put one in Peter's brain pan right then and there. But Peter had a wife and a kid. And Ben for sure did not want Huang on his ass, too.

He stood and without another word safed the automatic and stuck it in his belt at the small of his back, and turned and ran toward the entrance to a lane.

The lane curved and wound its way between walls and high buildings without windows. He ran past large, metal roll-up garage doors. Anemic, yellow lights every hundred meters or so only served to emphasize the shadows and ruin his night vision. Other lanes crossed the lane he was on. The lights and the way the lane snaked made it difficult to tell which direction he was headed. He had assumed that he would come out at either the canal or the mountain. Instead, he was in a maze of lanes and walls and buildings.

He stopped, his skin itching from a combination of sweat and bonfire smoke. Sweat trickled down his sides. The Beretta was beginning to chaff the skin above his hip.

He pulled the automatic out of his belt and stuck it in his pocket, and then pulled off his sweatshirt and threw it over a wall. The air was cool on his bare arms. He was thirsty. A little sleepy, now that the adrenaline had worn off.

He slid the pistol back inside his belt, behind his hip and, as he did, an old man hunched over handlebars came out of nowhere and pedaled past on an ancient, black tricycle, a large wooden box filled with old boards and corrugated sheet metal on the back. He stared owl-eyed at Ben as he pedaled past.

Ben relaxed his grip on the automatic, trying to slow the thud of his heart. Under the odor of smoke and sweat he smelled other smells now, older smells. Rotting vegetation, open sewers, fish and unwashed people—as if the asphalt and concrete and old buildings were merely part of a deteriorating mantle covering more organic decomposition.

He heard the soft wheeze of the old man's lungs, and realized that the creaking and groaning of the old tricycle was in fact a blend of noises made by both the old man and the tricycle, so that it was impossible to say which was groaning or creaking. He watched until the dim figure blended with distant shadow and dark.

He blew air out in a long, soft sigh. And turned and began jogging down the lane, keeping to the side and the shadows as much as possible. Imagining that the smell of rotting vegetation and sewer was stronger to his left, and probably coming from the canal, he turned left at the next intersection. If he could find the canal, he could find his way back to the Ishida compound.

What did she mean, they wouldn't hurt her now?

His footsteps echoed softly in the lane, and he stopped to listen. In the distance, he could hear the festival. It was seriously eerie running up and down empty lanes. Everyone must be at the festival. He had the feeling that he'd made a half-circle in the maze of lanes and was headed back toward the festival. Maybe it would be best to go back to the festival and then skirt the temples and shrines to the canal. He'd seen other bridges further down the canal.

He heard the distant warble of sirens and a spasm of fear and adrenaline widened his eyes and jerked his hand toward the automatic as from across the lane in a recessed entryway a priest of some kind, close-cropped head and shapeless black clothes, squatting next to a gray, mold-encrusted wall, lifted his head and looked at him. The priest's head nodded, weaving like an animal searching a scent, and as Ben slowly drew closer, he could see that the priest's skull was worn and raw, his eyes dull and jaundiced in the yellow light, his clothes filthy layers and folds. And he remembered, as the abnormally narrow head elongated toward him, that this was Japan, not other places in Asia, and it was not a priest at all, the begging bowl not a begging bowl, but a partially eaten rice cake lying on a piece of cracked roofing tile. A retard of some sort—probably in all the commotion at the Shrine he had become separated from whoever watched over him. Japan was much too fastidious a place to allow someone like this to be out on his own.

The creature's eyes focused on him with a brightness and an intensity that only animals and the insane are capable of, and Ben felt another jolt of fear, his stomach hollow and sick at the same time, seeing with sudden clarity that the idiot's fingernails were black crescents at the side of a pink, open mouth, and that bugs crawled on the narrow, scabbed head. In his mind, he saw the bear rear up, its open maw and bloody

264

teeth reaching for him. Red-rimmed eyes shifted, widened, and he whirled to look and saw fifteen meters back a man standing arms folded across his chest. Big. As tall as him, but bigger. Military looking even in loose brown shirt, dark warm-up pants, running shoes. Tough. Competent.

Familiar.

The man smiled and nodded, and started toward him. A black car, a Toyota, pulled across the lane behind the big man, blocking the lane. The big man glanced back at the Toyota and Ben turned and ran, ran as hard as he could, ran flat out for the festival and the people, the light and noise, the lane a long, dark alley stretching ahead, sickly yellow light bouncing off walls and concrete, as he sprinted for the crowd and the confusion. He heard his shoes squeak on pavement and after a while again heard his footsteps echo—knew now that the echo was the big man coming behind him.

His jeans were already too tight at knee and thigh. Leg muscles heavy. Lungs raw. Fear crawled at the back of his neck.

The Toyota would never be able to get around in front of him, no matter how well they knew the lanes. He dodged left into another lane. Bounced off the far wall. Sprinted five or six steps, then turned right into another lane, again bouncing off the far wall, almost going down this time. He heard a grunt and the sound of the big man hitting the wall behind him. The slap of shoes behind him was not so loud now.

Ahead, where the lane emptied into the Shrine grounds, there was light and sound, fireworks, fire, a mass of people, most of the people staring up at the fireworks. He slowed, dodged women and children, an old man, heard surprised voices behind him: the big Japanese bulling his way through.

He ran up stone steps to a shrine, taking the steps three and four at a time. Ran around the back of the shrine, down another flight of steps, into an uncovered, concrete passage-

265

way leading to another shrine. And slammed into a man in a dark suit, and felt himself graze concrete wall. Out of the corner of his eye, he saw the big Japanese keep his balance by running sideways down the steps, and saw, as he ran out of the passageway, that the wide, stone-covered path leading to the main shrine was crowded with people walking or standing looking at small shrines, candles of varying height lit in front of tiny representations of houses and people.

He grabbed at arms and shirts, a jacket, the back of a dress, pulling people behind instead of pushing them away. He stepped on a heel and stumbled and nearly fell. He glanced back and saw the big Japanese ten meters back shove a woman to the side.

The wide walkway he was on crossed another equally wide walkway. If he continued straight ahead, he would be on the other side of the temple complex and it would be impossible for the Toyota and the men in it to head him off. But the men in the Toyota and the man behind him probably expected him to cross to the other side. They'd have radios. Others would be waiting.

He ran around a row of small shrines into a mass of people milling around more bonfires, knocking a lit incense stick out of the hands of a woman wearing an orange dress and sunglasses, the sunglasses spinning away end over end. Why was she wearing sunglasses at night? Trying to run through the crowd was like running through too-thick undergrowth. He was like one of those bears he'd hunted, fighting its way through heavy brush. The stink of sweat and fear—his, this time—sifting through it all.

He stopped. The people ahead were too many to force his way through. He had nowhere to go. *He had nowhere to go.*

A woman sat faced pressed to a concrete pedestal of some kind on the bottom step of a row of steps leading up to a shrine, a baby strapped to her chest. The eyes of the little girl sitting next to her went wide. His mind screamed for him to step on the mother and the baby and the little girl if that was the only way out of there. But reflexes and the memory of a bear rising roaring and bawling out of the grass forced him to pivot back to the left, left hand and forearm rigid and parallel to his body to protect face and chest, as simultaneously his right hand reached behind underneath loose t-shirt to the grip of the Beretta, thumb flicking up the safety. His rigid left arm came around partially deflecting the thrust of a knife aimed just under his left shoulder blade, the knife slicing his right shoulder, a line along the right side of his back burning as skin and muscle parted.

He looked down at the back of the big Japanese twisted almost onto one knee by the force of his lunge and by Ben's unexpected pivot. Saw clearly black bristles at the small of the neck, as the Japanese threw his left arm up and back, knife cutting toward his face.

He brought the Beretta up and shot the big man four times in the rib cage, the four shots a stutter of sound lost in the clamor of voices and exploding firecrackers–four forty-five caliber slugs that slammed the big man's body to the ground, leg arrested in mid-kick, blood and pieces of something splattered on the concrete step.

The knife bounced, skittered across concrete steps.

He stood, sweat sliding down the side of his face, his breathing too fast and shallow, smelling the sour stink of ruptured viscera. The sweet smell of blood: all the elk and deer and birds he'd ever gutted. All the bears he'd massacred.

Adrenaline hissed in his veins. And abruptly, like a camera lens brought into focus, he was aware of the people about him, some of them comical in their wide-eyed reaction to the body that lay draining at his feet.

The woman who had been resting on the bottom step scrambled backwards up the steps behind her, trying with one hand to protect the child strapped to her chest. His finger convulsed against trigger and another bullet smacked into nerveless flesh, the sound of it hitting lost in the boom of the automatic.

People scrambled, screaming, shouting, pressing against small shrines.

He turned to run and nearly tripped over the little girl still sitting white eyes around an open mouth. He stepped over her and keeping to the edge of the walkway ran bent over, so as to not be taller than those around him, across the open area, fighting his way through tangles of people either trying to escape or trying to get closer to see what was going on.

He ran across a bridge—not the one he'd crossed to enter the Shrine—and sprinted across a paved street, across a narrow, tiled sidewalk, through the open, sliding doors of a shop.

Inside the shop a blur of white, fearful eyes watched him. His hip bumped a stack of red, plastic cases, Asahi beer written on the sides, toppling the cases to the floor. Bottles of beer hit and smashed and scattered, rolling across the floor and under a counter. He spun off balance, the Beretta striking the counter top, kicking upward, booming in the crowded room, muzzle blast searing the side of an old woman's wrinkled face. A neat hole appeared in the white door of a small refrigerator.

The old woman screamed in his face, her mouth a black oval edged with crooked, gold-encrusted teeth. His fingers easily wrapped over her forehead and ears and he shoved at the wrinkled face and the old woman fell out of sight behind the counter.

Ears ringing, he ran through a beaded doorway, through a room piled with boxes and beer crates, out the rear entrance, into a lane.

And stopped. Out of breath. Reacting, reacting. Wanting

to shoot something, anything, most of it a blur from the moment he'd seen the idiot's eyes widen and he'd turned and seen the big man *that motherfucker, he should have shot him again.* Bits and pieces of it sharp and clear—a black knife skittering across concrete steps.

The lane was little more than a paved alley bordered on one side by backs of buildings so similar they appeared a single gray construction. Narrow sewers covered with thick, concrete tiles lined both edges; a group of rats sat hunched at the edge of several broken tiles. He began to shake. Afraid of inadvertently firing another shot, he reached across with his left hand to set the safety and discovered the slide stopped all the way back. He'd fired his last round into the refrigerator. That was what? Six rounds? No seven, counting Peter. There'd been seven rounds in a gun that could carry eight. Probably didn't want to ruin the magazine spring. Stupid.

Cops would be coming from everywhere. There was a busy street a block away. He couldn't be far from the Ishidas' compound.

He thumbed the slide release and the slide chunked forward and, not bothering to lower the hammer, he put the automatic underneath his shirt, in the belt at the small of his back, aware of its warmth as he trotted toward the busy street.

Ten minutes later, he stood in the shadow of a concrete utility pole just inside the entrance to the lane. He'd been forced to stay on a major street in order to find the lane. There'd been plenty of traffic and a few pedestrians, but no cops. No cops in cars. No cops on bicycles. No cops walking. No cops anywhere. He'd even walked past a lit *koban,* a neighborhood cop shop. The *koban* had been lighted, the red light on above the door, but as he passed, he'd seen through the windows that no one was there.

No black Toyota either.

He leaned against the rough concrete and allowed a sudden

lethargy to wash through him. He was safe for the moment. The lane was empty; he was sure of that. It had the feel of no-man's-land. Hell, the whole city had the feel of no-man's-land.

Ah, well, he thought. Back in the shit. He'd thought he'd bought it for sure back at the temple. Fuck that big bastard. And fuck Peter, too. Shoot both of them again if he could. *Blood all over the concrete. He could smell it.* How many days since he'd seen Carlos die? *Muscle and skin parting in his shoulder, ugly ugly liquid feeling.* Some of these people were not being nice at all. If he got out of this, he'd tell them all to stick it up their ass. Go back to Montana. Nothing was worth this shit. Walk the mountains. Fish his grandfather's favorite hole. *Big motherfucker all over the step, I should have wasted you that time before your black eyes.*

Huang. Jim. Those two assholes in Coffee Shop Cha Cha. *Peter. Peter. You ain't the Pumpkin Eater no more.*

Friends. Fuck *that.*

His t-shirt felt glued to his back and it wasn't because of sweat. He knew he'd been cut good because it was starting to ache from the inside out.

He eased out from next to the utility pole. Keeping to the side of the lane, he walked as much as possible from shadow to shadow. The bleeding made the Beretta feel as if it had been dipped in oil, sliding up and down inside his belt every time he took a step. He was doing his best, but he was beginning to slow down a little. There was a sick feeling in his stomach that he could not remember ever having before. No doubt his heart had been maxed out for quite a while back there. A heart pumping at max output was not exactly what you wanted when you were bleeding like a stuck pig.

The door to the entrance to the Ishida compound slid open with a bang, and before he could react, Kei rushed out, and as she did four or five shadows closed on him from behind and to the side, his heart lurching into another gear, neck muscles braced, as two more appeared from the shadows on the other side of the entrance.

"Ben! Are you okay?"

He stopped, hands raised, palms out, as black-clad figures surrounded him and Kei. He saw now that they were men in SWAT gear. All but two had their backs to him. Night vision devices were clipped to their helmets. They had been watching him since he entered the lane. He dropped his hands to his sides. So much for being worried about Mr. Ishida's ability to protect himself and his family.

He felt her hand on his arm. "Ben." She shook his arm. "Ben!" He looked down at her. "Are you all right?" she asked.

"No."

Holding onto his arm, she pulled him to the doorway and, shifting her grip on his arm, she turned and backed through the doorway, pulling him through with her.

Inside, the compound was well lit by floodlights mounted high on all the buildings and at intervals along the walkways. He released her hand and straightened. There seemed to be a lot of men walking around dressed in camouflage. A man walked between buildings, a German shepherd on a short leash at his side. Everyone had on web gear, automatic rifles slung barrel down.

Damn shoulder was beginning to smart.

"What is it?" she asked. "Are you hurt?"

"Just a cut," he said, thinking, *fucking aye just a cut.* He was probably bleeding to death but, hey, when had he ever had a better chance to play John Wayne? A platoon of soldiers in the compound. A SWAT team outside. A damsel all beautiful and worried next to him. *Ain't but a scratch, ma'm. Shot of whiskey and a bandaid, and I'll be good as new.*

Damn thing was *really* starting to ache. He sure hoped he hadn't pissed his pants somewhere along the line.

271

"Follow me," she said, and led him down the walkway to the main house. The door was open and what seemed like a lot of people, some in suits, some in police uniform, some in camouflage, were coming and going, all of them looking at him without expression as they went past. He kicked off his shoes. From the sound of things, there was a crowd of people in the big room where earlier in the day they had met Sato and the Major.

"Go into the other room—the dining room," she said. He heard a quick intake of breath as she saw the back of his shirt and pants.

"Go sit at the table," she said. "I'll get some help."

Just a scratch, ma'm," he said, or thought he said. Whatever. It didn't matter because she was already gone. Damn, he was thirsty. He probably had a serious case of dragon breath, too. Maybe that was why she'd left in such a hurry.

He wandered through the Western-style living room, past leather couches and chairs, the glass coffee table. One wall held large, framed photographs of Mr. Ishida and, he assumed, the late Mrs. Ishida. No judge he, but the photographs seemed first rate. Kei's probably. An artist, for sure.

Another wall was covered with bookcases and cabinets with glass doors. Books, lots of books. Souvenirs and knick-knacks from around the world.

The carpet was soft and spongy under his stocking feet. He should lie down on the carpet. Take a little snooze. Rest his weary limbs. Nah, he couldn't do that. John Wayne would never do that.

But Mr. Slide sure would.

The dining room was a formal dining room. Hardwood floor. Antique-looking sideboards, crystal stuff on top. Huge hardwood table—teak, it looked like. Eight high-backed matching chairs, three on a side, one at each end. He walked

272

to the far end and pulled the chair out and sat–and stood and pulled the Beretta from his belt. He gently placed the Beretta on the table, careful of the polished surface. The oiled metal and dark plastic grips against the rich hardwood looked like an advertisement in a gun magazine–except that the end of the barrel and the slide were streaked with carbon and blood. He sat down and waited.

Mr. Ishida hurried into the room. Ben smiled at him. Mr. Ishida started to say something but stopped. He frowned at Ben for a moment and then turned to Kei. "A doctor will be here soon," he said in Japanese. He turned back to Ben. "Are you all right, Mr. Tails?" he asked in English.

Ben grinned at him. "Peachy," he said. He looked down at the carbon and blood caked on his right hand. *Just peachy.* He felt a tingling throughout his body.

"They were going to take your daughter," he said, trying to keep his voice quiet, wondering if he had.

Mr. Ishida's eyes darkened, his forehead turning shiny. "Are you certain?"

"Dead sure," Ben said, and heard someone giggle. He looked around to see who was giggling.

He heard the rasp and rush of someone opening and closing the *genkan* door. A voice Ben didn't recognize called for Mr. Ishida.

"In here," Mr. Ishida shouted in Japanese.

A big man–the uncle he'd seen at Danny's place–came in. Thick neck and shoulders. Bullet head. Gray, conservative suit. Paisley tie. No jewelry this time, but the suit must have cost a pretty penny, Ben thought. The uncle was accompanied by two men in fatigues. The first was an officer, a semi-automatic pistol of some sort held loose at his side; the other was in black SWAT gear, automatic rifle to his shoulder, barrel pointed down, finger next to the trigger guard.

Mr. Ishida said something in Japanese, and the officer

holstered his pistol, and the SWAT guy safed his rifle and walked over to the wall and stood with the rifle cradled in his arms.

Mr. Ishida went over to the uncle and the officer and they began talking, now and then glancing without expression at Ben. Their voices sounded distant, metallic, as if they were talking in an empty room.

It was amazing how calm he felt. Especially since he might be spending the rest of his life in a Japanese jail, or somewhere out in the nearest bay, food for the sharks.

Kei came back into the room. He hadn't noticed her leave. She stood arms folded across her chest watching him. *Nice chest, no doubt about it.* He couldn't read her eyes. *Yo! Wasn't this where the girl was supposed to look all dewy-eyed?*

Mr. Ishida and the uncle and the officer talking quietly reminded him of one of Carlos' parties, the room filled with Japanese—hard men despite their smiles and polite voices.

A gold tooth glinted as Mr. Ishida talked.

Ice cubes had clinked in whiskey glasses.

The one in black with the automatic weapon watched him. *It was amazing how relaxed he felt.*

He frowned.

"This is. . . ," he heard Mr. Ishida say, and Mr. Ishida and the other three men were standing next to him, looking down at him.

"Nice to meet you," Ben said, and then for some reason he didn't understand he repeated it in Mandarin. Oh, well, he thought.

"I attended Ohio State," the officer said in English. His opaque eyes studied Ben.

Ben frowned. He glanced from the officer to the other men. He licked his lips, *What a strange party. Where was the music?*

"How many were there?" the officer asked.

274

What was he talking about? How many what? Why was he looking so worried?

And what was a Beretta, slide dulled with carbon and blood—*he felt the recoil in the web of his hand*—doing on the table? *I attended Ohio State.* Attended, not went to. And who gives a flying fuck, anyway? *Damn, Sam. Bodies all over the place and he was talking about Ohio State.*

His mouth tasted like dead snakes—whatever dead snakes tasted like. He smiled to himself. Actually, he knew what dead snakes tasted like. But sure as God made little green apples, Mr. I-attended didn't.

He held out his right hand, turning it slowly, studying the dried blood. *The mascara of death.* He laughed out loud. *What a stupid thought.* He giggled. What comes around, goes around—or was it what goes around comes around? He could never get it right. No matter. It was the key to the secret of the universe, whatever way you said it.

He smiled at the officer. "Sneaky little bastard, aren't you?" he said. And not knowing it, he continued to smile, his eyes soft and liquid, like the eyes of an animal that is just beginning to understand the nature of its wound.

His body began to tremble, muscles cabling forearms and neck.

Mr. Ishida said something to someone in the doorway.

"Shit, shower, and shave," Ben said.

Kei placed a hand on his shoulder. "Relax," she murmured. "Relax."

He nodded. Yellow droplets of sweat appeared on his forehead. He grunted and gripped his thigh to stop his right leg from jerking up and down. His pant leg was speckled with dried blood. His shoes were gone. *Where were his shoes? He couldn't run very far without his shoes.*

Another soldier appeared in the doorway, carrying a small

bag that looked like a cheap plastic shaving kit. The soldier walked directly to Ben, watched him for a moment, put several fingers to the side of his neck, checking his pulse, and then unzipped the small bag. He took a small vial of clear liquid and a syringe and needle in a sterile, plastic wrap from the bag.

"What is in the vial?" Kei asked in Japanese.

"A morphine derivative. It's all I have with me. He's lost some blood, but not as much as it looks. He is in shock and probably dehydrated."

The room was silent as the man retracted the plunger, drawing liquid into the syringe. "I'll start an IV, as soon as this calms him down."

"Don't want . . . any . . . of that . . . shit," Ben said through clenched teeth.

"Can you take care of the shoulder?" Kei asked.

"In a hospital, yes. Here, I don't know—and won't know until I look at it." With his free hand he pushed up Ben's shirt sleeve. "Get him to relax a little," he said.

Kei leaned close to Ben, her voice low so that the others could not hear. "Relax, Coach," she murmured. "You are safe with me."

Ben squinted, and as his head turned toward Kei, the muscle in his arm eased a little, and the waiting doctor in one quick motion inserted the needle into his arm and shoved the plunger down.

Ben's head snapped toward him.

The doctor pulled the needle free.

Ben glared at him. He looked down at his arm. And looked back up, finding Mr. Ishida. His face softened, and he sagged, arms loose on the table top.

"You gave him too much," Mr. Ishida said.

Ben sighed, staring at the Beretta on the table next to his forearm.

"He is big and very strong. He'll be all right." The doctor closed the plastic bag. "Help me get him up on the table, and I'll do what I can for the shoulder."

"Don't mean nothin'," Ben slurred, his eyes closing to slits.

Kei was saying something to him. But all he could see was pillow and hardwood floor. Amazing how much time they spent making the floors. Strips of hardwood interlocked into eight-or ten-inch squares, the grain in every other square running the opposite way. Did that make sense? "Ol Luke the Gook is cleverer than any spook," he mumbled. The muscles in his right shoulder felt immensely tired, as if he was holding a rifle in one hand, arm straight out from his side. Someone was plucking his shoulder muscles as if his shoulder muscles were guitar strings. *God damn, it ached.*

"Almost finished," she was saying. "A few more stitches. Try to sleep."

Sleep? It felt as if he was holding a safe in his right hand. How the fuck was he supposed to sleep? He felt a tiny, sharp sting in his right buttock.

That's how, he thought, as a rushing blackness rolled through him, thrashing like out-of-control rotor blades.

Chapter 15
The Blue Captain

The dark felt warm, comfortable, a tangible presence that filled the room and padded noise. Even the hard bed felt molded to his body.

He smiled at the darkness, feeling the morphine, or whatever it was, pull him back toward sleep. Dark blurs in the corner smiled back: a dresser, a lamp, books and stuffed animals on top the dresser. There was a reproduction on the wall that even in the gloom he recognized as Chinese. Sung Dynasty, he was pretty sure.

He began to nod off and the door slid open and a lighter darkness bounced against the closed window across from him. He watched as Kei crossed to the window and slid it open. A warm breeze unaccountably smelling of ripe mangoes gently plucked at the sheet. He wasn't sure if he was awake or not. It felt like a dream.

She kicked off her slippers and began to undress in front of the window, her blouse and slacks falling without sound or substance to the floor. She stepped out of her panties and, lifting her pony tail from neck and shoulders, faced the breeze washing though the window.

He watched the rise and fall of her breasts.

She turned her head toward him. "You're awake," she said, and dropped her arms to her sides. She crossed to the bed. "How do you feel?"

He felt the mattress give as she sat next to his chest. Felt her touch light on his arm. Smelled her. Her perfume. Her. His hand ran along the inside of her thigh.

She stilled his hand with hers. "Do you remember waking up?"

"I remember–" He cleared his throat. "I remember someone walking me to the toilet." He frowned. "Was that you?"

"That was my uncle–the driver. And not once, but three times. You've been asleep for nearly twenty-four hours." Her hand squeezed his. "Ben, do you remember what happened?"

"I remember my shoulder aching as if I'd been holding a heavy weight for a long time."

"You killed three men. Do you remember that?"

The darkness stirred. Tendrils of warmth coming through the window caressed the skin below his eyes and at his throat. He closed his eyes and breathed deep; tasted death.

"Yes," he said.

She released his hand and slid in under the sheet, her body smooth and cool. She put her face against his chest, arm around his waist, and pulled herself closer. Her breath smelled of sex, and he felt himself grow hard. Her hand shifted to the small of his back, bringing their bodies even closer together.

He kissed the top of her head, and she tilted her head back, and he kissed her forehead, her eyes, and she wedged herself between him and the mattress, pulling him gently over on top of her, her legs spread, ankles and feet wrapped behind his knees. He felt his shoulder tear and at the same time felt her move beneath him, her stomach warm and soft and smooth against his, until–with a soft, quick sound–she found him. And lifted her head. Lips greedy as his.

• • •

A warm breeze dried their sweat. His shoulder throbbed,

279

ached like the socket of a tooth newly pulled. He concentrated on the feel of their bodies, still damp where joined at leg and hip and shoulder. His shoulder felt solid. Too solid.

Kei turned on her side, and he felt the breeze where they had been pressed together. She propped herself up on one arm and leaned over and kissed him lightly on the forehead. "You need to sleep," she said.

"What I need is a toothbrush and a shower."

Her fingers massaged his temple. He closed his eyes. Felt her smile. "Sleep," she said.

"What did your father say?" he asked.

"He said for you to rest."

"Yeah?"

"That is exactly what he said."

"Okay."

• • •

The dresser was metallic in the moonlight. Random edges of books and bottles glinted like fresh shrapnel. Blood flowed through the open window. Steamed in icy-white puddles.

His eyes snapped open. The dream again—or a version of it. He knew that, but even knowing it didn't stop blood from curdling along the window edge. Plants and shrubs outside swam in a sea of it. Leaves glistened with it. His heart thudded, rippling the stream of blood. He closed his eyes.

And saw hundreds of corpses waxen and contorted, their eyes watching him no matter which way he moved. Watched him without emotion or life. Watched him watch the square body bag.

He woke again. Moonlight flowed through the open window, sterilizing the floor and the mattress and the sheets he lay on. The dope, he thought.

He looked out the window at the plants, their long, thin leaves gleaming in the moonlight, and was gone again.

To the cane field. The head rebounding off the ground, gunpowder acrid against the fertile humidity of the sugar cane. Dark tendrils of blood crept from the head. But the head was not that of the Frenchman, was instead the Pumpkin Eater's.

The head began to move, eyes black holes, as it oozed over the window, down the wall, onto sterile floor. And flowed across the floor, up onto the bed. Onto his chest.

He tried to scream—a soundless scream that echoed from the throats of the piled and scattered corpses.

Light flooded the room, blinding.

Kei screamed.

The snake on his chest rotated toward her, its body big around as a man's wrist, tail hanging to the floor. Its tongue darted, and it elongated away from him, and flowed down onto the floor, across the floor to the window. A large, gray snake that from the shape of its head he could tell was harmless. The same kind of snake he'd seen at temples and shrines.

The snake flowed effortlessly up the wall, over the windowsill. Its tail paused for a moment draped over the sill, before it, too, disappeared out the window.

Ben struggled to a sitting position. His chest and face were pallid with sweat. The stink of fear permeated the room. His eyes darted from the window to Kei.

He knew what she was thinking: an omen. A ghost of some kind. An enemy from a previous life, maybe.

"It is only our *ao dai sho*," she said.

"Your blue captain?"

"A lot of older houses and temples have them," she said. "It is bad luck to hurt them. They protect the house." She blinked. "This one has lived in the garden for as long as I can remember. He is harmless. He eats rats and mice."

"Harmless, unless you are a rat."

"Yes."

He swung his legs over the edge of the mattress, forgetting that he was naked. "Does he often come in through your window?" he asked, but even as he asked, he could see the answer in her eyes.

Once in Cambodia, he'd been on the roof of an apartment building with Huang, and a snake had found them. A long, green snake, head the shape of a smooth leaf, sliding out of the darkness under a concrete water tank, passing next to Huang sitting in the shade arguing with him—Huang trying to understand why anyone, even an American, wanted to lay baking and sweating on an air mattress in the bright sunlight.

Huang had jumped up, and kicked down, the heel of his shoe crushing the head of the snake, smashing it into the white gravel of the rooftop, the long, thin body coiling and uncoiling spastically around his ankle as the snake died—a bamboo snake that had probably been transported there in the bamboo the construction workers had used.

All the times he'd sunbathed up there, next to the water tank, sleeping in the hot sunlight. . . .

Now it was an ancient, ugly-gray snake, a "blue captain." What next; why him? He leaned forward elbows on knees, feeling a ripple of pain in his shoulder. He ran his fingers through his hair.

He could feel Kei staring at him.

He pulled the sheet across his lap. "Excuse me," he said, but he felt it, too.

The stench of opened graves.

Chapter 16
Dancing

Early morning sunlight made bright the *shoji* screen closed over the window. He remembered getting up in the middle of the night to take a piss and seeing the snake shadowed by moonlight against the screen, its shadow swaying, as if by a breeze. He had watched it until he'd fallen asleep again. An inexplicably dreamless, comfortable sleep.

The stitches in his shoulder felt tight, and there were a few spots of dried blood on the sheet, but other than that he felt no discomfort–thanks in part, no doubt, to the wonders of modern pharmaceuticals. His stomach growled and he realized he was hungry. He rubbed the side of his face, surprised by the rough bristles. A shower and shave wouldn't hurt either. He'd brushed his teeth when he'd gotten up to take a piss–stumbling around in the dark until he remembered that he was in Kei's little house, and not in the guest house.

He stretched his leg and his foot brushed another leg, and Kei stirred behind him. She must have crawled into bed with him after he'd fallen asleep, he thought. Maybe that explained why he'd slept so well. His shoulder wouldn't let him turn over to look at her.

He pulled the sheet off his legs and sat up, feet on the floor, and turned to look at her.

The cover was to her chin, her face tilted up, mouth slightly open, braid tossed over the pillow.

He eased off the bed, and knelt on the floor, and pulled his pillow toward the edge of the bed so that he could lean forward, chin and throat on the pillow, face to face with her.

Evy had been a restless sleeper. She would kick and hit to keep her space in the bed and never wake up. When she woke in the morning, she awakened wide awake and raring to go. For a moment, Kei's face melded into an image of Evy, and Evy's gray eyes stared at him, her pupils tiny and out of kilter. He'd heard and felt her thrashing around in the night, but he'd thought it was just her being her usual restless self. Cerebral aneurysm, the doctor had said. A broken blood vessel in the brain stem. Rare, but sometimes found in women her age—especially in women with Native American ancestry. The bleeding into brain tissue made it easy to detect at autopsy.

She closed her mouth and swallowed and her eyes opened brown and soft and full of sleep. "What are you doing?" she asked. Her smile was hazy.

"Looking at you."

"How is your shoulder?"

"My shoulder is fine. Do you ever wear your hair loose?"

Her eyes focused. "Would you like me to?"

"I would."

"If you let me take your picture, I'll wear my hair loose."

He lifted his face off the pillow.

"Please?" she said.

"Okay."

"Okay?"

"Okay, you can take my picture—but only after I shower and shave."

"Oh!" she said, and raised her head off pillow. "I'm sorry. You must be hungry."

"I am very hungry. But right now I want a shower more than I want food."

"You are supposed to keep your shoulder dry."

"Maybe you could tape plastic wrap or a piece of plastic garbage bag over the stitches?"

Her eyes flitted over his face, and he understood that she was waiting for something from him that at least acknowledged their lovemaking. But she was such a rare and exotic creature that looking at her lying there it seemed impossible that they had made love. It was only moments ago that he'd met her in coffee shop ChaCha.

He pushed himself away from the bed, and stood, and then sat on the bed next to her. "In Montana, I lived with a woman named Evy for nearly three years," he said. "We got along, but we didn't get along–if that makes any sense. Most of the didn't-get-along was my fault."

"Where is she now?"

"She's dead," he said, and saying the words out loud, he felt something untangle in his mind. Not a relief exactly, but his mind was suddenly lighter, more ordered, his thoughts for the first time meshing with his memories of Evy. "I woke up in the morning and she was dead. She had died in the night."

Kei was quiet, her face showing nothing, and he understood that it was the Japanese way sometimes to show no emotion when the emotion was too strong.

"I once asked Jim-san why he had never married," she said. Her eyes were intelligent. Careful.

"What did he say?"

"Lie down next to me, please."

He smiled. "Jim said that?"

"You know what I mean."

Careful of his shoulder, he lay down on his back next to her, his feet hanging over the end of the mattress. He folded his arms across his chest and looked up at the ceiling. "Okay, doctor. I'm ready."

"Jim said that men who know death rarely choose women they love. He said that because such men have experienced the reality of losing someone close, they unconsciously pick women whose loss will not be as traumatic as would be the loss of someone they could be truly close to."

"Jim said that?"

"Well, not in those words maybe. But, yes."

"I suppose that would help account for the divorce rate among combat veterans and cops."

"Perhaps Jim-san was speaking only for himself," she said.

Ben was silent, staring at the ceiling, as he considered her words. It was true that his friends who were cops, or who had been in a war—men like Manfred and Robert Lee—had a talent for ignoring the women they were most attracted to. "That might be part of it," he said. "But for me it's more than that. I think her death was payback for some of the things I've done."

"Isn't that being a bit egoistic?"

"What do you mean?"

"Her life was her life, Ben. How she lived it, who she was, who she lived it with—all that was her choice, not yours. Her life was hers, and so was her death."

He closed his eyes, seeing a water trough. A rusty old manual pump on the side of the trough. Bird feathers in the mud next to the trough. "I miss her," he said.

"Of course you do. And you probably have regrets. But her death was not some kind of payback."

He turned his head. "So, vat are you sayink, Herr Doktar-san? Are you sayink that I am being full of it?"

"Oh, no. A proper Japanese woman like me would never even imply such a thing—let alone say it."

"You didn't seem all that proper last night."

"That was last night."

"I see."

286

"I see? What does *that* mean?"

"Well, I'm just wondering if a proper Japanese woman like yourself would like to take a bath with a big, hairy *gaijin* like me."

She laughed.

"Of course," he said. "Manners and good breeding prevent me from mentioning that the *gaijin* in question suffered a life threatening wound in an attempt to rescue said proper Japanese woman from the clutches of men of questionable intent."

"Is that a long-winded way of saying you're angling for a mercy fuck?"

"As a former Marine, I am aghast," he said. "Shocked and taken aback by your choice of vocabulary."

"Well, Big Hairy *Gaijin*-san, get used to it. I discovered long ago that crude and rude vocabulary is one of the perks of using the English language."

"Do you think women look at death different than the way men look at death?" he asked.

She laughed. "Boy, when you change the subject, you change the subject."

"Well," he said. "Do you think what Jim said about men who have been to war not picking women they love applies to women, too? I mean, do you think the kind of experiences he's talking about would stop a woman from choosing someone she could be close to?"

She stretched her arms toward the ceiling and wiggled her fingers. "Someone once said that the mystery of life appears to most women when they look into a child's face." Her fingers stilled, and she dropped her arms to her sides. She turned her face toward him. "But it appears to a man when he looks into the face of death."

"Malraux," he said.

"Yes," she said, surprised.

"Do you think Malraux is right?" he asked.

"I don't know. I've never had a child."

"I can help you with that."

"I'm sure you can."

They were silent for a moment, comfortable with each other and with the sexual tension between them, both aware that they were not going to do anything about it until he'd bathed and eaten.

"Don't you think it strange that two people such as us could have met—and not only met, but be here together in this bed?" she said.

"Is that a question, or are you just thinking out loud?"

"How *did* you come to be here, Ben?"

"Aliens."

"No, seriously."

"Seriously . . . I don't know. I suppose once upon a time it started as an adventure—something to tell the people back home."

"And now?"

"Now it's just life."

"If you were asked to—if you had to describe yourself in a single sentence, what would you say?"

He smiled at the ceiling. "Another moth-eaten bear hanging on the wall in a bar in Montana."

"I don't understand."

"Are we being serious here?"

"Yes, we are."

"A warrior, I suppose."

"So! A warrior. And what is that, a warrior?"

"Kind of like a *samurai*."

"When you say it, you make it sound noble."

"I used to think it was."

"And now?"

He smiled. "And now it's just life."

She propped herself up on one elbow to look at him. "You are worried about prices to be paid," she said. "Aren't you?"

"I guess." This was getting a little close to the bone, he thought. He'd never talked like this with anyone, not even his grandfather.

He looked up at the ceiling.

Neither of them were able to say what they were really thinking, he thought. A kind of dance. Trying to talk out loud about the things they were thinking was like trying to thank the mountains at the end of a hard day of hunting. He'd tried more than once to thank the mountains, but the more he tried, the further he went from it, until, if he persisted, he was just a man standing on a mountain, talking to himself, while he looked at a sunset. He knew—because the mountains had taught him—that the more he tried to talk to her about the things he wanted to talk to her about, the more he'd sound a fool.

"You had dreams last night," she said.

"Always."

"Sometimes there is nothing worse than dreams."

His eyes met hers. "Sometimes there is waking up," he said.

Chapter 17
A Fine Figure of a Man

Kei gently pressed strips of adhesive tape on his back. He hated it when someone, anyone, messed with his back. A doctor stitching a cut was one thing; he could tolerate that. But this—he didn't even like back rubs or neck massages, never mind someone taping Saranwrap over his stitches.

It had probably started in Vietnam—the way the skin on his back and neck would shiver when bad guys were out and about. The touch of her fingers, as she smoothed tape over the plastic wrap, was sensual and uncomfortable at the same time.

"Maybe you better take a bath with me," he said. "You know, in case the tape comes loose or something."

She smiled, and kissed his shoulder. "You take a bath. I'll make us something to eat."

And later, the bathroom warm and steamy, he was glad she hadn't joined him. He washed and rinsed several times. Shaved. Brushed his teeth. Washed and rinsed again. And then soaked in the *furo* until she knocked on the door and told him that for the sake of his stitches he probably shouldn't be in there so long.

He toweled off, and put on clean underwear and a *yukata* that she'd left for him on top the washing machine. The *yukata*, sort of a combination bathrobe and *kimono*, ended short of his elbows and above his knees. He was careful to fold it closed to the right, away from his heart. Only the dead wore

290

a *yukata* closed to the left. He tied the sash belt around his waist, and feeling ridiculous in the tiny *yukata*, padded barefoot into the kitchen area.

The house was new, small by American standards, but by Japanese standards too large for a single woman. Maybe twelve-hundred square feet, one half devoted to a combination living room, dining room, kitchen.

The floor of the kitchen and dining room was wood parquet. The living room floor was *tatami,* but most of the *tatami* was covered with Persian rugs and leather furniture. Large windows and a sliding glass door in the dining area looked out onto fruit trees of some kind and onto a small patio surrounded by a combination vegetable and flower garden. A section of the ancient gray wall surrounding the compound could be seen through the trees on the far side of the garden.

There were large bookcases filled with books in the living room, and where there were not bookcases there were clusters of framed photographs.

The other half of the house he already knew: bathroom, toilet, a small nook containing washer and dryer, a bedroom— and a study that he hadn't been in.

The dining table was set with place mats, knives and forks wrapped in linen napkins. Glasses of orange juice. Mugs of steaming coffee. Small bowls of diced, green melon. "Smells good," he said.

Kei placed plates of scrambled eggs and ham and English muffins on the place mats. "I hope this will be enough," she said. "The last time I went shopping, I didn't know I'd have a cowboy from Montana staying for breakfast." She was wearing a blue apron that said ChaCha on the front. Her hair was loose and shiny, brushed back and parted so that the left side of her face was half hidden by a fall of hair. She looked at him, and her eyes widened, and her mouth made an Oh! of surprise. She burst into laughter.

291

"What?" he said. "What?"

She looked away, trying to control herself. "I'm–" she started to say but, glancing at him, began to laugh again, laughing so hard she had to put one hand on the back of a chair to steady herself.

He pulled the chair out opposite hers and sat. "Is this better?"

She wiped tears from the corners of her eyes. "I'm sorry," she said, tucking loose hair behind her ear.

"Now might be a good time to take a picture," he said.

"No. No," she said, waving her hand in front of her face, as if to ward off the thought. She turned and hurried to the kitchen counter. He could see her back shaking.

She took a deep breath. "Hooo!" she said, and turned and walked stiffly to the table and sat down.

"Please help yourself," she said. There was a slight quaver in her voice.

"Thank you," he said, his mouth already full of English muffin and scrambled egg. "I will."

She unwrapped her silverware and put the napkin primly on her lap.

"Oops," he said, and stuffed his own napkin into the cleavage of his *yukata*.

"Please," she said, refusing to look at him. "I'm doing my best."

He took the napkin out of his *yukata* and placed it on his lap.

"You were starved," she said, watching in amazement as the food disappeared from his plate.

"You have a weird laugh sometimes," he said.

"Oh, I know. Everyone says so. My sister calls it my Betty Boop laugh."

"Does everyone also say how beautiful you are when you wear your hair down like that?"

She blushed and picked up her fork.

He stopped chewing for a moment, fork filled with scrambled egg suspended over his plate. He put the fork down. "I have to say it," he said. "You've probably heard it all your life. But I have to say it anyway."

She looked up, one eye peeking at him, the other hidden by her hair. "Have to say what?"

"That you are the most beautiful woman I've ever seen."

"Oh," she said, and blushed. She looked down and put her fork on her plate.

"And. . . ," he said.

She looked up. "And?"

"And are you going to eat all of that English muffin?"

She smiled. "You can have it."

"Really?"

"Really."

"You're sure?"

"I'm sure," she said. "Especially since you've already eaten half of it."

"This is great," he said. "I can't tell you how great this is."

"*Do itashimashite*," she said, giving him a formal little bow.

With his coffee mug, he gestured behind him. "Are all those pictures yours?"

"Yes."

He swiveled in his chair to look at the pictures. "I thought you only took pictures of people?"

"I make my living taking pictures of people. These pictures are for me."

"Well, they're really good." He turned back toward her.

She smiled and took a square of melon from the bowl, and with her finger she slowly pushed the square into her mouth, her lips sucking at the melon, and then at her finger.

He blinked, not sure what he had just seen.

She smiled. A Mona Lisa smile if he'd ever seen one. Man
. . . He coughed, and cleared his throat.

"Are you okay?"

"Why were they after you?" he asked.

"Kidnapping in this part of the world, as you perhaps know,
is not usually the heinous crime that it is in America. More
often than not it has more to do with influencing someone
than with money."

"They wanted to kidnap you to influence your father?"

"Not only my father; my family."

"Would it have worked?"

"They know that my father is ready for retirement. Perhaps
it would have hastened his retirement."

"Keep quiet and retire and you get your daughter back,"
he said.

She put another piece of melon in her mouth, but this time
there was nothing sensual about the way she ate it. Maybe
he'd imagined it—a delayed effect of the drugs he'd been given,
or something.

"I still don't get it," he said. "What do they want?"

"They want Raven. Captain Sato thinks he can assume my
father's place."

"But your father's influence is the result of a lifetime of
experience. It's taken him all his life to acquire his connections."

"You know that, and I know that, but men like Sato. . . ."
She ate another piece of melon. Definitely nothing erotic
about it, he thought. He must have been imagining things.

"Will they try again?" he asked.

She selected another piece of melon. "No. I don't think so.
It would do them no good now. My father is angry. And my
uncle is . . . beyond angry."

"I expected to wake up in jail," he said.

With her finger she poked the melon piece into her mouth,

sucking for a moment on her finger after the melon had disappeared. Her smile was innocent.

"That was not even discussed," she said. "My uncle had a chance to talk with Major Ishii and, in the course of that conversation, found out it was me they were after. I wasn't as safe from them as I'd thought. Apparently you were a bonus."

"What do you mean, a bonus?"

"A target of opportunity. Sato doesn't like you."

"That little—"

"That little what, Ben?" Her eyes were cool.

"Sato has had a hard on for me from the moment we met."

"Yes. Sato is Sato. But look at it from his point of view. You broke his face."

"And I'm an American."

"And you are an American."

"Imagine if he knew I had eaten your English muffin."

She didn't smile.

"The issue is still in doubt," he said. "Is that it?"

She nodded. "That's why we are both here."

"No cops. Nothing in the newspapers."

"A fight between Yakuza gangs at the festival," she said. She selected another piece of melon, thought about it, and dropped it back in the bowl.

"Why do you want to take my picture?" he asked.

She studied him for a moment—a professional evaluation.

"For me it is always the eyes," she said. In Mandarin she said, "Monkeys touch dead eyes with puzzled fingers."

"You lost me."

"When you told me about your Evy, I could see you mentally touching her eyes with puzzled fingers. It's what people do, when they look at death. But for someone like you who has seen so much death—who has been an instrument of death—to still be puzzled . . . that is unique."

"You want a picture of me looking puzzled?"

295

She smiled. "Yes, something like that. But now that you've told me about her, it will be difficult to capture that look, because—"

"Because once you bring it out and look at it, it is gone." He was unaware how harsh his voice had become.

Her eyes looked suddenly stricken. She ducked her head, a fall of hair hiding most her face, but not before he saw her eyes water. "I'm sorry," she said. "I didn't mean—"

He reached out and covered her hand with his and as he did the room darkened, as if the light outside was controlled by a rheostat. Clouds, he knew, but the coincidence—the room darkening at the precise instant he touched her hand—startled both of them.

"I didn't mean to sound so strong," he said. "It's got nothing to do with you. It's something I've thought about, that's all."

There was a sudden hiss of rain hitting the garden and the small patio, and a breeze damp with the smell of garden and earth swept through the screen door, cool on his bare feet and legs.

He released her hand and sat back. "So what's the plan?" he asked.

"Plan?"

"What am I supposed to do now?"

"My father wants you to stay here for a few days, if that's okay with you. Rest. Make sure your shoulder is healing properly."

"And then?"

"And then I'm afraid you'll have to leave Japan for a while."

"What about you?"

"Until some kind of accommodation is reached with Sato and his American friends, my uncle insists that I stay here."

"You mean Sato has not been dealt with yet?"

She shook her head. "There are many here in Japan who agree with him."

"But he won't try for you again, right?"

"My uncle is only being prudent. For the last five years or so I've been my father's connection to the world. I control the bank accounts, okay my father's appointments." She smiled. "I represent him in the interminable meetings we Japanese are famous for."

He looked at her, at her almond eyes and her long, thick hair shiny even in the gray light. Her perfect lips. And wondered why she was there with him. She had been educated at the best universities—a Japanese blue blood, if such a thing existed. His education had been at the hands of his grandfather and the Marine Corps. His professors had been people like Peter and Shia Ling and Huang. She was—sleek. Sleek in mind as well as body. He was a scruffy bear looking in through the window. She had a future; he probably did not. One of these days, someone—probably someone like the Frenchman—was going to see him coming, and that would be that. It almost was the other night.

"Seriously," she said. "Don't you think it strange that two people such as us—two people from such different worlds—have come to be sitting here, across from each other?"

"Strange, if you look at it one way, I guess. Not so strange in other ways."

She frowned, and he realized he liked it when she frowned. When she frowned, he could see the girl in her. "It's not so strange," he said. "At least not for me. I know it sounds like a cliché—hell, it is a cliché. But one day—this is going to sound melodramatic . . . "

"Please," she said.

"Well, one day I should have died. And since then nothing has been the same. Nothing since that day has seemed strange."

He turned his head and looked out the window, at the rain sheeting into the fruit trees and bushes against the compound

297

wall. In his mind he saw himself and the others he'd been with kneeling in the dust at the side of the road, hands clasped behind their heads.

The Khmer Rouge had taken their watches, passports, cameras, their backpacks, but even the Khmer Rouge were not interested in the ancient, beat-to-shit GMC pickup they'd been trying to drive to Thailand.

The Khmer Rouge–kids, really, if not for the war–had tired of playing with the stuff they'd taken and had started to terrorize the two guys to his right–playing with them like cats play with mice. The guy next to him had pissed his pants, and he'd known for sure they were dead. To the Khmer Rouge only one thing could be funnier than making someone piss his pants: shoot him. Make him die. That'd be a real hoot.

The leader, an old man of twenty, had knocked his straw cowboy hat off with the barrel of his AK, and seen the scars on his forehead, and looked in his eyes, and had taken a step back and said something, and then the whole bunch of them had clustered around him, one of them with the flash suppressor of his AK pressed hard into his forehead. The leader had barked something, and they had formed up in a loose line and, leaving the piles of personal stuff lying in the dust, had moved off into the desiccated paddies. Mean, tough, veteran Khmer Rouge, most of them younger, and some of them not much taller than the AKs and RPGs they carried, their interval and discipline and professionalism the equal of any Marine Corps squad.

He squinted at the rain. That was weird enough, but then as the last of them stepped off the road into the paddies, an ancient C-47 more beat up than even the GMC pickup roared over a line of tall palms behind them, passing no more than fifty feet over their heads, one prop feathered–so close he could have hit it with a rock. Roared over them and over the squad of Khmer Rouge, somehow gaining enough altitude to clear the next line of palms before it crashed. There'd been a long, grinding sound, not very loud, followed by a small explosion. He remembered a weak tendril of smoke rising above the palms, as the file of Khmer Rouge double-timed toward it.

He rubbed the side of his face.

To this day, he didn't know why the Khmer Rouge had not killed the bunch of them. Something to do with him, but what?

He'd assumed that Huang had known he would never trust any of the planes that Chinese businessmen were paying American pilots who'd flown in Vietnam—most of whom were at the end of their rope because of dope or booze or both—to fly in and out of Phnom Penh. If one out of three planes made it, the Chinese businessmen had been happy; they'd made money. He had assumed that Huang had known he would be coming out on the ground and had put out the word with the local KR cadre.

But Huang denied doing any such thing. And Huang would not lie about something like that.

He would never know why the Khmer had not shot him. All he knew was that from the moment that squad of Death Monsters stepped away from him, nothing had ever been the same. It just hadn't.

He grinned at her, and with both hands grasped the lapels of the *yukata*. "Sitting in a house in Japan. At a table with the most beautiful woman I have ever known. Stitches in my shoulder. Rain outside—for me the only thing strange about all this is that none of it seems strange at all."

She smiled. "When Jim-san described you, I pictured someone different."

"Someone like. . . ?"

"Someone like Jim, I guess, only younger. A hard man."

"Hard is good," he said, and bobbed his eyebrows lewdly at her.

She rolled her eyes. "But you look years younger than you should—you look like you have few cares or worries. A retired athlete is what I would have guessed."

He spread his arms wide, the loose sleeves of the *yukata* ridiculously short. "A fine figure of a man," he said.

She laughed. "Well. . . ."

He dropped his arms to the table. "If it seems as if I have few cares or worries, it's because I don't. I mean, I care about a lot of things, but the truth is, most of my life has been a freebie."

"Haven't you ever wanted a family?"

"You mean like house and kids and car, that kind of thing?"

"You should at least have someone to care for you in your old age."

"My old age?" He laughed. "It's flat amazing I've lasted this long."

Outside the rain picked up again, the sound of it a heavy drumming on roof and patio. His nostrils expanded, sensitive to the wet, humid smells coming through the screen.

"Are you cold?" she asked. "I can shut the door, if you like."

"How about you sit here and listen to the rain, and I'll hunt up my clothes and get dressed and help you clean up."

"Oh, no," she said. "The doctor said you should rest. You go back to bed, and I'll clean up. The bed will be very comfortable, especially on a day like this."

He looked out the patio door. Gray sheets of water slanted through leaves, battering young plants against the earth, the sound of it triggering an eerie rumble-jumble in his head. A white-out of sound, fueled, he knew, by the residue of drugs in his system. He could almost feel the bed and the covers.

He imagined an envelope of well being created by the little house and Kei and the sound of the rain. He watched her mouth as she inserted a piece of melon between her lips, her mouth closing around her finger, sucking for a moment as she withdrew it.

"I think I will," he said.

Chapter 18
Dead Dogs and Hurt Pigs

He half woke to the feel of a painful erection held in warm, lubricated suction. He felt her hair brush his inner thigh and his erection engorged to the point of real pain tried to relax and, as he did and before he could fully wake and control it, felt everything give and spill in a spasm of electricity that arched his back and cramped his foot. Waves of it, as she drew him deeper and with more insistence into her mouth.

"Ah," he groaned, and reached to pull her head away. "What are you doing?" His muscles felt weak, drained, aching from the inside out, as if he'd had a malaria attack. His hands moved to the backs of her arms and he pulled her up onto his chest.

Her face hung suspended over his, her eyes mischievous behind a screen of hair. With one hand she pulled hair away from the left side of her face and tucked it behind her ear. Her lips were swollen. He felt a rush of heat in his crotch and in his face and neck.

"Please," he said, and rotated his body to the side, gently pulling her over on the bed next to him, her face on the pillow. "I'm an injured man."

She squirmed closer, eyes wide and full of guile, and he realized she was naked—of course, she was naked. From the waist down so was he. She reached behind and pulled a down quilt over both of them.

"Okay," she said. He felt her hand softly cup his balls. "I'll do something else."

He heard the music of Sade coming from the living room. Subtle, sensual Sade, melding perfectly with the sound of the rain outside and the feel of the creature next to him, her limbs twining warm and smooth with his. He felt himself slipping inside her, the rhythm of the music matching the movement of her body.

Rain drummed against the house. Over her shoulder he could see fan blades going round and round on the ceiling of her study. He imagined that he could feel blood moving through his veins, circulating the residue of the pill he'd taken before crawling back into bed. All of it—the music and her heavy-lidded eyes and swollen lips and hard nipples, the rain and the whip of the fan and the rustle in his blood—all of it melding into a weird montage of half-remembered sights and feelings: the drum of rain against forest leaves, the dull thud of distant rotor blades. Dead dogs and hurt pigs. Blood slick and sweet as her lips, as he lifted her leg and buried himself deep into her. He heard mewing sounds, and felt his shoulder rip a little, as he forced himself up kneeling behind her, pulling her legs back behind him so that he could lay stomach on top of her buttocks, both of them somehow pointed now toward the foot of the bed.

She arched her back and drove her ass upward, and ignoring his shoulder he rose onto his knees and grasped her hips. The room seemed to rotate in perfect counterbalance to the fan blades on the ceiling in the other room. Music pulsed. Sweet, sensual music building to a jumble of voices and sounds in his head.

A heavy rumble of thunder outside registered in his mind as the threat of an approaching storm. He knew snakes always waited out the monsoon in dark places. Wind sluiced against the window. And fear, like the rustle of dry garlic skins, shivered through him, Evy's gray eyes looking at him out of a black pig dead in the center of a ville. In his mind he heard the eerie ululation of a warrior's death song mixed with the sound of Jimi Hendrix's guitar.

On the far wall of the study a rogue's gallery of faces.

He relaxed his grip on her hips slippery with his sweat.

Through the doorway he could see that the entire far wall of the study was covered with framed pictures of faces, most of the pictures black and white. Faces of evil. Faces that mocked him. The face of a young Khmer Rouge, checked scarf around his neck. A recon soldier, eyes luminous in dark face paint under a bush hat. An old woman with beetle nut-stained teeth, her eyes black holes devoid of any human emotion. A man in coat and tie. A woman wearing pearls and earrings, hair perfectly coifed. All of them with the same eyes.

He felt her pressing against him, her voice coming from a long way off.

Evil faces. Every one suffused with some bent, awful facet of human potential.

He felt a thudding in his ears.

And the faces on the far wall, the knowledge of what they were, the opiate in his blood, the smell of sex and rain, the music—all of it congealed into a gray, pink-tinted mist that corded his muscles and made the veins prominent at his throat and forehead. Rage uncoiled cold in his limbs and in his stomach and he looked down and saw her perfect ass, the long, sleek curve of her spine, her beautiful black hair draped on the sheets.

And not knowing it he gnashed his teeth, the sound causing her to turn her head to the side.

"Are you all ri–" she started to say.

And cried out as he jerked himself out of her, and grasping his cock with one hand, her hip with the other, jammed himself into her anus.

She gasped, and tried to pull away, tried to drop her hips to the mattress, but he held her tight, his fingers sunk deep into the soft tissue of her hips.

"Ben. . . ," she said.

He felt himself push further inside her.

"Don't," she said in a smaller voice.

He looked down and he was a naked man impaled in a rigid, protesting woman. Music played in the other room. Jimi Hendrix. *Foxy Lady.* It was raining outside and he felt clammy and cold, his shoulder one large ache, a feeling of nausea spreading from his stomach into his limbs. He felt himself shrivel, no longer inside her. Heard her groan.

On the far wall of her study faces leered.

He sat on the edge of the bed and, looking for his underwear, felt her get up and hurry from the room. Heard the bathroom door open and close. The sound of the shower turned on. No crying. Of course not. She'd be too tough to cry.

Fuck her. Japanese kinky bent. Getting off on being next to—getting off on bedding someone whose picture belonged on that wall.

Hurting her or hurting himself, he didn't know. Didn't care. He knew his rage was directed more at himself, than at her, but so what. By doing what he'd just done, by being the person he'd just been, he'd only confirmed what both of them obviously already knew: there was no intrinsic difference between himself and people like those in the photographs.

Intrinsic! Did he just say intrinsic? How was that for a Jesuit word? The fact was, and she knew it, there was no difference, *intrinsic* or otherwise, between himself and someone like the Frenchman, or that squad of Khmer Rouge.

He found his underwear and put them on. *What a piece of work he'd turned out to be.*

He stood and pulled on his pants, ignoring the ache in his shoulder, and padded barefoot into the study. *Might as well see if he recognized anyone.*

She was truly talented, he had to admit. The eyes, the expressions, the way she managed to capture light and shade—the wall was stunning in its malevolence. There were no names or dates or titles, only pictures of slightly different sizes, all glass covered and all set in light gray matting with narrow, dark brown frames.

The Frenchman smiled at him, his eyes familiar in the gloom of a dimly lit bar. He knew from the array of bottles in the background that it was the bar in Bangkok. The Frenchman's pupils were flat black, the light glinting off bottles behind him emphasizing their utter lack of emotion.

Off to the side, a few pictures from the Frenchman, was a mirror framed the size of the pictures on the wall. The mirror was about chin height—eye level for most people. He stepped forward until his face was framed in the mirror.

He looked at the faces to the side. Looked at the faces above and below. Looked at his face in the mirror: his face was nothing special; it was nothing more than the face he saw when he shaved in the morning.

He smiled at himself and the smile changed the shape of his face, and the eyes that stared back at him above the smile matched the eyes in the other pictures. Before he could look away, he saw fear.

He pulled the chair out from the desk and sat, leaning forward, forearms on knees, head down between his legs. There was a metallic taste in his mouth. He breathed deep, felt the nausea recede.

He sat upright, his eyes glittering with anger.

A fine fucking how-do-you-do, he thought. Sitting in a room

306

in Japan surrounded by faces that defined what it was he thought he had been fighting. Sitting here feeling lower than whale shit—which, as every Marine knows, is at the bottom of the ocean. Sitting here feeling abused and used, and no one to blame but himself. He hated it when he started feeling sorry for himself. He'd made his choices. Live with it, asshole.

It wasn't her fault. She wasn't perfect. She had a little kink about the people she wanted to photograph. So what? Given her life—working with her father and Raven, and all—and given the fact that being Japanese she was not constrained by the kind of Judeo-Christian bullshit that the Jesuits had shoved down his throat—it would be *beaucoup* strange if she did not have a few kinks.

He took a deep breath and felt the stitches tighten. They must still be in there if he could feel them tighten. He stood, his thoughts arrested by the sudden realization that the other walls of the study were also covered with framed photographs. All the photographs were about the same size as the photographs on the wall he'd been looking at. One wall had pictures with green frames; the other had red frames. How had he missed them? The photographs on the other walls were in color. Vibrant colors that reflected people laughing, people crying, people smiling, people happy, sad, bemused, confused. A little Asian girl with a caterpillar on her finger, eyes round with wonder. An old Japanese man smiling around a half-smoked cigarette, molten sunset reflected on his creased face. Mourners at an Irish wake—probably Boston, where she'd gone to school. Jim in the middle of a stream, same old patched and leaky waders, his face turned slyly toward the photographer as the line, lit like his face by the light, snaked toward a trout just breaking the surface. How had she done that? he wondered, walking toward the picture. The trees and bushes in the photograph were bright with fall colors. Water bubbled against Jim's waders. Sunlight was on the line and on Jim's face. The rocks were slick and dark. And the trout—the trout was breaking the surface of the water, greedy for the fly inches above its open mouth.

He could spend days in here, he thought. Looking at her pictures was like looking at the creature on the bottom level of the Palace Museum in Taipei.

Each wall had a framed mirror. Obviously the idea was to compare the face you saw in the mirrors to the faces in the pictures on that particular wall

The Pumpkin Eater was on the wall with red frames. Only he wasn't the Pumpkin Eater. He was Peter in a suit and tie, seated alone and pensive on a bench near the Japanese garden at the other end of the Ishida compound, the black of his skin complimented by the green foliage behind him. From the photo, Ben would not have guessed he was an American, let alone the Peter he knew so well. A diplomat, perhaps. A businessman from Belgium or the Netherlands. European, at any rate, by the cut of his clothes. For sure, the antithesis of the Pumpkin Eater he remembered blending so perfectly with the jungle: it was a photograph of Peter as perhaps he would have been if not for Vietnam and Laos and Cambodia.

He turned slowly around. In their eyes and in their faces, the wall he'd seen from the bedroom was filled with evil in all its human forms. The intelligence in them was all too apparent.

The other walls ran a gamut of people and emotions: kids, women, men, young, old, in between. Happy, sad, wise, laughing, crying, sexy, aesthetic, strong, weak—the room was a representation of humanity as seen through her eyes and mind.

He tried his face in each of the mirrors. Smiled. Frowned. Made his face do whatever the people in the adjacent photographs were doing. When he did that, his face seemed to fit on each of the three walls. He found a piece of white paper on the desk and used it to hide his lower face. His eyes had no warmth. Not cold, exactly. Nor without emotion. But lit with an emotion he could not define. What made them like that? With Manfred and Robert Lee, he'd compared himself, and them, to a grizzly, but his eyes were not those of a grizzly—especially not those of the grizzly that had charged across the clearing, its eyes hot black sparks.

He stepped back. No, not a grizzly, that was for sure. More like the eyes of the cobra that had periscoped above the high grass.

Was that why it had left him alone? The two cobras had to have known that he was there. Hidden in the leaves and grass, waiting for his prey.

He felt a gray melancholy eel through his veins.

He was no warrior. He was merely a human version of that cobra—mature, now, and experienced, and because of that experience and maturity oh-so-lethal.

The big Japanese with the knife, the two men with leaded pipes, they'd made themselves the enemy, but they had not been in the same league as someone like the Frenchman or the Khmer Rouge. They had families and friends. And they believed in the task they had been given as much as he believed in the tasks he was given. They had been soldiers. And this was their country, not his. Their country, that is, until Ben Tails, hunter, sniper, Motorcycle man, venomous snake had wrenched life from them, and, in its place, left a hole, a dead circuit in the lives of those whose lives had twined with theirs.

That was part of it.

But most of it—the way he felt right now—was the fact that he'd crossed a line with her. Never mind that it was a line that he hadn't even known existed until he'd crossed it.

Drugs. His wound. The aftermath of the killing. He could blame it on a lot things, but the simple fact was that she made him feel life was precious. A fragile word, precious. One that neither fit him, nor what he knew to be real. But there it was: a fragile word that made him even more dangerous.

Man, was he fucked up, or what? Shrinks could write books about the snakes crawling around in his brain.

Since Vietnam and the death of his grandfather, there had not been much reason to give a damn. There'd been just himself and whatever he was doing at the moment. Even with Evy, he'd never had much to lose except himself.

He wasn't a father or a husband, an artist, doctor, or builder. He contributed nothing except his ability to hunt and to kill. If he died pushing the envelope, no big deal, not even to himself. No big deal, that is, until he met her.

He couldn't get a handle on it. It felt as if there was glue in his brain. He felt like banging his head against a post.

A few days with her, and he'd learned something that could not be unlearned. It was in there now. He looked around the room, at the pictures. He'd give anything to take back the last half hour.

He heard the door to the bath open and close, the shuffle of slippers.

She was like the bamboo, he thought. Strong, supple, capable of withstanding even the strongest wind. She was the antithesis of men like him—men who thought they were strong, but who were really nothing more than bull pines. Solid until the wind, and not enough give, had them down, shallow roots torn from the ground.

Time to go face the music, he thought. Bend as much as he could. He smiled to himself. Better yet, lie down on the floor. Stick his legs in the air. Grovel like the dog he was.

She was at the kitchen counter, her back to him, making what smelled like hot chocolate, her hair in a pony tail that reached nearly to her waist, stray strands damp at the collar of her blue and white *yukata.*

He cleared his throat. She poured more hot water into a mug and then placed the kettle back on the stove. She picked up a long-handled spoon and put it into the mug, hesitated a moment, and began stirring. She glanced back at him, and her eyes were vulnerable.

He looked out the window. He'd expected anger, contempt, disgust—anything but what was in her eyes. His throat felt thick. He tried to clear it, but there was nothing in it. "I'm sorry," he said, his voice sounding flat even to himself. "I saw—"

She picked up the mug, and turned and brought it to him.

She left the mug in his hands, the smell of the hot chocolate and the heat of the mug so out of place in his mind that he unconsciously raised the mug to his lips and took a sip. She walked past him into the living room.

He put the mug on the dining table, thought about it, and picked it up again and followed her into the living room.

She sat in a large, over-stuffed chair, drawing her feet and ankles up under her—a graceful movement that women seem to do effortlessly, but that most men, himself included, could not do at all. She looked out the window, her face in profile, long, slender throat exposed.

He walked to the window and holding the cup with both hands sat cross-legged on the floor between her chair and the window. He leaned forward elbows on knees, feeling the warmth of the mug in his hands. "Which wall were you going to put my picture on?" he asked.

She slowly turned her head. "You mean, on which wall of the study?"

"Yes."

Understanding and something else—anger—bled through the

look in her eyes. "I would not have put it in the study," she said.

Unable to hold her gaze, he looked down at the mug and the hot chocolate in it. He raised the mug to his lips and took a sip.

"Do you understand the mirrors?" she asked.

"I think so."

"Did you look in them?"

He took another sip of hot chocolate.

"If you looked in the mirrors, then you know you don't fit any of them."

He set the cup on the floor.

"None of my family or friends are on that back wall," she said.

He cleared his throat. "I saw the pictures through the open doors, and I recognized some of them, and, well, I thought—"

"You thought *what?*"

Startled by her tone he looked up. Her eyes had turned dark. Brittle. He'd never imagined her lips could look so thin. He looked past her to the kitchen.

"Tell me what you thought, Ben," she said, and he knew from the quiet in her voice that she already knew. What he had thought might be a reasonable excuse for his actions was in fact no excuse at all—had been an excuse only if she had intended to put his picture on that far wall. He had judged her and passed sentence and started to carry out the sentence all in an instant. From her voice he knew that to her that was the heart of it: that he had not considered, not even for a heartbeat, that there might be more to it. He had no excuse. At best he'd insulted her, at worst . . . *God damn it,* he thought.

"I'm sorry," he said, and met her eyes. His gaze slid back down to the *tatami.* "For what it's worth, I've never done anything like that before."

312

"Kinky little Japanese slut is what you thought." Her voice was matter-of-fact.

He looked up. Her eyes were hot.

With a speed that surprised him, she uncoiled from the chair and stood and went into the bedroom. He heard dresser doors open and shut, the quick hiss of a *shoji* door sliding open, a loud bang as it was slammed shut. "Asshole," he heard. *"Bakka* Motherfucker. . . ."

Anger is good, he thought.

"You could have hurt me," she shouted.

He grinned in the direction of the bedroom; felt his pulse in the stitches in his shoulder.

She reappeared in the doorway, wearing a plain, green dress with short sleeves and high neckline. She was genuinely furious, he could see that. She stared at him for a long moment, and then wheeled and went back into the room.

Oh, man, he thought. He'd just done it again. He'd misjudged the depth of her anger—just as he'd misjudged everything else about her. It was going to be a long time, maybe never, before she got over this. He sighed. Well, there was nothing he could do about it now except be himself. There was no way, not with her, that he could hide behind words or charm. He looked toward the empty doorway. Still . . . It was probably nothing more than wishful thinking, but he had the feeling that she hadn't yet made up her mind about him.

The killing, his wound, the drugs, maybe she was taking those things into consideration. He didn't think she knew— except maybe in a felt way—what lurked under the parts she knew. There was no way she could know about the adrenaline and the fear and the *get some.* She could not know that all he had to do was close his eyes and fire and festival, dark lanes lit with sickly yellow light, temple stones, a priest that wasn't a priest—all of it was right there and would always be right there, another memory added to those that already lived in him. She could not know that his mind was forever coated with the gray knowledge that he had taken lives, or that she had been for a few brief moments his only relief from that knowledge.

In this house with her, in this country, he knew none of it would surface the way it would someday back home. Later, when he was home, and when he was least prepared, it would creep out, the memory of what had happened at the Shrine. And that memory would lead to another, and then to another—memories tangled together like the roots of too many plants in a planter, so that if you tried to remove one and look at it, you found its roots inseparable from the roots of the plants around it. He was okay now, here with her, but he knew someday, in the sunshine next to a mountain stream, or maybe in a place as innocuous as Manfred's bar, sunlight would refract off water, or off a bottle of cold beer, and a memory would be there full and complete. He was okay now, but later the memories and the gray melancholy that always accompanied them would be there.

In the end, it would be not her but the people in his memories who judged him; who weighed his reasons against fear and blood lust and choice.

"And on that happy note," he muttered to himself. He picked up the mug of chocolate and stood and walked to the kitchen and set the mug on the counter. He stood for a moment looking down at the mug of dark liquid, and then picked it up, and forced himself to drink the entire, lukewarm, too-sweet contents.

He put the mug in the sink, and then crossed to the sliding glass door, and looked out at the rain and the well-tended little vegetable garden. Tiny, green tomatoes clustered under leaves shiny with rain. Behind the garden was the ancient, mold-encrusted wall of the compound.

The shrill, muted trill of the telephone interrupted his thoughts. He heard her voice low and indistinct as she answered it.

No regrets, he thought. I yam who I yam. And if I wasn't, I never would have met her in the first place.

He heard her hang up.

"That was Huang-*xiansheng*," she said from the doorway. "He wants to meet you at a coffee shop he says you know."

"The old sake brewery," he said.

"Yes. It is nearby. You can walk."

He turned. Her hair was in a braid, and once again she was beautiful and healthy, with not a hint of what had happened between them.

"When?" he asked.

"He is there now."

Chapter 19
Shedding Skin

The walk to the coffee shop was uneventful, her directions easy to follow, the lanes and streets and sidewalks sparsely populated—old people and housewives, for the most part. There might be a battle going on between the Ishidas and their allies and whoever it was that Sato represented, but walking to the coffee shop you'd never know it. The events of a few nights ago had obviously not affected the daily comings and goings of the local population.

He knew he was safe. No one would harm him here. The Ishidas had made certain of that. But knowing it and strolling down empty lanes in broad daylight, no weapons and a shoulder full of stitches, was a different thing entirely.

The coffee shop was a large, barn-like structure—an ancient, two-story storehouse dating back to the days of commerce along the canal. In its second incarnation it had been a *sake* brewery. Now it was a coffee shop. Its white walls and exposed beams made him think of German architecture—Hansel and Gretel, the Black Forest, that kind of thing.

Inside, the large open space under the vaulted ceiling was crossed by large, rough-cut wood beams. White walls. Dark wood floor. Dark wood tables and chairs and window moldings. Lofts at both ends of the room. When he was here before, he'd joked about how all the place needed were pink-cheeked German waitresses in pigtails and low-cut dresses, steins of beer clutched in their hands.

Reality was Mozart and pottery, small, earthen vases with real flowers, chair cushions covered with the burlap-like material used to filter *sake,* the smell of green tea.

Light came from windows high above the exposed rafters and from small, latticed windows set in the walls. Part of a giant willow could be seen through an open side door.

To his left, two old ladies ignored him as they sipped thick, foamy green tea from large ceremonial bowls. A young woman, her back to him, moved behind a wooden bar on the other side of the room. Huang was at a table at the far end of the room, seated on a bench that spanned the entire back wall.

Huang raised his hand, and Ben nodded, and headed for his table, all too aware of the empty tables. He itched to look up at the loft. The open side door remained empty.

An earthen cup and saucer and a black, lacquered bowl of what looked like vanilla ice cream were on the table in front of Huang. The ice cream was untouched. The one and only chair at the table would leave him with his back to the room.

Huang smiled, and gestured to the chair. "Please sit," he said in Mandarin.

Ben pulled out the chair and sat.

"Coffee?" Huang asked.

Ben flinched as the girl put a hot towel on a slender piece of lacquered bamboo next to his left hand. He had not been aware of her approach. Huang had undoubtedly noticed his flinch.

"*Kohii, onegashimasu,*" Huang said in Japanese, coffee, please.

Wordlessly, the girl left, and Huang sat back against the wall, arms folded across his chest. He was wearing a cheap, short-sleeved, white cotton shirt, a white, sleeveless undershirt underneath. Thick veins raised the skin of his forearms.

"Relax," he said in Mandarin. "No matter what has happened, we are friends."

"How is Peter?"

"He will lose his arm."

"He's lucky he didn't lose his life."

"Yes," Huang said. "And because he knows you, he knows that. Do you understand now that he was there to help?"

"And just how the hell did he expect me to know that?" Ben said in English.

"That was my fault." Huang inclined his head. "I should have made it clear the last time we met. He was there as a favor to me."

The girl put a cup and saucer in front of Ben, and in the middle of the table put another saucer with a tiny earthen container of cream. She put a matching sugar bowl next to the cream container, and left as silently as she had come.

"You said he has a wife and child."

"Two children actually. There's a new baby boy."

Ben turned away from Huang and looked out the open side door. In his mind he saw the Pumpkin Eater mottled with green camouflage and mud and sweat slide his AK forward through the leaves and point it in the direction of the Hmong they'd spotted hidden on the opposing slope. The Hmong had been unaware that they were there and that they had been running from at least a company of hunter-killer NVA who were about to flank them. He'd felt the blast as Peter fired half a clip, hot brass bouncing off his hat and cheek and neck, as one of the Hmong slid down the slope, M-16 caught by its sling around arm and shoulder. He'd found out when they got back that it had been a kid they'd both known from the big base at Long Tieng.

A breeze rustled through the big willow, streamers of leaves swaying across the open doorway.

In his mind he heard the lead NVA elements open up on

318

the Hmong position, he and Peter up and running, sliding, crawling, clawing their way up a steep slope, across a ridge, as mortar rounds began to impact the far slope where the Hmong were. Peter had gambled that the NVA would hear his AK and see or hear the body sliding down the slope and assume that it was one of their own opening up on an ambush. The distinctive sound of the Hmong M-16s, as the Hmong returned fire, further convincing the NVA that it was the Americans they'd been tracking who were shooting at them. It had taken him a while, what with the frantic scramble up and down steep, slick slopes, leg and arm muscles numb, lungs raw, to fully realize what Peter had done.

If not for Huang and Huang's men, he would have killed Peter, instead of merely kicking the shit out of him.

That same day, he'd caught an Air America bird to Udorn. From Udorn he'd hitched a ride to Bangkok, and from Bangkok he'd flown to Taipei.

Looking back on it now, it was easy to see that what Peter had done by sacrificing the Hmong was neither more nor less wrong than a lot of what they had been doing for years. The body of that Hmong kid sliding down the hillside had been the proverbial straw that broke the camel's back, that's all.

The Hmong were going to die anyway, Peter had said. And that had set him off. But really it was not so much what Peter had done or said as it was that—in that context—Peter was right to have done it

To the hill peoples, the Pumpkin Eater had been more than human. To them he had been a creature created by the horror and death that stretched in an unbroken line from the First IndoChina War and the fall of Dien Bien Phu to the present. If not exactly a God, then at least a black monster invincible in its luck.

Before Huang's men had pulled him away, he'd broken

319

the God's nose, cracked a couple of ribs, and left him with balls swelling to the size of baseballs.

Wandering around Taiwan, he'd realized that he was done with Asia, and he'd gone home, the memory of that Hmong kid sliding through dead leaves forcing him to leave everything behind–the money he'd made working with Peter, his collections of pottery and calligraphy, even most of his clothes.

As if by leaving all that he could shed memories and responsibility as easy as a snake sheds skin.

He pushed the chair back and stood and walked over to the doorway, and leaned for a moment against the sill. Leaves rustled as a breeze shivered through the willow.

To his left, behind the coffee shop, was a small stone patio with wooden benches. A stone path led in an undulating line from patio to canal. He pushed off from the sill and walked over to one of the benches and sat down.

The myth of the Pumpkin Eater. Always in his mind it had been about the Pumpkin Eater. But what about his own myth? How much of it had been disgust with what Peter had done, and how much of it had been Mr. Slide adding a final punctuation to his own myth?

He'd shot Peter. Shattered his arm. Had in fact killed him if Peter had been anyone other than the Pumpkin Eater. Strong enough not to pass out. Experienced enough to use his belt as a tourniquet. Strong and experienced enough to get up and walk away before the Japanese found him and killed him, too. *Ahh, damn,* he thought, not aware that he'd groaned out loud. He'd give anything to take that shot back. Give anything to sit down with Peter and find out how he had managed to find a wife and kids.

Peter had been exactly right: there wasn't much that the Pumpkin Eater had done that Mr. Slide hadn't done, too. And like he'd said, they'd done a lot of it together. He smiled wryly. They must have made a pair. The Pumpkin Eater and Mr. Slide; Mr. Slide and the Pumpkin Eater. Any way you flipped that coin, you lost. The two of them caught in a time and in a place where the weird and the lethal were the norm.

He shook his head. Even as he had pulled the trigger, he'd known that Peter would never expose himself like that. The Pumpkin Eater had been a master of the ambush. No way he would step out in the open like that. Except that he had. And feeling righteous and full of kill, Mr. Slide had pulled the trigger.

Well, fuck him if he couldn't take a joke, he thought. He'd only pulled it once, not many times like he usually did when he used a handgun. If the Buddhists were right, he'd atone for it in his next life by coming back as a slug or a rock or something.

He stood and walked back inside. Huang was sitting arms across his chest, his head bowed, as if asleep. His ice cream was a small slick mound in a puddle of cream.

Ben sat down.

Huang looked up and smiled. "I thought perhaps you had left."

"Still the same old shit, isn't it?"

"Fate," Huang said in Mandarin.

"Peter has a family. Is that fate, too?"

Huang shrugged. "Perhaps. Who can say?"

"I'm sorry I shot him."

"Yes," Huang said in English. "I can see that you are. But you acted correctly. If Peter had known that you had taken a gun from one of the men who attacked Miss Ishida, he would not have exposed himself."

"He told you that?"

Huang nodded.

"Still–"

"I was told that you had been wounded?"

"A knife. My shoulder. Stitches, is all."

"I am also told that you will be going home soon."

"I don't mean to be rude," Ben said in Mandarin. "But can I ask you something."

"Of course."

"Do you have a family? I mean, a family like Peter now has a family?"

"I have no family. You know that."

"I know your family were killed in 1948—you told me that. But I thought maybe—"

"I have no family."

"Well . . . why?"

The fingers of Huang's right hand tapped the table top. His eyes were black, unreadable.

"You said I could ask," Ben said.

"Let me tell you something," Huang said in Mandarin. "There is great danger in letting yourself reach a point where you believe that death is the same as life. . . . If you begin to see only death and what lies behind it—if you believe that what you see is life—then you have lost yourself."

"I don't understand."

"For me, after my family was killed by the Kuomintang, death was all there was."

Ben shook his head. "I can't even imagine."

"And I hope you never can. That is not the point. The point is that this is not China in the late 40s. It is not Cambodia in the 70s. You still have choices, Ben."

"Don't you consider it stupid that men like you and I are willing to exchange life for an idea? For a belief?"

"Ben, the fact that you have become surfeited with death and killing is precisely what makes you so valuable. It is why Raven hired you: your experience makes you careful with your decisions."

"I feel like a rat in a cage forever running on a wheel. I

chase life, but all I find is death or life so bent that the faster I run, the further I am from living."

"Then, perhaps you should stop running."

"Is that what Peter did?"

"He has now."

"Even if I stop running," Ben said, "I'm still in a cage."

"You have found a woman." Huang smiled. "That is good."

"Yeah. Found. And already lost."

"I see."

"What do you see, Huang? Today I looked in mirrors and I didn't recognize what I saw."

"Listen to me, my friend. No matter how much your own people have taught you to denigrate yourself, it is people like you, with your sweat and blood and sacrifice who have mastered the world in a way that nothing or no one ever has. Take comfort in that, and perhaps the rest will fall into place."

"Four men are dead that I know of, including Carlos, and I killed three of them. Peter is going to lose an arm. My shoulder was sliced open like a fish in a *sushi* shop. And you are trying to make me feel better by elevating all that to some. . . ." Ben paused, and shook his head. "Why can't you say what it really is? We are nothing more than wild dogs fighting and killing mainly for the sake of fighting and killing."

"Action is easy," Huang said, reversing a saying he knew Ben was familiar with. "Knowledge is difficult. But what is most difficult is when action becomes knowledge."

Ben smiled. "The ingratiating Chinese," he quoted in English, "ever moving with the current, is in any case inclined to tell a man what he thinks he would like to hear, rather than the unpalatable truth. And to his knack for tactful distortion may be added his isolation from the facts of life."

Huang chuckled. It had been something Ben had read when he had first started studying Chinese, a joke with them for almost as long as they'd know each other. "That be me," Huang said. "Mr. Don't-give-anyone-a-cold-shower."

"I don't think I can do this shit anymore, Huang."

"You are still a young man. Go back to your Montana. Rest. Jim is moving Raven's corporate offices to Montana, anyway. There'll be plenty for you to do there."

"To Montana? Why Montana?"

Huang shrugged. "Lower profile. Easier to protect from people like Sato. Friendly banking laws." He smiled. "Good fly fishing."

Ben smiled. "Well, there's that–good fly fishing."

"What will you do now?" Huang asked. "I mean today, when you leave here?"

"Go back to Ishida's until they tell me I can leave, I guess."

"Do you understand what is happening with the Ishidas?"

Ben snorted. "This is Japan. Does *anyone* understand what is happening?" He frowned, knowing that Huang had not lightly asked the question. "Sato used killing Carlos as a way to precipitate a confrontation between factions I know little about." He looked at Huang. "But of course it's more than that, or you wouldn't be here, and Raven would not be involved. Boxes within boxes, if I know you and Jim. Something to do with the custom in Asia of using drugs to finance agendas that cannot be financed through normal, legal means." He shook his head. "The only thing I know for sure is that I didn't sign on for anything like this."

Huang nodded.

Ben shifted in his chair. "But there's something else, too. They were going to snatch Kei and they were going to kill me–kill me for no other reason than, near as I can tell, the simple fact that Sato doesn't like me."

Huang slid out from behind the table and stood. Ben stood also, and Huang extended his hand. His grip was dry and callused. "We will meet again, my friend. Despite what you are feeling and thinking now, your fate is in Asia." He released Ben's hand. "The bill has already been taken care of by Ishida-san."

Ben watched him leave through the side door, a whip-thin man of indeterminate age, weathered, fit, gliding out of sight along the stone path that led to the walkway along the canal. Huang had been grateful that he had not killed Peter. Peter and Huang went way back. Peter was married to a Chinese. Peter and his family were living in China. Maybe Huang was responsible for the marriage, he thought. Maybe Peter had become family. It would sure explain a lot.

Huang had not eaten his ice cream, though, and he did not know what to make of that.

He watched Huang disappear from view. China. The Revolution. The Great Leap Forward. All those battles and political upheavals that had resulted in millions of deaths. How had Huang survived? Huang who could speak many languages. Huang who could live invisible in any country in Asia. Huang who always had connections.

He's right, he thought. It's time to go home.

Chapter 20
Clarity

School was out. Clusters of little boys dressed in matching blue shorts and shirts, square, black leather backpacks, and little hats that reminded him of Cub Scout hats ran past, white socks and black shoes flashing, jostling each other as they shouted, *"Gaijin! Gaijin!,"* or "Huh-roh! Huh-roh!" They reminded him of a litter of puppies at feeding time.

A group of junior-high girls dressed in long, black wool skirts and matching long-sleeved jackets rode toward him, stately on clunky, black high-handlebar bicycles. If the boys reminded him of puppies, the girls reminded him of Mennonite women riding their bicycles to town or out to the men in the fields. The girls giggled, watching him out of the corner of their eyes as they passed.

An old woman hunchbacked and bent nearly double, dressed in a stiff-looking brown kimono, smiled a toothless smile at him. Holding on to her walking stick, she bowed, her gray hair a wispy knot at the back of her head.

He smiled, and nodded, and continued past, for once comfortable with the day and the place and the people.

He'd done his part. Jim and Huang had inserted him into the mix in the hope that his presence at the Ishida house would provoke Sato to some kind of reaction. Not the reaction that had occurred maybe; nothing that extreme could have been anticipated. But at least a reaction that would help get the situation off dead center. No pun intended, he thought.

He turned into a smaller, even narrower lane that led to the back of the Ishida compound. He glanced up, searching the balconies seen here and there on the second story of houses set back from the walls that lined the narrow lane. Except for a woman watering plants, and another beating *futons* hung over metal rails, the balconies were as empty as the lane.

Other places in Asia, affluent neighborhood or not, the balconies and the lane would be alive with children playing, housewives and old people gossiping, neighbors calling to each other. Of course, the flip side of that was that in the rest of Asia instead of tile, the walls lining the lane would be topped with broken glass or concertina wire or both.

Eerie, though, he thought. Real eerie to walk down an empty lane in the middle of a city in the middle of the day, the only sound the distant dull slap of someone hitting a *futon*.

He figured he had the rest of the day—and maybe some of the night, if he was lucky—to make amends with Kei. He didn't give himself much of a chance—her eyes when he'd left had told him that. But, hey, he'd give it his best shot. And if his best wasn't enough, well—

He frowned. The small wood door set into the wall of the Ishida compound was ajar. He distinctly remembered the feel and the sound of the latch as he'd pulled the door shut behind him. Maybe Kei had gone out. He felt the skin prickle at the back of his neck. And then again, maybe not. Adrenaline shivered through him, his hand shaking as he stepped to the side and gently pushed the door open.

He peered around the doorway into the compound. Nothing moved. Kei's little house was silent. The latticed glass door to the *genkan* was open. His heart thudded heavy in his chest.

Go now, a voice in his head said. And without thinking

about it he slid inside the doorway and stood upright and walking on the sides of his feet walked at a normal pace to the doorway. Anyone could walk down the lane, he thought, and as he'd just done, open the stubby, little door set in the wall, and enter the compound. It would be risky, though. Enough of a risk that, even with the empty lane and neighbors that might not say anything, if it was him, he would not do it. It would have to be someone with very large *cojones.*

Or someone very arrogant.

He stepped out of his shoes and as he did saw a partial shoe print on the polished hardwood floor above the *genkan.* He heard movement to his left, in the living room. A grunt. The sound of something heavy being moved. A low mutter—a man's voice. A laugh that he recognized.

He stepped up out of the *genkan* onto the wood floor and keeping to the wall that separated the living room from the *genkan,* eased his head into the doorway, and saw Kei lying on the couch, dress bunched around her waist, panty hose torn, white panties exposed. Face swollen and misshapen, covered down one side in blood. Left eye half out of its socket. Dress torn, bra ripped or cut in two. One breast exposed. Red, raw marks on breast and ribs. Rib cage a nasty red-purple. Broken ribs, he thought. Broken cheek and eye bones. His mind calmly categorizing her injuries in a fraction of a second. Handcuffed hands. Handcuffed feet. Yellow-white, bloody bone protruding through bloody skin below her elbow. Dress and couch and floor and coffee table spackled with blood. Sato in a suit bending over her. Syringe in his left hand.

He stepped inside and, as he did, Sato glanced toward him, his eyes widening as Ben silently closed the distance between them and before Sato could react as hard as he could heel-kicked Sato in the right temple, knocking him down onto the couch and floor, the syringe propelled from Sato's hand, sticking in the couch next to Kei's shoulder.

He reached across Kei and with his left hand pulled the syringe out of the couch and grasped Sato's hair with his right and stabbed the syringe deep into Sato's neck. He depressed the plunger, and left the syringe in his neck.

Sato's eyes bulged and his body stiffened. His eyes rolled up and Ben slammed him face down on the floor and kneeling one knee on his back with one hand grasped Sato's chin, and with the other the back of his head, and with all his strength twisted violently, feeling and hearing vertebrae rupture and part.

He pushed the limp head away, and rolled the body over. The suit jacket fell open, exposing a 9mm Browning High-Power in a shoulder rig. He jerked the automatic free of the holster and worked the slide, ejecting a round. He'd carried a Browning High-Power whenever he worked with Peter in Laos and Cambodia, and he knew this model was not double action. By working the slide he'd made sure there was a round ready to fire.

He thumbed off the safety, and put the Browning on the coffee table, and turned to Kei.

Her one good eye was half shut, glassy with pain and shock. It watched him, waited for him to notice, and then swiveled toward the kitchen and hallway at the other end of the house. He sensed movement at the end of the hallway–the toilet door opening–and he snatched the Browning from the table and took two quick steps to the hallway and saw a figure coming from the toilet, the gun in the man's hand firing, two quick explosions, rounds snapping past and into the side of a bookcase inside the living room door. He felt his elbows and chest and knees hit hardwood floor, sliding forward toward the man, both hands wrapped around the grips, the automatic extended up, barely aware of the recoil and the stutter of explosions as rounds impacted into a picture hanging at the end of the hall and into hip, chest, chest chest chest throat, the man twisted and snatched to the side by the throat shot and by an aimed shot that took off the top of his head, the man's arm and the gun in his hand breaking glass doors on a cabinet set into the hallway wall, Ben unable to stop a final shot that splintered molding under the cabinet.

Ears ringing, he scrambled to his feet, arms extended, the Browning tracking windows, the sliding door to the patio outside the dining room, the *genkan* behind him. Kei's eye stared at him from the living room.

He walked quickly to Sato's body and checked the shoulder rig for another magazine. Found one. He ejected the half-used magazine. Inserted the new one. Put the ejected magazine in his back pocket.

"Are there more?" he asked, his voice sounding as if it was coming from the bottom of an empty barrel. Something bloody drooled from around the gag in her mouth. Her eye squinted shut.

He walked back to the hallway, automatic extended. The hallway reeked of cordite and draining body. He looked quick in the other rooms, ignoring the stink coming from the corpse in the hallway. A white man. A *gaijin*. Something familiar about him. Clumps of pink brain made slippery the floor at the far end of the hallway. Dark blood pooled outside the empty skull cavity. Jeans. Running shoes. Blue polo shirt. Without the top of his head, the man looked Neanderthal. It was the short, aggressive one from Coffee Shop Cha Cha. Bits of brain matter clung wetly to wall and to broken cabinet. He was careful not to step on any broken glass. He safed the Browning, and returned to Sato's body, and put the automatic on the coffee table. He searched Sato's pockets for a handcuff key.

With both hands he flopped the body over onto its stomach

330

and chest. The body felt as if it was filled with wet sand. His ears were numb, ringing. The key was in the back pantpocket.

He felt strange—not like he usually did. He looked toward the body in the hallway. Looked at Kei. He didn't feel anything. No rage. No fear. No trembling muscles. Only a cold clarity free of any emotion or excitement whatsoever. It felt kind of good. All he wanted to do was kill.

"Your ankles and wrists are swollen," he said. "I'm going to release the cuffs so I can put you on your back. You are going into shock. It's going to hurt. Ankles first."

He inserted the key into the cuff and squeezed the cuff tighter, allowing the key to turn. The cuff sprang free and, as it did, he heard a small, muffled sound, and felt her ankle go limp. Good, he thought. The cuffs are bad, but the broken arm will be a lot worse.

He freed the other cuff, and rolled her onto her side and freed her wrists, dropping the cuffs onto the floor next to the other pair. He gently removed the gag—one of her socks—from her mouth. A tooth came out with the sock. As carefully as he could he laid her back on the couch, using both hands to place her broken arm across her stomach. She was very pale and had lost blood and there was no way he could tell if she had internal bleeding. Her breathing was shallow, but at least her lungs were working. He put cushions under her feet, made sure by putting his finger in her mouth that her airway was clear, and then put an afghan that he found on one of the stuffed chairs over her.

He picked up the automatic, and thumbed the safety off, and walked to the hallway. He'd call someone, he thought, if only he knew who to call. *Where was everyone? It must have sounded like a war in here.*

Pieces of skull, like pieces of broken pink pottery, were scattered about the floor. Random line-designs decorated the curved inner surfaces—crazing, potters called it. The whole place stunk of cordite and blood and feces. His ears were ringing; his body felt swathed in cotton. The pieces of skull and the stench were proof that he had survived, but, like always, survival felt surreal, his connection to time and place and normal emotion corroded by a sick, cold energy that skittered in his blood and in his stomach.

What to do about her? He had to get help. But if he went running out the door, there might be others waiting. He looked around once more, a vague memory of the *hit hit hit* into the web of his hand insufficiently related to the carnage in the small house.

He whirled toward the *genkan* and saw an old man standing outside the door. Straggling gray moustache. Wispy goatee. His eyes cringed. Ben stared at him over the front sight blade of the Browning.

The old man slowly raised his arms up and out, palms toward Ben, as if trying to push Ben away.

The uncle, Ben thought. The driver. He lowered the Browning. "Get some help," he said. *"Wakarimasuka,* do you understand? Go get some help. God damn it!" he shouted, and raised the Browning. "Don't fucking bow at me!" He stepped forward, the Browning pointed at the old man. "Get some help! Now!"

• • •

Ben watched the ambulance as it inched along, edging past dark sedans and marked police cars parked along the compound side of the lane, the sound of its siren echoing between walls and buildings. As the ambulance passed the last car, it picked up speed, and he watched it recede down the lane—watched until it turned a distant corner and disappeared, the eccentric, obnoxious up/down sound of its siren marking its passage through the city.

Once he'd gotten the old man motivated, it hadn't taken long for help to arrive. Two old women, gray hair in tight knots at the back of their heads, and wearing matching tan aprons over nondescript dresses, had hurried down the path, stopping only to bow deeply to him as they entered the house. They had both ignored the gun in his hand and the body in the hallway, intent only on finding Kei and tending to her. All business, the two old woman, talking to each other and to Kei in breathless, rapid-fire Japanese impossible for him to understand. Local healers, he'd assumed. Midwives, nurses, whatever. He'd half expected them to throw salt or something.

Next it had been two policemen in blue uniforms and Sam Browne belts running down the path, revolvers in hand, the hat on one falling off when he stumbled on a pathway stone and nearly fell. The two policemen had been too excited by the bodies and the injured Kei to even notice the Browning inside his belt at the small of his back. They had tramped back and forth between the bodies and Kei and him, totally destroying the crime scene, one of them talking excited into a portable radio. *Gaijin* this and *gaijin* that was about all he'd been able to make out. He had gone outside and sat on the same bench that Peter had sat on when Kei had taken the picture of him—the one on the wall in her study.

More cops had arrived. Suits, this time. One with reasonably good English had politely asked him to stay where he was. The same cop had assigned a young patrolman to stay with him. He had ignored the patrolman, choosing instead to watch Kei's little garden, bemused by the juxtaposition of the perfectly healthy green, growing garden with what was inside the house.

Fifteen minutes or so later, Kei's uncle, the rich, bull-necked one with the jewelry, led an entourage of silent, grim-faced expensive suits and power ties down the path, the whole bunch of them, including several large and very fit individuals

333

in less-expensive suits, sweeping past as if he were not even there, a doctor and several EMTs with a wheeled gurney in their wake, their only sound the clatter of expensive shoes, the swish of expensive cloth, the metallic sounds made by the gurney bouncing over the uneven surface of the walkway. Grim, determined faces. Game faces. He would have laughed out loud if he hadn't been so pissed off that it had taken them that long to get there.

They'd disappeared inside, bodyguards and all. It was amazing how many people had gone into that little house. Hell of a crime scene. Kei all chewed up and lying there, while a bunch of well dressed assholes trying to look tough and officious rubber necked.

The young patrolman, to his credit, had by turns looked nervous, then worried, then embarrassed.

Sitting there, trying not to think of the cluster fuck going on inside Kei's house, he'd wondered briefly if Huang might have known what was coming down. But he'd dismissed the thought almost as fast as he'd thought it, embarrassed with himself for even thinking it. Huang would never countenance something like this. Clearly, the two men had not known he was still there or they would have been better prepared. Especially the American.

Where had everyone been? Where was Mr. Ishida? Sato, that piece of human garbage, would never have attempted something like this, no matter how desperate, unless he'd felt he had a good chance to pull it off.

The two EMTs had carefully wheeled the gurney out of the house, Kei covered by a blanket, bags of plasma or glucose or who-knew-what, this being Japan, swinging from thin, metal poles at the head of the gurney, tubes from the bags leading to her good arm lying on top the blanket. He'd stood and watched her go by, her one eye covered by a moist-

334

looking wrap, the other nearly shut. He hadn't been sure but he thought she had seen him standing there.

He'd followed the gurney around the main house and out into the lane, and watched as they loaded her aboard, the doctor and one EMT and one of the old ladies squeezing into the narrow van with her.

He could still hear the ambulance as it wended its way through the city to the hospital.

He turned to go back inside and saw that the young patrolman assigned to him had been joined by another, equally young and nervous patrolman. Their eyes darted to each other, back to him. He bent forward to clear the doorway and as he did felt the Browning at the small of his back. That's why they were so nervous, he thought. They must have seen the grips over the tops of his belt when they followed him out into the lane.

Kei's uncle was coming toward him from the direction of the main house. Face stern. Muscles bunched at the jaw. Ben stopped and waited.

One of the patrolmen stumbled to the side to avoid colliding with him. "*Shitsurei,*" excuse me, the patrolman blurted, hastily stepping back behind him.

"Mr. Tails—" the uncle began, his voice and his manner those of an executive too busy to brook any nonsense.

"Where was everyone?" Ben interrupted, letting what he felt leak into his voice.

The uncle paused.

The patrolman who had nearly collided with Ben quickly said something to him.

The uncle frowned at Ben. "Are you armed, Mr. Tails?"

"Of course, I'm armed."

The uncle squinted. "Then would you please give me your weapon?"

"Where was everyone?"

"Your weapon, Mr. Tails." He held out his hand. "If you please."

Ben reached behind and pulled the Browning from his belt and brought it around in front of him, barrel pointed to his left, toward the compound wall. Holding the other man's eyes with his, he pushed the eject button with his right thumb and let the loaded magazine fall to the ground. With his left hand he pushed the slide back, ejecting the chambered round, the round bouncing off the uncle's suit, and pushed the slide lock up, locking the slide open.

He handed the automatic to the uncle.

"It's Sato's," he said

The uncle handed the Browning to the patrolman on Ben's right. The other patrolman bent and picked up the ejected magazine. Without taking his eyes from the uncle, Ben handed the patrolman the partially loaded magazine from his back pocket.

"Mr. Tails—"

"Where was everyone?" Ben asked again. He knew that even if the two patrolmen could not understand the words, they for sure understood the tone of his voice. The uncle was losing face. But he didn't care. In fact, he was going to hit the son of a bitch if he didn't get an answer pretty damn soon. See about face then.

The anger in the uncle's eyes was plain to see. "Mr. Ishida must have a body check every week," he said, his voice almost a bark. "His heart and his blood must be checked by machines at the hospital. Of course, we went with him. You were here with Kei—" His eyes widened.

"That's right," Ben said, the sarcasm in his voice making it clear that no one had told him that he should have stayed. "I wasn't here."

"Huang-*xiansheng*," the uncle said, more to himself than to

Ben. He seemed to deflate, his broad face turning pale. He turned away, right eye twitching. He muttered something in Japanese.

And then grated a series of commands to the two patrolmen. The two patrolmen came to attention, and bowed, and hurried past Ben, down the path that led to Kei's little house.

The uncle squared his shoulders. With his right hand he made sure his tie was tucked into his suit. Chin jutting, he faced Ben. "It is my fault," he said. "I was told you would be meeting with Huang-*xiansheng,* and I forgot. They knew Kei was alone because we told them you had left Japan."

Ben nodded. What had gone down at the festival was almost unheard of in a country like this–and then only between Yakuza factions. What had happened to Kei here, in her own house, on the estate of a respected family, was something that even he had not imagined, let alone anticipated. Like everyone else, he had assumed that Kei was safe as long as she stayed in the sanctuary of the compound. "It was my fault as much as yours," he said.

The uncle briefly inclined his head, acknowledging Ben's attempt to share responsibility.

"Will she be okay?" Ben asked.

The uncle sucked air through clenched teeth. "It is difficult to say. . . ."

They were silent for a moment, each with his own thoughts of Kei. Ben seeing her at the dining table that morning, one eye hidden by a fall of shiny black hair. Morning seemed like days ago.

"Can I see her?" he asked.

The uncle regarded Ben in that half-smiling way that in Japan was the precursor of news that would cause great embarrassment or loss of face. "Mr. Tails–how can I say this?"

"Just say it."

337

"Of course, we are very grateful to you for saving Kei." He smiled at Ben, and Ben recognized the smile for what it was: an attempt to allay the impact of what he was about to say. "But I am sorry to say that you must leave the country immediately. Those are Mr. Ishida's instructions."

"He knows, then?"

"Yes. He knows. But he does not yet know the extent of her injuries."

"I was never here, is that it?"

"Yes. That is exactly it. You were never here. I am instructed to give you money adequate for your journey, and adequate to compensate you for any loss of business or personal property."

Ben stared at him.

"It was a near thing with the man in the hallway," he said. "Most men would have passed out from such injuries, but she was able to warn me."

"Kei Ishida is a special woman, Mr. Tails."

"So I've noticed."

"No," the uncle said, surprising Ben. "I think perhaps you have not. Kei is her father's right hand. His confidant. She, and not I, will succeed him as head of the family. Kei is educated. Traveled. At home in many countries. She speaks English, Mandarin Chinese, and French. She has been schooled in arts and music, and in traditional Japanese martial arts. Our family has invested much in her, Mr. Tails. She well understands her responsibilities. And her responsibilities are to her family first, not to the organization that you and my elder brother are a part of."

Ben was silent.

"There is a long history of such women in Japan, Mr. Tails. But even among them, Ishida Kei is special." He paused. "Do you understand what I am telling you?"

He understood all right. She was special, that was for sure.

338

But no matter what this asshole was telling him, she was not *that* special. The real message here was that there was no way the family was going to let him get close to Kei. The fact that he had been sharing more than her hospitality had obviously already caused serious consternation–though he wondered what Mr. Ishida thought about it.

One thing was clear, though: they were not going to let him near her. Not even to say *sayonara* on the way to the airport.

"I understand that I am a *gaijin*," he said.

"That is not wha–"

"Sure it is," Ben said.

The uncle flushed, his neck reddening around the collar of his shirt. He bowed a short bow. "If you have your passport and Alien Card, I will see that you are driven to Nagoya International Airport. There is a Delta Airlines flight to Portland this evening."

"I have my passport and Alien Card on my person," Ben said. "I do not wish to go back in that house. Please give my best wishes to Miss Ishida for a quick and complete recovery. And please convey to Mr. Ishida my sincere regret for not being here when I should have been."

"I will tell–"

"I'll wait in the lane for the driver," Ben said. He turned and walked toward the entranceway. *"Vaya con dios,* mother-fucker," he muttered.

At the gate, he turned for one last look at the compound. The uncle was already walking back toward the main house. Take care, Kei, he thought. Be strong.

And turned and slipped through the doorway.

Chapter 21
Monsters

The best thing about Nagoya International Airport was that some of the small restaurants tucked away on the second floor of the Departures building were as good as any he'd found in the city. The food was quick and good and—miracle of miracles, this being Japan—it was not expensive.

The hallway was sparsely populated, the window of a souvenir shop reflecting the images of two uniformed cops and three or four—the number seemed to vary as he moved through the airport—plainclothes cops who had followed him since he'd climbed out of the car.

He hesitated outside a small restaurant, looking at the display window containing plastic models of food served inside. *Katsudon. Tendon. Soba* noodles. The usual suspects.

He was hungry, thirsty, and he needed a shower, but he'd settle for food and drink.

In the restroom, he'd scrubbed dried blood from his right arm, and soaked his hands in hot water to loosen blood caked under his fingernails. Looking at himself in the mirror, he'd thought that if it was up to him, he wouldn't have let the person he saw in the mirror within sight of an airplane, let alone on one. But the two women at the check-in counter had smiled, processed his ticket and passport, bowed, and

340

wished him a good trip. No luggage. No carry on. Only a Business Class seat to Portland, Oregon, with open connections to Salt Lake City and Missoula, Montana. Well, he was a *gaijin,* after all. And *gaijin* by their very definition were expected to behave unnaturally. No luggage? Dried blood on your arm and under your fingernails? Have a good trip, Mr. *Gaijin,* sir.

He'd had a bad moment in the restroom when someone had come out of a toilet stall and the body in the hallway had jumped out at him again. But a little water splashed on his face had taken care of that. Right now, he felt as if he'd gone three rounds with someone stronger than him. His arms and shoulders had that kind of soreness, and his back burned where the stitches were. The stitches hadn't come apart, but he could tell that the skin had stretched away from them. He was going to have a hell of a scar.

He ducked under the cloth banner across the entrance.

"Katsudon teishoku hitotsu," he said to the square-faced, middle-aged woman behind the cash register, one *katsudon* set. *Katsudon* was a breaded pork cutlet fried with egg and onion in a slightly sweet soy sauce placed on top of a bowl of steamed rice.

He paid the woman and she handed him his change and a ticket. When his order came, whoever brought it would tear off half of the ticket. The other half served as a receipt.

There were three empty tables along the far wall, two chairs at each, and three larger tables, four chairs each, down the center. All the center tables were occupied.

He selected the middle table along the far wall, and sat facing the entrance.

"Biiru ippon," one beer, he said to the master, when he arrived with the inevitable cup of green tea.

Paper sheets filled with elegant Japanese script–menus that

341

changed with the season—were tacked to the walls between large beer and *sake* and whiskey posters.

The master placed a sweating bottle of Sapporo beer on the table, a small glass next to it. Drinking from the bottle was a major no-no in Japan, and he poured and quickly drank a glass, the feel and taste of the cold beer excruciatingly sensual. *"Mo ippon,"* another bottle, he said to the master, and by the time the next beer arrived, he was finished with the first.

He started on the other beer, and the food came on a tray, and until he finished eating, he thought of nothing except how good the food tasted, only vaguely aware that other customers and the master and the woman at the register were watching him out of the corner of their eyes—watching, as the Japanese always watched, his improbable skill with chopsticks.

The Chinese expected everyone to use chopsticks, but to the Japanese finding a *gaijin* able to use chopsticks was sort of like finding a monkey that could read.

The woman left her place at the register and went to the back of the room and brought him a cup of *hoji cha*, roasted tea. The cup was a piece of *Tokoname* pottery—pottery done in the natural, reddish-clay style that he liked so much.

He admired the cup for a moment, and then sipped the tea. His only regret—besides Kei—was that he could not return to his apartment and pick up his tiny collection of Japanese pottery: a small vase with a delicate, subtle glaze; an antique tea set, the mottled, pewter-gray cups thin and light as expensive crystal; five, ancient *sake* cups.

He set the cup down and sat upright, arching his back to stretch it, and as he did felt something in the front pocket of his jeans. The envelope. He'd forgotten all about it. The driver, a young guy, probably a cop, had handed it to him just before he'd climbed into the car, and he'd stuffed it in his pocket, asleep in the back seat before the car had even left Ohmi-hachiman.

He opened the envelope and took out a bank draft. One hundred thousand dollars. He looked again, making sure he'd gotten the number of zeros right. Damn, he thought, not sure whether he should feel flattered or offended.

The bank draft had come at the instruction of the old man, he reasoned. Not the uncle. If Mr. Ishida thought he was worth that much, then who was he to argue. After all, he'd saved her life.

Maybe he'd buy his grandfather's house back.

A *gaijin* came into the restaurant. The other man from coffee shop Cha Cha. Tall. Thin. Blond. Late thirties, early forties. Hair short on the sides, long at the back. Preppy in pleated tan slacks and woven leather belt and dark blue polo shirt. *What now?* Ben thought.

The man paused at the cash register. He spotted Ben, and raised his hand in greeting, as if he and Ben were old friends, and made his way between tables and chairs and staring customers to where Ben sat.

"Mr. Tails." He pulled the other chair out from the table. "How are you?"

"Go away."

The blond man laughed, as if Ben had made a joke, and sat, sitting at an angle so that he could cross one leg over the other. He picked particles from the knee of his trousers. Watching what his hand was doing, he said absently, as if it was of no particular importance. "I want you to know that I am not in a particularly happy state of mind at the moment, Mr. Tails." His hand paused and he looked up, giving Ben the full weight of his blue eyes. "So if you don't mind—" His eyes widened.

In his mind, Ben could feel his hand wrap in the man's hair, could hear the sound of his face smashed down onto the table top, the sound like meat slapped hard onto a butcher's block. He grinned crookedly, not aware that he had grinned. It was the same weird clarity that he'd felt looking at Kei on the couch.

"Whoa!" the blond man said, uncrossing his legs and raising both his hands palms out. "Slow down, pardner."

"I'm not your fucking pardner," Ben heard someone say. He blinked. The blond man across from him had his hands raised like a banker being held up in a bad Western.

Two plainclothes cops came in and said something to the woman at the register. They walked over and sat at one of the tables against the opposite wall, both of them making no attempt to hide the fact that they were there to observe Ben and the blond man. Outside, on the other side of the display window, were two men in United States Marine Corps uniforms–khaki shirts, blue, red-stripped trousers, barracks hats. A master sergeant and a corporal.

"Put your hands down," Ben said. "You're embarrassing me." The top sergeant was trying to peer inside through the display window. "What do you want?" Ben asked the blond man.

"I just want to talk to you for a minute."

"Hang on," Ben said, and stood, and threaded his way between tables.

"I'll be right back," he said to the two, blank-faced cops, *"Chotto matte, kudasai,"* and walked past the register, ducking underneath the cloth hanging over the entrance, out into the broad, brightly-lit hallway.

The top sergeant had three up and three down, crossed rifles in the center. Tall. Lean. Grizzled. Jug ears and a nose that had been broken more than once. Scars above and at the sides of his eyes. A boxer.

"Top," Ben said.

"Sir?"

"Are you here with that limp dick civilian—the one just went inside?"

The corporal came up beside the sergeant. The corporal was much younger. Big. An all-American kid with the kind of arms and hands that come from hard work and not from pumping iron in a gym. Both men had expert rifle and pistol badges; no ribbons of any sort. The sergeant's name tag said Whaley; the corporal's said Power.

"Sir?" the sergeant again said, his face and the tone of his voice polite.

"Do you know who I am, sergeant? Did James Bond, or whoever he thinks he is, brief you at all?"

"Sir, we have no knowledge whatsoever of who you are."

Ben smiled, and extended his hand. "Former United States Marine Corps Staff Sergeant Ben Tails."

The Sergeant, hesitated, and then shook his hand, his grip polite.

"Corporal," Ben said. The Corporal's hand engulfed Ben's, and Ben realized he'd never met anyone with a more powerful grip. "Damn," he said.

"Iowa State wrestling champ," the Sergeant explained.

"You guys must be Embassy guards?"

The top sergeant snorted. "Not hardly fucking likely," he said. "Excuse the French."

"No?"

"You were a Marine, you say?"

"Two tours and change in-country," Ben said.

"With. . . ?"

Ben smiled. "With not hardly fucking likely," he said.

The top sergeant looked more closely at Ben. "You have a handle when you were in-country? One of those guys with his own call sign, maybe?"

"Mr. Slide."

"Oh, hell, yes. I saw you a couple of times up by the Rock

Pile. You were always by yourself, that's how come I remember. Saw you again–where was that?" He looked at the corporal as if the corporal ought to know. "You came through the wire on the tail of some Recon FNGs who didn't know you were there until you were all inside the wire."

"Could be."

"Could be?" He shook Ben's hand again, and this time his grip was strong and heartfelt. "Damn sure was." He turned to the corporal. "Bear, you boot camp. You know who this is?"

Corporal Power looked confused.

"This man has his name on that board at the sniper range. It's about three from the top. We're Force Recon," he said to Ben. "We're supposed to be getting familiarized with the embassy. You know, see where everything is in case–well, you know. In case." He looked disgusted. "But so far all we've done is baby sit that asshole in there."

"Who is he?" Ben said. "I'm asking because for some reason he wants to talk to me."

The sergeant glanced at the corporal. "Don't really know. His name is Cyr–*Mr.* Cyr to us. DEA, FBI, CIA–one of them. It don't really matter to us. They're all alike."

"Think their shit don't stink," the corporal said.

"Well, he wants to talk to me so I guess I'll go talk to him. C'mon inside and I'll buy you a beer."

"We're on duty, sir," the corporal said.

"Yeah. We're on duty," the top sergeant said sarcastically. "What's wrong with you, Power? This man is a Marine and he just offered us a beer."

"Tea, maybe?" Ben said to the Corporal. "Coffee? A rice ball?"

"You would not believe today's Corps," the Top said to Ben. "You just would not believe."

"That's exactly what the old salts said about us, Corporal,"

Ben said, as he led them inside the restaurant, both Marines uncovering as soon as they were inside.

"We'd best sit over there," the Top said. "Next to those two cops." He looked at Ben. "You must be a popular guy."

"My lucky day. Hey, look. If I don't get a chance to talk to you later. . . ."

"No sweat," the sergeant said. He stuck his hand out. "It was good to see you again, Mr. Slide." Ben shook his hand. He extended his hand to the corporal.

"Yeah. Semper Fi, old dude," the corporal grinned, his grip merely crushing this time.

Ben watched as they seated themselves. He turned to the woman and gestured to the two Marines. *"Biiru ipon,"* he said. *"Katsudon futatsu,"* a beer, and two orders of *katsudon*. He gave her a 10,000 yen note, and refused the change. Tipping was not done in Japan, but he knew customers would turn away as soon as they saw the two cops and so many *gaijin* in the restaurant.

The blond man was giving the Marines a look that said they would answer to him later. The two Marines studiously ignored him.

"They weren't doing you much good outside," Ben said, as he sat down.

"Mr. Tails. Ben. I apologize for my bad manners. One of my associates—in fact, the man I was with the other day in that coffee shop—was killed today in a traffic accident. We were on our way to the scene when I received word you were here at the airport."

"Gee," Ben said. "I sure hope no one else was hurt."

"I understand the body is burned beyond recognition."

"The body?"

"My associate."

"A crispy critter. How awful."

347

The man studied him for a moment. "You really are a wise ass, aren't you?"

"Actually, what I am is a motorcycle salesman on his way back to the States for a little R and R."

"We both know exactly who you are and what you do, Mr. Tails. According to Japanese Immigration you departed Japan several days ago from Osaka International Airport."

"Really. Well, as you can see, unlike your crispy-crittered friend, I are not yet 'departed'."

"You sonofabitch—"

"Ah-ah," Ben said, and wagged his finger at him.

The blond man flushed, and glanced toward the two Marines. "You think I'm just some CIA, Ivy-League twit, don't you?"

"Perish the thought."

"I'm FBI."

"Well, that certainly changes things."

"I was twelve years on the street before I was sent here."

"No kidding? Twelve whole years. Gosh. Tell me, what school did you attend before you became a G-man?" He smiled to himself at his use of the word "attend."

"I did my graduate work at Columbia."

"There you go."

"What does that mean, there you go?"

Ben watched the two Marines digging into their *katusdon*. Both men were proficient with chopsticks. The bottle of Sapporo was already empty. The Top caught his eye and raised his chopsticks in a gesture of thanks. Ben smiled. Marines. The good ones were always polite.

"I thought the FBI left drug stuff to the DEA," he said.

"Is that what you think this is about? Drugs?"

Ben shrugged. There was a weakness in the blond man's face that he could not define. "It doesn't matter what I think. I'm just a motorcycle salesman."

"You underestimate your worth, Mr. Tails."

What was it about him? Ben wondered. Columbia meant he'd talk in terms like Realpolitik and Collateral Damage and You Can't Make An Omelet Without Breaking Eggs. Machiavellian by nature, a bureaucrat by training. The sacrifice of lives in the pursuit of the political flavor of the year would be a way of life to him.

"Raven is an anachronism," the blond man said. "A dinosaur," he added, in case Ben didn't understand the word "anachronism." *"Terry and the Pirates*–and how long has it been since you've seen *Terry and the Pirates?"* He slouched back in his chair. "Raven International is rickety and inefficient and, worse, it allows people like you to function as little more than vigilantes."

"I don't go looking for people, Mr. FBI, or whoever you are. I especially don't go looking for people like Carlos Montoya. I always–repeat, *always*–have background. Usually a whole box of it. Everything from satellite surveillance to high school transcripts. And it is people like you who compile the information in that box. It is people like you who request that someone like me get down and dirty and find out if the person in that box is who or what you think he or she is."

"Not so loud, please, the blond man said. "There are two policemen over there, and they probably speak English."

"DRUGS," Ben said. "I DON'T GOT NO DRUGS!"

"Okay, okay." The blond man held up his hands. He shook his head, as if reminding himself that there was no accounting for people like Ben.

"Look," he said. "It's always about drugs. The Japanese in World War Two used heroin tablets to pacify the Chinese population. The Vietminh used the opium harvest to buy arms–selling most of it to the French so the French could market it in their Government-owned or licensed opium dens to help finance their war against the Vietminh. The CIA

349

borrowed a page from the French and Vietnamese and used opium and heroin to help finance CIA-sponsored operations. Chou En Lai and the People's Republic of China marketed heroin to American troops in Vietnam. I could go on and on. It's always about drugs in this part of the world, Mr. Tails. The Japanese know that. *You* know that."

"I could care less about what people want to stick up their noses or in their veins," Ben said.

"Drug use is inevitable," the blond man said. "You know that, too. So why not do something useful with the money? Streamline Raven, for example. Make it more responsive. More efficient. Think about it," he said.

Ben stared at him. The overlapping webs of connections and intelligence and influence that allowed Raven to function depended on a handful of men—Jim and Mr. Ishida and Huang and a few others like them. Their connections went all the way back to the old OSS days of World War Two, when Americans had worked with everyone from the Vietminh and the Chinese Fifth Route Army to the Thai Royal Family and fledgling Yakuza gangs. *Terry and the Pirates,* like the blond man said, filtered down over the years to a few hardcore, principled, tough-as-nails remnants—Raven International Trading Company, Ltd.—determined to act for the common good, rather than for the naturally selfish interests of their respective governments. He hadn't thought about it until now, but despite what the blond man was saying, Raven seemed plenty efficient and responsive to him. There was no hurry up and wait. No receipts. No written reports other than his final evaluation. He was given a target, background on the target, and the rest was up to him. If he needed advice or help, all he had to do was ask. What could be more efficient and responsive than that? That someone else might get the job done in less time for less money mattered not at all. Lives, not money, were at stake. Money was merely a tool used to get the job done. How did you streamline all that?

You couldn't. Raven's ability to do what it did was directly related to its ability to field people capable of getting close to sociopaths like the Frenchman, or to outlaws like Carlos. How much the organization could do was directly proportional to the ratio of burn-out to capable people, and not to efficiency or to responsiveness or to money.

But knowledge and money were power. And the knowledge and fiscal autonomy gained by Raven over the years must seem like a potential source of power and money to people like the blond man.

"When you say 'we,' who are you talking about?" he asked.

"People like you and me, Ben. People who are sick and tired of seeing their hard work and sacrifice come to naught—or worse, of seeing their hard work and sacrifice result not in a better existence for the people we work to help, but actually result in their destruction. People like us who have seen lives ruined by faceless men and women who have no knowledge of the real world."

"See those two cops over there?" Ben said. "They're here to make sure I get on a plane. I'm out of here. Never to return. I'm no use to you at all."

"Not here, you aren't. I agree with that. And I can see that you need a break. But the man who recruited you has returned to the States—to Montana, as a matter of fact. And—"

"And what? What are you talking about now?"

The blond man licked his lips, and Ben knew he was about to hear a lie. "I'm saying that the Chief is in it up to his ears. He wants personal control of the importation of illegal drugs into this country. That's why Carlos Montoya."

"The Chief?"

"He's Native American, isn't he? Everyone calls him the Chief."

"His name is Jim."

"Jim, then. What you need to understand is that *Jim* was the one behind the assassination of Montoya."

"How do you know that?"

"Ben, we know. Trust me, we know. We are the American Government, and we know."

"And what exactly does the American Government want with someone like me?"

"In addition to this problem with the Chief. . . ." The blond man shifted in his chair. "Special unit operations is a growth industry, Ben. But it is very difficult to find enough people with the proper training, experience, and, most important, the proper mind set. People like you are far and few between." He showed Ben his perfect teeth. "Whether or not you realize it, you are on the cutting edge of new theories and tactics—especially those concerned with how to keep in check the growing number of individuals and small groups capable of doing catastrophic damage."

Ben laughed. "What is this? The Henry Kissinger manual of how to win hearts and minds? Do you really believe what you are saying, or are you just saying it?"

"I believe, Ben. Make no mistake, I believe. I might seem like a government candy ass to you, and maybe in your world I am, but in my world I have a wife, a beautiful woman whom I love very much, and two, small, wonderful daughters whom I'd give my life for. It's because of them that I believe, Ben. The world today is too small, the dangers too great to wait for politicians or bureaucrats or strategists who have no knowledge of the real world to make decisions."

"So let me get this straight. You—and I assume others like you—are going to save the world by taking matters into your own hands. You are going to get your seed money to do this from the dissemination of illegal drugs. And you think that taking over Raven will help to facilitate all this. Is that about it?"

"Well, that is a rather crude and simplistic, and I suspect sarcastic, way to put it. But, yes. Essentially that's it."

"So what's in it for me? I mean, sure, there's a certain amount of personal satisfaction in ignoring constitutions and Bills of Rights and freely elected governments, things like that. But other than that, what's in it for me?"

The blond man smirked. "You don't disappoint, Ben. I am happy to say, you do not disappoint. Some of the others said personal gain would not appeal to you–that it would be a mistake to even bring it up. But I know you are only human. And considering the sacrifices you have made–" He paused. "What's in it for you, Ben, is employment. More money than you ever imagined. Perhaps even," he smirked again, and Ben realized that the man did not know he smirked, "if it's important to you–and somehow I think it no longer is–the chance to influence the course of world events."

The course of world events, Ben thought. He could see Kei sprawled on the couch. "Tell me exactly what it is that you want me to do," he said.

"When you get back to Montana, we want you to talk some sense into the Chief. Convince him to turn control of Raven over to us. It's time for him to retire, anyway. His way of thinking and of getting things done has been obsolete for decades. Do you know that he barely knows how to use a computer?"

"And if he doesn't want to retire. If he refuses to turn his files over?"

The blond man looked over at the two Marines, and then back at Ben. "Well, then, I guess you do what you do best."

Ben shook his head. "I don't know," he said. "Let me think about it. It's been a difficult week."

"Take all the time you need–just not too much time, okay?"

"Or what?"

"There is no 'or what.' That's not what I meant to imply. The issue is simply one of time. We are in a window of opportunity, and we don't know how long it will last. If you are not up to it, tell me now, and we'll get someone else. You can work with us later, after you've rested."

"Who will you get?"

"Oh, I don't know." The blond man smirked. "Me, maybe."

"Didn't you just say you have a family?"

"Yes, and I'd like you to meet them some day, Ben. I really would."

"Old man or not, he's a handful."

"The Chief might be a handful, but when all is said and done, he's small stuff." The blond man stood to leave. He extended his hand, and Ben took it without getting up. "We'll be in touch. You take care, Ben."

"Yeah. You, too. Hey, sorry about your friend."

"Me, too."

Ben watched him leave, the two Marines getting up to follow him out. The corporal made a jerking off motion with his right hand. Ben smiled.

The top sergeant gave the corporal a shove and rolled his eyes at Ben.

Ben raised his hand in farewell.

The two cops trailed the three men out.

He took a deep breath and let it out. He had to get away from this shit, he thought. He had to get away from these people. What he had been doing for Raven was like pissing into the wind. Nothing ever changed. People like the blond man were humanity's version of shark teeth. Break one off and another dropped into its place. It had been this way since Time One. It was only his conceit and his ego that made him think he could make a difference.

He stood and walked to the entrance. He would go home. Buy back the house he had grown up in. Go fishing. Hike the mountains. Bullshit with Robert Lee and Manfred at the bar—

He laughed out loud.

"Domo arigato gozaimashita!" the cook and the woman at the register shouted.

. . .

Outside the window the lights of Nagoya glittered beneath a sky black at the bottom, bruised ugly purple and red on the horizon. The bruised sky reminded him of blood-shot meat. Elk muscle traumatized by the shock wave generated by a bullet travelling at 3,000 feet per second. The subdermal bleeding and torn muscle tissue beneath Kei's flawless skin.

Rage bitter black and ugly as the night descending on the city below rippled through him, making his gut burn, stretching the skin tight around his eyes and at his temples. A gutteral sound, not unlike the groan an aircraft will sometimes make, issued unknown to him from between his clenched teeth. Rage at himself or at others or at God, he didn't know, knew only that Kei had given him a tiny taste, a few moments away from what he was—a few moments filled with the promise of a future he'd never considered. The hugeness of it was like a boulder in his chest.

He made himself relax.

Gone now. All of it, gone now, except the memory. Ripped from him by the same monster, the Death Monster, he and Peter had called it, that had stalked the forests and high grass of Vietnam and Laos and Cambodia. The years in Montana had allowed him to trick himself into believing that the Death Monster had been only a figment of their imaginations. He'd forgotten about the something glimpsed at the extreme periphery of his vision. Forgotten about shadow where

355

shadows weren't. Sunlight weirdly polarized at the edge of a clearing. Beneath the grumble of an approaching storm a thin, musky scream heard more in his mind than in his ears. In Montana, he'd convinced himself that if not his imagination, then the Death Monster was something that lived and found sustenance only in places that he had no intention of ever again visiting.

In fact, it had been with him all along. Watching with interest as he looked at Evy's dead eyes. Laughing when the sow grizzly reared up and fainted back down into bloody grass. Spreading itself over the cane field, infusing the night and the sugar cane and his mind with the Frenchman's evil. And it was out there now, reminding him with the brutal sky that it would always be there on a gray, poorly-lit street in Nagoya. In pieces of crazed pottery scattered across polished hardwood floor. In a knife skittering across temple steps. Forever there no matter where he went or what he did. The Death Monster. The cobra had seen it. That's why the cobra had not come for him.

The plane banked wing up, turning toward the ocean and home, and he felt the last vestiges of his rage dissipate, his stomach settle, the will and want to do damage replaced by a deeply felt, fatalistic understanding that the street he walked had never, from the first step, offered more than the illusion of choice.

The plane leveled, and outside the window the sky turned to stars and ghostly white clouds.

But between the stars he could see the dark forever spaces.

Part III
Montana

Chapter 1
The Old Homestead

The mountains stood proud and aloof, in his mind like women long neglected, suspicious of any sudden affection, their creases and cliffs above the tree line dusted with the first snow of the season, peaks etched against a sky so blue it didn't look real. The larch had turned yellow, easy to see against the greens of Douglas fir and Ponderosa pine.

As the old International rattled and bounced down the severely washboarded gravel road, he rolled down the window, letting in air crisp with the smell of river and pine and, from somewhere, the smell of apples.

Always when he came back, it was as if he had never left, only the accusing, suspicious presence of the mountains, and a scattering of new, very large custom log homes to remind him that it had been years, not days, since he had last driven this road.

He slowed to watch a group of whitetail does and fawns feeding at the edge of a cropped grain field white with frost. No bucks. The bucks would be nocturnal until rutting season. He'd have to dig out the .308 and shoot himself an elk this year. He'd grown up on venison and elk and he missed it.

An image of his grandfather slid into his mind. His

grandfather standing in his ratty old long johns, an even older pair of his grandmother's fuzzy slippers barely covering the front half of his feet, cooking eggs and elk sausage on the ancient wood stove. He could almost smell the eggs and sausage cooking. Grizzled, unshaven Grandpa. A big, burly, florid bear of a man who drank rarely and smoked never. A retired Montana Power linesman—a linesman back in the days when roads were few and often not passable in the winter. A hard man who should have been bitter, but wasn't. Corny jokes and twinkling eyes. A piece of old hardwood flooring next to the stove to stir the fire, and to whack his bottom. Two pair of boxing gloves hanging from a nail in the woodshed when he was older.

His grandmother had died from diphtheria when his father was a teen. And then his mother and father had died in a car accident when he was an infant. Looking back on it now, it explained a lot about his grandfather's attitudes and philosophies. "Nothing more important than these mountains," he'd say. "When you are in some God forsaken corner of the world, feeling low as beaver shit, you remember that."

A piece of work his grandfather. A fanatic about house and land and equipment. If he had the woodpile out of square, his grandfather would tear it down, make him re-stack it. Beds made. Clothes folded. The ancient linoleum in the kitchen once a month stripped and re-waxed. God help anyone who wore shoes in the house. "Damn," Manfred had said the first time he'd used the outhouse. "You got the only shitter in the entire world that don't hardly stink."

Three fingers shot off at Belleau Wood, another two lost and his innards forever messed up when someone had ignored the note at the power station and thrown the switch for a couple of seconds before realizing what he'd done. Grandpa had been up on that line.

His grandfather would delight kids by pretending to stick

358

one of his missing fingers all the way up his nose. He'd blink his eye and make it water, claiming he was tickling the back of his eye with his finger.

He never talked about his war, or about his son's war in the Pacific. But he'd taught him how to track and how to shoot and how to move in the forest. Once, when he was eleven, he'd shot a chipmunk for no reason other than the chipmunk was noisy and telling the whole forest they were there, and his grandfather hadn't spoken to him for a week.

At the end of the week, his grandfather had said, "You go spend a few nights up on the mountain. No need to take a rifle or your knife. What you got on right now is plenty. No, don't say anything. You bring me a quartz rock from that old mine shaft so I know you went at least that far. Go on. Git."

Ben smiled. Up on the mountain, he'd taken off his jeans and tied the legs and then he'd filled his pant legs with rocks from all over the top of the mountain and hauled them home. Together they'd built a new sweat lodge in the big stand of aspen down where the creek emptied into the trout pond, using the rocks he'd brought back for the fire pit. Had themselves a fine sweat. The best sweat he'd ever had. The sweat had hid his young tears.

He blinked to clear his vision. The truck had come to a stop in the middle of the road. He stepped on the gas, and the truck chugged ahead. Tough as nails his grandfather. Thick as a tree trunk. Not afraid to look ridiculous in his long johns and fuzzy slippers. He understood now that the old things his grandfather had been ferocious in defense of were part of his grandfather's memories.

Manfred had been home on leave and had come out to see his grandfather and found him sitting in the swing on the front porch, his skin still warm to the touch. His grandfather's heart, scarred and weakened decades before by the jolt of electricity he'd taken up on that line, had finally given out. It

359

had been an easy and perhaps a welcome death. He liked to think that his grandfather had known it was coming, and had gone out on the porch to look at the mountains as he died.

He squinted toward the snow-dusted peaks. When he'd come home on emergency leave for the funeral, he'd been glad, and he was glad now that his grandfather had not lived to see him when he came back from Asia. No amount of staying on the mountain and bringing rocks home and sweating in the sweat lodge would have helped.

He understood exactly what the blond man had been trying to say in that restaurant at the airport in Nagoya, even if the blond man did not. He'd lived it. Been it. Vietnam, Laos, Cambodia. Johnson. McNamara. Westmoreland. Krulak. Nixon. Kissinger. None of what they schemed and thought would have happened without men like him.

He'd read books, educated himself, hoping to discover that the men in control were smarter, more able. Instead, he'd discovered that they were not especially able at all; they were merely bent. Ambition or fanaticism had turned them into men who were capable of anything. They didn't waste time shooting chipmunks; they saw to it that men like him killed every living thing in the forest.

The Street Without Joy didn't begin on Highway One in Vietnam; it began when the United States allowed the British to re-arm the Imperial Japanese Army so that the French would have time to ship fresh troops to their colony in IndoChina. America, land of the free and home of the brave, his country, and his father's country, and his grandfather's country, re-arming the people who were responsible for Pearl Harbor so that the French could have their colony back.

But as much as he hated those men, he loved this place, Montana. He'd stayed in Asia and done what he had done because he knew by then that he was lost anyway. That he hadn't died was something that made no sense whatsoever.

He'd come home to his grandfather's funeral out of place and time. He didn't know how else to put it. Manfred had lined him up with a sexy blonde sorority girl in Missoula. Soft skin. Soft pink sweater. A really nice girl who before he had gone to Nam would have had him behaving like a puppy. She hadn't asked if he'd killed anyone, or how many. Hadn't even asked what it had been like. But still he hadn't been able to talk. Not a word after the brief introductions. Afraid of what might come out if he said anything at all.

The four of them, Manfred and his date, the blonde girl and him, motoring up Highway 12 to Lolo Hot Springs. He'd stared out the window, mortified at himself for the way he was behaving.

Manfred had left him at the hot springs, and driven the two women back to town, and then returned to pick him up.

They'd been silent most of the way back. "Guess I'll be finding out for myself, huh?" Manfred had said. He'd said that as they were crossing the bridge outside Missoula, where Ben's parents had been killed, and for a moment Ben had been confused.

"What do you mean?" he asked.

"How do you think I've been able to afford school?"

"I don't know. Jobs. Scholarships."

"Yeah. ROTC scholarships."

He had known immediately what Manfred was talking about, and he'd told Manfred not to do it. "Don't do it, Manfred. Don't fucking do it. Go to Canada."

"Got to, man. I owe it to this country."

That was the bottom line for Manfred, his family's debt to America. Manfred's father had been a professor in Germany before the war. When Manfred was ten, the Americans had brought the professor and his family to America and made them American citizens. The Americans had meant it as thanks for the professor's involvement in the anti-Nazi underground. Moving to the United States had been great for Manfred, but for his mother and father, who had been respected, upper-class intelligentsia in Germany, it had been exile to a language they barely knew, and to a place, Montana, they understood not at all. Manfred's father had never learned English very well and had no skills with which to find a decent job.

He'd died when Manfred was still in grade school. Ben had only a vague memory of a shadowy, taciturn figure.

A few days after the debacle with the blond sorority girl, both of them drunk on apricot brandy, he'd matter-of-factly informed Manfred, "I am now going to break your leg. I am going to hit you with this baseball bat."

Manfred had seen that he was serious and had jumped up and run out the front door.

"I talked it over with your grandpa," he'd said from the other side of the porch railing. "It's not about the war, Ben. It's about being able to say that I'm as American as you are."

Ben downshifted the old International to let it creep, swaying, over some deep pot holes. Well, Manfred had found out what it was really all about, no doubt about that. And look at him now. Look at all of them now. Manfred and Robert Lee had been through God knows how many women. Robert Lee was married to his job; Manfred to the bar. An elected official and a bartender, for Christ's sake. Manfred was bilingual in English and German, fluent in Russian, and once upon a time could get by in Vietnamese. Robert NMI Lee had gone from Special Forces sergeant to Special Forces captain in two tours in Vietnam. A politician and a barkeep in a backwater Montana county. And him. What about him? Hell, he was so fucked up, he didn't even count.

The three of them, three of the best this country was capable of producing, made the way they were by politicians and bureaucrats. By strategists. Made the way they were by men

362

with out-of-control egos. God, if there was a God, had to be one bent sonofabitch. How else could you have these mountains and that sky? Deer in a field of white frost. How else could you have someone like himself, who had done the things he'd done, be healthy and alive and enjoying it all, while someone like Kei Ishida lay all busted up and mangled in a hospital bed?

What had his grandfather felt to see him march off to war? His grandfather could have prevented it by simply writing a letter to the Marines or to Senator Mansfield. Sole surviving son.

He smiled to himself. His grandfather had known that he would have found a way, letter or no letter. All his whining and crying about the men who had conducted the war—all that was bogus as far as it applied to him. Those men hadn't turned him into anything; the war had simply brought out who he really was. He was just glad that his grandfather had died with the memory of the boy who'd brought home pant legs full of rocks, and not of Mr. Slide.

He pulled the truck off the gravel road into the gated entrance to the old place, and turned the engine off. The exhaust pipe ticked and popped in the sudden silence. The open gate was a new, green, Forest Service-style metal gate, hinges bolted through a thick railroad tie set deep in the rocky ground.

He'd wondered many times if the young couple who had bought the house and five acres—a young couple from Seattle who wanted to write and to paint and to grow organic vegetables—had kept the place up, or if the local economy and the snowpack had driven them back to the coast. From the looks of the gate, they'd done fine.

The road was the same—two wide tracks indented into rocky soil, grass growing sparse between the tracks. The tracks meandered between stands of lodgepole before breaking out into a big meadow. Grandpa had seeded the place with a variety of prairie bunch grass, and from what he could see it looked as if the bunch grass had finally taken over.

He started the truck, excited suddenly to see his land, to walk through the grass and under the big pines.

All that dicking around in Japan with gardens and temples and shrines, and all along he had this place to come to.

A fleeting image of being inside the sweat lodge with Kei rose unbidden and unwanted in his mind. Forget that shit, he thought. Thinking about things like that would only make him more crazy than he already was.

The truck grumbled and bounced, springs squeaking, as he steered it out of the trees and into the big meadow. The house and fields were in morning shadow, the roof of the house and the surrounding field white with frost. Smoke curled from the old brick chimney. The house was over a hundred years old, built on the ruins of other, much older houses. But it looked new thanks to the dark-gray siding, new windows, and metal roof that he'd put on before he'd sold it. Only the chimney gave away its age.

He stopped the truck, frowning. There was smoke coming from the chimney, but where the woman had planted her gardens there were no plastic tarps protecting herbs and tomatoes from frost. Instead there was tall, yellow grass and raspberry bushes grown too thick and bushy. A pair of what looked like hip waders hung upside down from the old, metal clothesline. Bushes grew nearly to the top of the old outhouse. A silver Jeep Grand Cherokee was parked between the house and the woodshed and what used to be the chicken coop.

The screen door opened and a man came out on the front porch. Small. Thin. Plaid wool shirt and suspenders. Carrying what Ben assumed was a cup of coffee.

The man on the porch walked over and sat down on the

old, wooden swing that he had built for a high school shop project, and that his grandfather had hung by steel chains from hooks bolted to porch rafters. The swing that his grandfather had died in. The man lifted a hand in greeting. He sipped his coffee.

Damn, Ben thought. Wouldn't you just know it. Oh, well. Now was as good a time as any. He shifted the truck into gear and motored slowly toward the figure on the porch. He was ready to get on with it. Get it over with. At Portland, he'd purchased a ticket to Hawaii, but no matter where he had gone or what he had done while he was in Hawaii—swimming at Ala Moana, running along beaches, watching sunsets and sunrises from the balcony of his room—the knowledge that it wasn't over yet had been a weight always there.

He stared without expression out the window at the man on the porch, and reached down and turned the engine off. He kicked the door open, hinges squealing, and climbed out.

"Morning," he said, as if meeting like this was something they did often—as if he was a neighbor stopping by for a morning cup of coffee. He bent backwards, stretching his back.

"Ohayo gozaimasu," Jim said. "Can I interest you in a cup of coffee?"

Ben swung the door squealing shut behind him. "Don't mind if I do," he said.

"I expect you know where to find it."

Ben walked up the steps. "Where are the people who own this place?" he asked.

"Help yourself to the coffee, and we'll talk."

"10-4, Chief."

"Chief?"

Ben pulled open the screen door and pushed open the old, solid oak door behind it and stepped inside.

The living room was bare, the hardwood floor as bright

and shiny as the day he'd refinished it. He smelled fresh paint. The dark finish work and moldings and banister on the staircase were shiny with new Verathane. The walls were painted an off-white, almost cream color. There were new-looking blinds on the windows.

He gingerly walked across the floor, uncomfortable with his boots on inside the house. His grandfather would have had a conniption.

A new, expensive-looking oak island with a stove insert—the kind with a fan in the stove top—and a half sink was in the middle of the kitchen floor. The cabinets were new. He pulled open a door. Solid oak. Damn. The shelves inside were empty, new shelf paper on the shelves. The counter tops were made of that gray stone-looking stuff. The old wood-burning stove was still there against one wall, but it looked as if it hadn't been used since he'd last cleaned and polished it. A small bay window had replaced the window over the sink, and he could see water rings where flower pots had rested on the wood shelf. Another, larger bay window had been inserted into the wall next to where they'd always kept the kitchen table. A mammoth stainless-steel, double-door refrigerator/freezer stood in what used to be the pantry.

A collection of fly rods, some of them old bamboo rods, an old wicker creel, and several green duffel bags were on the floor next to the back door.

Looking out the big bay window he could see a redwood deck and a gazebo twenty yards out into the yard. There was a large covered hot tub on the deck under the gazebo. A new stand of young alders and three baby maples were further out, chicken wire protecting the trees from deer. The lawn looked as if it hadn't been mowed for at least a couple of months.

He opened more cupboard doors. All the cupboards were bare. The new shelf liner was patterned with a bull elk, head thrown back, mouth open as it bugled. Not a pattern he would expect a woman to pick.

The refrigerator took up the entire pantry. They'd kept flour and preserves, enough for a couple of years, in that pantry. His grandfather would have loved the damn thing, though. As old-fashioned as he could be, his grandfather had never had a problem with technology—as long as the technology was something he thought useful. No TV, but an expensive stereo that he was constantly updating. New cross-country skis every time something new and better came out. Same old truck, because he said no one had yet improved on it. He'd used the old cook stove a couple of times a week instead of the electric one because that was what his wife had cooked on, and cooking on it reminded him of her.

Five blue-gray ceramic mugs were on the counter next to a handful of sugar packets and a plastic gallon jug of skim milk. An open package of clear plastic spoons was next to the milk. The mugs were pretty decent, he thought, the glaze exceptional even by Japanese standards. A ten-cup Mr. Coffee coffee maker hissed and popped on the expensive counter top. The pot was filled with very black coffee.

He filled a mug, added milk from the jug, took a drink, grimaced, and added more milk. He liked strong coffee, but this was beyond strong. Even with the milk it was bitter and oily. He retraced his steps back through the living room and out onto the porch.

"You sure this coffee is legal?" he asked.

Jim sipped his coffee, looking off across the fields. "There were about fifty head of elk out there in that far meadow, evening before last."

"Where the elk were is mine, but this house and five acres aren't. I hope you didn't break in thinking that it was."

Jim took another sip. "Is now," he said.

"What?"

"Ishida-san bought it back for you. The kitchen and the deck and hot tub were his idea." He glanced up at Ben and smiled. "I got it back for less than you sold it. Those hippies you sold it to had had it. Something about the local inbreds and the long winters."

"I see."

"You don't sound very excited about it."

"Well, it isn't like I earned it."

"There was a little money left over so I figured, what the hell. Had a new gate put in, the inside painted, ordered king-size beds for the rooms upstairs. They'll be here next week."

Ben half-leaned, half-sat on the porch railing. He took a drink of coffee, looking at Jim over the rim of the mug.

Jim glanced at him. "Not much else to do," he said. "Go fishing. Go for a hike. Dick around with this house, while I waited for you to get tired of Hawaii and come home."

"Mr. Ishida already gave me some money; I was going to buy the place back with that."

"I told him I thought you would. But he was adamant about buying the place back for you."

"He's being a little over the top, don't you think?"

Jim shrugged. "Not from his point of view." Sunlight was beginning to make golden the dry grass and the leaves on the alders in the far meadow. "The elk were noisy as hell just before dark last night. But I haven't heard a thing so far this morning."

"How's the fishing?"

"The fishing is good. Why'd you call me Chief?"

"That's what they call you."

"They being?"

"They being the people who want me to have a talk with you. Bring you to your senses. Those people."

Jim chuckled. "Who specifically are we talking about, this time?"

368

Ben shrugged. "He didn't tell me his name—and I didn't ask. I knew he'd lie, anyway."

"What did he look like?"

"Blond. Blue eyed. Early forties. All-American preppy."

"Getting a little thin on top? Long at the back?"

"Yeah."

"That'd be Kent."

"Claimed he was FBI."

Jim took a drink of coffee. "When he wants to be, I believe he is. But he's really head of a special Anti-Terrorist Task Force. His position has allowed him to recruit a handful of like-minded people from Federal intelligence and law enforcement agencies."

"Like-minded?"

"Men who feel they have been used and abused."

"Men who want their just desserts, is that it?"

"That's it."

"And control of Raven will help them get what they want?"

"So they think."

"But in order to get at Raven they've found it necessary to ally themselves with people like Sato?"

"It's the way these things generally work, Ben."

Somewhere at the base of the mountain beyond the far meadow a bull elk screamed. Ben turned toward the sound, his nostrils unconsciously searching the crisp morning air for the scent of elk.

"How was Hawaii?" Jim asked. "Looks like you got a little sun. Hard to tell, though, with that pony tail and all that stubble on your face."

"Hawaii was good." Twenty-odd elk—cows and calves, near as he could tell from there—walked rapidly in a line across the far clearing, moving away from where the elk had bugled. "How is Kei Ishida doing?"

Jim leaned forward and set his cup on the porch floor, and

369

then sat back arms spread along the back of the swing. "According to Ishida-san, they almost lost her a couple of times. Internal bleeding. Shock. That kind of thing. She even had a severe reaction to the antibiotics. But apparently she's going to make it okay."

"Why did they do it? Did he say anything about that?"

In the distance the bull again screamed challenge, and this time was immediately answered from close to where the string of elk had crossed the clearing. The answering bull had a much deeper, more throaty bugle.

They waited, but the first bull was silent.

"Hel-lo." Jim said. "That shut him up. He doesn't know," he said to Ben. "According to Mitsunari they were supposed to go in and sedate her, and then call for a van that was waiting to pick them up. But for some reason Sato went nuts, and things got a little out of hand."

"A little out of hand! You should have seen her."

"I've known her since she was a child, Ben."

"Sorry."

"Did she tell you how I met the family?"

Ben shook his head.

"You okay?" Jim asked. "Help yourself to more coffee, if you want."

"I'm okay. Hawaii was good. I did a lot of running and swimming. I'm okay." He looked out across the meadows in the direction of the elk.

"Manfred tells this story about how you killed an elk with a spear when the two of you were in high school."

"Manfred always could tell a story."

"It's not true?"

"It's true, but it's one of those stories you can't tell. It's kind of like a fish-that-got-away story. You can tell it, but no one will believe you if you do."

"Humor an old man."

"Manfred threw javelin for the track team, and we were out here—over there where the hot tub is—screwing around with his javelin, and I threw it through the side of the chicken coop. I said, I bet I can kill an elk with this." He took a sip of coffee. "One thing led to another, and Manfred got a guy who worked in the machine shop at the pulp mill in Missoula to make a bladed tip for it. We found a spot above a draw not too far from where we just heard that first elk bugle, and Manfred talked a spike in with a cow call. I damn near threw the javelin right through it."

Jim looked up at him.

"Hey, I told you it was one of those stories."

"You must have gone in the Marines soon after that?"

"The next spring. Right after graduation."

"I ever tell you I was a Marine?"

Ben sat against the railing. "Is this one of those stories you can't tell because no one will believe it?"

Jim laughed. "No. Not at all. Frozen Chosin. Maybe you've heard of it. I was a second lieutenant. That's how I met the Ishidas. Chosin to a hospital in Japan. Met Mitsunari a few months later at a *sushi* bar in Kyoto."

"You walked out of Chosin?"

"I was one of the lucky ones. I was evacuated by plane from a makeshift runway at a place called Hagaru."

"And that's how you got started in Asia?"

"I suppose so. I was at the hospital in Japan, and the Agency sent a guy down from Tokyo to recruit me—for Southeast Asia Area Studies. I had a degree in anthropology. Never mind that my area of expertise was American Plains Indians, they thought my looks would help me pass for someone other than a white Anglo-Saxon American. Damn," Jim said, sitting bolt upright. "A big bull just ran across that meadow."

371

"He's going after his harem," Ben said without turning to look. "The bunch that ran across earlier."

They were both silent for a moment, watching as bright, golden morning light crept across fields and forest toward the house. "A javelin," Jim said.

"Just remember you heard it from Manfred, not me. Why are you here, Jim? I mean why are you here and not in upstate New York or Colorado or Thailand—anywhere but here?"

Jim shrugged. "I like it here. Montana is like another country. Even the banking laws are different."

"Huang tells me you are moving Raven here."

"It's always been here. You just didn't know it."

Jim sitting there like that reminded Ben of his grandmother's people—their creased, weathered faces and dark, obsidian eyes.

"So I own this place again," he said.

"Indeed you do. The paperwork is in a drawer in the kitchen. All you have to do is sign it and have it notarized and take it to the county assessor's office."

"Do you think I got a good deal? Do you think the Ishidas are being fair?"

Jim looked up. "Now, listen to me, Ben. This is important. Whatever happened between you and Kei Ishida, this house has nothing to do with that. You know how it works. Don't complicate it. He'll never be able to repay you. This gives him a little face, is all."

"Her uncle wouldn't even let me say goodbye."

"Well, that's between you and her uncle, then. This house is not part of that."

"But you know what I'm talking about," Ben said.

"Yeah, I know. But so what, huh?"

Ben sighed and uncrossed his arms, and turned and picked the mug of coffee off the railing and threw what was left of the coffee out into the yard. He squinted against the sunlight as it hit the porch and glinted off the windows and the hardware on the swing. "You ever meet my grandfather?" he asked.

"Never had the pleasure."

"He wasn't much for books. But he loved poetry. Whitman. Sandberg. Kipling. Especially Kipling."

"We are not soldiers by the side of the road, Ben. Don't make it something it's not."

"Strange words coming from someone who was at Chosin."

"Why? You think I'm some sort of super patriot? I'm not. Harry Truman and Douglas MacArthur fucked my war up every bit as much as did the people who ran your war. Asia sucked me in much the way it did you, that's all.

"Your grandfather's mother came across those mountains in a covered wagon, Ben, and I know exactly how those people felt. Area Studies translated meant organizing oxen trains–covered wagons, if you will–to explore the interior of Southeast Asia. Or taking long treks with what little I and a few porters could carry on our backs. No roads. No hospitals. Back then, a bad sprain was serious business. A broken bone or a snake bite meant you were probably going to die. I found people who had never had contact with the outside world. I tape recorded their languages and filmed them when they'd let me. I learned their customs. Ate what they ate. Even wrote articles about them for some pretty well-known publications."

"You sound like you miss it."

"Oh, you bet I do." He smiled. "But these are my mountains, too, Ben. At least the east side of them–the Rocky Mountain front, and the high plateaus of the Great Plains. Most of my people still live there. But, like you, those Asian mountains and countries are in my blood, too."

"You make it sound romantic."

"Well, isn't it?"

"Not lately."

"Well, there is that other part that Kipling wrote about. The part where our blood and the blood of our comrades stain foreign lands."

"I sure hope you're not going to say something about prices to be paid."

"Let me ask you something, Ben. Do you think you have paid a bigger price than, say, your neighbor down the road who lives in that old double-wide—your neighbor who gets up every day and goes cheerfully to work so that his wife and kids can have a life in a place like this, rather than in some polluted, crime-infested city. Is that what you think?"

"Apples and oranges," Ben said.

"The hell it is. You just think it is because you've never done what your neighbor does every day. You think he doesn't get burned out? You think people don't fuck him over? You think people don't die on him? His life is no less a never ending series of choices and decisions than is yours. Truth be told, the only thing special about you, Ben, beyond your experience, is your hunter's reflexes, and your hand/eye coordination. In terms of willingness to sacrifice for what is right, you haven't got a damn thing on your neighbor."

"My neighbor hasn't had to kill people."

"You made your choices, Ben."

Ben looked down at the wood floor on the porch. He scuffed his boot back and forth. "I don't think I can do it anymore, Jim. I felt like pieces of me were flying off. I would do something, pull the trigger, or something, and it was like a mist would fly off me. By the time they loaded me in a car for the airport, I was losing it big time."

"Losing it how?"

"I wanted to keep killing until someone killed me."

"Do you think you would have reacted in such a manner if it had not been Kei?"

"I–" Ben hesitated. He looked out at the two old apple trees, scraggly and heavy with fruit, in one of the far meadows.

"You didn't answer me," Jim said.

"No," Ben said. "It would not have been the same if it hadn't been Kei."

"You need time, that's all."

Ben snorted. "Yeah, right. Time. As if that Kent asshole and his buddies are going to give us time." He looked at Jim. "They are coming for your scalp, Chief. And believe it, they are just as mean and ignorant and full of themselves as the Yellow Legs were."

"My," Jim said. He chuckled. "A little too much time on the beach, perhaps."

"You can make fun of me all you want. But these boys play for keeps. Just ask Kei Ishida."

"That was a cheap shot, Ben."

"I didn't mean it to sound the way it did."

"I get the feeling that you think these people are something new and different in my experience?"

"I think they are something new and different in everyone's experience. Technology. Communications. Money. Weaponry. Computers that practically think. Satellites that can see us here on the porch or inside the house. I think they are the new Renaissance men–and they've got exactly the same care about human life that the Conquistadors had."

Jim was silent for a moment. "There might be something in what you say," he said.

"You sic people like me on serial killers, rapists, child molesters–the criminally diseased, or whatever you want to call them. But we do nothing about the people who do the real damage," Ben said.

"The people you speak of are products–or byproducts–of our institutions, Ben. It is not for us, you and I, to act on our judgement of our institutions. If we were to act, then that would make us no different than people like Sato and this Kent fellow."

"Who is it up to then? My neighbor? How in the world could someone like him ever know who these people are and what they are capable of?"

"No government exists without the will of the people, Ben. I really believe that."

"When they start killing us. When they start fucking up people like Kei Ishida, I say it damn sure is up to us."

"You never felt this way before?" Jim asked.

Ben leaned forward both hands on the railing. He squinted toward the mountain. "It was never this personal."

Jim was silent for a moment. "She is special woman," he said.

"So I've been told."

"Well, give it time. You have your house back. Fall is here. Your favorite time of the year. Have a few drinks with your friends. Have a sweat in that sweat lodge out there in the trees. Talk to your grandfather. He'll tell you what to do."

Ben straightened and crossed his arms, looking at the mountains and the high, thin clouds coming in from the north. His grandpa would know all right, he thought. His grandfather had taken his grandmother's family name when they were married because she was the last of her line. Then he'd lost her, and then he'd lost his only son—not to disease or to war, but to something as stupid as a bridge abutment. "They are not going to go away," he said. "They want Raven's connections and bank accounts. They want to know where the bodies are buried. And since you are not going to give them any of that, they are going to do the next best thing. They are going to kill you and Huang and Mr. Ishida and anyone else at Raven who might not want to give them what they want."

"This is not the first time someone has made a run at Raven, Ben. And it won't be the last."

"My grandfather used to say, 'Sometimes you eat the bear; sometimes the bear eats you.'"

"We have eaten a lot of bear, Ben."

"Yeah," Ben said, shading his eyes against the glare as he looked toward the far meadow. "We have, haven't we?" He dropped his hand to his side and turned toward Jim, "But this time the bear is one mean sonofabitch."

"Kent, you mean?"

"Some of the people he's with are pretty good. His partner in Japan had his pants down around his knees, but he still put two right by my ear. If he would have kept shooting, instead of using that bullshit double-tap technique, he would have killed me."

"Your point being?"

"He might be a wimp and a snake, but he's going to have people with him who are for real. People who don't mind a few dead bodies. The guy who almost got me was in the can taking a dump while Sato was doing his thing with Kei. That's how much it bothered him."

They both turned in unison toward the distant, dull thump of rotor blades. A helicopter, but not a logging helicopter, Ben thought. Most logging helicopters were Vietnam-vintage, heavy-lift helicopters, and he recognized them by their sound right away.

The sound grew louder. They both shaded their eyes, searching the horizon.

A large black helicopter flew low and fast against the backdrop of trees and cliffs at the base of the mountains across the valley. A Blackhawk without any markings that they could see.

They watched, their heads turning in unison as the

377

helicopter continued past on the far side of the valley, headed toward town.

"That will be Kent and his merry band of anti-terrorists," Jim said.

"And you are the terrorist they are looking for."

"I am."

Ben smiled. "Here to terrorize the trout population."

Jim chuckled. "I'm trying. But they don't seem to respond very well to my brand of terrorism."

"So what are you going to do?" Ben asked.

"What am I going to do?" Jim yawned, and stretched. "I'll tell you what I'm going to do. Today, I am going fishing. And tomorrow I am going to get up at first light and go for a long hike. Rain or shine, tomorrow I am going to follow that old logging road up over the ridge and back down to the river." He looked without emotion at Ben. "That is exactly what I am going to do."

They stared at each other for a moment.

"You don't mind if I stay here for a few days, do you?" Jim asked.

"Stay as long as you like. I'll probably stay at Manfred's tonight, anyway."

"Well, good. Have a beer or two for me."

Chapter 2
The Book of Odes

Y ou're back," Manfred said, as if Ben had been gone
only minutes, instead of years. "You look like shit."
"I'm glad to see you, too. What happened to this place?"
"Thanks for writing."
"You're welcome."

Manfred put the dishcloth down that he'd been wiping beer
glasses with. He threw open the trap door in the bar, letting
it bang down on the bar top. "You asshole," he said, and
grabbed Ben in a bear hug.

"Sorry about not writing."

Manfred laughed, and went back behind the bar, and picked
a pint glass off the back counter, flipped it in the air, caught
it, and held it under a tap with one hand, and pulled the tap
with the other. "If we ever got a letter from you, we'd be
worried."

"Made some changes, I see."

"A few."

The old, massive, ornate back bar had been stripped and
refinished. The mirrors were new; they no longer had that
faded, grainy look. The counter top had been refinished with
cherry wood or some other hardwood, and stained the same
mahogany color as the back bar. Ben ran his hand along the
counter top. The finish felt like smooth plastic.

He looked around. Same old moth-eaten heads on the walls, but the walls had been painted a rich cream color, the moldings along the floor and ceiling painted forest green. Fake, antique-looking columns and half-columns, also painted forest green, were scattered about the room and along the walls.

The old linoleum floor had been replaced with glossy hardwood. The tables and chairs were blond pine. Even the bar stools were new.

Tiny black speakers hung from the edges of the ceiling and in clusters around the tops of the columns. In the back there was a huge, square television screen. The side wall, from the back all the way to the first fake column in the middle, had been wainscoted with blond pine, the wall above the wainscoting filled with what looked like framed black and white pictures of sports teams and athletes and pictures of the old sawmill and Main Street the way they had looked fifty years ago.

Large, stained glass panels depicting elk, bear, and mountain lion respectively were hung in front of the three front windows. Real plants grew in giant clay pots on either side of the big windows. In the center of the bar, there were at least ten draught spigots, all but two or three offering micro brews. Even the neon beer signs on the wall and on the mirrors advertised micro brews. A small, wooden sign glued to the top of the cash register said, Veterans Drink For Half Price, and in smaller letters, Double Price If You Tell More Than One War Story, and in even smaller letters, A Round For The Bar If The Story Takes More Than Five Minutes.

Manfred put the pint of beer on a cork coaster on the bar in front of Ben. "Pretty spiffy, huh?"

"You've got ferns in front of the window."

"Those are bamboo plants—as you well know."

"They might as well be ferns."

380

"I knew you'd hate it," Manfred said. He grinned like a kid with a new bike. "Damn, you don't know how good that makes me feel."

"No poker machines," Ben said. "I'll give you that."

"Oh, you'll give me that, will you?"

Ben took a long drink. The beer was cold and bitter and good. Real good. He held the glass at arm's length. "What the hell is this?"

"That's called beer. Beer is something you thought you knew, but now that you've had a drink of real beer, you realize you didn't."

"Why did you do it?" He put the beer on the bar next to the coaster.

"Why did I do it?" Manfred put Ben's beer back on the coaster, and wiped the bar free of moisture where the glass had been. "To me this place was nothing more than a seedy, fucking bar. And I had to work nearly every day of my life in it. That's why I did it. It was getting to me.

"The worm has turned," he said. "You've been gone three years, and these days three years in Montana is like dog years to human years. Manny's Place is keeping up with the times, that's all."

"Well, I like the beer."

Manfred laughed. "You like the whole place; you just don't want to admit it yet."

"But *Manny's Place?* You hate to be called Manny."

Manfred shrugged. "These days we get movie stars in Beemers and Humvees. Twenty-somethings who yesterday were the class nerds in Lexus' and Grand Cherokees and Turbo'd Somethings from Sweden. Rich, middle-aged professionals motor over from Spokane or Seattle, fly into Missoula and Kalispell from Portland, San Francisco, L.A., Denver, Minneapolis. Hell, they fly in from everyfucking-where. And that doesn't even count the Canadians. People are coming here to go hiking, skiing, mountain biking, hunting, fishing—and they love to bar hop to all the funky little bars like Manny's Place scattered around Montana."

Manfred gestured at the ratty old heads on the walls. "People these days, even the people from here, want the ambiance of Montana, the romantic version of The Way It Was. These old heads and the old pictures I put up on the wall over there, this old-but-restored bar, the sound system with subwoofers big as your new refrigerator—this is what they want." He frowned and picked up the towel and started wiping the counter again.

"And you are happy to give it to them."

"Bet your ass, I am. I make more in bar tips in one night than I used to make total in two weeks. And the women— well, you'll see."

Ben grunted.

"What. You got something against good-looking women now?" Manfred frowned again. He took Ben's glass and put it in the sink under the bar. Ben heard a sealed door slide open, and Manfred placed a frosted glass under the tap and filled it. He set it on a fresh coaster in front of Ben and put the used coaster to the side of a stack of coasters next to the beer taps.

"Why didn't you give me one of these the first time?"

Manfred grinned. "I wanted you to see me flip a beer glass."

"Yeah, how many did you break before you got it right?"

"A few."

Ben raised his glass. "A few cases, you mean." He put the glass down, and raised himself up both hands on counter top, and looked over. "Padded floor," he said. "I should have known." He sat back. "Seriously," he said, "all this must have cost a pretty penny."

"Worth every cent."

"Where'd you get the money?"

"I borrowed it; what do you think?"

"You just waltzed into the bank and borrowed more money that the whole block is worth."

"Most of the banks are now owned by out-of-state banks, and the out-of-state bankers see what is happening to this place, Ben. Missoula has more banks than hamburger stands, and that's not much of an exaggeration. You won't believe it."

"I'm not sure I want to."

"Lost some weight, didn't you? I haven't seen you this thin since you came back for your grandfather's funeral."

"It's been—interesting," Ben said.

"You want to, you can bunk in your old apartment. It hasn't been used much since you left."

"How'd you know I was back?"

"Roger down at the Conoco said the International was gone from the storage lot when he went over to run it around for awhile this morning." He laughed. "Man, you and that truck. You're worse than your grandpa sometimes."

"How'd you know about my new refrigerator?"

"Refrigerator?" Manfred tried to look confused. " What are you talking about?"

"You said—" Ben picked up the beer and took a drink. He carefully put the glass down on the coaster. *Manny's Place* was printed in thick black Old English letters over a Special Forces patch—the patch that Manfred and Robert Lee had earned in Vietnam.

They were both silent for a moment, Ben studying the beer in his glass, Manfred looking worried at him.

Ben looked up. "What did Robert Lee have to say about all this?"

Manfred grinned. "Oh, about what you'd expect. Pissed and moaned. Took to calling me Manny Money in front of the old farts used to come in here." He wiped non-existent moisture from the bar. "All that changed when he walked in one night wearing his uniform and discovered a couple of carloads of good-looking women drinking micro-brews with lemon slices."

Ben smiled, seeing in his mind Robert Lee's sly, crafty look as he took in the women and what they were drinking. That look replaced by a big grin and a Southern accent so thick it was practically troweled on.

"Yeah," Manfred said. "You got it. The next week, he went to Missoula and had a special going-to-Manny's Place uniform tailor made. Now, he wears a Glock nine and a name tag with Sheriff Robert Lee in big white letters. Keeps his old duty belt and his .44 in his truck."

"I drove by the S.O., but there was a Blackhawk helicopter parked in the field so I didn't stop."

"Yeah, I'm not sure what that is all about. Feds are here on a training exercise, I guess. Happens a lot these days."

"I also noticed quite a few new Sheriff Department vehicles, and a new addition on the jail."

Manfred nodded. "Don't tell the little shit I said so, but he has put together a really professional department. He's been hiring guys with a lot of big-city experience. Family men, most of them, looking for a better place to raise their kids."

"Must be a helluva salary cut."

"Well, you know him. He's finagled some sort of long-term Federal subsidy that pays for a lot of salary and equipment. The new jail addition was something the taxpayers voted for."

"How does he do it?"

Manfred shrugged. "Has the knack, I guess."

"I'll bet it sure helps at election time, though?"

"Nah, he'd get elected no matter what."

"Maybe it has something to do with that Blackhawk."

"What does?"

"The Federal money he gets."

Manfred stopped polishing the bar and looked at him.

"How's your mom?" Ben asked. "Still using a tennis racket to keep her boyfriends in line?"

"Man, you *have* been gone for a while, haven't you? I had to put her in a nursing home. She's totally senile now. Won't wash. Speaks only German."

"Damn, Manfred."

"Yeah, I know. But it happens. She's never been right since the old man died–and that was what? Thirty years ago."

Manfred emptied the rest of Ben's beer into the metal grate below the taps, and refilled it. He smiled. "It's good to see you, bro. Real good. Every time you leave, I think, well, that's the last I'll see of *him.*" He wiped the bottom of the glass on his bar towel and put the glass on Ben's coaster. "But here you are."

"It's good to be back."

"What are you going to do now?'

"I don't know. Listening to you, and looking at this place, I'm starting to feel like Rip Van Winkle." He eyed Manfred. "I've got the old place back, you know."

"The hell you say. When did that happen?"

"Just happened."

"I couldn't believe it when you sold it."

"I know. I couldn't believe it either."

"Those two hippies or whatever they were did pretty good by it, though."

"Grandpa would like it."

Manfred shook his head. "I sure miss that man. He was more a father to me than my own father."

"Broke the mold," Ben agreed.

"Remember the time he caught us–Oh, oh. Here comes trouble. You should have parked around back."

"Must be Robert Lee."

"Himself."

Ben smiled and turned his back to the door.

"There's a vehicle parked out here ain't been licensed in three years," he heard a loud voice say from the door. "And the asshole driving it probably don't have a valid driver's license no more, neither."

Ben hung his head for a moment, and then pushed away from the bar, and stood and turned. He grinned. "How you doin' Robert Lee?" he said, extending his hand.

Robert Lee grabbed Ben's hand, his grip ferocious. "You look like shit," he said.

Manfred laughed, and flipped a glass.

"Not when I'm in uniform," Robert Lee said. He gave Ben's hand another squeeze. "Damn, it's good to see you, Ben."

"I'll just set it here on this coaster," Manfred said. "You don't have to drink it if you don't want to."

Ben stepped back from Robert Lee. Robert Lee was wearing light brown trousers and matching long-sleeved shirt, a dark brown stripe down the trouser legs that matched the dark brown pocket flaps on his shirt. The trousers and the shirt were obviously tailored, sharp creases on both. Gold Sheriff's star and matching gold collar insignia. A brown turtle neck instead of a tie. Glossy, dark brown cowboy boots. Black, polished duty belt complete with black leather holster for the Glock, black leather extra-magazines holder, cuffs. No mace, no nightstick, no radio—nothing to make him look bulky around the waist. His face was tanned and fresh shaved, and Ben could tell from his skin color and clear eyes that Robert Lee hadn't been drinking as much as he used to.

"Regular poster child, ain't I?"

"I'm speechless."

Robert Lee picked up the beer. "How do you like what dickweed here has done with the bar?"

"I thought you weren't going to drink in uniform," Manfred said.

"I was gone for nearly ten years the last time," Ben said. "And when I came back it seemed like nothing had changed. This time, if it weren't for the mountains, I'd think I was in the wrong state." He raised his beer to Robert Lee and they touched glasses. Ben took a drink, and put the glass on the coaster. "Beer's better, that's for sure."

"Wait until you see some of the new clientele," Robert Lee said. He exchanged a glance with Manfred that Ben could not read. Both men looked worried.

"What?" Ben said.

"What, what?" Manfred said.

"You guys are looking at me like I'm walking around with my dick hanging out or something."

"It's been a long time since we've seen you with a pony tail," Robert Lee said.

"Your clothes look worse than your truck," Manfred said.

"Well, don't be shy," Ben said. "Tell me what you really think."

Robert Lee took a big drink of his beer, and set the glass on the bar.

"Put it on the damn coaster," Manfred said. "How many times I got to tell you? Put it on the damn coaster."

"I've still got your badge in my drawer," Robert Lee said to Ben. "Pay is a lot better since you left."

"It must be. I saw your helicopter."

"There I was sitting at my desk, doing paperwork, and all of a sudden a Blackhawk helicopter is squatting in the field outside my window, shit blowing everywhere. The Feds who came in on it tried to commandeer the entire S.O. I actually had to have a few words with them."

"What do they want?" Ben asked.

"Oh, they're after—I'm quoting here—'an international

387

terrorist who makes Carlos the Jackal seem like a Boy Scout.' They have apparently located this 'man with no remorse or conscience'—that's a quote, too—and 'under no circumstances, Sheriff, are you to even consider apprehending him.' Turns out they've had a team on the ground for a week—posing as road surveyors, if you can believe that."

"If he's that dangerous, you'd think they'd have more than a helicopter and a handful of SWAT."

"HRT," Robert Lee said. "Us little people have SWAT; the Feds now have HRT."

"You know what I mean."

"Yeah, I know. And I'm making fun of them, but make no mistake. HRT or not, these guys are the real deal. You should see their equipment. The problem is, I don't think they are here to do any apprehending."

"What do you mean?" Ben asked. Out of the corner of his eye, he saw Manfred give a barely perceptible shake of his head.

"I think they are here to assassinate this dude," Robert Lee said. He looked at Manfred.

"What makes you think that?" Ben asked.

"Most of them are ex-SEAL or Delta Force or something like that. You know what I mean: Quiet. Polite. Watch everything like they're figuring fields of fire or how much explosives to blow it up with. The two in cammies even look like they are still in the military."

"Do they look like they could be Marines?" Ben asked. "The two who look like they are in the military?"

Robert Lee looked him up and down. "Hell, you are the only Marine I know, and they damn sure don't look like you." He laughed, glancing at Manfred as he did.

"You ever meet up with the Pumpkin Eater?" Manfred asked, his voice casual.

Too casual, Ben thought. He looked past Robert Lee out

the window. On the other side of the tracks small maples were scattered about what looked like a new park. He could feel Robert Lee and Manfred watching him. "Yeah, I met him."

"Well, since you're here," Robert Lee said, "I guess that tells us something."

"He has a wife and kids."

Robert Lee and Manfred were silent.

"Why don't you go up to the apartment," Manfred said. "Take a shower. Shave. Change your clothes. Your stuff is still in the back bedroom."

"My rifles, too?"

Manfred glanced at Robert Lee. "I guess. The only time I've been in there was to vacuum, or to put out new D-Con."

"I thought I'd spend the night camped out on my land," Ben said. "Have myself a sweat in the morning. Listen to the elk."

"You probably shouldn't do that," Robert Lee said. "Not for a few nights, anyway. Somewhere out that way is where all the Feebies are going to be."

"Fuck them. It's my land."

Manfred opened his mouth to say something.

"I was out there this morning," Ben said, before he could. He turned toward the bar, feigning interest in Manfred's collection of bumper stickers stuck in one corner of the big mirror. One of them said, JANE CALL HOME: 1-800-HANOI.

"New everything in here," he said. "New vehicles at the Sheriff's Office. New addition on the jail. Decent pay for the deputies. A county of what? Thirty-forty thousand?"

"About that," Robert Lee said.

Ben could see himself in the mirror. Grungy, no doubt about it. Five-day-old beard. Sweatshirt and jeans that he'd bought in Hawaii and hadn't washed since. He felt good, though.

389

All that running and swimming and biking had cleaned the old tubes out. He just didn't look like he felt. In the mirror Robert Lee and Manfred were watching him.

He took a drink and carefully set the glass down on the coaster.

"How long have you known me, Manfred?" he asked, his voice quiet.

"I don't know, since I was ten, I guess. Since I came to this country."

"Robert Lee?"

Robert Lee looked at Manfred.

"I'm not here for Jim," Ben said. "I'm not point man for the people who came in that Blackhawk. I was out at the place talking to Jim this morning."

Manfred and Robert Lee stared at him.

"The damn refrigerator," Manfred said, and Ben could hear the relief in his voice. "I could not believe it when I said that. I said something about his new refrigerator," he said to Robert Lee.

Ben shook his head. "Amateur night at Manny's Place."

"Oh, is that right?" Robert Lee said. "Well, us *amateurs* managed to–"

"Keep it from me, Robert Lee?" He looked at him. "Is that what you were going to say?"

Robert Lee held up his hands.

"You must have met Jim when the two of you were in Vietnam," Ben said to Manfred.

"He debriefed us after a mission into Laos–one of the last we went on. Told us about Raven then."

"This is where we come," Ben said. "To hide. To rest. To try to put the pieces back together again."

"What did I tell you," Manfred said to Robert Lee.

"I could never understand how you made money off your

apartments and cabins," Ben said to Manfred. He looked around the bar. "All this."

Manfred threw a coaster on the bar top next to Robert Lee, and wiped his hands on the bar towel. "No. This place is all me. I bought it with my own money. I took out the loan without any help from anyone."

"And you being Sheriff, was that part of the plan?" Ben asked Robert Lee.

"It just sort of happened."

"Surprised everyone when he won the election," Manfred said.

"But Raven saw the opportunity, and made sure you got the money to turn the Sheriff's Department into a first-class operation," Ben said.

"What's wrong with that? The money spent to upgrade the S.O. works both ways: it helps the people of the county, and it helps us protect people like you. None of the money goes for political campaigning, if that's what you're worried about."

"We never lied to you," Manfred said. "You just never asked."

"And if I would have asked, would you have told me?"

"I would have told you," Manfred said.

"Jim had his eye on you way before you came back here," Robert Lee said. "He knew about you through some Chinese guy. It was coincidence that you are from here, that's all. It had nothing to do with us. In fact, dickweed here convinced him to wait and see what shook out between you and Evy."

"It isn't easy," Manfred said. "The people Jim sends—most of them didn't grow up the way we did. This place calms them down. Helps them find a balance. If they need it, Jim sends first-class medical and psychiatric help to stay with them. There's a nice old lady in Seattle who finds new lives for the ones who are finished, if that's what they want."

"Remember that suicide you had?" Robert Lee asked.

"Right after you started as a deputy? Guy in a VW bug? Shot himself with a .41?"

Ben nodded.

"We've had a couple of those." Robert Lee looked at Manfred. "Manfred tries to help. He's pretty good at it. But sometimes—"

"All the king's horses, and all the king's men. . . ," Manfred said.

"Ever had anyone go bad?" Ben asked.

Robert Lee shook his head. "Not really. DUI. Speeding. Some drugs. Little things like that."

"I mean *really* go bad."

"You mean like the Frenchman?" Manfred asked. He laughed at the expression on Ben's face. "Hey, everyone who works for Raven knows about the—"

"Oh, fuck a duck," Robert Lee said. "Here comes Mr. I-got-my-own-helicopter. You all are going to love this guy. Asshole does not even begin to describe."

The door opened and the blond man Ben had met in the Nagoya airport came in, plaid wool shirt, jeans, well-used hiking boots, his black, FBI-issue HRT baseball hat at odds with his clothes.

He caught sight of the Sheriff, and strode over to the bar, his walk and his look-you-in-the-eye manner projecting purpose and can-do leadership.

"Sheriff Lee," he said, extending his hand to Robert Lee— shaking hands with Robert Lee, as if they were good friends and it had been a while since they'd last met. "I've been looking all over—" He paused, looking around the bar. "My word," he said. "Look at this place."

"What can I get you?" Manfred asked.

"Oh, nothing for me, thank you. I'm on the clock." He chuckled. You know us Feds, his voice suggested. "Maybe later, though." He eyed Robert Lee's half empty glass, his raised eyebrows immediately replaced by a look that he probably thought masked his thoughts, but that to the three men watching him clearly said, *well, what can you expect from a Sheriff in a place like Bumfuck, Montana.*

"Agent Wayne Anderson," Robert Lee said. "Meet some of the local color. Manny, the proprietor of this emporium. And Ben Tails, resident mountain man and part-time prodigal son."

"Howdy," Ben said.

"Pleased to meet both of you," the blond man said, not shaking hands with either of them—a serious breach of Montana manners. Or maybe not, Ben thought. Maybe the blond man knew the role he was playing.

Manfred reached beneath the counter and produced a small beer glass, and filled it with dark beer from a spigot marked with a Moose Drool label. He put the glass on a coaster and slid both toward the blond man. "Just a taste, Agent Anderson. Some of Montana's finest."

"You are a gentleman and a scholar," the blond man said. He tilted the black baseball cap up on the back of his head, and picked up the glass of dark beer. He sniffed it, and then took a small taste, rolling the beer around in his mouth before swallowing it.

Watching him, Ben realized that the blond man wasn't playing a role at all. He wasn't being a Motorcycle Man. This was who he was. For a brief moment, he almost felt sorry for him.

"Very nice," the blond man said, and drank half the glass. "Very nice indeed." He set the glass on the bar, ignoring the coaster. "Sheriff Lee, could I have a moment of your time?"

"These men are sworn deputies," Robert Lee said. "You can say whatever you want in front of them."

The blond man eyed Ben. A secret communication that Ben understood: you've made your decision, the blond man's look said. Stay out of it.

"Well, not to sound dramatic," the blond man said, his voice making it clear that he was about to tell them something dramatic. "But I'm here, my men and I, to apprehend one of the most dangerous men on the planet."

Ben smiled, seeing in his mind Jim sitting in the swing on the porch, feet up on the railing, coffee in hand.

"I have a team of bad boys with me who will have no trouble capturing this man—as long, and let me emphasize, *as long* as this individual has no idea that we have ascertained his whereabouts." He looked sober-faced at the three of them. "In the interests of public safety we are biding our time, hoping to catch him when he is away from the house. He is an avid fly fisherman, and several times a week he goes on long hikes. When he hikes, he always hikes the same route; and when he fishes, he always fishes the same section of the river."

"Bad boys," Manfred said, his tone bemused. He was careful not to look at Robert Lee or Ben.

"What? Oh, yes. Some of the best."

Ben flipped a coaster onto the bar top next to the blond man's beer. "Check it out," he said.

The blond man picked up the coaster. "Vietnam?" he asked Manfred.

"Yes, sir."

The blond man tossed the coaster on the bar. "Before my time," he said. He looked at Ben. "One of my men was there, though."

Shit, Ben thought, *I knew it.*

"Sheriff Lee," the blond man said. "What we need from you is detailed information concerning any civilians who might be in the A.O.—the area of operation," he added, in case the three men might not know what A.O. meant. "We'll also need you to keep the area clear of civilians once we go in. Our helicopter is outfitted with FLIR, and with other, classified, search equipment; however, given the number of large mammals in the area, we would rather not rely on technology to find and fix this individual."

Translation, Ben thought. We don't want anyone watching us assassinate this guy.

Robert Lee shook his head. "What's the world comin' to," he said. "Pretty soon y'all will have machines and computers doing it all. Won't be any need a'tall for the likes of people like me."

"Where is this 'individual' supposed to be?" Ben asked.

"He's east of town about ten klicks. At what used to be an old homestead."

"Why don't you just take him down there?" Manfred asked.

The blond man smirked. "There is no telling what sort of equipment and weaponry he might have in that house. We know he has seeded the area around it with motion detectors and heat sensors, and we know the house has a backup generator, but we don't know what else he might have."

Bullshit, Ben thought.

The blond man paused. "Let me repeat, gentlemen. This guy is as good as it gets. My bad boys are good, but I wouldn't bet on the outcome if any one of them had to go one-on-one with this guy. He's a Native American. A Korean War Marine with access to state-of-the-art weapons and surveillance equipment. By taking him down when he is away from the house, we are trying to minimize the chance of anything going wrong."

"Hell," Robert Lee said. "Why don't y'all just surround the place and wait him out."

"My recommendation exactly," the blond man said. "But the Powers That Be want to keep this out of the public eye. That much manpower and equipment running around for that long would inevitably bring the press."

"Well," Robert Lee said. "I'd sure hate to think my department was assisting what some folks hereabouts might regard as not much more than a government hit squad doing their thing in our backyard."

"Sheriff Lee," the blond man said, looking Robert Lee in the eye. "You have my personal assurance that my men will not use deadly force, except as a last resort."

"Are you going to be there personally?" Ben asked.

"Yes. As a matter of fact, I will be."

Ben looked away, as if acceding to the message in the blond man's eyes. He smiled a weak, crooked smile.

"I've got the maps y'all wanted in my truck," Robert Lee said. "Y'all decide on the perimeter y'all want, and my men will make sure none of the locals wander inside it. There ain't but a little logging going on out that way. A couple of phone calls will fix that."

"Great," the blond man said. "We're good to go, then. Gentlemen," he said. "It's been a pleasure. I'll be back," he said to Manfred.

"Look forward to it," Manfred said.

"See y'all later." Robert Lee winked at Manfred and Ben.

Ben and Manfred were silent as the two men went out the door. They watched the two men split up outside the door, the blond man walking past the window.

Ben sighed. "Too many fools."

"Too many sacrifices," Manfred said.

Ben looked at him. "Too many games in the real world."

Manfred grinned. "Believe it or not, I play Boz Skaggs in here now. Hardly any Country Western at all."

"I was at a coffee shop in Nagoya, and Boz Skaggs was playing on the sound system. . . ." He had to fight for a moment to keep Kei out of the memory. "I went to the can, and when I came out, Boz Skaggs wasn't playing any more, and that blond asshole who just walked out the door was at a table with another guy."

"You met him in Japan?"

"Small world, isn't it?"

The sky had turned gray, and there were snow or rain squalls in the small valleys and folds of the mountains across the valley. Robert Lee's truck drove by.

"Remember how in Vietnam sometimes you'd meet someone, and you'd know they weren't going to make it?" Manfred asked.

"I was just thinking the same thing."

"He's got a family, doesn't he?"

"So he says."

Manfred sighed, and shook his head. He scooped up the glasses and coasters from where Robert Lee and the blond man had been, and busied himself behind the bar. Outside a gust of wind sent a few stray snowflakes fluttering along the street.

Ben watched him.

Manfred dried his hands on a towel. "Walk away from this one, Ben. This is where you live. Let Jim and Robert Lee handle it."

An image of Kei's face in Coffee Shop ChaCha, as she turned from her cousin and saw him sitting there, leaped unbidden into Ben's mind.

Outside, long, gray slants of snow and rain hid most of the mountains across the valley.

"You once said that an evil action has evil consequences," Manfred said.

"Words," Ben said.

"You didn't kill the Pumpkin Eater, did you?"

"No. I didn't."

"Because he has a family?"

"That was part of it."

"Well, Agent Wayne, or whoever he is, has a family, too."

Ben stood, and stretched.

"I was watching you there, right before they left." Manfred began polishing the draught beer spigots with his bar towel. "You were real slick. I didn't know you could be that slick."

"The people I've been dealing with aren't exactly the local dopers, Manfred."

Manfred stopped his polishing and looked at him. "Some of the people Raven sends through here, it isn't that they are cold, or don't have any emotions. It's more like—" He resumed his polishing. "It's like what happened when I caught that shrapnel in my foot and leg and I lost some of the nerves around my ankle. Everything still works okay; my ankle just doesn't feel anything, is all." He glanced at Ben. "For some reason, I never equated you with the people coming through here."

"And now you do."

"Watching you be that slick, I do."

"This is personal, Manfred."

"Which is all the more reason why you should let someone else handle it."

"You don't know."

"I know you."

"Manfred, trust me. You don't know."

Manfred looked away, and Ben could see the glisten in his eyes. "There's no talking to you. Never has been."

Ben smiled. "You're talking to Mr. Slide, remember?"

"You know that Chinese saying you have framed on the wall of the bedroom in the apartment?"

"The one written in Chinese characters?"

"One of the women who came through translated it for me."

"And?"

"And think about it, that's all."

Ben looked around the bar. At the old, moth-eaten heads and the wall filled with framed photographs. At Manfred standing behind the glossy countertop, the refurbished bar massive and beautiful behind him.

"I like what you've done to this place," he said. "It fits you."

"You take care," Manfred said.

Ben smiled.

"You hear me, Ben?"

"I hear you."

• • •

Outside, he breathed deep, letting the cold air clear his mind. The Book of Odes, he thought, that's what Manfred had been referring to:

Even in your secret chambers you are watched. See that you do nothing to blush for. Though only the ceiling looks down on you.

He breathed deep again. *Fuck it,* he thought. This one was for Kei.

Chapter 3
The Death Monster

Inside the grove of ancient cedars a fine dusting of snow on mossy forest floor muffled all but the sound of the creek. Gray light and the silence and the huge, dark cedars rising from white ground like giant pillars made him feel as if he was walking through the ruins of an ancient temple. As a young boy he had imagined a huge hallway created by beings other than men—the ruins of an alien civilization overgrown and eroded by the passage of time and the encroachment of mountain and forest.

He crossed diagonally through the silent grove, stepping easily over the narrow creek, and followed a game trail thick with deer prints up the steep, brush-covered slope on the far side of the cedar grove, until the trail broke out onto a grassy bench. The upper end of the bench blended into a steep, fat ridge forested with old, second-growth bull pine, the ground under the pines bare of all but a thick carpet of pine needles and old, rotted stumps and small rock outcroppings. Looking uphill, he could see the dark horizontal lines of long-ago fallen trees, the ground in front littered with broken chunks of skeletonized branches.

A small, rectangular plot surrounded by a sturdy, thigh-high, green, wrought-iron fence occupied the end of the bench closest to the cedar grove. Two rounded gravestones stood upright and dusted with snow inside the enclosure. The

400

wrought iron fence looked as if it had been painted within the last year or so, the area inside kept free of weeds and fallen branches. Manfred, he thought.

Only a small portion of his grandparents' ashes were buried beneath the stones. Most of his grandmother's ashes had been released to the wind blowing across the Blackfeet reservation; his grandfather's were scattered here and there across meadows and among trees on the flat below and across the top of the mountain above. In truth it was more a place for him than for them. It was a place, like ancestral altars in Asia, designed to give him a connection to his grandparents, and through his grandparents to his other ancestors.

He'd thought of putting his parents here, too, but his parents were strangers seen in photographs. Two people he could neither remember nor feel. An ill-defined link between him and his grandfather. His parents were buried together in the old Catholic cemetery in Missoula. When he visited their graves, they felt comfortable where they were.

He propped the shotgun against the wrought-iron fence, and unslung the rifle, automatically checking to make sure the small piece of camouflage cloth was still rubber banded to the end of the barrel. He placed the rifle, an old, heavy-barreled Ruger .308, next to the shotgun.

The Ruger might not look like much, the wood stock scratched and marred by contact with rock and brush and by elk antlers carried across his shoulders, but the action had been worked and the barrel glass-beaded by his grandfather, and both he and Manfred could drive nails with it at 150 meters.

He unsnapped the wide plastic buckle on the butt pack and let the suspenders slide down his shoulders and arms, allowing the pack and the sleeping bag fastened to the suspenders to fall to the ground.

It wasn't much, the fenced plot and the two stones, but the

gentle bench and the huge, ancient cedars rising out of the steep ravine next to the bench made it a special place. His grandfather had told him that his grandmother had loved to sit and nap in the sunlight on this bench.

It had stopped snowing, but the heavy gray light and the stillness told him that it would soon start again, and when it did, it would be a heavier, wetter snow.

He would move when it started snowing again. The snow would cover his tracks. If he heard the helicopter—on the off chance that it had the capability to fly in this kind of weather—he'd get into the shake 'n bake bag that he'd kept after fighting fires the first summer he'd come back from Asia. He figured that if the bag could save him from the heat of a forest fire, it would make his heat signature invisible to whatever search equipment was on that helicopter.

And if it didn't, well, there were so many warm-blooded critters—elk and deer and bear, even raccoons and badgers and mountain lions—scattered about the flat and on the mountain that he figured as long as he wasn't moving upright the helicopter wouldn't be able to tell him from all the other mammals. It would take a people sniffer to do that. And if the helicopter, or the men who would be coming in the night, found him—well, that was why he was here at the gravestones. To talk to his grandfather and grandmother. To tell them what he'd been up to. To talk about Kei. To apologize for the way he'd turned out. To say he was sorry for being the last of the line.

He stepped over the fence and sat cross-legged on the ground to the side of the gravestones, facing the cedars. The cedars were dark, forested columns rising toward gray-white light.

It took a while, but gradually his shoulders relaxed, and the jumble of thoughts and emotions in his mind faded into the gray light.

In his mind the cedars seemed to rustle, and without warning a hot, burning sensation rushed through his gut, into his chest, his feeling of well being abruptly charged with a malevolence that was as terrible as it was unexpected. He felt death wished upon him, that wish, that utter lack of pity for him or for anything human, spreading from the ancient cedars. His grandfather's voice fluttered at the edge of his consciousness. *Ben,* a woman's voice, not Kei's, not Evy's, not anyone he recognized, called. *Ben.* No urgency. Only *Ben,* clearly heard.

"What?" he said, and the word spoken out loud left him alone and sitting cross-legged next to his grandparents' gravestones.

A breeze passed across his face, snowflakes sticking to his forehead and to the skin under his eye. The snowflakes reminded him of cherry blossoms on a bridge over a river in Nagoya, Japan.

He rose. Bowed to his grandparents. Bowed to the cedars. And then stepped back over the fence and knelt in front of his pack and his weapons. He unzipped the butt pack and took from it a pair of soft, cotton coveralls, several sizes too large so that they would easily fit over his wool pants and heavy wool sweater. He stood and pulled the coveralls on over his boots and up his legs, shrugging into the arms and shoulders, and then zipped the thin, camouflage material to his neck.

He knelt again and took out his grandfather's old yellow tobacco pouch and opened it and poured sandbag ash into the palm of his hand. He put the pouch down and mixed snow into the ash, mixing it until it turned into a paste, and then rubbed the paste into the skin of his face and neck and ears and into the stubble of his beard, the back of his hands, the paste leaving his skin mottled, the same colors as the bark on the cedar trees. He put the pouch away, and took a wool camouflage stocking cap from the pack and put it on. He zipped the pack shut, and stood and picked up the pack and put it on, fastening the belt and chest clips, and pulling the waist strap tight. The camouflage pattern on the hat and coveralls was a faded brown-and-gray pattern that featured leaves and tree limbs. The butt pack was a woodland green pattern.

He slung the Ruger barrel down so that the sling went over his right shoulder, diagonally across his chest, the scope and receiver wedged tight against his side under his left arm.

The blond man believed that Ben Tails was going to go quietly, without a whimper, into the night. They were watching Jim, not him. But even if they were expecting him, this was his land. He knew this land and this mountain better than he knew anywhere else in the world.

He picked up the short-barreled shotgun, its ammunition tube longer than the barrel, and jacked a round into the chamber and pushed the safety button on, and then reached through a slit in the side of his coveralls, into his pant pocket, and pulled another shotgun shell from his pocket and inserted it into the tube. The shotgun shells were double-ought—nine .32 caliber pellets per round, seven rounds in all.

The men who would be coming would probably have night vision equipment. They might also have acoustic ears and a people sniffer. He'd have the snow and the wind and his knowledge of the terrain and the forest and the fact that they wouldn't be expecting him.

Watch this, grandpa, he thought. I may not be worth much as a human being, but I am damn sure good at this. He walked to the end of the bench and down the flat, open ridge, moving, the moment he left the bench, in a fluid line from tree to tree to anything, rock, bush, blowdown, that he could blend with, his figure receding steadily down the slope until even his movement through open areas beneath trees and between rock outcroppings became more a trick of light and shadow than the passage of a man through forest.

And behind him, in the dark recesses beneath the giant cedars, something far more ancient than the giant trees, as old as mankind itself, stirred and followed, its darkness spreading like a dark stain through the growing dusk.

Chapter 4
Welcome to Montana

Pitch dark, and he was standing motionless next to a large bull pine. A few yards behind was a dense stand of lodgepole. Against the backdrop of lodgepole, he knew he would be invisible to anyone coming down the track. Even with night vision gear it would be difficult to pick him out.

The wind had picked up, snow gusting in a wet, biting slant from his right, the trunk of the tree protecting him from most of it. The track was already covered with several inches of white slush. If he stepped out of the lee of the tree, he would be able to see the lights of the house about half a mile away.

Wind gusted, and snow swirled around the tree trunk, across his line of vision. Trees groaned and creaked, rubbing together in the darkness. He kept his eyes moving, trying not to look directly at anything. If he looked too long, branches laden with wet snow became men in dark clothes wearing packs and carrying rifles. He blinked snow out of his eyes; resisted the urge to rub them. As long as he stayed next to the tree, he was okay. The mitten flaps on the wool half-gloves were keeping his hands plenty warm.

If it was him, he would try to do without night vision equipment. Wet blowing snow would stick to the lenses, blurring the view. It would be better to let your eyes adapt to the night.

406

Snow made the track two ghostly white lines meandering through the forest.

By morning, footprints would be hidden under a frozen crust of snow. A cold front was supposed to dip into Western Montana overnight; the National Weather Service in Missoula had predicted as much as six inches before morning. But by mid morning, if the Weather Service could be trusted, the cold front would be replaced by clear skies and temperatures in the sixties.

Montana, he thought. If you don't like the weather, wait ten minutes.

The elk herd was bedded somewhere nearby. He'd smelled them when he'd come off the ridge. He'd have to be careful in case the men he expected to come through here in the night got the elk up and moving through the trees. What with the dark and the snow, it was difficult enough without a bunch of elk ghosting through the trees.

Wind whipped around the tree, and snow slapped his eyes. He blinked rapidly to clear his vision, and the wind died– one of those inexplicable pauses–and all around him was still, as if even the wind and the snow had paused to listen.

He and Manfred had grown up playing in this forest. Counting coup on each other in the dark. Scaring themselves until, inevitably, they found themselves running hell bent for leather, side by side along the track. Running from ghosts or monsters–real or imagined, they never had the courage, no matter how much they talked about it beforehand, to wait around and find out. Once they started running, that was it. Running verified the existence of the thing that pursued them, and they would not stop running until they were home.

The wind gusted again. No games tonight, he thought. Real monsters were out and about tonight.

His eyes caught movement that went across the wind–a

brief shift in the darkness along the edge of the track. His heart hammered.

Gusts of snow blew across the track. He smelled pine and gun oil.

The fingers of his right hand crawled from under the mitten flap and reached under the action to the safety button. His thumb and trigger finger pinched both sides of the button, and he eased off the safety.

Nothing moved except tree branches and blowing snow. But unseen and acknowledged only in the deepest recesses of his mind, a deeper darkness, not his, stirred.

Whoever was out there was good, he thought. Whoever was out there had felt it, too, the Death Monster. But just as it had been with the NVA sniper, it was he who had the lock. Whoever was out there was telling himself that what he'd felt was only a product of wind and snow and darkness and unfamiliar forest. Whoever was out there, his intellect was telling his gut that it was only his imagination.

If the man out there was good, he would take time to scan the area with his night vision gear. And then, about now, he'd take it off, or flip it up, and stand there until his eyes had again adapted to the darkness. If the man out there was better than good, he'd move off the track into the forest to flank whatever had made him feel uneasy.

He heard a wet, slushy sound under the wind. A boot trying to be quiet in wet snow.

A bulky mass mottled dark gray and black moved along the right side of the track. He couldn't see anything behind whoever it was, but that didn't mean anything. They might have headsets to communicate with.

The figure stopped about six feet from him, and he could see there was no night vision device or any other kind of device. The weapon the figure carried was slung barrel down. No face paint: the face was a pale oval that seemed to brighten, then dim, as snow swirled around it. Web gear. Small backpack. Black, bulky-looking gloves.

Welcome to my forest, he thought.

His fingers silently squeezed the safety back on. He waited for the figure to move, and when finally it did, he raised the shotgun and speared the barrel into the chest, feeling it hit vest or chest strap. The man's legs shot out from under him and he fell heavily onto his back. His rifle made a dull clunk as it fell off his shoulder into the snow at the side of the track.

"Twelve gauge," Ben said in a normal tone of voice. "Double ought."

He waited, the safety off, his finger on the trigger.

"Who are you?"

"I'm your worst fucking nightmare, Top."

There was a long silence, the figure on the ground breathing heavily. "Shit," the figure said. "What are you doing here?"

"Who's behind you?"

"I'm alone."

Ben stepped to the side and kicked him hard in the thigh. The figure on the ground grunted, pain evident in the sound.

"How many, Top?"

"I'm alone, Goddamn it."

"Roll over on your stomach, away from the rifle, hands out to the side." Ben kicked him in the thigh again. Hard. Kicked him a third time. Harder. The man rolled over face down in the snow, arms to the side.

With his left hand, right hand holding the shotgun extended over the head of the figure on the ground and pointed down the track in the direction the man had come, Ben reached through the slit in his coveralls and found the handcuffs in his belt. He pulled the handcuffs out, and dropped them next to the man's head.

"Take your gloves off and cuff yourself behind your back."

The figure did not move.

Ben stepped back in the lee of the big pine. "Fine," he said. "I'll just shoot you."

The figure on the ground levered himself up on his elbows and pulled his gloves off with his teeth. Ben heard a handcuff ratchet shut on one wrist, and then the figure was back face down in the snow, hands groping behind his back. Ben heard the other handcuff ratchet shut.

He stepped forward, shotgun pressed into the back of the man's neck, and with his left hand checked the cuffs. He tightened the cuff on the man's right hand.

"If you fight them, they'll tighten," he said. He backed next to the tree. "Come over here."

The man struggled to his feet, his leg where Ben had kicked him spasming out to the side as his thigh muscle cramped.

Ben grabbed his pack and pulled him backwards onto his ass, next to the tree.

Down the track, there was only the movement of wind in the trees. Snow swirled through the darkness. The rifle was in the snow next to the track, but that was where it would have to stay, he thought.

"I am going to shoot whoever comes along next," he said.

"It's Corporal Power. He's about five minutes behind me."

Ben crouched behind the man, shotgun aimed down the track.

They waited, neither man moving.

A figure abruptly materialized out of the snow and darkness, and halted ten yards away, and turned sideways, back to the wind, and took off his gloves and put them under his right armpit. Ben heard the sound of a zipper being unzipped; the sound of piss hitting the snow.

He slowly stood and then walked forward down the track as fast as he could, the shotgun held straight out in front of him.

"Quit fucking around, Top. I knew you were there before you even moved," the figure said.

"I'm not the Top."

The figure whirled, gloves falling to the ground.

"And this is a shotgun. Let the rifle fall off your shoulder."

"Do what he says," the Top shouted.

The rifle clattered to the ground.

"Turn around."

The figure turned.

"Drop your pack."

The pack toppled back into the snow.

"Tuck your dick in."

Ben heard the sound of a zipper being zipped.

"Is this all of you?"

The figure in front of him was silent, but Ben knew it was only the two of them, or the Top would not have spoken so loud, and the corporal would not have been diddy-bopping along the way he'd been. "Kneel down," he said.

The Corporal kneeled.

Ben fished around under his coveralls and found the other pair of cuffs. He draped them over the Corporal's shoulder. "Cuff yourself behind your back."

"Do it," the Top said. Ben could tell from the sound of the Top's voice that he'd leveraged himself up and was standing leaning against the big pine.

"I'm real nervous," Ben said to the corporal. "I've never captured anyone before, and I'm probably going about this all wrong."

The figure still did not move.

"Goddamn it, Corporal. He will *kill you,"* the Top shouted.

The figure reached up and took the cuffs and Ben heard one ratchet close, and then the figure put his hands behind his back.

411

"Top is right," Ben said; "I will kill you." And for a moment, his finger on the trigger, that black thing was all around them.

He heard the other cuff ratchet shut.

Ben stepped forward and with his foot shoved the man face down in the snow. He placed the barrel of the shotgun against the back of the man's neck and checked the cuffs, tightening both against the man's wrists.

"Get up," he said, and backed off the track, the wind at his back. "Come over here, Top."

"I can't use my leg."

"Yes, you can. Get over here."

He waited for the Top to shuffle over. "Straight ahead into the trees, Corporal. Follow him," he said to the Top. "Hey, welcome to Montana, guys."

Chapter 5
Secrets

"What were you thinking of?" Ben asked the Top. They were seated in a thick stand of aspen, both Marines with their arms and legs wrapped around tree trunks. He'd freed the Top Sergeant's cuffs and had the Top free the corporal and then handcuff the corporal around a tree. Then he'd had him handcuff himself around another tree. He thought for sure the corporal was going to bolt or otherwise do something stupid, but the Top had held tight to his cuffs, and ordered him to sit and put his arms around a tree. It was a good thing the corporal had not done something stupid because by then he had decided that he was not going to shoot these two under any circumstances. His days of killing Marines were long over—especially Marines like these.

"This has to be about the dumbest thing you've ever done," he said.

"Not really," the Top said. "I've been married four times."

Ben laughed.

"Mr. Cyr has some kind of juice with the Colonel," the Top said. "We didn't have a choice."

Ben felt the cold seeping in around them. There were still leaves on the trees and because there were, there wasn't much snow on the ground, but there was enough snow and his night vision was acute enough to make out their forms wrapped around the trees. He'd been surprised to find no other weapons besides a couple of knives. It was obvious the

413

two Marines had not taken their recon seriously—at least not the night portion of it.

The Corporal carried a scoped rifle and forty rounds or so of extra ammunition. An M-16 outfitted with a small scope for the Top. Four thirty-round magazines for the 16. A GPS.

A couple of nifty Motorola radios that were more like cell phones than radios. MRI's, candy bars, plastic bottles of water, packets of survival and medical gear—standard-issue stuff that, along with the ammunition, they had probably dragged along more out of habit than anything else. Oreo cookies for the corporal, a couple of stogies in plastic tubes and two cans of beer for the Top. An entire roll of toilet paper for the corporal. New, unused containers of face paint. Their night vision goggles had been in their packs.

It must have been that sixth sense, and years of doing it by the numbers, that had made the Top slow up and move the way he had.

"Tell me again why you are here?"

"The Colonel knows I'm going to retire soon, and he jumps at any chance to have me train new guys like Corporal Power here. But it's been a civilian operation from the minute we left Japan. We shouldn't even be here."

Wind rattled the branches, and a clump of wet snow splatted to the ground somewhere in the darkness. Ben knew that by mid-morning the grove of aspen would be raining ice water as the sun melted snow in the branches and leaves.

"Why is it you have a sniper rifle and plenty of rounds for both weapons?"

"Power here is a sniper. It's what he normally carries. If we would've had a clue that this was going to be for real, we would have been packing handguns, grenades, all the fun stuff. Instead we've got poggy bait. There's even some cigars and beer in my pack. Tell me we were out here doing anything real."

Ben was silent. The corporal hadn't said a word, but he could feel the corporal's anger–the slow-to-come anger of someone who'd grown up on a working ranch or farm. He thought the corporal might be strong enough to break the small chain holding the cuffs together.

He unzipped the top pocket on his butt pack and took a couple of thick, plastic wire ties from the pocket and went over and fastened them, one to each man, so that the plastic ties held the cuffs tight together.

"Where are the other people you flew in with?" he asked the Top.

"Down by the river. We were supposed to set up on the mountain and let them know if the old man went for a walk up the road."

"And then?"

"What do you mean, and then? And then nothing. Oh, I see. You think–There's no way, man. No way in God's green earth we'd light up a civilian on the say so of another civilian."

"Light up a civilian?"

"Hey, I been on enough ops to know that those people are not here to *apprehend* anyone. They are here to kill that old man, whoever he is."

"They said that?"

"They didn't have to."

"Well, let me tell you who that old man is. He's my boss. And for your information, both of you, he's a Chosin Marine. You know, the Korean War. Chosin Resevoir," he said to the Corporal.

"I know what a Chosin Marine is."

"It speaks," Ben said.

"Fuck you."

"Didn't I tell you this was going to be a cluster fuck," the Top said to the corporal. "Didn't I fucking tell you."

"Yeah, you told me."

"I still don't understand why the Marine Corps has you working with these guys," Ben said.

"These days they use us for a lot of stuff like this," the Top said. "Not here in the States so much, but overseas. They use us to sniff people out, or to provide security that most of the time they don't need. Way too much of it is sneak and peak bullshit–like we thought this was–hatched by civilian idiots in a secure room somewhere." He paused. "But since it's you, let me tell you. These days the other side–the ragheads and the dopers and the Russians and the used-to-be Russians, and most especially the Chinese–those people are for real. It's not like it used to be. Except for the satellites and the communications, their equipment and training are as good as ours. That's why the Colonel jumps at any chance to give us real-world, real-time experience. But no way we'd be here if the Colonel had known this kind of bullshit was going to go down."

"You're sure of that?"

"I'm sure."

"How about you, Corporal, are you sure?"

"Fuck you."

"Ask yourself who you're pissed off at, Corporal. Me? Or the people who got you into this?"

The corporal was silent.

"Okay. Both of you. Listen up. You are alive because this is my land. I mean *this is my land.* I grew up in that house back there. Some of my ancestors were already here when Lewis and Clark wandered their sorry asses down the Clark Fork. I *own* the trees you are hugging. Are you hearing me, Corporal?"

"I hear you."

"This is my land, Corporal, just as that farm you grew up on in Corncob, Iowa, is yours. The old man you were tasked to observe is a guest in *my* house on *my* land."

The Corporal grunted.

"Un-fucking-real," the Top muttered.

"It gets worse," Ben said, his voice taking on an edge. "Your Fearless Leader, whoever he is, was one of the people responsible for nearly killing a woman I like a lot. She will be in a hospital for months—and even at that she will probably never be the same again." He paused, letting his mind open enough to see Kei on the couch, Sato bent over her.

Deep in the forest trees groaned against each other, and at the base of the mountain the bull elk and the lead cow stirred, snow cascading from their hides as they stood, nostrils searching the wind for whatever it was that had gotten them up. The bull raised his head and screamed defiance, the eerie, piercing sound carried by the wind into the aspen grove, making it seem to the three men as if the bull was right outside the screen of trees.

A gust of wind cold as Ben's thoughts rattled the trees.

"She did nothing to warrant the attack," he said. "They would have killed her."

"Would have?" the Top asked.

Branches rattled and scraped in the darkness. The Death Monster was near, Ben thought. He could feel it. He could hear it in the groan and creak of heavy trees moving against each other. It was here, and it didn't like the fact that it had been cheated.

He stood and walked over to the Corporal and pressed the shotgun against his head. The corporal tried to jerk his head away, his arms sawing against the tree, pieces of bark falling to the ground. Ben shoved the barrel harder against the corporal's head. The Corporal jerked frantic against the tree.

Ben pulled the barrel away, and for a moment stood silent between the two figures hunched around their trees.

"We've been talking like we are friends," he said to both of them. "But make no mistake, we are not friends. Do not let our conversation confuse you. If you were not Marines, you would be dead."

The two men sat silent, each in his own way feeling the breath of the thing that had infiltrated the stand of aspen, both of them acutely aware of the shotgun in his hands, their ears unconsciously straining for any movement on his part.

"What's supposed to happen tomorrow?" Ben asked the Top.

The Top started to answer, but his voice came out a thick, phlegmy sound. He cleared his throat, and spit. "There's a team," he said. He cleared his throat again, and again spit. "HRT, they say. But I don't think so. I worked with one of them a couple of years back on a DEA operation in Burma. They're down by the river. That's where they expect the old man to be in the morning."

"They expect him to go fishing even with the snow?"

"They say rain or shine he either goes fishing or he goes hiking."

"Who says? They haven't been around here long enough to know that."

"The Sheriff, maybe. They think the Sheriff is some kind of hick fool, but you ask me, it's an act. That man knows what he's doing."

"You have no idea," Ben muttered.

"What?"

"Special Forces," Ben said. "Three tours."

The Top was silent for a moment. "I'm going to retire," he said. "Soon as we get out of here, I'm going to fucking retire."

"Why don't they assault the house?" Ben asked. "Shoot him on the porch, or something?"

"Most likely because there's always a deputy following them around like a dog that won't go home."

"Use the Blackhawk, then."

"The Sheriff doesn't want it flying around. He raised all

kinds of hell with the Governor and a senator. Says there's too many folks in these parts get all excited when they see unmarked, black helicopters flying around. There was a real to-do between him and Mr. Cyr over it before we left to come out here."

"I'll bet."

"I have to take a piss," the corporal said.

"So piss," Ben replied. "Let me get this straight," he said to the Top. "There are two teams. You and the Iowa State Wrestling Champ here, and a group of guys pretending to be HRT-trained FBI types. Is that right?"

"That's right."

"How long you going to keep us out here?" the corporal asked.

"Be quiet," the Top said. "Jesus."

Ben sighed. He clicked the shotgun safety off and on to make sure it was on, and then leaned the shotgun between a branch and the trunk of a tree.

"So if he goes for a hike, what are you supposed to do?"

"We're supposed to direct people to his location."

"So they can kill him?"

"Well, like I said, no one is talking search warrants, arrest warrants, any of that. All they talk about is what a bad-ass international terrorist he is. *'Don't take chances,'*" he mimicked. "*'Under no circumstances are you to initiate any hostile action, except by my direct order.'* The old guy goes hiking with an old ski pole for a hiking stick, fishes with an old bamboo fishing pole, and we're supposed to be worried about him? Give me a break."

Ben was silent.

"It's all classified beyond my C.O.'s eyes," the Top said. "I can't even tell him what bullshit this is when we get back."

"But you are going to."

"Fucking right, I'm going to."

"Well, don't." Ben zipped his pack shut and, and pulling it up by one suspender, put it on, the clack of the waist and chest buckles as they fastened a sharp, alien sound in the dark.

"He wants to do it the old-fashioned way," the Top said. "That's what I think. Low tech. Like we did in Nam."

"Low tech? A Blackhawk helicopter with infrared and who knows what else. An unarmed old man on a mountain road?"

"Man, this is nothing. You would not believe the shit we have now. You are one of the best ever, no doubt about it. But if we would have been serious, you would be in a world of hurt."

"I wouldn't even be here if I thought you were packing equipment I couldn't deal with."

"What do you mean?"

"Didn't you tell me the Sheriff got the helicopter grounded?"

"Yeah?"

"Well, then, tell me. Where are all those nifty little black boxes that came in on the helicopter?"

"They're locked in a room at the–" He paused. "Sheriff's Office."

Ben picked up his rifle and slung it over his shoulder. He'd hide the shotgun and their weapons and gear in the sweat lodge, then head up the mountain.

"It's personal for them, too," the Top said. "They think the old guy was responsible for what happened to some of their people in Japan."

"Well, he wasn't," Ben said. "I was."

Leaves rustled.

"So what are you going to do?" the Top asked.

"He's gone," the Corporal said.

Chapter 6
Ravens

Ben stood in the dark at the base of a rock outcrop, next to the rough, fissured trunk of an old-growth fir. His thigh and calf muscles ached, and his breath was still raspy as his lungs struggled to compensate for the abrupt change in altitude, and for the physical exertion that had been required to climb straight up the slope. To his left as he stood with his back to the rock outcrop was a long, broad, easy ridge leading down to a saddle. For some reason that he'd never been able to figure, the ridge all the way to the saddle had never been logged.

As a boy he'd loved being on that ridge, the long, dark, grassy expanses under the ancient trees the kind of mysterious forest found only in books like *The Hobbit*.

He cleared his throat and spit and unbuckled the pack. When he was a kid, he could *run* up this mountain. And had—more than once. He placed the rifle against the tree, and shrugged out of the pack, letting it fall to the ground.

He was sweating pretty good. Hot now, but in a few minutes, after his heart calmed down, it would get cold in a hurry.

The good news was that, contrary to what he'd expected, there was little wind and what snow had fallen at this altitude was dry and cold. The bad news was that the temperature would probably dip to around zero before dawn. Colder, if the sky cleared before then.

There was a place in the rocks where he'd built fires, and he'd build one if it got cold enough, but Manfred claimed the bag was waterproof and good to twenty below.

With his feet he cleared a space free of branches and small rocks between roots at the base of the tree. Even lying down he would be able to see anyone coming up the slope long before they would be able to see him.

He was tired. He checked his watch. Only ten o'clock. Dealing with the two Marines and then climbing to the top of the mountain had taken more out of him than he wanted to admit. After he'd stashed their equipment and his shotgun, he'd gone back to where the two Marines were and put their gloves on their handcuffed hands. They'd be cold by the time the sun came up. But, hey, they would also be alive.

It had occurred to him that as soon as they were sure he was not coming back they would climb the trees he had handcuffed them around, breaking off branches as they went, eventually breaking the tops off the trees and freeing themselves. So with plastic ties he'd bound their ankles together so that both their legs and their arms were fastened around the trees. To their credit, they had both remained silent, stoic in their predicament.

"Someone will come and get you," he'd told them. He smiled to himself. There had to be something politically correct about tree-hugging Marines.

He pulled the sleeping bag out of the stuff sack and spread it on the ground, and then made a low half shelter, open on the downhill side, out of rocks and tarp and long, thick pieces of fallen branches. He unzipped his wet coveralls and worked his arms and shoulders out of the damp material, and then sat down and pulled the coveralls off. He stood and pulled off his wool sweater and the long-sleeved polypropylene shirt underneath. He wiped his chest and arms and ribs and the back of his neck with the shirt, and then took another, similar shirt from his pack and put it on. His long hair, pony tail or not, was getting to be a real pain in the ass. He looked forward to having it whacked off. Cold was already seeping into his chest and arms and bare head.

He pulled the sweater back on—wool was a good insulator, even when damp—and unzipped the sleeping bag and folded the coveralls and put them at the bottom of the bag: it would not do to wake up and find his camouflage frozen stiff as a board. He reached in the pack and found a black polyproplylene balaclava and a wool stocking hat. He took out a bottle of water and a Snickers bar, and then pulled open a velcro pocket flap on the side of the pack and took out a small baggie, a thin line of pills at the bottom of the baggie. A couple of Advil would stop him from stiffening up, and one Sudafed would keep his sinuses and lungs clear.

He washed the pills down with water from the bottle. When he was younger, he'd wipe his nose on his sleeve and spit a lot. He put the baggie back in the pack and put the other things to the side of the sleeping bag, and then put the wet shirt in the pack and zipped it shut.

He carefully placed the rifle on the inside of the shelter. He debated taking his boots off, but decided there was a chance, albeit a very remote chance, that some idiot would use a flashlight to climb the mountain in the dark, and left them on.

He sat down on the end of the bag and drank the water and ate the Snickers bar. No matter how many times he'd done it, it always amazed him how good a Snickers bar tasted after climbing a mountain.

He stood and walked a few steps to the side and took a piss. And then put the empty bottle and candy wrapper in his pack, and placed the pack at the head of the bag so that he could use it for a pillow. He pulled on the balaclava and the stocking hat, and climbed in the bag. With his hips and feet and shoulders, he worked the bag sideways under the shelter, and then put the top of his head in the head piece at the end of the bag, and zipped the bag all the way up.

He relaxed his head against the lumpy pack and, looking up at branches barely seen in the darkness, fell asleep.

• • •

The sky behind the ravens was a weird, fluorescent, otherworldly blend of reds and purples. He'd been walking down a mountain road somewhere, footsore and tired, his head down, not really paying attention, his thoughts on dinner and a hot shower, and he'd looked up and before his mind could register what he was seeing, the forest ahead was abruptly filled with dark movement, the fluorescent sky above the ridge and in the spaces between the trees alive with the effort of huge black wings. And in that instant of recognition— not of ravens but of what they must have been at—he felt a rush of adrenaline. Not the bright electric rush of finding an elk. But a greasy rush, dark and familiar as a favorite song from those bygone days spent in other mountains. And for a moment—one of those moments he thought he'd locked away forever—he wasn't sure where those dark wings had come from.

For a moment it wasn't the body of an animal that the ravens had been at, but the body of a woman with long hair the same lustrous black as the ravens. One eye gone. The ribs and one arm picked clean. Raw, red holes in the skin and in bruised meat on the haunch.

• • •

He opened his eyes and the sky above the branches was filled with star fields so bright and so close it felt as if the

424

giant tree was moving into them. Ghostly clouds, soft and rumpled on top, blanketed the valley below. Distant peaks were black islands against the stars.

He'd expected to wake chilled to the bone, but apparently Manfred was right about the sleeping bag, because he felt warm, the hard ground comfortable beneath him. The stars were so bright he could see down through the trees below.

He closed his eyes. First light was still an hour or so away. And thought of his dream, seeing the ravens, their wings against the strange horizon. He was surprised that he even remembered it. He almost never remembered his dreams, knew only that he had them. What did the dream mean? Evy? Kei? One of the women from the village the Marines had been massacring? The most unsettling thing about the dream was that his empathy had not been with the body, but with the ravens, as they escaped through the branches.

He opened his eyes, unwilling to go back to sleep. He was back in his land, but a part of him, maybe even the most important part of him, would be forever in those other mountains. For too long he'd walked among people—Vietnamese and Chinese and Thai, Hmong and Cambodian and, yes, of course, American—so replete with killing and death that had they been part of those dark, lubricious wings rising off the carcass in his dream, they never would have made it off the ground, would instead have continued to gorge, intent, even as their brittle eyes registered what was coming, only on that last bite, that last savage peck and tear before they themselves became food for the feast.

Gentle air—a chill breath on the skin under his eyes and on his eyelids—passed across his face, gone as easily as it had come.

Looking up at the stars, at mountain tops like black islands in a ghostly sea, at times like this he knew there was a right and a wrong, a yin and a yang, a dark and a light. There is a

425

God that dwells in the mind of mankind, he thought, and Gods that dwell in animate and inanimate objects. There is all that and, he knew in his bones, much more. But no one, least of all him, understood any of it. In the morning, the blond man was going to chase death, imagining that with death there comes an understanding, not realizing that the death he chased was his own.

The blond man had a family. But at first light, family or not, the blond man would be on this mountain, under this same sky, intending to kill a man for no reason other than the man he intended to kill had something he thought he needed. That was his excuse. But what he really wanted was to experience first hand what it was to look through a rifle scope and mete out death.

It was amazing, he thought, the death and pain that a few men in the right place at the right time could cause—Carlos, the three Japanese killed at the festival, Peter's arm, Sato, the American in the hallway, Kei. Shooting the blond man was going to be no more difficult that it had been to shoot those feral dogs that had chased a doe up this very mountain, intending to kill her for the sport of it.

What was going to be difficult was to shoot a man on this mountain. He could not understand why Jim was letting it play out this way. He knew that it had to do with him and what had happened to Carlos and to Kei. But he also suspected that part of it had to do with Jim blaming himself for letting things get so out of hand. Not only was Jim like an uncle to the Ishida girls, but the murder of Carlos, and the fact that one of his men had been wounded and nearly killed, had to weigh heavy on his mind.

Or maybe not. Maybe it was none of that. Maybe it was the cumulative effect of a lifetime spent doing the things Jim had done. Maybe he was just tired and didn't give a damn. Sort of like running up this mountain had been.

To run up the mountain he'd had to maintain short, even steps, and a pace that was less than twice the speed he could have walked it. At the bottom it felt ridiculous to run so slow and with such short, careful steps, but half way up the mountain, the pace was just right, and by the time he was on the last, steep slope, his thigh and calf muscles burned and his lungs felt torn and each step was the last he could take. Reaching the top became possible only because he knew where the top was. Without that knowledge he doubted he would have made it.

Jim's life must have been like running up this mountain, he thought. Only Jim could not have known what pace to keep, and he could not have known where the top was. Many times he must have expended his energy thinking that what he could see before him was the end of it. He must have done that again and again, far beyond the stamina of an ordinary man.

Maybe Jim had gone as far as he could, and had decided that, fuck it, he was going to sidehill for awhile, let whatever happened happen.

Ben smiled at the tree above him. There might be something to all that, he thought. Jim was only human, after all. But the man he'd seen on the porch enjoying his coffee and the morning was a long way from running out of energy.

Fact was, he was probably transposing his own fucked-up, burned-out feelings on to Jim. It was he, more than Jim, who wanted to stop, let happen whatever happened. And Jim wasn't going to let him do that. Jim was going to force him to take that next step, no matter how leaden his legs felt. That's why Jim was letting it play out this way.

He sighed. It would be something, he thought, to be able to see how many warriors had over the centuries come to this place and sat or camped cold beneath this tree. Not men who were like those black-winged creatures he'd seen in his dream, but men who appreciated the trees and the stars— men who knew the minds of those black winged creatures, but were not them.

Until now these mountains had been a refuge. When he was a child, full of too much energy, and mean from his inability to understand why he, and no one else, had been cheated of parents, his grandfather would give him a sack lunch and tell him to take the dog and be back at sundown. Bow and arrow in hand, he'd cross meadows and walk up on the mountain where he and his dog would find deer and elk, now and then a black bear, rabbits and porcupines and skunks, squirrels and chipmunks, maybe Mr. Badger, song birds of all shapes and sizes, a hawk or two, occasionally an eagle or a great horned owl. Looking back on it now, he realized that what he'd liked most about this mountain was how full of life it was. The mountain had made him realize in a felt way that his concerns were merely the selfish, thoughtless concerns of someone who already had what he needed. It did not matter that he did not have parents. He had his grandfather, and he had the mountain.

But now those other mountains had finally followed him home, and before the day was out, what he had been in those other mountains was going to end the magic of this place. In a few hours, those black lubricious wings would no longer be in his dream. They would be real, and they would be him, and this place would never again be the same.

Humping up the mountain in the dark and in the snow, he'd felt the weight of his memories and he hadn't been sure he would be able to go through with it. But lying here in this familiar place, beside the same tree and under the same stars that his father and grandfather and generations of men before them had sat or lain, he knew that he was going to.

He would go through with it because even here in this place with the tree reaching into the stars, the memory of Kei lying broken on her couch, the sour stink of her urine and shit and blood mixed with the carnage in the hallway–that memory was far too strong. When he thought of the blond man coming up the ridge in a few hours, the magic of this place was a price he was willing to pay.

He unzipped the sleeping bag to his waist, and pulled off the balaclava, the air crisp and cold on his cheeks and under his chin. He fished out the radio from the front pocket of his pants and turned it on.

He looked once more up at the tree and the stars, and down the ridge through the fairy-tale forest of his youth. And then he keyed the transmit button, and began to talk, his voice the impersonal, matter-of-fact, slightly cocky voice of a professional Marine reporting in.

Chapter 7
No Choice

The sky above was the kind of deep blue that in a photo or in a painting does not look real. Moisture sparkled the air. The trees looked like the artificial, snow-flocked, too-perfect trees in Christmas displays. Shading his eyes with his hand he looked out across the clouds covering the valley. Snow-covered peaks delineated the far horizon.

Up where he was, it was silent and perfect, everything clean and white and crisp, but down below, the slush and snow of the evening before would be crusted hard, making it impossible to drive a vehicle quietly down the road, or to walk across meadows and up the old logging road without being heard.

In a little while the sun would begin to burn off the clouds, and the frozen crust would melt. Walking through the trees below would mean walking under a drizzle of ice water, clumps of ice-cold snow splatting onto the ground or onto your head and shoulders.

Jim would keep to the old road to avoid all that. The old road began at the National Forest boundary at the back of his land, and rose following the contours of the mountain for about a mile before it became a series of short, steep switchbacks. Nine switchbacks in all. Once beyond the steep

430

switchbacks, the road climbed steadily, following the contours of the mountain.

Far below to his right, the road crested a bench in the middle of a long, finger ridge, and then disappeared into a fold that he could not see from where he stood. He had decided to set up on that ridge. From his hide, he would be able to see where the old pack trail crossed the road.

If you followed the road up, and the pack trail down, it was a reasonably comfortable nine- or ten-mile hike. He was sure that Jim had found the old pack trail. Saplings and bushes cut close to the ground and a path chain sawed through the trunks of large blown down trees made it obvious that the trail was manmade and must therefore lead down to the valley floor.

He dismantled his makeshift shelter and stuffed the sleeping bag into the stuff sack, and then wrapped the sleeping bag and his wet, sweaty clothes from the night before, along with candy wrappers and empty plastic water bottles, in the tarp, and placed large rocks over and around the tarp. He would come back for everything when he could. Right now he did not want the extra weight and bulk.

The sun had risen in the short time it had taken him to get organized. The sparkle was already gone from the air, the first drips beginning to fall from the tree above. He pulled the cloth from the end of the rifle barrel, and then removed the bolt, keeping it in one hand against the stock as he pushed the magazine plate release and unloaded the rifle.

He set the cartridges on his stocking hat, and turned the rifle barrel toward him, holding it like a telescope toward the eastern horizon. The barrel was free of moisture—or at least as free as it was going to get, he thought. He closed the magazine plate and re-inserted the bolt. Checking the cartridges one by one to see that they were dry, he reloaded the rifle, and put the cloth back over the end of the barrel.

431

He leaned the rifle against the tree, put the pack on, and fastened the plastic buckles over his still damp coveralls. He picked up the rifle, jacked a round into the chamber, and set the safety.

Holding the rifle in the crook of his left arm, he started down the hill, moving from tree to tree, careful to stay well off the ridgeline as he worked his way down the slope. This mountain had been his backyard. Ben Tails was at home on this mountain. But Mr. Slide was not. And working his way down the slope he felt edgy and off-balance. The cover was too sparse, the open spaces too great. The ancient trees brought back memories, and the memories were distracting.

A part of him wanted nothing more than to find a place in the sunlight, where he could stretch out, arms behind his head, face turned toward the sun. Ben Tails the boy had done that many times—fallen asleep in the morning sun—waking more than once, his eyes and the inside of his mouth gluey from the hot sun, to his grandfather bouncing pine cones off his head and chest.

"You're just like your grandmother," his grandfather had said the first time he'd found him that way. He had expected a lecture, but instead his grandfather had sat down next to him and leaned back against the hillside and closed his eyes.

"Take her hunting and she'd end up picking flowers or leaves or some damn thing. Fall asleep in the sun just like you. Herd of elephants come by and neither one of you would know it."

His grandfather. Eyes closed. Smiling at the sun.

What do you think of me now, grandpa? he thought. You got to see the Marine who had won a promotion and dress blues in boot camp, but you never got to see Mr. Slide.

He stopped next to the trunk of an old-growth bull pine, one of the last before he moved out of the mysterious forest, and leaned against the thick, rough bark.

It was hard to accept that his decisions had followed him

here to this place, but they had, and there was nothing he could do about it now.

Never again would the boy who could sleep in the sun like his grandmother walk this way. From this day forward, in some form or another, it would be Mr. Slide who walked this mountain—as out of place as that cobra would be if it made its home the tall grass of the meadows below.

But just as there had been no choice when he'd watched those Marines rape and pillage and murder, there was no choice now. The blond man and his buddies were the people with the choices. Not him. Not in this place. Not with his ancestors watching.

He left the protection of the giant tree and moved down the mountain. And gradually, as he descended toward the road below, the juxtaposition in his mind of this mountain with those other mountains was forgotten, his awareness, as he worked his way across the slope, heightened far beyond any boyhood consciousness.

Chapter 8
Warpaint

Late morning now, and all but a few wisps of cloud in the folds low down on the shaded, north slopes across the valley had burned off. The ridge he was on was free of snow, the ground wet and treacherous. From his hide, he could see the road below where it crossed a small knob and turned and ran in a long, winding horseshoe up onto the ridge with the old pack trail.

The slope below his hide looked open, populated only by a scattering of mature larch. But what looked open was in fact a cover of grass and weeds and chest-high bushes hiding the rotted debris and churned ground left behind by loggers.

It was amazing how much animal life could be hidden on a slope like this, he thought. He'd once sat on a slope like this to eat lunch, and thinking there were no large animals around, unzipped his pack to get a sandwich, and the sound of the zipper had caused a whitetail buck to bolt from not more than twenty yards below. The buck had run bounding across the hillside, and another twenty or thirty deer in its path had also jumped up, scattering across what he had thought was an empty slope. For a moment, it had seemed as if the entire forest had jumped up and taken a column right into the trees.

That was not going to happen today. He had a 180 degree

field of fire, and for the several hours that he had been here nothing had moved below. A few minutes ago, way off to his right, he'd seen through the Nikons Jim walk up the last of the steep switchbacks and come out onto a long stretch that led eventually, winding in and out of folds and over small ridges, to the small knob below.

Ben was talking whoever it was–the blond man, he assumed; it was hard to tell over the radio–up what he knew was the steepest, most rock-strewn spine on the mountain.

The radio bounced an ultra-high frequency signal off a solar- and battery-powered repeater that the Blackhawk had dropped off on a peak on the far side of the valley. The radio had been programmed for two frequencies only–one for the "talk," the control who had stayed back at the S.O., and one for the man he was bringing up the mountain.

He'd kept his messages as terse as possible. The last time he'd called, the talk had informed him that the Blackhawk was down for some kind of maintenance gripe. They were on their own.

"No problem," the man Ben was directing up the mountain had said. Most certainly the blond man, Ben thought. Talking as if this was some kind of hunt in Africa, and the helicopter being down merely made it more interesting.

The knob on the other side of the road below was so open, the good shooting positions so limited, that distance for Ben was not a factor. He was burrowed into an old pile of slash– a gray, rotting, jumbled pile of logs and stumps–and there was no way he could be seen unless someone crawled in with him. The place that the blond man could shoot from was about 250 meters walking distance down the slope and across the road, but only about 120 meters in a straight line.

Earlier he'd heard something come down the slope on the other side of the slash pile and root around for a while–Mr. Badger or Mr. Bear, he hadn't been sure which–and he had been worried that maybe he was near its den. Whatever it was had paused at what it had been tearing apart, and he'd shouted, "Get out of here." One thing he did not need was a bear wandering around looking for huckleberries or ground squirrels. A long moment of silence had passed before it had taken the hint and moved off, probably up the slope behind where he was burrowed into the slash pile.

Jim emerged on a far bend in the road–about fifteen minutes from the knob below at the pace he was walking.

Ben keyed the transmit button. "Where are you now?"

"Thirty meters or so below the knob. I see the target coming around a bend."

"Hold your position," Ben said. "Move on my say in about twenty-five."

"10-4."

The voice on the other end sounded tired and out of breath. Too bad he had so much time to recover from what must have been a truly shitty climb, Ben thought.

Once Jim passed below, it would take another twenty minutes or so for Jim to follow the road around to the next ridge. The shooter would have plenty of time to climb the last pitch and get into position. From the knob below to the ridge would be an easy shot of not more than 350 meters. He'd bet the blond man would be carrying a long-barreled seven mag. with at least a ten-power scope. He'd heard that was what a lot of the government types, especially the Secret Service, were using these days. The ammunition was supposed to be accurate to inside six inches at a thousand meters.

In the real world, what the blond man wanted to do was something best left to claymores or automatic weapons fire. "Vectoring" someone "in" was apparently some kind of new jargon developed by people who'd had no experience fighting people like the NVA or the Hmong who had worked with the NVA–or the Russian and Chinese special forces advisors who had been in Vietnam and Laos and Cambodia. Pull any of this "vector me in" bullshit against those people and they would laugh as they handed you your head.

Which, as a matter of fact, now that he thought of it, was exactly what was going to happen. The blond man was going to get his head handed to him. Too bad they couldn't make a video of it, complete with all the radio traffic. A mini documentary of how the real world had a nasty habit of changing the best laid plans.

In his experience, whenever someone got cute or made a sport of it, the real world tended to be sort of like a grizzly wandering around a mountainside. If the grizzly was in the mood—and who knew when a grizzly might be in the mood— and if you were in what the grizzly considered its own private space—and who knew what a grizzly might consider its own private space—you were pretty much screwed—at the mercy of whatever the grizzly felt was an appropriate response. It might decide to run away. It might decide to eat you. Or it might decide something in between. The real world was like that. The old joke was to go hunting in grizzly country with someone who ran slower than you.

People like the blond man, always, sooner or later, seemed to forget that the grizzly cares nothing about how golden the person who has invaded its territory might be. It cares nothing about agendas.

The blond man was down there waiting for Jim to walk by the knob so that he could get into position to put a bullet into Jim as Jim walked unsuspecting up the road. He could tell from the voice on the radio—a voice trying to be cool—that it had not even occurred to the blond man that perhaps the bear had winded him, and was no longer the bear he thought it was. It had not occurred to him that he might have already crossed a line visible only in the bear's mind.

People like the man down there, with their rationales and

437

their agendas and their high-tech equipment, people like that rarely had the ability to sense that it was the Death Monster, and not a doofus bear foraging for bugs and berries, that had scented them. The blond man was rare only in that he wanted to get bloody himself, rather than "vector in" someone else to do it.

He had left the two Marines unharmed because they were no threat, and because he wanted to believe that the Top would not have allowed the corporal to pull the trigger in circumstances like this, no matter what kind of slick, reasonable-sounding bullshit the blond man or one of his people had tried to feed the two Marines. But had they slipped past him and made it up here in the dark, they, too, would have crossed that invisible line—they would have violated the bear's space—and he would have done his best to kill them. Based on what he wanted to believe of them, and on the fact that they'd been so half-assed about it, he'd left them handcuffed to trees. For the corporal—the shotgun pressed to his head—a lesson learned.

Jim came around the corner below, the old, blue cross-country ski pole that he used as a hiking stick clicking on the rocky road surface. It was so quiet and still that even from where Ben was he could hear Jim's footsteps on the hard-packed road.

He turned the volume all the way down on the radio, and turned it on. He waited for Jim to pass across the knob and go around the corner, out of sight, before he keyed the transmit button.

"Go for it," he said, and then, "This transmission brought to you by Force Recon. We *are* the best. Have a great day. We are *out* of here." He turned the radio off and set it to the side.

He'd been winging it all morning with the radio jargon. Even in Vietnam he had never used the radio unless he absolutely had to—usually for artillery or for an extraction. Never for this kind of thing. He had tried to sound like he imagined the Top or the corporal would sound, and that last had felt like something the Top would say. The Top's way of saying, don't call us, we'll call you.

To his left, he could see Jim walking in the shadow of the next ridge, the road surface white with snow in places. He watched him for a moment—a solitary figure walking up a white, snow-covered road—and was reminded of that big old yellow dog padding dejected down a snow-covered logging road.

He turned from Jim, and eased the rifle forward, resting the stock on the soft, damp surface of a gray, rotted log, and waited.

He felt more than saw him—a subtle difference in the light and shade in the trees and bushes at the far edge of the knob. Whoever had taught him how to move in a forest had known what he was about. No quick head or arm movement, his posture when he stopped adapted to the foliage around him. The man below was doing it by the numbers, he'd give him that. The man below knew that by now Jim was well on his way to the next ridge and could not see or hear him no matter how clumsy or noisy had been his progress up onto the knob, but he was still playing his fantasy out by the numbers. If not for his choice of camouflage material—a gray-white material printed with large branches—it would have been a lot more difficult to pick him out. A few hours earlier, at the base of the mountain, the ground still covered with snow, the material had probably been a good choice. But he should have known that up here on the south-facing slopes, the snow would be long gone and winter camouflage would be out of place against the greens and yellows and rich browns.

He blinked, not quite believing what he was seeing. The man's face was painted so that one side was black and the

439

other side ocher red. He'd shaved his head, and that, too, was painted half black and half red. Warpaint. He was hunting an Indian and he'd painted himself the way he'd probably seen an Indian warrior in a photograph or in a movie. A Crow or a Sioux warrior, maybe. Hell, a Huron or a Mohawk, for all he knew.

If it was the blond man, the fucking guy had a house and a family somewhere and here he was sneaking around the mountains of Montana looking like a cross between a Russian Spetsnatz in cold-weather gear and a Huron war chief. What a total asshole. He deserved to be shot for his costume alone, never mind the rest.

Jim knew that he was being hunted. There was not a doubt in Ben's mind. And it boggled his mind that the man down there had such an ego, such a disregard for someone of Jim's experience, that he thought he could simply waltz up the mountain, painted like an Indian he'd seen in a movie, and shoot someone who, if he so willed it, was probably impossible to sneak up on. A man who had discovered hill people. A Marine who had been at Chosin Reservoir. No doubt about it, he thought, the human imagination could be an ugly thing.

The figure below ghosted out of the trees and moved quickly across a small, open bowl at the top of the knob to the thick trunk of a large bull pine uprooted and lying on its side along the edge of the knob facing the next ridge. The pine had been blown over recently; its needles were still green.

The figure knelt on one knee and unlimbered a long-barreled rifle and placed it leaning against the tree trunk, and then shrugged out of a small backpack made of the same camouflage material as his clothes. He placed the rifle across the tree trunk, his arm and head obscured by branches and pine needles.

There was a large patch dark with sweat covering the figure from the back of his neck to his waist, the material plastered flat across his upper back, making it obvious that he was not wearing body armor. Ben wasn't sure a .308 would penetrate some of the new armor; it was nice to know that the man had none.

The figure stood and picked up the rifle and moved to the base of the fallen tree—to the gnarled and twisted root system that lay exposed on its side. Standing upright, knees slightly bent, he inserted the rifle into the bend of a thick root, his camouflage clothes and his painted head easily seen. Ben watched him sight on the distant bench. Watched him fiddle with the scope. Maybe one of those new scopes with a range finder built into it, he thought. The scope looked big and fat enough to house the electronics that it would take.

It was the blond man, all right. Even with the ridiculous paint and the shaved head, he recognized the profile. God, he thought. It was truly depressing to know that people like the man down there won more often than they lost. Hell, they won most of the time. How else could the world be so fucked up? It was usually people like the two Marines cuffed to trees down below who paid the price.

The blond man no doubt assumed it was his right by dint of, name one, intelligence/breeding/education/leadership ability/all of the above, to waltz up here and get himself one of those stories like his story of killing an elk with a spear. The paint and the shaved head were designed to contribute to the myth. A Pumpkin Eater wannabe was what he was. That it was the men he sent into the night, the men who took the risks and paid the prices—that it was only the best of those men who became legendary—had probably never even occurred to him.

In business or politics or war, he thought, it was always someone or group of someones with too much education and not enough conscience who were responsible for creating monsters.

441

What would it be like, he thought. To know for sure that the man down there was a future Kissinger or Westmoreland, an Ayatollah Khomeni or a Kim Il Sung, the CEO of a bank or an automobile company or a chemical company who cared not a whit that his policies resulted in the death and maiming of thousands, sometimes millions. What would it be like to have in the crosshairs a Joseph Stalin, or that stone-cold Colonel who had been responsible for sending the 101st again and again up Hamburger Hill?

Never happen, he thought. Men like that, unlike the man below, restrained their fantasies. They let people like the two Marines sacrifice their lives and their sanity in the unknown and even less understood pursuit of someone else's bent needs. From the sacrifice of others, if they had any emotion at all, they obtained a vicarious thrill. A God-like high.

Every once in awhile, though, the laws of probability being what they were, some of them were still young and stupid enough to forget that someone like himself occasionally got to shoot one of them before he could grow up and do some real damage.

Ben rotated the binoculars toward the far road and immediately found Jim striding along, twirling the ski pole like the conductor in a marching band, letting the pole fall straight down onto the road and bounce back up into his hand. Jim was still a couple of minutes from where the road crossed the ridge. The blond man would be able to see him now, but for sure, with the way the blond man's face was painted, he would wait to shoot until Jim was in sunlight and on the road at the top of the bench, silhouetted against blue sky. At 350 meters with that rifle and that scope and the ammunition that he certainly had, no matter how nervous he might be, no matter how jittery from the adrenaline that was by now making his legs and stomach weak, it would be an almost impossible shot to miss.

442

He put the binoculars down next to the radio, and squirmed into a comfortable position, the old Ruger firm in his shoulder, and put the crosshairs on a spot under the blond man's left armpit. He would give him the benefit of the doubt until the last second.

He breathed slow and easy, time, like always, suspended, the man below frozen with his left arm straight out, palm against the tree trunk, the stock of his rifle resting in the bend of a large root. In his mind, Ben saw clearly the evolving geometry of Jim approaching the bench and the man below aiming a rifle at Jim and himself, hidden inside the slash pile, the barrel of his rifle completing the triangle.

The blond man's shoulders tensed and Ben breathed in and held and a rifle went off so close it sounded as if it had gone off in his ear, the stuttered explosion causing the Ruger to recoil into his shoulder. He knew immediately that the other rifle going off had made him flinch. His round had gone high and right, somewhere into the tree root to the right of the blond man's shoulder.

Not taking his eye from the scope, he cycled the bolt with his little finger, ejecting the brass, pushing the bolt forward with his thumb, chambering a new round, and, as he did, saw that the figure below was hanging by one hand, his right, from the root system. The rifle was on the ground at his feet, barrel pointed back away from the tree trunk.

The rifle behind the slash pile stuttered again and the body below jumped into the root system, and fell slumped into a sitting position, legs bent together to the side like a woman sitting with her feet up on a couch, head down, arms and hands splayed to the side, shoulder propped against the roots. Like a puppet left sitting limp on the stage, he thought.

He pulled the bolt back slowly so that the cartridge would not eject away from the rifle, and pushed the round down into the magazine, holding it down so that he could push the bolt forward without loading a round into the chamber. Rifle in one hand, radio and binoculars in the other, he snaked backwards out of the slash pile and stood and set the rifle against a small fir, the radio on the ground next to it.

He raised the binoculars to his eyes, and saw Jim at the edge of the embankment. Jim raised his arm, ski pole held sideways, and then turned and picked his way down the rocky embankment, disappearing into the trees where the old pack trail began.

Ben sat next to a clump of bear grass, and unzipped his damp coveralls, and worked his shoulders and arms out of the coveralls. Behind him he heard the clatter and scrape of Manfred working his way around the slash pile. He leaned back and closed his eyes, the sun warm against his face. He heard the unmistakable sound of a metal magazine being ejected, a bolt pulled back and locked open. Manfred sat down above and to his left.

"I would have shot him," Ben said.

"You damn near did."

"I told you to get out of here."

"You knew that was me? Man, I about pissed myself when you yelled. Listening to you on the radio, I thought you were up the mountain somewhere."

Ben tilted his head back and cracked open his left eye. Manfred was wearing gray, heavy-wool bib overalls and a woodland-green camouflage long-sleeved T-shirt, the sleeves pulled up to his elbows. On his head was his old, goofy, dirty wool and leather cap with ears that tied on top. He had worn that hat since high school. The ears were hanging loose, one side higher than the other, like the ears on a cartoon dog. His hands and face were streaked with random smudges of green and black face paint. It was a homely, uniquely Montana sort of camouflage that even sitting there on the open slope blended better than did Ben's coveralls. Ben closed his eye and turned his face to the sun. "A bear would have worked its way around until it winded me," he said.

Manfred was silent. Ben could almost hear his mind working. Manfred sitting there like some squat, German gargoyle made him think of that ancient, stone creature on the bottom floor of the Palace Museum in Taipei.

The sun felt good, yellow and red behind his eyelids, hot on his face. His ears were still ringing, but he could hear the buzz of a grasshopper off to his left. The air was rich with the smells of fir and earth and composting slash pile.

Barely heard through the thermals blanketing the valley below came the sound of automatic weapons fire. Robert Lee taking care of business. The dull, flat smack of a grenade. Twenty seconds or so of sustained fire, and then it was silent except for the sound of insects. A whisper of warm air blew up the slope, caressing the side of his face and neck. Manfred shifted his position. From below came a scattering of shots.

Ben opened his eyes. The treeline far to his left was etched against deep blue sky. Larch scattered about the slope were spindly and yellow, most of their needles already gone. A single shot drifted up to them. He wondered what the two Marines were thinking.

"I did it for your grandfather," Manfred said. Ben could hear the shake in Manfred's voice, the after-effect of muscles trembling from unexpended adrenaline.

"I know that."

"I know what this place meant to him . . ."

Ben heard him get to his feet and pick up the rifle and sling it over his shoulder. He glanced up. An H and K sniper rifle, with a selector switch for three-round bursts, the action so fast the burst sounded and hit like a single round. Big. Clunky. German. Run over it with a truck and it would still fire. The perfect rifle for Manfred walking squat and broad backed down the mountainside, his doggy ears bouncing as he jumped from one mound to another.

"Hey, Manfred," he called.

Manfred stopped and turned uphill. "What?"

"Thank you."

Manfred shook his head, and turned and continued down the hill. "Fuck you," he shouted.

And Ben didn't know if Manfred meant him, or if he meant the body slumped against the uprooted pine tree.

Chapter 9
Be Honest

Ben slowly made his way up the center of the ridge along an old skid trail, headed toward the peak to retrieve the tarp and the sleeping bag. The skid trail was steep, crunchy with broken shale and twigs and fallen branches. To his right was the south-facing slope, reasonably open but well treed with mature pine and fir in all the gullies and cuts, high grass and low bushes where there were no trees. The kind of country elk love, he thought. Lots of feed. Lots of cover.

The skid trail petered out where it crested a long, open expanse of almost flat ridge about the length of a football field. The open expanse ended at the base of the final steep pitch to the peak.

Ahead, on his right, was part of the old forest inexplicably left uncut by generations of loggers, the area beneath the old trees shaded and park like. On his left, on the north side of the mountain—out of sight of everyone down in the valley— was a steep slope clearcut several decades ago, the ground still littered with the rotted carcasses of trees too small to market. Farther down, dense thickets of lodgepole or bushes too tall and too thick to walk through had taken the place of fir and larch and ponderosa pine.

A breeze brushed cool and refreshing across his sweat-streaked face and neck. Overhead the sky was a deep blue bowl.

He stopped, his heart thudding. Thirty yards in front of him was a Muley buck. His eyes had seen the deer, but it was a long moment before his mind had fully accepted what he was seeing; the buck was so obvious and so close.

For what seemed like minutes they stared at each other, Ben shocked that he hadn't at least felt the proximity of the buck. He could not remember ever blundering upon an elk or a deer the way he just had.

The buck was a beautiful, healthy animal in its prime.

He unslung the rifle and brought it up into the offhand position and sighted through the scope, finger on the trigger, thumb on the safety.

The buck turned broadside, as if to offer a better target. It lowered its head and went back to feeding.

Ben lowered the rifle and watched the deer feed.

The buck jerked its head up, and looked toward the peak, its oversize ears moving independent of each other, hearing sounds that no human could ever hope to hear.

Its neck swelled, and it snorted, and it began high-stepping diagonally across the open ridge, down onto the north slope, headed sidehill toward the peak.

Probably going after a doe in heat, Ben thought, watching until the buck disappeared around a distant finger ridge.

A file of elk abruptly materialized out of the thick timber, crossing the path of the buck. He blinked. First the buck, and now a herd of elk. Damn.

The elk were headed sidehill directly toward him, moving as only elk can—a relaxed, almost casual walk that belied the speed with which they were closing the distance.

He dropped to the ground. On hands and knees, his right hand holding the rifle off the ground, he scuttled over to the hulk of a long-ago downed pine. The trunk of the pine was maybe three feet in diameter. Old, gray branches, like desiccated bones, littered the ground around the trunk.

He stood, crouching, and placed the rifle into a fork in a thick, broken branch sticking almost straight up from the trunk.

The elk were going to file past not more than fifty meters below.

The lead cow was unusually large. Five cows behind her was a massive bull with a six-or seven-point rack. Behind the bull came more cows and calves. A gaggle of spikes and raghorns brought up the rear.

Time slowed, the adrenaline rush of seeing such a big bull replaced by a reflex of breath control and sight picture, distance and speed and angle all calculated in a moment of time that always seemed much longer than it was. The crosshairs settled on a spot low and behind the shoulder of the bull, and his thumb pushed off the safety. His finger put pressure on the trigger and the firing pin snapped on the empty chamber, the crisp metallic sound echoing in the still mountain air.

He raised his head, grinning to see elk moving faster. The bull, his massive rack tilted back, great shoulders and haunches flexing, hurried toward the saddle, one eye baleful and looking back toward Ben.

He watched as the last of them—the lesser bulls and a few calves—disappeared over the saddle, and then the forest was still.

He could feel the mountain looking at him, weighing his choices against his reflexes. What made him want to count coup on a herd of elk, anyway, he wondered. Blood lust or the residue of other mountains or just the pure simple joy of the hunt, he didn't know. Would probably never know.

He guessed it didn't matter. What mattered was that he'd felt destined to be a stranger to these mountains and now—

thanks to Manfred—he was not. The mountain had just shown him that there was still a lot to live for. No family, perhaps. But like the lesser bulls and barren cows, most of whom would also never have a family, he would always have this place and the creatures that inhabited it. And that was enough. It was more than most men like him could hope for.

If the mountain could accept him for what he was—if the mountain could live with him crippled by his past, then he could learn to live with himself, too.

He leaned against the husk of the old tree and looked out across the mountains. In Vietnam and Laos and Cambodia he'd many times looked out the open doorway of a helicopter at those other mountains so impossibly green and humid and forested, and seen huge stretches of land denuded by chemicals or made by bombs into a moonscape of water-and mosquito-filled craters and torn trees.

Someone had said it was legal and right to inflict that kind of pain and damage.

Free-fire zones. No-fire zones. Fire-by-permission-only zones. Rules of engagement, they called it. Implying that since there are rules, the rules are therefore legal and right.

His rules of engagement had included, but not been limited to killing VC, NVA, renegade Marines, Chinese Special Forces troops supplying dope to Americans, Japanese cops, a stone-cold psychopath nicknamed the Frenchman, and a sociopath-in-development, a Captain in the Japanese National Police named Sato. The people he worked for said that the Rules of Engagement made it right for him to have done the things he had done.

Somewhere along the trail, he had forgotten how to listen to these mountains. In these mountains he could feel how far he had strayed from what was natural and right.

He wondered if Manfred really understood the favor he'd done him.

He pushed off from the fallen tree and continued across the open expanse and up the ridge to where he'd stashed his gear.

After he'd put the tarp and his garbage and the coveralls in the pack, and fastened the sleeping bag to it, he shouldered the pack and the rifle and climbed up on the rock peak.

In the distance, he could see the snow-capped peaks of Evy's mountains.

Standing there on the peak, he tried to thank the forest and the mountains. But, as always, as soon as he tried the emotion began to slide away. And he stopped his thanks because he knew that if he persisted, the feeling would be gone entirely. And if the feeling was gone, then he'd be nothing but a man standing on top a mountain. A stranger even to himself. As ridiculous in his efforts to say thank you as the ears on Manfred's hat.

He stayed on the peak, seated next to a small but very old fir gnarled and weathered—*bonsaied*—by wind and altitude—stayed there until the evening sky turned to gold and yellow on the horizon. And then he stood and picked his way down off the rocky peak, down through the secret forest.

At the bottom of the forest he walked out of blue-gray shadow, onto a grassy ridge bathed in blood-red light. Warm air coming out of the valley below carried the smell of sun-baked grass and earth. To the west red sky streaked yellow outlined the ragged peaks of the Bitterroot Mountains. To the east, a great, bald valley, its bare hills and ridges cast in golden relief, stretched toward snow-capped peaks, a silver ribbon of Interstate running more or less through the center of the valley. Above the distant peaks the sky was bruised purple.

Around him everything, each blade of grass, each rock, the barrel of his rifle, the air itself was charged red.

Turning back the way he'd come, he could see across the saddle the elk had crossed Evy's mountains, their ridges and valleys etched in sharp relief by the light.

Another thermal wafted afternoon heat and forest smells over him and, turning again toward the sunset, for a moment—a moment as religious as it gets—he felt whole.

But it was only for a moment, and then he was merely comfortable, his mind already occupied with the logistics of getting off the mountain, and making sure that Manfred had found the two Marines.

And thinking of the seven- or eight-mile walk out, he sighed, abruptly footsore and tired. He slung his rifle over his shoulder and, as he did, heard the unmistakable throb of rotor blades—a large helicopter to the west—and the sound of rotor blades echoing between mountains, and the sunset, and perhaps his fatigue, combined to trigger a montage of memories seen but not seen: phantom images sifting through the red light. Memory that made little sense: a black and green-faced Peter, teeth gleaming white beneath green foliage. Bodies and pieces of bodies, Marines and NVA alike, stretched out in the red dust and clay. Bodies jiggling on a helicopter floor. Bodies of NVA hung on trees and fences as warning around a Hmong village. An old man grinning toothless around a bowl of rice. A Hmong man and his wife dressed in traditional clothes trudging along a busy road in Missoula, Montana, their faces almost comical in their bewilderment and fear.

And unknown to him tears, the first tears of his adult life, spilled from his eyes, as images marched phantom-like through the red light. Faces and places shuffling through the light, fading away as the wind changed direction, and he could see the first stars brittle in the night sky to the east.

Other mountains.

Other places.

Evy, I'm sorry, he thought. I really am. But how do you suppose we—men like me and Manfred and Robert Lee—got this way? Our childhood washed by Monsoons that wept gray adrenaline. Our sanity too many times caught between reason and panic. Children we were, growing old trying to escape the stench of graves, knowing even then that our sacrifices were for naught. Don't mean nothin', we learned to say.

But standing here on this mountain, under a sky turning from blood red to night, smelling mountain and elk, at times like this, Evy, I am inexplicably made whole again.

The double beep of a car or truck horn echoed up the ridge. Manfred and Robert Lee and maybe Jim on the road below, he thought. He wouldn't have to walk all the way home after all.

He turned one last time toward the sunset and spread his arms wide—a puny, corny gesture that nevertheless felt good.

Be honest with yourself, Ben Tails, he thought. You have eaten well. Your dreams edible. Nourishment enough for someone like you.

Walking the trail.

Epilogue

Montana,
Ten Months Later
Tight Lines

L ate summer, and afternoon light streamed in smoky lines through the stained glass panels in front of the windows, refracted sharp and golden off bottles arrayed in front of the mirror. Three big, new ceiling fans whisked and creaked, stirring the air not at all.

"These fans are useless," Ben said. He was seated on a stool at the end of the bar closest to the windows, his back against the bar, elbows behind him on the counter, hands hanging limp.

Manfred had the newspaper spread open on the counter. He peered at Ben over the top of his new half-glasses. "Atmosphere," he said.

Ben snorted. "Yeah. Legends of the Fall meets Casablanca."

Manfred licked his finger and turned a page. "Whatever works," he said. "I hear you're on your way out again."

"Unh," Ben grunted. Out the windows, past the tracks and the new park, above trees green with summer leaves, he could see blue mountains.

Manfred sighed, and straightened away from the bar. He folded the paper closed. "I hate it when you get like this," he said. He took off his glasses and put them in a glasses case. The case snapped shut with a hard, muffled sound. He put it

454

next to the cash register and, with one hand, picked up two cups–the thick, white ceramic, no-nonsense kind that a half-century ago were standard in most bars and restaurants–and grabbed the coffee pot out of the large, stainless steel coffee maker, and walked behind the bar to where Ben was seated.

He set the cups on the bar and poured black, steaming coffee. The coffee had the rich, expensive smell of fresh ground beans. "You want a doughnut or something to go with this?" he asked.

"You got any?"

"No, but I thought I'd ask."

Ben reached behind with his left hand, his other arm still on the bar top, and brought the cup of coffee around in front of his face. He inhaled the aroma. Out-fucking-standing, he thought. Coffee like this would have been a sacrilege in the old bar. He took a sip.

"Too hot," he said.

"Too hot," Manfred mimicked. "Too black, too oily, too bitter, too weak, too strong–someday you're going to tell me how good it really is, and I'm going to keel over with a heart attack."

Ben took another sip. *Really* good coffee, he thought. Growing up, the coffee had been so bad he'd never learned to drink it on a regular basis. This was way better even than the coffee he'd had in Japan.

"I like the cups," he said.

"He likes the cups," Manfred muttered, shaking his head as he walked the coffee pot back to the coffee maker. "Dickhead."

Outside a thirty-something couple dressed in matching chino trousers and blue denim shirts walked past the window to the door. The man tried the door knob, rattled it, and then they both peered inside, hands cupped around faces pressed to the window. The woman had a pony tail. The man was wearing a green baseball hat turned the correct way.

Ben took another sip of coffee. The woman had strong Nordic features. Her shirt had a lot of embroidery at collar and pockets.

Manfred walked to the door. "Closed," he said, pointing to the closed sign hanging in the middle of the window.

The man pointed to his watch.

"Closed," Manfred said again, and walked back to the bar.

The couple scowled at each other. The man shrugged. What can you expect? his body language said. They turned and walked away.

"It's your coffee," Ben said.

"I know it."

"Maybe you could make this an expresso bar by day, the yuppie bar that it has become by night."

"Fuck you."

"You know: Lattes. Americano. Thimble-sized cups of expresso."

"It's *es*-presso, not expresso."

"You could serve *es*-pressso in shot glasses. Call them Rocky Mountain shooters, Casablanca Cappuchino, something like that."

"Why don't you go fishing."

"I'm tired of eating fish." Ben sipped his coffee.

"Throw them back."

"Fuck I want to go fishing for if I'm not going to eat them?"

"It's called sport. You know, the zen of fly fishing. That kind of thing."

"Right. Fly fishing. Get in touch with your inner self, become one with nature and the universe by being cruel to a creature with a brain the size of a contact lens."

"That creature with a brain the size of a contact lens seems to have no trouble outwitting you."

456

"You have surely got my fishing prowess mixed up with that of Robert Lee." He sat upright and pivoted toward Manfred. "The other day, I got out of the truck, and there's this woman standing there at the trailhead. No pole, or anything, just a small day pack. I figured she'd been hiking. She asked me what I was fishing with. I was planning to use flies, but there was something about the way she asked. "Grasshoppers," I said, and showed her an old tobacco can that I use to put hoppers in.

"Man, you should have seen her face. It was like she'd suddenly come face to face with the Charles Manson of fishing. I'm telling you, Manfred. These people. It's okay to torture fish with hand-tied flys, but it's not okay to catch them with worms or hoppers. Heaven forbid if you actually take one home and *eat* it."

"It's a good thing you're getting out of here soon."

Ben drained his cup, and stood and walked to the opening in the bar, and pulled out the coffee pot from the coffee maker and refilled his cup. "I'm serious," he said. "Next thing you know these people are going to be wanting us to catch and release elk."

"You must of got up on the wrong side of the bed this morning or something," Manfred said. "You are sure wound up today."

"I got up on the right side of an *empty* bed," Ben said. "That's what I got up on."

"Hey, you've got no one but yourself to blame for that. Every time you come in here in the evening, for the next week there's some woman calling long distance wanting to know how to get in touch with you."

"Yeah, right."

"Look, Ben—" Manfred hesitated. "Can I be serious for a minute?"

"Knock yourself out."

"Well, look. Evy isn't—"

"Isn't what?"

Manfred threw his hands up. "Forget I said anything."

Ben walked back to the end of the bar and sat on the stool. He looked out the window.

"I hear Raven is going to try you out in management," Manfred said. "And Robert Lee's latest took you to Missoula to buy some suits."

Ben was silent.

"She says you dress up real nice."

"Fuck you and the horse you rode in on."

Manfred laughed.

"You ever look out these windows?" Ben said. "And think of us when we were kids running up and down those tracks out there?"

"You know what your trouble is?" Manfred said. "You been spending way too much time with creatures that have brains the size of contact lenses. You need to watch more TV, or something." He switched off the coffee maker and put his cup in the sink under the bar. "Why don't you leave early," he said. "Take a little detour and go see that woman you told us about. Kay or Khe Sanh, or whatever her name is."

Ben stared blankly out the window, the cup of coffee forgotten in his hand.

"Hello," Manfred said. "Earth to Ben." He switched off the fans and overhead lights.

Ben blinked, roused himself. He put the cup of coffee on the bar. "What are you doing?"

"It's too nice out. No one is going to come in here for hours." He walked down the bar and picked up Ben's cup. "And talking to you is about as much fun as having my prostate examined." He poured the coffee out and put the cup in the sink. "Robert Lee called and wants me to bring him out a few cold ones." He opened the cooler and took out a couple of six packs. "If your *schedule* permits, you can come along."

"You don't have to be so sarcastic."

"Well, I'm tired of watching you wander around whimpering and sniveling like some junkyard dog that got its ass kicked."

"I *can't* go see her. I told you, her family won't let me."

"I had a dollar for every family didn't want you seeing their little girl, I wouldn't need this bar anymore."

"That's different."

"You say."

"Japan isn't like here, Manfred. There's no way."

"Well, I don't believe it," Manfred said. "But, hey, it isn't my life going down the toilet. Here take these."

Ben took the six packs from Manfred. "Where's Robert Lee, he wants this beer?"

"Robert Lee is communing with nature," Manfred said. "He's learning the zen of fly fishing."

Ben followed Manfred out the back door. "And where exactly is he doing this?"

Manfred held the door for him. "Even as we speak, he is standing next to your favorite fishing hole, untangling his line from bushes, wondering why his zen isn't as good as your zen."

Ben waited while Manfred locked the door. Hot sunlight reflected off the back of the building. "Actually, drinking beer and watching that idiot try to catch fish sounds like an excellent idea."

"Since I'm supplying the beer, we'll take your truck."

"Whatever you say, bwana."

• • •

Ben's old, beat-to-hell, faded-green International shuddered and bounced, rattling down the dusty gravel road, the back end coming around every time it hit a series of washboard bumps. A strong breeze coming through the cottonwoods and willows along the creek blew the rooster tail of dust behind them off toward scree fields and rocky outcrops at the base of the mountain.

He slowed the truck, and turned off the main road onto a track that went over a series of small, grassy hillocks, across the dry gravel bottom of a feeder creek, up an embankment into a large shady area under mature pines. Fire rings and broken bottles and crushed beer cans in and around the fire rings identified it as a place the local teenagers used for keggers. At the end of the summer, and every spring, the local Kiwanis club came out and policed up the area.

Ben steered the truck through the trees, engine grumbling.

On the other side of the trees was a large alfalfa field bordered on two sides by leafy trees and bushes, and on the other by a steep, rock-strewn mountainside, bull pines clinging to outcroppings and in small, steep gullies.

A lone set of tracks led across the field toward the base of the mountain.

The camping area they'd just driven through was known only to locals, but even the locals didn't visit this part of the creek. There were rattlesnakes in the rocks at the edge of the alfalfa field, and at night the snakes hunted for rodents in the alfalfa and along the creek. There weren't many rattlesnakes because the area was also home to bull snakes and hawks and owls, but every time someone saw one, or mistook the buzz of grasshoppers for the buzz of a rattlesnake, the number and size of the snakes increased exponentially. Ben had never even seen a rattlesnake near this part of the creek, but since the tall stories about snakes tended to keep other fisherman away, he never disabused anyone of the notion that this part of the creek was overrun with rattlesnakes.

Ahead, parked behind a thick peninsula of willow bushes was a marked brown-and-white Sheriff's Department Chevy Tahoe. The back end was open, fishing poles and boxes of tackle next to brushed-aluminum crime-scene cases and black duffel bags filled with SWAT and Search and Rescue gear.

Ben pulled the International up to the Tahoe, and shut off the engine. "I can't believe he has the balls to use a public vehicle for his private fishing and hunting trips," he said.

"He claims that since he's the Sheriff, he has to be prepared always for any emergency."

"And the citizens eat it up."

"Of course, they do." Manfred kicked his door open, hinges grating.

Ben shoved his door open and climbed out. Two dark lines meandered from the Tahoe through the damp alfalfa to the trees and bushes at the end of the field.

Manfred reached into the bed of the pickup and pulled out the two six pacs. "These ought to be well shaken," he said. He turned and began following the two tracks in the alfalfa.

"Two people," Ben said from behind him.

Manfred stopped and put the two six packs down in the alfalfa. He crossed his arms and looked at Ben.

Ben stopped. "What?"

"Let me remind you that this is public land," Manfred said. "Just because you go out of your way to make people believe there are giant rattlesnakes around here doesn't make it yours."

"Who's he with? It better not be one of his bimbos or some fucking tourist."

"Why don't we sit for a minute?" Manfred said. He grinned. "Have a beer. Enjoy the sunshine. Smell the alfalfa. Look for snakes."

Ben stared hard at Manfred. "Son-of-a-bitch," he said, and

461

stalked off toward the creek. Manfred picked up the beer and followed.

Ben plowed through the screen of bushes, not bothering to follow the tracks. On the other side of the bushes were mature pines and spruce, the ground underneath mostly bare.

Twenty yards ahead through the trees was the creek—actually more a small river than a creek—white river rock and sand bars and thick stands of willow bushes in bright sunlight on the other side.

The side they were on was shaded by cliffs barely seen through the trees. The creek next to the steep, undercut bank on their side was deep and fast. He followed a well-worn trail through the trees, over mossy rocks and tree roots, headed up stream, into the shade of the cliffs.

"You know Robert Lee," Manfred said from behind him. "Most of the time he doesn't know what he's going to do until he does it."

"This is not funny," Ben said. He stopped and turned toward Manfred. "This is not a laughing matter."

"Hey, you're the one who showed it to him."

"Yeah. To *him*." He paused. "I showed it to him because I knew he'd never be able to catch any fish there—and he hasn't." He turned to continue walking, but wheeled back toward Manfred. "That's what you think is so funny, isn't it? He's brought someone here who knows how to fish a place like this. You two think it will be funny as hell to watch me watch someone else catch fish out of *my* fishing hole."

Manfred laughed. "You've got no one to blame but yourself."

"If it's some L.L.Bean chick, that's one thing, but if it's someone who knows how to catch fish. . . ."

"What are you going to do? He's the sheriff."

"I never even took Evy here, you know that?"

Manfred sobered. He stared at Ben for a moment, and then

462

looked toward the creek. He frowned. "I didn't know that," he said. He looked at Ben. "Why not? Because you knew she'd catch fish?"

"Isn't that what Grandpa taught us? A woman who knows how to fish will always catch more fish than the man she is with." In unison, they both said, "SO DON'T EVER TAKE A WOMAN FISHING."

Ben turned and began following the trail

"Why do you think that is?" Manfred asked.

"How do I know. Maybe it's got something to do with brain size."

"Contact lens size, you mean?"

"Kiss my ass, Manfred."

"Hey. Hold on a minute."

Ben stopped, and turned toward Manfred.

"Look, you're leaving soon," Manfred said. "And like always just before you take off for God-knows-where, you either walk around with your shorts pulled up too tight, or in some kind of funk. Robert Lee wouldn't bring a woman out here if he knew you'd never brought Evy here. Not in a hundred years." He shifted the beer in his arms. "So cool your jets. Knowing him, he probably blindfolded whoever he's with anyway."

"You think?"

"Well, it's a theory."

Ben turned and began walking. After awhile, he laughed, his laugh lost in the rush and chuckle of the water next to the path. He stopped and pointed across the creek. "There's a new beaver pond over there on the other side of those cottonwoods," he said. "It's full of fish that even Robert Lee can catch."

"And?"

"And there's a mother moose and her calf over there, too. The last time I saw them, she raised her hackles at me."

"And you think it would be funny if I tell Robert Lee about the pond and the fish but not about the moose?"

"You said it, not me." Ben half jumped, half ran up a rise in the embankment.

Manfred scrambled up next to him. To the left, the creek flowed dark and deep beneath a cliff. Moss and small fir clung to tiny shelves and benches in the dark cliff face. On the other side of the creek a wide expanse of river rock was bright white in the sunlight.

Ahead, twenty yards out in the shallows on the other side, in a line on the water delineated by shade and sunlight stood two figures, fly rods in their hands.

Manfred put the beer down next to a tree leaning out over the water, and they both sat on the embankment next to the beer.

"We'll just sit here and drink this beer in front of him," Ben said.

Robert Lee was dressed in chest waders and red t-shirt and faded-green fishing vest, a net clipped to his side, old camouflage bush hat festooned with flies stuck in a broad felt band that he'd had sewn to the hat. The hat had come from the head of a dead NVA officer; the felt covered a bullet hole that was still visible on the inside: Robert Lee's lucky hat.

Next to Robert Lee, the other fisherman, his back to them, was dressed in chest waders, long-sleeved khaki shirt, khaki fishing vest, a hat that Ben thought was the same kind of hat that Humphrey Bogart wore in Casablanca. The fly rod looked expensive even from twenty yards away.

Robert Lee reeled in his line. "Hey," he said, without looking at them.

"Hey, yourself," Ben said absently, watching as the other fisherman pulled his line out of the water and began flicking the pole back and forth, drying the fly, the line snapping back toward them in a graceful, relaxed movement that no amount of lessons could ever teach.

He felt his stomach go suddenly hollow, a sudden rush of heat enveloping his upper body. The movement of water where shade and sunlight met, the deep water moving deceptive beneath the cliff—all of it was abruptly clear and discrete and in slow motion.

The fisherman gave a final, languid flick of the pole, slender, tanned forearm and wrist tuned perfectly to the water and to the air and to the feel of the pole.

"Beautiful," Manfred said, as the long, slow "S", the dark speck of a fly at the end of it, snaked toward a shiny, dark gray rock in the water beneath the overhang. Because the overhang blended into the cliff face, most people never noticed the overhang until the fly landed on the cliff face, instead of the water.

Exactly right, Ben thought, as the fly settled toward the space between the rock overhang and the water below.

He focused on the slender neck, her hair shaved short on the long muscles at the back of the neck, and as he did, her face turned in profile, one eye closing in a wink, a broad smile on her lips, a network of red weals, tender-looking even from there, radiating from the edge of her eye down next to her nose and the corner of her mouth.

Surgery scars, he thought, as, at the edge of his vision, the fly settled on a tiny ripple behind the rock and in a sudden slap of spray and wagging tail a trout came out of the water, into the air, and fell back into the water.

He leaned back, his hands in the moss and earth behind him.

"She's just like you," Manfred said, as the line went taut.

A natural.